# DUDLEY PUBLIC LIBRARIES

The loan of this book may be renewed if not required by other readers, by contacting the library from which it was borrowed.

KT-146-862

scribbling in h... She's a former So You Think You Can Write and former RWA Golden Heart finalist. Kat, her husband and their two boys live in north Texas.

**Robyn Grady** has sold millions of books worldwide and features regularly on bestsellers lists and at award ceremonies, including The National Readers Choice, The Booksellers Best and Australia's prestigious Romantic Book of the Year. When she's not tapping out her next story, she enjoys the challenge of raising three very different daughters as well as dreaming about shooting the breeze with Stephen King during a month-long Mediterranean cruise. Contact her at www.robyngrady.com

**Maureen Child** is the author of more than 130 romance novels and novellas that routinely appear on bestseller lists and have won numerous awards, including the National Reader's Choice Award. A seven-time nominee for the prestigious RITA™ award from Romance Writers of America, one of her books was made into a CBS-TV movie called The Soul Collector. Maureen recently moved from California to the mountains of Utah and is trying to get used to snow.

000003069450

# Scandalous Secrets

# Scandalous Secrets:
# The Billion Dollar Secret

**KAT CANTRELL**

**ROBYN GRADY**

**MAUREEN CHILD**

MIX

Paper from
responsible sources

FSC

FSC C007454

This book is produced from independently certified FSC™ paper
to ensure responsible forest management.

For more information visit: www.harpercollins.co.uk/green

Printed and bound in Spain
by CPI, Barcelona

**MILLS & BOON**

All rights reserved including the right of reproduction in whole or
in part in any form. This edition is published by arrangement with
Harlequin Books S.A.

This is a work of fiction. Names, characters, places, locations and
incidents are purely fictional and bear no relationship to any real
life individuals, living or dead, or to any actual places, business
establishments, locations, events or incidents. Any resemblance is
entirely coincidental.

This book is sold subject to the condition that it shall not, by
way of trade or otherwise, be lent, resold, hired out or otherwise
circulated without the prior consent of the publisher in any form
of binding or cover other than that in which it is published and
without a similar condition including this condition being imposed
on the subsequent purchaser.

® and TM are trademarks owned and used by the trademark owner
and/or its licensee. Trademarks marked with ® are registered
with the United Kingdom Patent Office and/or the Office for
Harmonisation in the Internal Market and in other countries.

First Published in Great Britain 2020
By Mills & Boon, an imprint of HarperCollins*Publishers*
1 London Bridge Street, London, SE1 9GF

SCANDALOUS SECRETS: THE BILLION DOLLAR SECRET
© 2020 Harlequin Books S.A.

*From Fake to Forever* © 2015 Kat Cantrell
*The Billionaire's Bedside Manner* © 2011 Robyn Grady
*King's Million-Dollar Secret* © 2011 Maureen Child

ISBN: 978-0-263-29879-6

| DUDLEY LIBRARIES | MIX Paper from responsible sources FSC C007454 |
| --- | --- |
| 000003069450 | |
| **Askews & Holts** | 18-Jan-2021 |
| AF ROM | £7.99 |
| 2LL | |

Th

# FROM FAKE
# TO FOREVER

**KAT CANTRELL**

# One

Normally, a surprise trip to Manhattan ranked high on Meredith Chandler-Harris's list of Really Cool Things. A visit to one of the most highly respected fashion houses in the world hit the list even higher than that. Having to tell the man she'd spent two years trying to forget that they were married, not so much. It pretty much ruined Manhattan, fashion and—hell, even martinis.

That had been Jason's drink.

Meredith shifted as unobtrusively as possible on the leather couch as she waited for the receptionist to admit her to the inner sanctum of Jason Lynhurst, chief operating officer of Lyn Couture. Who was also Meredith's husband. Apparently.

"Mr. Lynhurst will see you now," the receptionist called in her frostiest voice.

Meredith always got frosty from women, who were largely unforgiving of the assets God had bestowed on her at birth. And she especially expected frosty from a woman who'd tried not-so-politely to show Meredith the door. She obviously had no clue who she was dealing with.

Lyn Couture bustled beyond the reception area, with sharply dressed men and women engaged in a myriad of tasks. Fascinated, Meredith craned her neck to peek at chalk outlines of sleek outfits stenciled on parchment and fabric swatches laid out on cluttered desks.

This was where the alchemy of fashion and style converged. It was enough to make a woman giddy. She adored everything about clothes: buying them, wearing them, owning them, matching them. But to a woman who wanted to buy half of her sister's wedding-dress-design company, Lyn Couture was so much more than a place of business—this was a mecca for like-minded people.

Even Meredith had a pair of Lyn jeans. Of course, she hadn't known who Jason was when she'd caught his eye across the dance floor at that club in Vegas. She'd only known that he moved like a man comfortable in his own body and had cheekbones to spare. And she'd wanted a piece of him. Only to learn two years later she'd bitten off a much bigger piece than she'd ever dreamed.

Curious gazes swung in Meredith's direction as she followed Frosty Receptionist to the corner office.

"Mr. Lynhurst?" the receptionist called through the open door. "Your visitor is here."

*Mr. Lynhurst.* Please. That man had done more wicked things to Meredith in one weekend than all the men since then…combined. Much to her chagrin. Wasn't there *one* who could make her forget the perfection of the man who had rocked her world so very long ago?

"Thanks, hon. I'll take it from here." Meredith skirted the receptionist and swept into the office as if she owned it because that's how you got people's attention.

And she needed Jason's attention. Because she had to talk him into a quiet divorce. Immediately. It was the only way she'd be able to stomach approaching her father about a loan so she could buy into her sister's business.

Plus, she wasn't ready to be married, to Jason or anyone. Not until she figured out who she was going to be when she grew up. That was why in the cold light of morning, the Las Vegas-style marriage ceremony from the night before had seemed like the opposite of a good idea. The paperwork was never supposed to be filed, but here she was. Married to Jason.

The man in question sat behind a glass desk, modern and sharp. Much like the man. As their gazes collided… and held…her breath stuttered. Oh, yeah. *That* was why no man in existence could erase Jason from her mind.

Those cheekbones. To die for. Artfully messed-up spiky pale blond hair, begging for her fingers to slide through it as she pulled him down for a scorching kiss. Witty, sensual and, God Almighty, he *listened* when she talked. Men rarely glanced above Meredith's shoulders, but Jason had asked her opinions, accepted her thoughts.

He was the man she'd compared to all other men and found them lacking. And two years hadn't diminished his potency in the slightest.

Jason rose from behind his desk, mouthwatering in a slim dark suit likely conceived, created and cut yards from his office.

"Meredith. You look well." If she'd surprised him with this unexpected visit, he kept it from his smooth voice.

"Thanks for seeing me on short notice." Well, wasn't this pleasant? Two people reacquainting themselves, who'd never thought they'd lay eyes on each other again. No point in beating around the bush. "We have a problem. The more quickly and quietly we can resolve it, the better."

A shield snapped over his expression. "I sincerely hope you are not about to tell me you got pregnant and are just now getting around to mentioning it to me."

What kind of woman did he take her for? She tamped back the ire. They really didn't know each other very well. Their wild weekend in Vegas had been about being at a crossroads, not about finding a lifelong mate.

The marriage had been a mistake. They both knew that.

"No, nothing like that." Meredith waved it off and perched on the edge of one of the chairs flanking Jason's desk, hoping he'd take the hint and sit back down. This was a friendly visit.

He relaxed, slightly, but didn't sit down. "Then anything else is manageable. What can I do for you?"

This was so weird. She'd spent hours upon hours sliding her slick body against this man's. Her tongue had tasted every inch of the skin hiding under that suit. They were strangers, then and now. And yet, not strangers. It felt oddly like they'd seen each other only yesterday.

"So, funny story." She grinned as if it really was. "Remember how we found that all-night marriage-license place and then thought it would be so great to tie the knot in Vegas to seal the Grown-Up Pact?"

*The Grown-Up Pact.*

It had seemed brilliant at the time…after four rounds of tequila shots and countless cosmopolitans and martinis. After that first initial meeting of gazes, they hadn't left each other's company the rest of the weekend. They'd embarked on a seemingly endless conversation during which Meredith spilled more of her soul to this man she'd just met than she ever had to anyone else. And he'd claimed the same. They'd both been searching for something, anything, to help them navigate the bridge between the caprices of youth and the rest of their lives.

The Grown-Up Pact had never been about staying married, but about proving they could do grown-up things, that a commitment like marriage wasn't so scary if they could do it together.

Ironic how the marriage that was supposed to prove they were grown-ups had resulted in a very adult problem.

"Of course I remember," he said. "It was the only time I've ever acted on a stupid idea."

She sighed. That made one of them. She did stupid things all the time. The Grown-Up Pact should have given her the fortitude to move past her beauty-pageant pedigree and find a place in the world where she could be appreciated for what went on between her temples. But she hadn't found that place, not yet.

"Turns out the marriage license got filed somehow."

"What?" Jason's expression turned flinty. "How did that happen? You were supposed to shred the license."

"I did! Well, I threw it away." She *had* to have thrown it away. The problem was she couldn't precisely recall the actual throwing away part. "No one said anything about shredding."

"That's what you do with something you don't want to fall into the wrong hands, Meredith." That seemed to be enough to get him to finally sit down. "Credit card numbers, legal documents. Marriage licenses that you realize the next morning you never should have registered for in the first place."

He threaded fingers through his messy hair and her own fingers flexed in response, aching to feel him again. It was a brutal reminder that she'd half thought they might catch up for old times' sake, once they sorted out this stupid mistake she'd made. One last roll in Jason's bed would probably cure her for good and then she could finally move on.

The fierce expression on his face didn't exactly put a warm fuzzy in her tummy.

"So, it happened," she said. "We're legally married and have been for two years. Now we need to deal with it. And then maybe we can, you know, have a drink or two later?"

The suggestion wasn't at all subtle, but no one did brazen better. She had a perverse need to see if any of the spark between them still existed.

"Deal with it? Oh, I see. You're here because you saw the announcement of my engagement and you want a payoff." He nodded wearily. "How much do you want?"

Jason was engaged? That was great. Obviously he'd want to handle this quickly and quietly, as well. She kept trying to convince herself of the greatness and failed.

The disappointment at learning he'd moved on so much

better than she had was bitter and sharp. There would be no catching up, then. No last wild weekend.

"I don't want your money, Jason. Just a no-fault, no-division-of-assets divorce."

"Sure." His sarcasm was thick. "As soon as you found out I was Bettina Lynhurst's son back in Vegas, little dollar signs must have danced before your eyes. Admit it. You filed the marriage license on purpose, hoping to cash in later. Frankly, I'm shocked it took this long for your trick to play out."

Her mouth fell open. "You've obviously forgotten I'm a Chandler *and* a Harris. I don't need your piddly fashion-empire fortune. My father's money built Houston. So keep your snotty dollar signs, sign the divorce papers and go about your business."

Of course, she'd cut up all her father's credit cards, but Jason didn't need to know that.

For God knew what reason, Jason grinned. The tension leeched away as he sat back in his chair. "I wish I could say I'd forgotten how sassy you are. If you're not here for money, what are you here for?"

"Is this rocket science?" Airily, she motioned to him so it would seem like something other than the really big deal it actually was. Her family could *not* find out she hadn't taken care of this problem. "It's in both our interests to get a quiet divorce. So I'm here to get that done."

"You already have papers drawn up? Great. Give me a copy and I'll shoot them to my lawyer. As long as everything's in order, I'll sign and mail you a copy. Thanks for coming by. I'll walk you out."

He stood. She didn't. "What guarantee do I have that you won't spill all of this to the media?"

If her father found out how supremely rash his daughter had acted, he'd never agree to give her a loan to buy half of Cara's design business. And Meredith wanted to prove once and for all she had what it took to make something of herself.

This loan was the key to the rest of Meredith's life. Finally, she'd be able to call herself something other than a pageant winner. Finally, other people would have something to call her besides a former Miss Texas: a grown-up.

Jason's laughter was harsh. "Why in the world would I want to advertise something so ridiculous as a spontaneous wedding in Las Vegas to a woman I'd just met who's boneheaded enough to accidentally file the marriage license?"

"Well, don't hold back, sweetie. Tell me how you really feel." She eyed him. "We're on the same page. I'd prefer no one found out I married someone boneheaded enough to have me. Here's a copy of the papers."

"I'll have my lawyer check them out. Don't go anywhere," he advised. "I want to settle this before you leave town."

"I'll be around for a few days, but no longer, so make it snappy."

With a flourish, she wrote the name of her hotel and her cell-phone number on a sticky note and pasted it to his lapel in a senseless effort to touch him one last time.

Shame about that fiancée. More was the shame that Jason Lynhurst was totally over Meredith.

But the biggest shame was that she couldn't say the same.

*Meredith.* Of all the freaking people to waltz into Jason's office on an otherwise unremarkable Friday.

She was the only woman who'd ever enticed him out from behind his all-business exterior, the only woman who could claim she'd slept in his bed, when normally, he kept women away from his personal space. Their brief relationship had been crazy, wild, the stuff of his hottest fantasies—and totally out of character.

Meredith was also the only woman he'd ever considered

truly dangerous. For his well-being, his future, his state of mind. And definitely dangerous to his self-control. Because he couldn't resist her back in Vegas and he had a feeling nothing had changed.

This was not the time, nor the place, to dwell on that.

He had a meeting with Avery in fifteen minutes and his sister was going to lord it over him for being late. And getting across town at this hour was more impossible than wishing himself invisible. Hefting his messenger bag to his other shoulder, Jason hailed a taxi instead of taking the company car because it would take too long to retrieve it from the garage.

Yet another disruption in his jam-packed day, thanks to that blast from the past.

Once Jason slid into the cab, his mind immediately flipped back to the bombshell Meredith had dropped on him. Apparently he couldn't resist thinking about her any more than he could resist that come-hither look she'd used so effectively in Vegas to drive him just this side of insane.

*Married. To Meredith.*

Once, it had seemed like a fantastic plan, to bond himself—symbolically, of course, as part of the Grown-Up Pact—to a woman who seemed to effortlessly understand his misery and pain and then take it all away.

Their brief affair had its place. In the history books.

Vegas had been a spontaneous trip, born out of his confusion and frustration over his parents' announcement. Not only were they divorcing after thirty years of marriage, but they were also splitting apart Lynhurst Enterprises, the company they'd founded. Lyn Couture to Bettina, Hurst House Fashion to Paul. Jason would stay at Lyn and Avery would go to Hurst House. Everyone seemed fine with it—except no one asked Jason's opinion.

He hated it. The legacy he'd been born to, depended on, planned for, was gone. Fractured beyond repair. All at once, he couldn't deal with it and jetted off to forget in Vegas.

Meredith had been a balm to his broken soul. Exactly what he'd needed at the time, and she'd honed his focus. If it hadn't been for the turmoil going on at home, he'd never have been open to what she'd offered, but thank God he'd decided to play by different rules for one weekend. He'd left her in that hotel room with a kiss and a thank-you and flown back to New York with new purpose.

He'd reunite Lynhurst Enterprises under one umbrella again or die trying.

That was what he'd hoped to gain with the Grown-Up Pact. A direction, a sense that he could take on this new paradigm and succeed. And the seed of his plan was about to bear fruit.

This meeting with Avery was the next step. Lyn belonged with Hurst House and Jason belonged at the helm as the CEO of the newly repaired company. At least in this, he and Avery agreed and they'd put their animosity aside to work toward it in secret. Today, they'd start putting their takeover plan into action.

Because he couldn't help himself, Jason did an internet search on his phone for the Clark County, Nevada, marriage registrar, and sure enough, a quick search revealed the plain-text record of his very legal marriage to Meredith Lizette Chandler-Harris.

A blip in judgment, one he couldn't imagine explaining to the people in his real life. That's why they'd tracked down the officiant who'd performed the ceremony and asked for the license back so it couldn't be filed. So what had happened? Jason called his lawyer to let him figure it out and jumped from the cab at the coffeehouse Avery had selected for their clandestine takeover bid, which was near her pretentious Tribeca loft.

As expected, his sister waited, not so patiently, at the back booth. Drumming her fingers in annoyance, she glared at Jason all the way across the room.

"Where have you been? I'm meeting with the *Project*

*Runway* advertising people in an hour." Avery's snootiness was in full force today. "Not all of us got a cushy position at Lyn doing Mother's bidding twenty-four seven. I have an actual job to do."

"Hello to you, too," he responded mildly. Avery liked nothing more than to rile him, so he never indulged her. "Since you're so busy, you should have picked a place closer to Midtown."

Jason pulled the paperwork from his bag, which detailed the restructuring of Lyn Couture and Hurst House Fashion back into one company, and set the document on the wooden tabletop. This had been his contribution, while Avery had managed the branding and design aspects, as they hoped to launch the re-formed company with a new spring line. The publicity would be great for all their labels. She also planned to give notice at Hurst House and take a job at Lyn in an effort to make a merger more attractive.

Avery glanced at the sheaf of papers he'd slaved over for weeks. Then she did a double take and raised her brows. "This says you're going to be the CEO. Except you aren't. I am."

"Are you insane? Why do you think I've been so passionate about this—so I can work for you instead of Mom?" Avery was delusional. She couldn't handle a CEO position and besides, it was his. He'd gone to Harvard to get a business degree in anticipation of it. "I'll take care of you, don't worry."

She tossed her long blond hair. "Why do you think *I've* been working on this? Lynhurst Enterprises is mine."

"Like hell." Avery had come to hate the split and wanted Lynhurst reunited as much as he did or he'd never have agreed to work with her. Why hadn't he seen that she'd also developed an appetite for power?

"I'm the oldest—it's a given that I'll take over the company once we get it back the way it was."

"It's not a given," Jason countered fiercely and lowered

his voice. "I've worked harder and longer than anyone, including you."

His entire life had been groomed toward the concept of stepping into his father's shoes as the head of Lynhurst. Avery and Bettina had critical roles on the design and marketing side, of course, but they weren't visionaries. They couldn't keep a huge ship like Lynhurst afloat *and* steer it in the right direction, especially not after merging the two halves. It took more than a good eye for color to manage a business.

"That's a complete lie." She flicked manicured fingers at Jason's face, a crafty smile playing about her thin lips. "Whose idea was it to tackle this puppy together? Not yours. It has more punch if we're united and take this proposal to Mom and Dad as fait accompli. Without that, you'd have nothing. Tell me you didn't think I was going to hand over the top spot to you, little brother."

A deliberate jab, like birth order meant something in the grand scheme of things.

"There's no 'handing over' of anything. I've earned that position with these merger plans, not to mention what I've accomplished as COO of Lyn Couture." Hell, he'd earned the CEO position with his coup of an engagement to Meiling Lim alone.

His fiancée's father owned the largest textile business in Asia, and Jason's marriage to Meiling would solidify the partnership between Lyn Couture and overseas manufacturing houses. It was a match negotiated over the boardroom table and made excellent business sense.

Meiling's delicate features and proper demeanor represented exactly the kind of wife an up-and-coming CEO needed. They liked each other and had similar goals for their union, namely, that it would benefit their families. Neither of them expected a love match and, in fact, they both preferred this sort of arrangement. He would gladly include her in his life and they'd have a calm, advantageous marriage…unlike the tumultuous, frenzied, crazy-making one he'd have with someone like Meredith.

The last thing he needed was a woman in his life who goaded him into making bad decisions. He'd leave that kind of woman to his father.

Jason was incredibly fortunate Meiling's traditional family seemed forward-thinking enough to overlook his Western heritage. He was a man navigating a world largely populated by women. He needed an edge. Meiling was it. Nothing could stop his careful plans.

Except for Avery's misguided notion of slipping CEO out from under him. Which would happen when camels learned to swim.

"Why don't we worry about who will be the boss when the merger is done?" Jason suggested smoothly.

They needed to focus on more important things or there wouldn't be a CEO position to fill. Bettina and Paul were very comfortable in their current roles as CEOs of their halves, especially Bettina since she largely depended on Jason to advise her, but the winds of change were upon his parents whether they liked it or not.

Avery scowled but nodded. "Fine. For now. But don't think you're getting away with something. I'm not going to back off. Let's get to work."

They hashed out details for the next twenty minutes until his sister had to jet to her *Project Runway* meeting. In the cab back to Lyn, Jason dialed Meiling. It was only appropriate she hear about the marriage-license snafu from him. Hopefully she would appreciate the expedience of already having divorce papers in hand. Once his lawyer looked over them, it would be a done deal and he'd never have to see Meredith again…except in his mind where her luminous eyes beckoned him into an upside-down world where pleasure and understanding and connection didn't seem like such foreign concepts.

He had to stop thinking about her. It was disrespectful to Meiling, if nothing else. There was no scenario in which Meredith being in his life—even briefly—made a bit of sense.

# Two

It was past seven o'clock, but Meredith's stomach seemed stuck on Central Standard Time and dinner had about the same appeal as a tetanus shot. *Nerves.* Everything rode on this very quiet, very quick divorce.

Lars, her father's lawyer, had been so patient when he'd explained that he'd found the marriage record during a thorough investigation of her father's beneficiaries. If her father hadn't decided to update his will, she might never have known the marriage to Jason existed and thankfully, it had come out *before* she approached her father about the loan.

Without a prenuptial agreement, Jason could claim to be a beneficiary to her father's billions if he chose to fight for them in court. Thank God Lars had been her father's lawyer since before she was born and was sweet on her. He'd agreed to keep her stupidity a secret until she took care of the divorce and then he'd advised her to come clean to her father or he would be forced to mention it on her behalf.

A legal marriage she didn't know about smacked of carelessness, and she couldn't stand the thought of asking her father for a loan in the same breath as admitting a mistake she hadn't yet fixed. Her sister, Cara, would never do something rash like a quickie Vegas wedding to a man she'd just met, let alone mess up the undoing of it. Meredith wanted to prove she could be as responsible as Cara. Once Meredith had Jason's signature, she could present the marriage and divorce as a package deal, and hopefully everyone would agree she'd handled it like an adult who deserved a loan and a partnership opportunity in a successful business.

Good thing Meredith wasn't hungry. If one of the trendy restaurants around her hotel tried to swipe her credit card to pay for the exorbitant menu prices, the plastic would probably catch fire and disintegrate. The credit limit on her Visa was laughable, but she'd qualified for it all by herself. No one could take away the satisfaction of paying her own way—that was what the Grown-Up Pact should have helped her realize, but it had taken a lot longer for the epiphany than she'd expected.

She hadn't counted on sticking around this expensive Manhattan hotel over the weekend, but she recognized Jason's wisdom in being available, just in case.

No biggie. She probably didn't need to eat anyway. Better to get used to lean times now because once she bought into Cara's business, she'd have a loan to repay on top of a paltry savings account.

Listlessly, she ran through the TV channels a fourth time. When her cell phone beeped, she greedily grabbed it in hopes of taking her mind off Jason.

Except it was a text from the man himself: I'm in the lobby. Text me your room number.

A quick, sharp thrill shot through her midsection. Oh, she didn't fool herself for a minute. He wasn't here to take her up on the ill-advised invitation for a drink. The man was engaged and she sincerely hoped he wasn't the kind of guy who'd fool around on his fiancée. If he *was* interested in "catching up," she wasn't—poaching on men in committed relationships wasn't her style.

She texted him back and hightailed it to the bathroom to splash on some perfume and freshen her makeup because Chandler-Harris women did not allow anyone to see their cracks.

The knock startled her despite her expecting it. *That was fast.*

She opened the door and the dark expression on Jason's face swept out to engulf her and not in a good way. The back of her neck crawled. "What's wrong?"

"Just let me in. I'm not having this conversation with you while lounging in the hall."

Silently, she pushed the door wide, forcing him to slide past her to enter the room. It was a deliberate ploy, but his solid body brushed hers deliciously and she wasn't sorry she'd done it.

Jason filled the hotel room and she couldn't tear her gaze from him. "I take it you aren't planning to ask me to dinner. Which would be totally fine, by the way. I haven't eaten yet."

"You've ruined everything," he said shortly. "Everything. I've worked so blasted hard for two years, and in one afternoon, it's gone. Poof."

"What are you talking about? I'm here to *fix* the problem."

"I told my fiancée the cute story of a torrid weekend in Vegas and how, get this, it's so funny, but it turns out I'm still married. She was not amused. In fact, she was so unamused, our engagement is over."

"Oh, Jason! I'm so sorry." Meredith's hand flew to her mouth involuntarily. How terrible. He had to be beside himself. No wonder his mood seemed so black. "I never imagined—"

"So here's how this is going to go. You cost me a very important contact in the textile industry. You owe me. And you are going to pay, starting right now."

She took a step backward as his ire rolled over her. "Uh, pay how?"

This was not the man she remembered from Vegas. He looked the same, had the same rocking body and a voice that should be required by law to talk dirty to her twenty-four seven. But this Jason Lynhurst was harder, more brittle. She didn't like it.

"In as many unpleasant ways as I can devise," he muttered and swept her with a look. "But not *that* way. This is strictly business, sweetheart. I need you to do something for me."

Since he'd just lost his fiancée, and likely was nursing a broken heart, she'd let the condescension slide. "I'm truly sorry that your fiancée is upset. I'm sure you can smooth things over. Do that thing with your mouth, you kno—"

"Meiling is not upset."

Fire flared from his gaze, giving her a great big clue who the upset party was in this equation. Since he'd interrupted her again, she crossed her arms and perched on the desk so he could burn off that mad.

"If she's not upset, what is she?"

Jason started pacing, rearranging his spiky hair with absent fingers as he stomped around in her small room, shedding his suit jacket as he went.

"She's unwilling to associate with someone who would marry a stranger in a crass Vegas wedding and then fail to follow up to ensure the marriage was dissolved. Her exact words." He tossed his jacket on the bed with a great deal more force than necessary. "I've embarrassed her in front of her family, and in her world, that's unforgivable. So there's no smoothing it over."

The light dawned. "You weren't in love with her."

Why that made her so happy, she couldn't pinpoint. But the realization moved through her with a wicked thrill nonetheless.

Jason shot her an annoyed glare. "Of course not. It was a business arrangement, and now I've lost the in I had into the Asian textile market. Lyn needed Meiling's connections. Since this is all your fault, you owe me."

Okay, this was not what she'd anticipated. Where was the sensitive, passionate man she'd spent many luscious hours with once upon a time? He'd been replaced with a coldhearted suit who possessed not a shred of romance in his soul.

"My fault?" She tightened her crossed arms before she used one to right-hook him to the ground. "Seems like your fiancée—sorry, ex-fiancée—called it exactly right. You didn't follow up, either. Actually, you should be thanking me that I came to you with the truth before you got married. You'd be guilty of bigamy. Imagine explaining *that* to your Meiling."

"I depended on you to destroy the papers." He made a noise of disgust. "I shouldn't have, obviously."

That stung. Mostly because the implication—that she couldn't be counted on and wasn't smart enough to handle a simple task—was actually true in this case. "You're not endearing me to your cause, honey. Doesn't seem like I owe you anything but an apology. Which I've already given."

"You want to play hardball?" He advanced on her, the look in his eyes enigmatic and edgy. "Fine. I can indulge you. I lost an advantage and you're going to help me regain it. Granted, you don't have Meiling's connections, but I'm sure you've got many tricks up your sleeve. Until I get back on track, what's my hurry to sign the divorce papers?"

He stopped not a foot from her as his meaning sank in. He wasn't going to give her the divorce unless she did whatever it was that he wanted. Which still hadn't been clearly established.

Poking a finger in the center of his chest, she held her ground. "You wouldn't dare."

"Try me. I've got nothing to lose."

Gazes deadlocked, they stared at each other. No way would she blink first. Or move her index finger from his hard torso.

God in Heaven, that beautiful face of his. She soaked

it in and something sharp tore right through her abdomen. Many a morning over the past two years, she'd woken in a cold sweat with no idea what she'd dreamed, but certain Jason Lynhurst had played a starring role in it. That face lingered in her mind's eye far past the time when she should have forgotten it.

And here he was. Her fingers relaxed and flattened against his chest, easily, as if her palm belonged there. He glanced down and back up, meeting her gaze again with lowered lids. As if the thrumming tension had wound through him with equal fervor.

"If you've got nothing to lose, then I'd be more than happy to try you," she murmured.

She bunched his shirt in her fist and reeled him in. He hesitated for an eternity and then their lips met. The sweet taste of Jason swept through her and it was as if they'd never been apart. She nearly wept as Jason's arms came around her, drawing her closer.

This was the Jason of Vegas, the one she'd worked so hard to forget and couldn't.

*Oh, yes.* Her heart burst into motion, pumping euphoria through her veins as if it hadn't beaten in two long years. Hungrily, he sucked her deeper into the kiss and sparks danced behind her eyelids.

She pulled back, chest heaving from the effort of not diving into him with abandon. As they stared at each other, locked in a long moment, a glimpse of the man he'd been flitted through his features.

Something pulled at her heart. Oh, that was not good. *That* was why she'd never forgotten him—he'd taken a piece of her she'd never meant to give.

"Now that we've gotten that out of the way, can we start over?" she asked, her voice more tremulous than she would have liked.

Because she'd just realized letting him go in Vegas might have been the biggest mistake of her life.

* * *

In spite of it all, a chuckle spilled from Jason's mouth and reluctantly, he let his arms drop from the siren he'd somehow wound up kissing. He'd come here to wring her neck, but instead, she'd expertly defused his mood.

But that didn't mean they'd be falling right back into a crazy-town affair, not when so much was at stake. Not when he couldn't seem to keep his hands off her. "Depends on what the definition of starting over is."

Meredith pursed her kiss-stung lips, and he decided it was better to put a little more distance between them. She was even more dangerous than he'd realized and he refused to follow in his father's footsteps. Paul had left Bettina for a younger, sexier wife, with no regard to the consequences to his company or his family. Obviously, it was in the Lynhurst blood to let passion rule, but that didn't have to be Jason's fate and *someone* had to step up where his father had failed.

Jason had a vision for putting the pieces of his life back together and no woman would sway him from realizing it. He was stronger than his father.

While he flopped into one of the overstuffed chairs in the sitting area of her hotel room, she crossed to the minibar and pulled two beers from the fridge, flipped off the caps expertly and handed him one.

"I don't want to be at odds, Jason. You're upset. I get that. But don't come in here slinging ultimatums and expect me to fall in line. Let's do this differently."

*What the hell.* He loosened his tie, guzzled a third of the cold dark beer and raised his eyebrows. "Which is how?"

She took the opposite chair and swung it around to face him, settling into it with her beer. Kicking off her heels, she curled her feet under her and propped her chin on her hand. "Talk to me. Like you used to. Tell me what you want in exchange for the divorce. I might volunteer to give it to you, for old times' sake."

*Like you used to.* As if they had history.

But really, didn't they? Just because it had only been one weekend didn't make it any less significant, whether he'd like to go back in time and erase it or not.

"What if what I really want is to stay married?"

It wasn't, but he was in a reckless mood after all his careful plans had unraveled in the course of an afternoon. One kiss wasn't enough to get him completely over the destruction this woman had caused. Plus, she'd piqued his curiosity about the divorce. Why was it so important to her? There were a lot of women who might find it convenient to be married to someone from a powerful fashion-industry family. The fact that she didn't intrigued him.

Of course, Meredith had always been one of a kind.

Her genuine smile hit him in the not-yet-cooled lower half, further proving the point. No woman had ever turned him on with simply a grin. Except his wife, apparently.

"You don't want to stay married any more than I do," she said. "The fact that you're threatening me with it tells me you need something very badly. What?"

His return smile shouldn't have been so easy, but her mind had always been the most attractive thing about her. He might never have left Vegas with a solid idea of how to heal the fractures in his life without her influence. Why not continue the trend?

"Do you remember why I was in Vegas?"

"I remember everything, including that cute birthmark on your butt. Your parents divorced and split up Lynhurst. You were a wreck over it." She waggled her brows. "Or you were until I distracted you."

It had happened two years ago. The memories shouldn't be so sharp, but they were…for both of them, obviously. "You did take care of me, quite well. And vice versa, if I recall."

"Oh, yeah. That was never in question." She shut her

eyes for a beat and hummed happily under her breath. "Best nineteen orgasms of my life."

"You kept track?"

She glanced at him from under lowered lashes, her gaze hot and full of appreciation. "Darling, I didn't have to keep track. Every one of them is burned into my center. Indelibly."

He let himself drown in memories of her for a moment. None of the barriers he easily employed with other women seemed to have an effect on her anyway. "Yeah. I can see your point."

The experience was scored across his soul, as well. Meredith had brought out a wild side he hadn't even realized existed. Or maybe it only existed because of her, which was all the more reason to stay far away.

"Was there a reason you brought that up?" Meredith asked. "We seem to be stuck on it, when I could have sworn you had something else entirely you wanted to chat about."

He shook his gaze free from the seductive depths of Meredith's gaze and cleared his throat.

Obviously, he needed to take a cold shower if he hoped to accomplish anything. Whatever power she held over him couldn't be allowed to interfere with the endgame. "I spent the last two years executing the plan I came up with in Vegas. It's simple. Reunite Lyn Couture and Hurst House under the Lynhurst Enterprises umbrella and step into the CEO position. Who better to run it than me, right?"

Slinging a shapely leg over the arm of the chair, she tossed back the last of her beer as her skirt rode up to reveal a healthy slice of gorgeous thigh. "Yep. You've got CEO written all over you."

"Meiling was a part of that plan." *A critical part.* She was the kind of wife a CEO needed, not the overblown sex goddess in the opposite chair. But he had to work with what he had. "Now that she's out of the picture, I have to come up with plan B."

"That's where I come in."

He nodded, relieved for some odd reason that she still read him so well. "I don't want to use the divorce as leverage."

"But you will."

Transparency meant she saw the not-so-nice-guy parts, as well, and that made him a little uncomfortable. He shrugged. "This is my legacy. I cannot fathom veering from the course I've laid out and that means I have to improvise if I want to fix the rift in my family's company. You fill the gap where Meiling's advantage used to be and I'll sign the divorce papers."

Meredith was a loose cannon—prone to dropping projectiles wherever she went. But she had a sharp wit and determination and best of all, she wanted something from him. That was the best combination possible under the circumstances.

"Why don't you sign them now and I'll offer to help as a thank-you?" she countered sweetly and that was the opening he'd been waiting for.

He cocked his head. "Why are you so hot for a divorce from a guy you didn't even know you were married to last week? Am I such a bad catch?"

Her giggle warmed his insides. A lot. Too much.

"I have never thought of you as a fish."

Which didn't answer the question at all. He should sign the papers right now and let her go back to Houston. But he couldn't, and he really didn't want to examine why it was so important that Meredith help him because he suspected it had too much to do with this nameless draw between them.

And that was a problem. One of many.

But he did need an edge; that much was still true.

If Avery would only drop her bid for CEO, he wouldn't have to play this game of chicken with Meredith. But Avery would definitely dig in her heels and she was a Lynhurst—that made her a treacherous opponent. He didn't for a min-

ute underestimate his sister's vindictiveness or her strategic
mind. He'd let her have the CEO position over his dead
body. Meredith was his secret advantage and she owed him.

Now he had to figure out how she could help.

"This goes both ways, you know." He flipped a hand
between them. "I'm talking. You have to talk, too. Tell me
why this divorce is so important."

She sighed and her expression blanked. It was wrong on
her. Normally, her beautiful face glowed with expressive-
ness and he was a little sorry he'd brought up the question.
But not entirely. She'd been trying to weasel out of spilling
this information for too long.

"You have a dream and so do I," she said and it was clear
she was choosing her words carefully. "I've been advised
that in order to pursue mine, it would be beneficial to have
my affairs in order. Correction—affair. I have no interest
in being married. To you, or anyone. So sign the papers
and everyone wins."

Now he was thoroughly intrigued, especially because
he'd never in a million years label the reuniting of Lynhurst as a dream. It was a fact. "What's your dream, Meredith? Tell me."

"Why?" she asked suspiciously. "More leverage?"

Oh, yeah, she was no dummy. And that turned him
on as much as everything else in her full package. More
maybe. The fact that she was so savvy about his motivation
changed it instantly. "No, because I'm curious. My mouth
has been between your legs. That gives me special rights
to know what's between your ears, too."

Her long, slow smile blew the blank expression away.
Better. And worse.

"You win. But only because that's a great point and I
happen to like it." She retrieved another beer and handed
him a second, as well, then settled into her chair.

He tapped the longneck. "Trying to get me drunk so
you can take advantage of me?"

She snorted. "Honey, I don't need alcohol for that."

Unfortunately, she might be right. All the more reason to nail down an agreement about their future interaction—which would be minimal. "So I made a great point. You liked it. Spill your beans."

"I'm buying into my sister's wedding-dress business." And then she clammed up with a show of drinking her beer.

There was more. He could sense it beneath the surface. "Seems like being married might be a bonus for that line of work."

"It's not, okay? Not this way." She shook her head. "I can't tell my family I did tequila shots in Vegas and wound up married to some guy. They'd never take me seriously again."

As he thoroughly and uniquely understood the sentiment, he grinned. "You make it sound tawdry. You can't tell them we fell in love?"

"Please. You can't even say that with a straight face and neither could I. They'd wonder why we haven't had any contact in two years, for one thing."

"Now that you mention it, I'm curious. Did you ever think about looking me up?"

He had briefly entertained the idea of contacting her on the plane home but then dismissed it as he hashed through mental plans about what it would take to get Lynhurst Enterprises back together. Besides, no one could be involved with Meredith long-term; the idea was ludicrous. She wasn't the kind of woman you settled down with. She was too lush, too distracting, too…everything. She'd compelled him to make stupid decisions without even opening her mouth.

He'd known then she'd spell disaster for his plans. Regrettably, he'd underestimated how catastrophic she'd ultimately be.

"Not once." Casually, she lifted the beer to her lips. Too casually, and he saw the guilt in the depths of her eyes. But why she'd lie was a mystery. "We agreed to part ways in Vegas. The Grown-Up Pact wasn't about actually staying married, right? It was about proving we could take grown-up steps. If we could do it together, we could do it apart. So why stonewall me on this divorce? Makes no sense."

"Does, too. Getting married had value. Staying married has advantages, too."

"For you. Though I have yet to hear how."

The time had come to lay it all on the line. "In order to reunite Lynhurst Enterprises, I have to take a strategic plan to the executive committees of Lyn Couture and Hurst House Fashion. My former fiancée's father owns the largest textile company in Asia and our marriage would have solidified a partnership with Lyn Couture, thus lowering production costs dramatically. Hurst House would want to benefit from this association and from my leadership."

Meredith could never fill that gap, but there had to be some way to spin this situation to his advantage.

"My sister, Avery," he continued, "was the second half of the plan. She runs the branding and marketing for Hurst House and we planned for her to quit Hurst House to come work for Lyn. Without her, the company would flounder, thus forcing my father, the current CEO of Hurst, to consider merging."

There was more, much more, but he kept those cards close to the vest. She didn't need to know his entire strategy.

"That's quite brilliant." Genuine appreciation shone from Meredith's gaze. "Sorry a weekend in Vegas a million years ago messed it all up."

The weekend in Vegas had helped him conceive this plan. Without it, he might never have come up with it. Ironic that the same weekend had come back to bite him.

"There's more. Avery's not on board with the plan anymore. She wants the CEO spot and I wouldn't put it past her to cook up her own scheme." Instantly, he knew how Meredith could provide that missing advantage. "I need someone she doesn't know to be my spy at Hurst House. Someone firmly on my side who can tell me what she's up to."

Meredith lit up but then quickly tamped back her excitement. "You want me to be a *spy* in a New York fashion house? In exchange for a divorce? That doesn't seem like a fair trade."

"Really?" Nonchalantly, he swallowed the last of his beer. "What would?"

A crafty glint in her eye raised the hair on the back of his neck.

"You have to put me on the payroll."

*That's* what she wanted? He'd expected her to ask for full marriage benefits, which would have been very difficult to refuse. Though he would have refused, for the sake of Lynhurst. He couldn't afford to let a woman cloud his vision. "Sure. I have no problem compensating you, though you'd have to be on the payroll at Hurst so no one suspects anything. What else?"

"The marriage stays a secret, now and after the divorce is final. I can't let it become known or my wedding-dress dream is over."

"That's easy. I don't care for anyone to know about it, either."

If Avery got ahold of that bit of information, she'd use it to her advantage somehow. The last thing Jason needed was to give someone leverage—someone other than him, that was.

She eyed him. "That's not what it sounded like a minute ago. You were all set to blab to your family about how we were in love."

"I was kidding. Love might make the world go round, but it tears businesses apart." Like his parents' failed marriage had done to Lynhurst Enterprises. He'd never repeat his father's mistakes. "The only reason to marry someone is if it gets you closer to where you want to be."

"I see. Marriage is your weapon. How romantic." She rolled her eyes. "Lucky me."

"Marriage is a tool," he corrected. "Romance is for losers who can't figure out how to get a woman into bed. I suffer from no such limitations."

"You might be surprised at what I consider romantic." She swept him with a heated once-over that slammed through him with knock-down, drag-out force.

"You're not going to be my wife in anything other than the legal sense. This is a strictly platonic deal, Meredith. I'm serious."

Her laugh rolled through him. "We'll see about that. It's not like you're suffering from a broken heart."

He had the distinct feeling he'd inadvertently challenged her to turn him into a liar. "So that means we're agreed?"

"I'll help you in exchange for the divorce, but only for a few weeks. I want twenty grand, not some measly minimum-wage salary. And you have to foot the bill for my hotel room."

He stuck out his hand and Meredith shook it. "Welcome to Lynhurst."

"Happy to be on board." She pulled him closer, skewering him with a sultry gaze. "What does a girl have to do to get the COO to take her to dinner?"

# Three

Meredith spent Monday morning shopping at Barneys and cursed her meager credit limit. She'd packed a few days' worth of outfits for her unexpected trip to New York, not nearly enough for the two or three weeks she now planned to stay. And nothing in her suitcase would fly as a wardrobe for an employee at a high-class place like Hurst.

She still couldn't quite believe *she* had landed a job in a real fashion house. It was a dream come true, but one of those usually unattainable childhood dreams like becoming an astronaut or ballerina. And part of the dream was getting to dress the part.

Asking Jason for an advance on her salary would have invited too many questions, so she made do with the sale rack. Most of the clothes were out of season. She'd be outed as a fraud in a New York minute. No pun intended.

But still, it was a morning shopping at Barneys in Manhattan and life did not suck. Except for the part where she still didn't have the divorce papers signed…and she'd have to take an extended vacation from her job with her sister.

For the past two years, she'd assisted Cara as she designed and sold wedding dresses to Houston brides. Cara had recently begun selling her dresses in an upscale boutique and business was booming. Meredith wanted to make more of a contribution than simply as an assistant. What else could she do but buy in as a partner? Wedding dresses were Cara's first love and she excelled at the design side. Meredith might as well help on the financial side. She had little else to offer.

This was her chance to prove she had what it took. To prove everyone wrong who thought there wasn't anything more to Meredith than the stuff they saw on the outside.

Cara was in Barbados. Or was it Saint Martin? Meredith could never keep track of which resort her brother-in-law had dragged her sister to. Keith, her sister's husband, ran around the Caribbean fixing up resorts in his consultant job and Cara traveled with him. Hopefully she'd understand Meredith's need for time off without asking too many questions.

Meredith made a mental note to call her sister later.

Her phone buzzed and she keyed up the text message from Jason: Where are you? I'm at the hotel.

She texted him back: Shopping. Be back soon.

What was that all about? Was she supposed to sit around and wait for His Highness to appear? He might have his precious leverage—and she was still a little miffed about it, make no mistake—but that didn't mean Meredith planned to jump when he said jump.

When she got to the hotel after dallying an extra ten minutes just because, Jason was waiting for her in the lobby. He didn't notice her right away. Unashamedly, she watched him as he talked on the phone.

The man was unparalleled in the looks department. Clean-cut, gorgeous cheekbones, equally comfortable in a suit, jeans or nothing at all. It was enough to make a girl salivate.

And then he saw her. A smile spread across his face and sent a shiver down her spine.

Platonic was not going to happen. She was in New York for a couple of weeks, they were married, for God's sake, and they'd certainly had plenty of sex in the past. Why would he even say something so ridiculous?

They'd walked away from each other once and it hadn't worked out so well. It was time to try *not* walking away.

He pocketed his phone and stood.

"You should give me a key," he suggested when she met up with him as he strode toward the elevator.

"In case you want to make a middle-of-the-night visit to your wife? Because I'm totally okay with that."

He chuckled and stuck his palm against the open elevator door so Meredith could enter ahead of him. "Because I'm paying for the room. I might as well use it to make private phone calls instead of letting everyone in the lobby hear about Lyn's strategic plans."

Why was he so against resuming their relationship? It wasn't as if she was asking him to stay married—that wasn't what she wanted, either. Once she got herself established in a career, then she could think about whether she actually wanted to get married. Some women—like Cara—dreamed of nothing but white dresses and bouquets, but Meredith had never thought marriage was all that great of a goal.

Figuring out how to be a grown-up was the scary, frustrating can't-see-the-light-at-the-end-of-the-tunnel quandary Meredith couldn't dig her way out of. That goal felt as out of reach as it had two years ago.

She stuck her tongue out at him and fished the extra card key out of her purse, then handed it over. "Seems like a waste of a good hotel room to me. Sorry you had to hang out in the lobby, sugar, but perhaps you should have told me to expect you and I would have been here," she said without a trace of irony.

She hadn't heard from him all weekend. Not that she'd expected to.

He waved it off and followed her to her room. "I was in the neighborhood, so I came by to go over all the arrangements I've made for you at Hurst House."

"Already?" Her throat got a little tight as this Machiavellian deal of Jason's got real.

What did she know about being a spy, in a fashion house or otherwise? The people at Jason's father's company would see through her instantly. If she failed at helping Jason get his plans back on track, would he refuse to sign the papers to spite her?

She should have gotten more of this established before she agreed. Actually, she should have told him no and demanded the divorce. But she well remembered how destroyed he'd been over the company splitting up, and she did have a *little* bit of fault in the marriage becoming legal in the first place, though how the paperwork had gotten submitted still baffled her. Her father's lawyer guessed that someone filed it on their behalf, probably a well-meaning hotel maid, but they'd never know for sure. Too much time had passed for anyone to remember.

She felt horrible about her part in it, and if she wished to prove she wasn't actually a scatterbrain, this was her opportunity. She couldn't abandon Jason. Adults took responsibility for mistakes and accepted consequences. Period.

"Yeah, already." His eyebrows went up. "You think I have time to waste? Avery doesn't rest, and she's too smart to underestimate. She'll have alternate plans in place in hopes of upstaging me. I can feel it."

"So what am I going to be doing?"

"You mentioned the other night at dinner that you'd been working as a designer's assistant. So it was a no-brainer to put you in that same role at Hurst House."

"Just like that?"

She would be working for a *God-honest designer*. If it was that easy to get a job working in the fashion industry in New York, could she have been doing it all along?

Her throat opened a little. At least she didn't have to learn a whole new job to be Jason's spy.

Except working with Cara was miles and miles away

from working with an established clothing label. Cara loved her and if Meredith occasionally messed up, it didn't feel like the end of the world. That's why buying into Cara's business was so important. It wasn't like Meredith could work with just anyone. It was the only opportunity available to her.

"Just like that. After I called my mother and asked her to recommend you, she called Hurst House Human Resources and informed them you'd be arriving tomorrow morning. The vice president of HR still has a guilt complex over defecting to Hurst House, so he'd pretty much do whatever my mom says."

"I see." How crazy was that? If only the rest of Meredith's appointed task went so easily. "And that's it? I show up, help one of the designers and wait around for Avery to stroll by? What if I never even see her?"

Why had she agreed to this again?

"You'll have to wing it. If you want the divorce badly enough, you'll figure out how to get the information I need."

Oh, so that's why he needed leverage. He didn't have any idea how this was supposed to go and hoped she'd be desperate enough to figure it out for him.

She snorted to cover her rising panic. "Lucky for you I'm a fast thinker."

"It's not luck." He shot her a strange look. "If I didn't think you could handle it, I never would have suggested this idea. You've got one of the sharpest minds of anyone I've ever met and I have no doubt you'll put your own spin on the assignment. In fact, I'm counting on it."

He thought she was smart. The revelation planted itself in her abdomen and spread with warm fingers. And of course, that alone motivated her in a way nothing else could. "You got it. I'm gonna be the best spy you've ever seen."

Jason was the only man who'd ever seen past her skin

to the real Meredith underneath. She'd never dreamed it would come to mean so much. Being here in his presence again, after all this time, had solidified why no other man did it for her.

But it had also brought home an ugly truth.

In Vegas, it had been okay to be clueless and spill all her uncertainty because Jason was at the same place. He'd grown up after coming home, like they'd planned. She hadn't. And that seemed to have everything to do with why he was so different.

She wanted the Jason of two years ago. And this unexpected extra time together gave her the perfect opportunity to peel back the layers of this new version of the man she'd married to see if she could find him again.

By ten o'clock the next morning, Meredith wished for a mocha latte, a bubble bath and that she'd never heard of Hurst House. Allo, the only-one-name-required in-house designer she'd been assigned to assist, hated her. Allo hated everyone as best Meredith could tell.

Allo called for shears yet again—the third time he'd changed his mind about whether he wanted chalk or shears—so Meredith trotted obediently to the table where all of Allo's tools had to be carefully stored when not in use. Even if he planned to use them in the next five minutes.

She placed the shears in Allo's outstretched hand and waited for the next round of barked instructions.

*"Non, non, non."* Allo threw the shears on the floor and kicked them across the beautiful blond hardwood. "I said pins. Take the cotton out of your head and pay attention."

"Pins. Coming right up," she muttered and cursed under her breath as she crossed to the cabinet yet again.

Tomorrow she'd wear flats. And bring cyanide to flavor Allo's chai tea. Not really, but she'd fantasized about it more than once after being told to remake the beverage four times.

Who was Meredith to question the genius of Allo, who had single-handedly launched Hurst House into the stratosphere with his line of ready-to-wear evening gowns? She'd even been a little tongue-tied when she'd first met him and secretly hoped she might absorb some of that genius. She still might. If she didn't kill him first.

None of Allo's assistants lasted longer than two months, according to the gossip she'd overheard in Human Resources that morning.

No wonder Bettina's phone call had netted Meredith a job so fast.

Now all she had to do was figure out how to casually run into Avery, pump her for secret information about her plans to thwart Jason's bid for CEO and then take over the world. Easy as pie.

At lunchtime, Meredith wearily contemplated the wilted salad and unidentifiable meat on offer in the building's cafeteria. The shopping trip to Barneys had been a wasted effort since everyone employed at Hurst House wore the Hurst House label, a small fact Jason could have mentioned. So her credit card was maxed out unnecessarily—though the off-the-shoulder Alexander Wang dress she'd found buried in the sale rack was amazing and she loved it. But having an amazing dress meant a low-cost and tasteless lunch.

All in the name of couture espionage.

"I wouldn't recommend the Salisbury steak."

Meredith glanced behind her and recognized Janelle, the girl from Human Resources who had performed Meredith's employee orientation. "Is that what it is? I wondered."

Janelle laughed. "They like to keep us guessing."

It was unusual to get such a friendly reception from another woman, and Meredith needed all the friends she could get if she hoped to score any information useful to Jason's cause. "What would you recommend for someone on a budget?"

Janelle pointed to the unrecognizable off-white lumps behind the Salisbury steak. "Chicken. Can't go wrong with that. It doesn't taste like anything in the first place, so it's hard to ruin it."

"Point taken." Meredith collected her lunch plate and inclined her head toward Janelle. "Any other first-day advice? I mean besides don't take a job working for Allo. That one I figured out on my own."

"Yeah, sorry about that." With a sympathetic smile, Janelle jerked her head in the direction of the dining room. "We made a pact in HR to do what we can to convince you to stay. Allo generates more paperwork for us than the tax department. Sit with me and I'll give you the scoop."

Oddly grateful for the support, Meredith followed Janelle to an unoccupied table as the other woman chatted about how to get around Allo's strident personality, how to win points and anything else she deemed worthwhile.

It wasn't until lunch was nearly over that Meredith got the break she'd been waiting for.

Janelle folded her napkin and glanced at her watch. "I've got to get back. I'll see you at the Garment Center gala tonight, right?"

"I don't know. What is it?"

"Samantha was supposed to invite you. I told her to send you an email with the details." Janelle looked annoyed. "Hurst House is a supporter of Save the Garment Center and there's a fund-raiser tonight. Avery Lynhurst—oh, she's the vice president of Marketing, if you haven't met her yet—is running the event and she wants all employees there. It makes her look good."

What better place to get in front of Jason's sister than a social event? And as a brand-new Hurst House employee, all the more reason to make sure she met everyone in attendance.

And it was a fashion-industry event that she got to attend. The thought made her downright cheerful.

"I'll be there," Meredith pledged and watched Janelle as she left the lunchroom.

As soon as Janelle was out of sight, she called Jason, who answered on the first ring.

"You have news, I trust?" he asked shortly, and the undercurrent said she was interrupting him, so she better make it good.

"There's an event tonight," she murmured softly in case anyone was listening in. "A Garment Center thing. Avery's going to be there, so I am, too. It's an opportunity to chat with her without raising any alarms."

"Excellent." Jason's voice warmed. "I'd forgotten about the gala, but you're right, it's perfect."

"There's one problem. I don't have anything to wear."

"That's the exact opposite of a problem," he said drily. "It so happens I know a couple of people in the evening-wear business. I'll swing by your hotel at six."

"You don't know what size I wear."

"Sweetheart, I'm a Lynhurst and that's plain insulting. Trust me," he advised with a chuckle. "See you tonight."

And that promise alone got her through the afternoon with Allo, the master of terror.

By tonight, she'd be one step closer to getting Jason's signature on the divorce papers. Then she could go back to Houston and get started on the rest of her grown-up life.

That had always been the plan. It should *still* be the plan. But she feared she'd spend the rest of her life dreaming of the man she'd divorced and continue to date lackluster men who couldn't begin to compare.

How had getting a man's signature on a piece of paper complicated everything so much?

# Four

Jason pounded on the door of Meredith's hotel room for the fourth time and juggled the zipped garment bags. Again. When had he become an errand boy for a woman who'd probably never owned a clock in her life?

Enough was enough. He'd said six. It was six-oh-seven and Meredith *had* given him a key. And all the clothes he'd brought were heavy. If he didn't let himself in, they'd be late to the gala, and it would be more difficult to enter separately, keeping up the ruse that they didn't know each other.

But what if she was in the shower or blow-drying her hair in a little satin robe? One or the other was the most likely reason she hadn't heard his many knocks.

That decided it.

It would serve her right to gain an audience if she was naked in the bathroom. A guy could hope.

Bobbling the garment bags until his fingers closed around the card key in his pocket, he cleared the threshold and dumped his cargo on the bed. His wife strolled from the bathroom at the same moment, clad in nothing but a skimpy towel, revealing miles and miles of legs and toned arms.

All that bare skin seared his retinas. The full force of her slammed into the backs of his knees, weakening them dangerously. It was one thing to barge into a hotel room on the possible assumption the female occupant might be undressed; it was another to get his wish.

His tongue went numb and every drop of blood in his body drained into the instant bulge in his pants.

How could he have walked away from *that* in Vegas? He couldn't tear his gaze from her and a half whimper, half growl crawled out of his throat before he could stop it.

She didn't even have the grace to look startled or embarrassed.

"Hey, you," she called and pulled some frothy concoction of lace from her suitcase without censor, like men appeared in her bedroom unannounced on a regular basis.

Maybe they did. He frowned. Why did that thought make the back of his throat feel as if it was on fire?

"Uh, hey." He cleared his throat as she slid a foot into the sexy panties.

Instantly, he whirled to face the window. Apparently she intended to get dressed as if he wasn't even here. And what had he expected when he'd cavalierly charged into her room?

"Surely you're not shy all of a sudden. You've seen everything I've got and then some."

He could hear the smile in her voice. "It's the 'and then some' that's the problem," he muttered.

This was ridiculous. The thought of his wife with another man made him want to claw the paint off the walls, yet she wasn't really his wife and they were not going to repeat the craziness of the first round of their relationship. They *had* no relationship. And that's how it was going to stay.

She laughed. "You're wearing a tux. Are you going, too?"

"Yeah. You don't think I expect you to do this all on your own, do you?"

Of course, the plan to accompany her had formed well before she'd reminded him what happened when they spent more than five seconds in a room together. Abrupt loss of focus. Instant desire to do nothing more than spend several hours in bed, with Meredith's soft laugh and softer skin against his.

The woman turned him stupid instantly.

"What, you don't trust me?" she asked coquettishly. "I'm dressed. You can stop pretending to have some misguided sense of modesty."

"I'm not pretending. Just because we're married doesn't mean I should get a free show."

He turned to face the interior of the room and got an eyeful of Meredith's idea of *dressed*—a bra-and-panty set skimpy enough that it should be illegal. God, she was going to kill him.

The freaking bath towel had covered more flesh. Her smile said she knew exactly what she was doing to him.

"Honey, you can fantasize about keeping this platonic to your heart's content. Just don't hold it against me if I give you something else to fantasize about." She raised her eyebrows suggestively. "What did you bring me?"

A hard-on the size of a subway train, apparently. "Clothes. I don't remember what."

She huffed out a sigh. "I'll check it out myself, then."

This heightened sense of awareness was merely the product of the close confines and distinct lack of sex over the past few months. Maybe if he could get a dress on her, and they got the hell out of this very private hotel room, he could breathe again.

Obviously, he had more in common with his hormonally driven father than Jason would have liked.

She unzipped the garment bag on top of the pile and squealed. "Oh, Jason."

His name in her throaty come-and-get-me voice washed over him, tightening the already massive erection he probably wasn't hiding as well as he hoped.

Who was he kidding? It didn't matter if they left the

hotel room; this evening was going to suck regardless because he couldn't think about anything *but* sex where Meredith was concerned.

He put some steel in his spine and pulled the glittery dress from the hanger. "It's one of Allo's. *Vogue* revealed it in a spread last week, but it's not in stores yet. I thought you might like to be the first woman to wear it out."

"What?" Her mouth gaped. "*Me?* You want me to wear a just-revealed dress designed by Allo to a *fashion-industry* event?"

Undisguised glee radiated from her expression and he forgot what he'd been about to say. Why did pleasing her make him feel as if *he'd* been given a gift?

"Put it on," he said, his voice husky and foreign. He cleared his throat. "I want to see it on you."

She complied, sliding her lithe legs through the opening at the top and gathering it into place against her torso. Then she presented her back, lifted her dark fall of gorgeous hair away and called over her shoulder, "Zip me up?"

Since his fingers were already straining for the zipper before she'd finished speaking, it seemed the answer was yes. He crossed to her and her heat reached out to engulf him. Slowly, he skated the zipper up its track, following the line of her bare flesh above it with his gaze.

*Wrong way*, his brain screamed. *Unzip! Unzip!*

He resisted. Barely. But his fingers wouldn't let go of the zipper pull, even though the dress was as zipped as it could be. Meredith's exotic perfume wrapped around him and somehow, his nose was nearly buried in her still-damp hair. It smelled like green apple. He sucked in a breath and the combination of scents and the essence of *her* wove through his senses.

She swayed, brushing his arousal with her shapely rear. He sought the curve of her waist, meaning to push her forward a step but instead rested his hands there as he drew her backward, flush with his body. Her head tipped back against his shoulder and she moaned so sexily, the answering spike of lust nearly blinded him.

So he shut his eyes and let his lips trail down her exposed throat. She tasted decadent and sinful and he wanted to sink into her.

"Jason," she murmured and twisted in his arms to peer up at him, her gaze heavy with unconcealed desire.

The kiss they'd shared roared back on a wave of unsuppressed memory and he ached to lay his lips on hers again. Her face tipped up, bringing her mouth within centimeters of his and paradise was within his reach.

But then she murmured his name again and said, "I'm absolutely okay with being really late to the gala. But are you?"

Rationality swamped him and cooled his ardor in a snap. "Yeah, no. Not really."

He stepped back. Meredith's mystifying and infuriating pull on him hadn't diminished, that was for sure. He didn't like it when someone had that much leverage over him, especially when he couldn't envision how she'd use it to her advantage.

Best-case scenario, she'd use it to get him into bed and leave it at that. He didn't ever count on best-case scenarios and besides, she'd have to try a lot harder to break his will.

His subconscious dissolved into gales of laughter and then reminded him that *she'd* been the one to halt what had almost turned into an invigorating reintroduction to the pleasures of his wife's body.

"All right, then." She smiled softly and he ignored the slight hitch it put in his gut. "Stop being so sexy and we'll have a much better shot of getting through the door."

He rolled his eyes. "The rest of the clothes are for you, too. I heard a rumor that you made a faux pas by wearing Alexander Wang your first day on the job. Allo is jealous of him. He wanted that Balenciaga job that Wang landed."

If Jason had known that weasel of a vice president in HR

would stick Meredith with Allo, he'd have specified otherwise. Too late now. He couldn't risk pulling any strings to get her reassigned or someone might get suspicious. But he could help her earn some points with her extremely difficult boss and the new clothes would accomplish that like nothing else. Allo was a narcissist to the core.

Meredith raised a brow. "Why, exactly, did you need me as a spy when you apparently already have plenty?"

"Nobody gossips about anything relevant to my merger plans." He waved a dismissive hand. "Only what people are wearing. Welcome to the world of fashion. And now you have a wardrobe worthy of the design floor at Hurst House."

The new wardrobe was also a bit of a thank-you, and he hoped she liked what he'd painstakingly picked out among the castoffs from Fashion Week.

"Wait, there's more than this dress? I figured the other bags held backups in case this one didn't fit." Meredith dug through the garment bags and squealed some more over the geometric dresses, skirts and angular tops from Hurst's newest line. None of it was available in stores yet, either.

"There you go insulting me again. You can try all of it on later," Jason advised. "We should leave. I have an out-of-the-way place in mind for a quick dinner. I'm sorry I can't take you to Nobu, or some place you might enjoy more, but we can't chance being photographed together."

She gave him an indecipherable look. "You don't have to take me to dinner at all. We're not dating. Just married."

"Which is why I should take you to dinner. Don't you think a wife should be treated better than a woman I'm simply dating?"

"Well…yeah." She tossed the four-hundred-dollar V-neck silk blouse on the bed. "But I thought you were Mr. No-Romance. Marriage is a tool, you said. I'm here to help you get a boring executive's job so you'll sign the divorce papers."

*Romance?* Dinner wasn't a precursor to seduction. Why was he torturing himself like this again? He threw up his hands. "Fine. Don't eat, then. We'll go to the gala and I'll shove you out of the car three blocks away so you can walk. Sound like a plan?"

"Good thing for you new clothes put me in a forgiving mood. So I'll overlook your bad attitude." As she stepped into a pair of sky-high stilettos—Miu Miu unless he missed his guess—she shot him a sunny smile. "And I would love to go to dinner. Thank you for asking."

Point taken. He groaned. "Meredith, would you like to go to dinner?"

She crossed to him and patted his cheek. "Maybe you should take some husband lessons if you hope to marry someone for real. Because, honey, you're obviously out of practice. For someone who thinks of marriage as a tool, you sure haven't figured out how to use it yet."

Her husky voice put plenty of innuendo in the statement, making it crystal clear she thought he was a moron for not taking advantage of what she was offering.

He followed her out of the hotel room and prayed her next suggestion wasn't an offer to be his tutor. Because he had the horrible feeling he might accept.

The third glass of champagne disappeared much more quickly than the second, and Meredith forced herself not to reach for a fourth. Avery Lynhurst still hadn't made an appearance and if Meredith was forced to watch another supermodel hit on Jason, she couldn't be held responsible for her actions.

It was bad enough that she couldn't keep her eyes off him. And worse, he didn't seem to be similarly afflicted. It was as if she didn't exist.

Meredith smiled at the buyer for Nordstrom who'd been chatting her up for ten minutes. Some of the most power-ful people in the New York fashion scene milled about in the Grand Ballroom of the iconic Plaza hotel and it was a bit dizzying to be in the midst of it.

Everyone in attendance dazzled in top-tier labels, and she voraciously soaked in the visual panorama. One lucky woman had somehow scored a Galinda Gennings gown adorned with real diamonds.

A hush fell on Meredith's right, but she didn't think anything of it until the crowd parted and Allo appeared on a tide of arrogance and condescending flair. She stifled a groan. Wasn't it bad enough that she had to spend eight hours a day being chastised? She deserved a night off.

"You." The designer waved his hand in Meredith's direction. "You're fired. See HR in the morning to get your exit papers."

What had she done now? A cold skitter went down her spine. Had someone seen her get out of Jason's car? They'd been so careful, separating on 58th Street a full two blocks from the hotel.

Allo's entourage tittered meanly and waited for the next round of fireworks with expectant expressions.

"Why?" Meredith narrowed one eye. "I did a great job working for you today. If you didn't think so, why didn't you say something earlier?"

*"Non."* Allo pursed his lips and muttered something in French that sounded uncomplimentary. "You have stolen my dress. You are a thief. That is the reason for your termination."

Meredith glanced down at the glittery dress Jason had given her. "This? You think I stole it?"

*Crap.* Why hadn't she and Jason discussed a good cover story? Of course a designer's brand-new assistant wouldn't have access to a dress that wasn't in stores yet. The photographers outside the ballroom had gone wild when Meredith hit the red carpet and she'd reveled in it a bit more than she probably should have. It had lulled her into a false sense of belonging that she clearly hadn't earned yet.

Meredith shook her head, thoughts racing. If she got fired, she couldn't be Jason's spy and there went her divorce. He'd never sign the papers if she screwed up this fast.

"I would never insult you like that, Allo," she countered smoothly. *Thank you, Miss Texas pageant, for training me how to brazen it out under the worst sort of pressure.* "I begged, uh…Samantha for this dress. It was on the rack in the…"

Which room at Hurst held the outfits for photo shoots? Someone had shown it to her during her orientation, but she'd been too busy gushing over the clothes to notice her surroundings. Meredith snagged a glass of champagne from a passing waiter and offered it to Allo as the name came to her.

"West gallery," she lied brightly. With no clue where Jason had actually scored the dress, she had to wing it. "I immediately recognized it as yours, and you're such a genius, I knew I couldn't wear anything else tonight. Only Allo will do for me from now on. The press ate it up."

"Of course they did." Allo sniffed, accepting the glass as if he'd asked for it thirty minutes ago and Meredith had been slow to fetch it. "You're too short to do that bit of brilliance justice, by the way. Don't be late tomorrow. We have much work to do."

He sailed off into the crowd and Meredith shook her head. Crisis averted. For now. "See you around, boss."

From behind her, Jason's warm chuckle flowed over her like honey.

"Don't turn around," he murmured.

"Why, because you don't want anyone to know I'm talking to you?" Meredith guessed and clamped down on the hard twist of need his presence had generated. He wasn't close enough to feel, but she could sense him, as if his heat had wrapped around her.

"Because I find myself entranced by your back."

"Yeah, you seem to have a thing for zippers." She bit

her lip as awareness ratcheted up a notch with the memory of his body behind hers as he'd helped her dress earlier.

He'd been hard and delicious, and while he might be lying to himself about not being into her, his erection against her backside had told her the plain, honest truth. He wanted her. And she wanted him. Sex between them had been mind-altering. Explosive. Unmatched.

So why all the theatrics over whether they'd eventually end up in bed? It was pretty much a foregone conclusion in her mind. Once she got him between the sheets, they'd laugh over private jokes and share their souls and he'd remember how great it had been in Vegas.

Maybe they wouldn't have to end things so quickly this time.

Jason cleared his throat. "Good thinking with Allo. It was impressive."

"Yeah, well you owe me." A spiky little thrill in her midsection that had nothing to do with sex surprised her. She'd been trying to save her job, but Jason's approval meant more than it should.

"Avery just waltzed in. Showtime."

Jason's heat vanished. By all rights, they should have been vanishing through the door together to make out in the car on the way back to her hotel room, where the big, lonely bed would actually be used for its rightful purpose.

All at once, it wasn't sex she craved, but the totally foreign desire to fall asleep in Jason's arms, like she had in Vegas, knowing they'd wake up together in the morning in perfect sync. Back then, they'd shared some kind of mystical connection that she desperately missed.

"See you around, boss," she muttered for the second time with a mental salute.

Here in New York, he wasn't on her side. In this sea of people, she was alone. It wasn't the two of them against the world, supporting each other and dreaming of how the

future could look. All of that seemed to have been left behind in the desert.

Maybe he'd changed more than she'd been willing to
admit. Was that why she couldn't find her footing with
him?

Maybe he was right about keeping things platonic. The
last thing she wanted was to get naked with Jason again,
only to have her perfect fantasy destroyed by reality.

Sadness cut through her heart. She was chasing a man
who didn't exist any longer. She had to stop wishing for
something that wasn't going to happen. Get the intel, get
the divorce and get home so she could ask her father for a
loan—that was her purpose here. This was nothing more
than a job.

It was bad enough to have one person to answer to. In
actuality, she had two. And she didn't like either one of
them at the moment. She elbowed her way through the
crowd until she caught sight of Jason's sister.

Meredith pasted on her best I'm-the-answer-to-all-your-
prayers smile and approached Avery Lynhurst. The blonde
woman oozed style and class in her Hurst House gown and
emanated the warmth of a barracuda. She and Jason shared
similar features, mostly around the mouth and eyes, and
they both had that sharp, attentive air as if neither of them
missed an iota of what happened around them. Meredith
had a feeling Avery used the information she gathered to
get what she wanted just as effectively as Jason did.

Avery was indeed a formidable opponent to Jason's
plans.

"Ms. Lynhurst, I'm Meredith Chandler-Harris." Meredith shook the other woman's hand as Avery took her measure. "I'm Allo's new assistant."

"Yes, I know." With a toss of her white-blond hair, Avery
swept Meredith with a condescending glance. "Nice of
you to deign to wear the label of the house that signs your
paychecks."

Meredith smiled as she clamped her back teeth together to keep the snarl from escaping. "Wearing Wang to the office today was a rookie mistake. I'm a fast learner, obviously."

Avery nodded to Meredith's dress. "That's one of my favorites. It's not my color, though."

To anyone else, Avery's comment would have seemed downright friendly, but Meredith had spent years in the trenches with pageant contestants and she recognized the need to tread carefully. Avery wasn't complimenting her, that was for sure.

"But only you could pull off that particular Allo." As she eyed Avery's dress, Meredith fixed the most appreciative and slightly jealous look on her face possible. "He designed it with you in mind, clearly. And his inspiration was well-founded."

"Yes, well." Avery cocked her head. "Where did you work before coming to Hurst House? I know every designer and designer's assistant in Manhattan. You're not from here."

"I'm from Houston." And the name Chandler-Harris meant nothing in New York, so Meredith didn't bother to toss in a mention of her connections. "I worked for a bridal design company. I feel truly blessed to have a chance to work for a top-notch label like Hurst House."

"Hurst is a long way from wedding dresses."

The disdain was thick. Meredith enjoyed working for Cara and liked wedding dresses, but she flicked a hand and bit back the name she'd really like to call Avery. "Honey, that scene is so limited. You know. Same fabrics, same colors. Same indecisive brides. This is where all the action is. Designers at Hurst House know what they want and how to do it and don't let anyone stand in their way. I'd like to learn that."

Avery's eyes glittered brighter than Meredith's dress. "Interesting. You're the first designer's assistant I've met who understands fashion is about more than the clothes. It's about owning your designs. No apologies."

Nodding, Meredith went with it, though it was really the first time she'd articulated how she felt about the fashion industry. "That's what makes working for Allo so amazing. You can feel the energy in the room. When he's creating, he makes no mistakes. It's brilliant simply because he believes that it is."

Avery seemed intrigued for God knew what reason.

"You know, if you're eager to learn from a mentor, I'm working on a project and I need a fresh perspective." Avery evaluated Meredith coolly. "It's hush-hush, though. I need someone who doesn't mind long, grueling hours far past the time regular people go home. I call the shots, you listen and follow my instructions to the letter. It's a chance to see what really goes on at a major house like Hurst. Behind the scenes. Interested?"

Not for any amount of money did she want to hole up in Avery's office at midnight. Especially since she had a sneaking suspicion Avery had only made the offer to keep an eye on her. Meredith must have tripped Avery's radar somehow. Why else would Jason's sister waste an opportunity like this on a new hire?

But Jason was paying her in currency far more valuable than mere money, and this was her golden opportunity to keep an eye on Avery in turn, regardless of the woman's suspicious motives. "I'm your girl. Long hours don't scare me. I don't even own a watch."

"I'll be in touch. You'll keep working for Allo, but we'll come to some agreement about your after-hours compensation. Welcome to Hurst House." Avery smiled and excused herself.

And now Meredith had three bosses. Four if you counted Cara, who was patiently waiting for Meredith to rejoin the wedding-dress business.

Meredith's head swam. For a woman who'd been floundering, she certainly seemed to have found a life raft full of opportunities.

# Five

Meredith and Avery talked far longer than Jason would have ever put money on. And Avery looked far too satisfied with the conversation for his comfort.

What were they saying to each other? Had Avery dropped any worthwhile information into the mix? No. Surely not. She'd just met Meredith, and Avery wasn't much of a blabbermouth. Everything she did came about through careful calculation.

Finally, his sister and Meredith parted, and Avery's smile was enigmatic and dangerous. He didn't like it. Anytime his sister smiled, it made him nervous.

His mother snapped her fingers in his face. "Earth to Jason."

"Sorry. I'm a little distracted." He refocused on Bettina and tried to put Meredith out of his mind.

With an indulgent smile, Bettina swirled her club soda and lime. "Yes, that's certainly one way to describe Avery's gorgeous new friend. As I was saying…"

She launched into a lengthy speech about ideas for her new swimwear line targeted at younger girls. Jason offered a half-formed opinion, wondering how his mother had known he was watching Meredith when he'd been careful to give everyone the opposite impression. Obviously, he was slipping.

Swimwear. That's what he needed to be thinking about.

Bettina had been running the company for two years and was ready to jump back into the design side. Perfect timing, in Jason's mind. If she eased away from her CEO role, he could slide right into the gap, ready to take over and execute his merger plans. His mother needed confidence in him and a new project to keep her busy.

Then Meredith left the ballroom in a swish of glittery dress and mahogany hair and Jason left his mother mid-sentence with a terse, "Be right back."

He had to know what Avery said to Meredith. The suspense was killing him.

Meredith ducked into the ladies' room, forcing Jason to cool his heels in the hall. He sipped his martini and tried to pretend he was getting some air.

When Meredith's distinctive dress flashed in his peripheral vision, he tilted his head toward the opposite end of the hall, away from the ballroom. He strolled in that direction without looking over his shoulder to be sure she was following him. She better be.

He turned the corner and lucked into a small alcove with a plush bench and side table. It was empty. Meredith's exotic perfume hit him a moment before the most striking woman in attendance appeared. The one-two punch put him on edge.

"What's up?" she asked. "Isn't meeting like this a little risky?"

He conceded the point with a small nod. "Yeah. So talk fast. What did Avery say?"

"Maybe you should learn the art of patience, hmm?" She perched on the edge of the bench and made a big show of fixing a buckle on her shoe.

"Don't be difficult. You talked to her for a long time. Avery doesn't chat. She strategizes. What angle did she play?"

Meredith flipped her hair behind her back and stole Jason's martini, which she downed in one gulp. "Pot, meet kettle."

"What's that supposed to mean?"

She arched a brow. "It means you two are cut from the same cloth, no pun intended. Maybe you should stop thinking about the angles once in a while."

With a growl, he snatched the empty glass from his wife's hand and checked his temper before he slammed it down on the side table and shattered it into a million pieces. Which might ease his frustration but wouldn't get the answers out of Meredith any faster. "What is your problem? I'm asking you to give me information. That's why you're here, Meredith."

"No, that's why *you're* here, darling." She raked him with a smoldering once-over that lit him up instantly. "I have my own reasons for agreeing to this stupid plan of yours."

His scowl didn't faze her and her calm rattled his cage even further. "Is this another cheap ploy to get me to hop into bed with you? Because it's getting a little old. Why can't you get it through your head that I'm not interested?"

Quickly, she smoothed the hurt from her expression. If he hadn't been so focused on her face, he would have missed it. Instantly, his ire drained away. "I'm sorry. That was uncalled for. Avery drives me mental."

It was a poor excuse and not fully accurate. Oh, his sister had her moments, but he'd never had any problem keeping his cool around *her*. It was his wife who altered his brain waves with merely a glance.

"It's fine." She waved it away dismissively, but her tone said it was anything but fine. "I decided you're right. Sleeping together would be a mistake. Much cleaner to stay out of bed and get through this as quickly as possible. No reason to complicate something that's already complicated enough."

Well, well. He was finally getting through to her. "Glad you see the wisdom."

He waited for a sense of relief. And kept waiting.

What had prompted this turnabout anyway? He didn't understand her motivation for her invitation to pick up where they'd left off in the first place, and he *really* didn't understand her motivation for backing off now. He had to know why.

Right after she spilled about Avery.

"Is there more you can get out of Avery tonight? If no, maybe we should go," Jason suggested.

Once they got back to her hotel, the stress of being caught together would be off and then he could pick through her strange mood until she told him what he wanted to know.

"No, my work here is done," she said flatly and stood. "I'll catch a cab back to my hotel. No need to see me out since this isn't a date. Later, Tater."

With the sarcasm of her parting comment still echoing through the alcove, she sailed down the hall without a backward glance. Jason barely got his mouth closed fast enough to scramble after her.

But not too closely. He slowed a bit as he passed the ballroom full of his colleagues and nodded to his father without stopping. *Nobody* would think it was strange they didn't exchange a word. Jason hadn't spoken to Paul in about six months and they both preferred it that way.

By the time he reached the sidewalk outside the hotel, Meredith had disappeared into a cab. He swore and signaled to his driver to get the car.

Where did she think she was going? She couldn't hide from him—he had a key to her room.

"Now this seems familiar," he muttered as he pounded on Meredith's hotel-room door for the second time that evening.

"What?" she called from inside the room.

"Candygram."

"Go away. I'm about Lynhursted out for the day."

"Come on, let me in so we can have a rational discussion like adults. If that's even possible."

The door flew open. "What kind of a crack is that? You think I can't act like an adult?"

At least she was still dressed. A small blessing, though that glittery dress with the tiny spaghetti straps and deep V over her cleavage had made him fantasize about unzipping it all night.

He pushed into the room, ignoring her protests, and went straight for the minibar. A fifteen-dollar shot of Jack Daniel's sounded like a bargain. The liquor slid down his throat and soothed his temper enough to allow a response. "That comment was directed at both of us. We're apparently only capable of insulting each other and I'd like to find a way to get past it."

She planted herself an inch from him, fists at her hips. "And *I'd* like a divorce. Maybe we can trade."

He threw up his hands. "Yet you stormed off from the gala when all I was trying to do was get us to the divorce faster."

Something shiny glinted in her expression and he did a double take. He'd never seen Meredith cry. She was a woman of many extremes, but sadness wasn't one of them. It threw him for a loop. His first response was to pull her into his arms and murmur nonsense into her hair.

She stiffened for a second and then liquefied against him, her arms snaking into place at his waist. Her head tilted against his shoulder, resting in a groove that had been waiting for her to fill it. Sniffling, she let him cradle her and the tension eased.

He pulled back so he could look into her eyes, the only way he knew to assess a person. The tears were still there, but she had a little of her normal snap back, too. His heart slowed.

"I don't pretend to be good at relationships, and we're

not even in one. But obviously I'm messing up whatever it is that we're doing here. Can't you give me some clues what I'm doing wrong?"

She sighed and slipped from his embrace, which grew cool far too fast. Surprising how quickly he'd gotten used to her heat.

"That's just it, Jason. I don't think you're doing anything wrong. This is who you are and I'm not above admitting I'm bitterly disappointed."

"Wait a minute." The buzzing in his ears didn't clear even with a hard shake of his head. "You're disappointed in who I *am*?"

Meredith evaluated him for a long, tense moment. "The man I met in Vegas wasn't so cold and calculating. He was passionate and open and I loved being around him."

She crossed to the bar and found her own fifteen-dollar shot of Jack Daniel's.

"He was also confused and misguided," Jason added. And that guy had been heavily under the influence of Meredith's seductive power. "I'd like to think you helped get me to the place where I am now. I owe you a debt for that, as a matter of fact."

She rolled her eyes and splashed Sprite in her highball along with the amber liquid, then downed it in two gulps.

"Great, so I get the credit for turning you into a zombie." She plunked the glass down and pierced him with her still-shiny gaze. "You want to know what Avery said to me? She asked me to work on a special project with her. After hours."

Elation warmed the cold place Meredith had left behind. "That's fantastic. It's perfect. You play your cards right and she might start to trust you. You can cozy up to her and get far more information about her plans."

"It's not perfect!" She poked a finger in his chest. "It's not even for real as best I can tell. You know why she asked me to work with her? She's keeping me close because she can't figure out my angle. I'm from Houston and have a background in bridal design. What am I doing horning in on New York couture, she asked."

Inwardly, he winced. They should have thought of a good cover story. Too late now.

"It's a logical question." How had Meredith figured out Avery's motivation so quickly?

He cursed as it dawned on him that Avery might be aware of his relationship with Meredith. Was that the reason behind the offer? "What did you tell her?"

Meredith was smart and quick on her feet. Their plans could still work.

"I told her exactly what she wanted to hear. Because I did not want to mess up a golden opportunity. The goal is for me to help you, right?"

"Of course. So thanks." Why did it sound like the incident had upset her?

She muttered a very unladylike curse. "Geez, Jason. You don't get it. I'm standing there listening to her talk and all I could think about was how the two of you are exactly alike. Cold-blooded and only interested in one-upping each other. And both of you are thrilled to use me to do it."

"I'm not using you," Jason protested instantly. He and Avery were not alike. He always used a situation to his advantage, but he wasn't taking advantage of *Meredith*. "We have a deal. You get something out of it, too, and I wouldn't even have the divorce to use as leverage if you hadn't allowed the papers to get filed."

Suddenly, he felt like a heel. He didn't like the thought of Meredith being disappointed in him, either. He hadn't always been so cold, but it was a necessity in the cutthroat world of fashion.

Nice guys finished last. And they didn't manage hostile mergers or win CEO spots away from their conniving sisters.

She strangled over a disgusted sound and leaned in, indignation sweeping through her expression. "There you go again. This marriage is not all my fault. You stood in front of that Elvis impersonator with me. *You.* I didn't drag you to the altar. If I recall, it was your idea."

He stepped back, away from her prodding finger, away from her anger and, most important, away from the truth. "Yeah, I can man up and admit it. I made a mistake in the heat of the moment."

She advanced on him again, charging into the space he'd created and bringing her sensual onslaught with her. "I'll say. And that moment was smoking hot. You can pretend that this—" she waved stiff fingers in a circle around Jason's tuxedoed torso "—is the place you were trying to get to, but I know the real you. The one you hide under this rigid CEO exterior. The man under there doesn't have a problem acknowledging his passion. He owns it, takes what he wants. That's the man I spent two years dreaming about."

Mesmerized, he watched the flicker in Meredith's gaze flare into something far hotter than any sane man should touch.

"Yeah? What do you dream about?"

That had not been what he'd meant to say. He cleared his throat, but it was too late. It was already out there.

"Your mouth." She reached up and traced it with her index finger, and his flesh sparked under her touch. "Your abs. The way you sigh after you come. The way my fingers look in your hair when you're under me."

Her fingers wound through his hair in a full-on demonstration. His body strained to close the small gap between them, begging to feel her one last time.

She was trying to goad him into losing his careful guard. It wasn't going to work. "I thought you didn't want to complicate this with sex."

"It's already so complicated it couldn't get much worse." Her smile turned wicked. "And I said that before you chased me back to my hotel room. Are you sure *you* know what you want?"

The smartest thing to do would be to keep his mouth shut. Because she'd called it—his middle name should be Mixed Signals. "Yeah. I know exactly what I want."

"Me, too. I want that man," she murmured. "Inside and out. I want to know it wasn't all a lie, that I don't misremember how amazing we were together. I want you inside me and to be so far from disappointed, I forget the meaning of the word."

The undisguised longing in her voice, in her touch, found the answering longing inside him. He hadn't realized it was there, waiting for her to unearth it, but it flared to life nonetheless. And in that moment, he wanted to give her what she wanted, to erase her disillusionment and embrace the devil-may-care Jason of Vegas again.

Would it really be so bad to indulge in a few hours of Meredith, burn it out of their systems and go back to real life tomorrow?

Yes, it would. Because he wasn't that man she remembered. That wasn't the real Jason Lynhurst. He'd only dabbled on the wild side because he'd been so messed up. Only that unique combination of confusion and Meredith could have enticed him to act so unlike himself and so much like his father.

Meredith's odd sway over him would only intensify if he gave in now. There would be no going back to real life once he tasted her particular brand of recklessness again. And then she'd use every bit of his weakness to her advantage. That he could never allow—he had a vision for the future of Lynhurst Enterprises and it did not involve Meredith. It would be unfair to her to let her believe he could be the man she seemed to want.

"It was a lie," he said. "You misremember. We can never get Vegas back and it would be madness to try."

He nearly choked on the words and immediately wished

he'd said something else, anything else. Because he knew good and well it wasn't a lie and she didn't misremember.

Worst of all, he wanted it, too. Wanted to indulge in a woman who made him feel, made him forget. An oasis of connection and understanding far removed from the ugly battles playing out across the remnants of Lynhurst Enterprises.

She banked the hurt in her gaze and nodded. "See ya. Don't call me. I'll call you."

Meredith gave up on the idea of sleeping at around 2:00 a.m. Tomorrow—correction, *today*—already promised to be brutal since she'd spend hours in Allo's torture chamber. But coupled with no sleep and Jason's thorough rejection, she might as well get on a plane back to Houston.

Surely a conversation with her father in which she admitted her mistake in Vegas and begged his forgiveness would be easier than the ups and downs of Jason's deal. The worst part was she'd known what would happen last night when she went for broke. But she'd done it anyway because she couldn't stop herself.

She yearned for the thrill Jason evoked when he slid into her and the kinship they'd shared. Then there was the communication and affinity—they'd had it all once upon a time, and for some reason, he refused to acknowledge how great the two of them naked had been.

But what if the Jason she couldn't forget never surfaced? Hanging on to that fantasy was the surest path to never moving on.

She slogged through the day, earning cutting remarks from Allo without even trying, a real bonus that went well with her mood. Avery never contacted her, and in an apparent attempt to give her what she'd asked for, Jason didn't call, either.

When she got back to her hotel, she booted up her laptop in an attempt to distract herself from the day, and an email from her mother put the cap on a supremely awful day. Thought you might want to see this, the note said and included a link to an online article titled: Miss Texas— Where Is She Now?

Dread knotted Meredith's stomach as she clicked the link. Exactly as she expected, a professional head shot from her pageant days filled the screen alongside the photos of two other women. She recognized Brandi MacArthur and LaTisha Kelley easily. Brandi had handed over her crown to Meredith when she won. And the following year, Meredith had handed her crown to LaTisha.

Kicking off her heels, Meredith sank down in the plush chair, determined to read every word on the screen.

The article wasn't a smear job or a puff piece. It was a well-written factual chronicle of the three women's lives since their respective reigns ended. Brandi was now a neonatal neurosurgeon working at the Baylor University Medical Center in Dallas, married to David Thomason, the renowned heart-transplant specialist. LaTisha had taken a different path, receiving a master's degree in theology and then signing on to become a missionary in Haiti. The writer expanded on their achievements in several glowing paragraphs, highlighting that the Miss Texas pageant had opened doors for these ladies, which they had walked through to enormous success.

Meredith's sole mention painted a sad but true picture— "Meredith Chandler-Harris works for her sister and is a second-generation Miss Texas. Her mother, Valerie Chandler, won the title in the eighties."

The article was kind enough to leave out the part where Meredith hadn't achieved a tenth of what her fellow titleholders had. But it was implied quite well.

Her mother hadn't sent the link to be malicious. She probably saw nothing wrong with the fact that of the two lines devoted to her daughter, fifty percent were about Valerie. As a major contributor to the Houston social scene, her mother thought nothing of seeing her name in print.

She also didn't have a shred of ambition. But Meredith, unlike her mother, had always wanted to be more than a wife to someone important. The Grown-Up Pact was supposed to help Meredith figure out what she might be good at besides smiling and traipsing down a runway.

Instead, she'd left Vegas hung up on a man who didn't long to recreate their connection the way she did. He'd rather lie about whether it had existed in the first place.

Perhaps part of her problem with not embracing her inner adult lay in being so stuck in the past. She sighed. She should really let Fantasy Jason go, get Real-Life Jason's signature on the divorce papers and move on.

Her cell phone beeped, and when she tapped open the new text message, her brow arched. It was from Jason, with the simple question: Thai for dinner?

Like last night hadn't even happened?

Of course. Because in his mind, it was business as usual. Two could play that game. In fact, she'd do herself a favor if she played the game his way and left her emotions out of it.

She texted him back: With plenty of red pepper sauce.

Jason replied: Be there in fifteen minutes.

She couldn't stop a tiny tendril of hope that dinner might be some kind of apology. A way to say, "Hey, I was just kidding. You rocked me in Vegas and I couldn't forget it even with brain damage."

He made it in ten, and when he swept into her hotel room looking devastating in his grey custom-made Lyn Couture suit, with spiky hair in delicious disarray, her heart fell out of rhythm and she couldn't breathe for a moment.

So much for leaving her emotions at the door.

"How was your day, dear?" she asked a touch more sarcastically than she probably should have, but her not-quite-a-husband had thrown her off balance.

He shot her a grimace. "We have a problem. Come eat and I'll tell you about it."

*Oh.* Of course that was the reason for his appearance so soon after the disaster of last night. She tossed the laptop onto the bed.

Meredith took the take-out box from Jason's hand and opened it. Pad Thai shrimp. It was her favorite, but far be it from her to read into the selection. There was no way Jason remembered that. Lots of people loved pad Thai. Jason had used his finely honed observation skills to make a good guess, that was all.

Listlessly, she picked at the food, washing down what little she could stomach with a beer Jason had retrieved from the minibar.

"What's the problem?" she asked.

"Avery put the first part of what must be her plan in motion today." Jason forked up a mouthful of his red curry beef and took his sweet time chewing. "Several reporters were tipped off to investigate potential labor violations against Lyn's factory workers. The press ambushed Bettina as she was leaving the office today, shouting for comments about how she was running a sweatshop right here in Manhattan."

Meredith scowled. "That's ridiculous. I hope Bettina put them in their place."

It wasn't like she *really* knew it wasn't true, but Jason was the chief operating officer and there was no way he'd abuse his factory workers. Nor would he let someone else force workers to endure difficult conditions.

Jason flashed a brief, grateful smile and sobered almost immediately. "I wish she had. But she's not a spokesperson. Put her in a room with reams of fabric and she's good for hours. Talking to the press, not so much. The whole thing upset her."

"And you think Avery was behind this?"

"I'd put money on it."

He dropped his fork and took a long pull from his beer, massaging the back of his neck as he swallowed. Tension put fine lines around his mouth and eyes, sullying his classically handsome face, and she could do without that.

Dropping her own fork, she stood and scooted around behind him to replace his hand with hers, kneading his taut neck muscles for him. He groaned appreciatively and his head tipped back.

"You don't have to do that," he murmured. "Don't you dare stop."

She laughed. "I wasn't going to. Your muscles are like concrete. Relax for a minute."

She wouldn't have realized how tense he was if she hadn't felt it with her own two hands. He'd been hiding it well, at least until these past couple of minutes.

Which of course led her down the path of wondering what else he was hiding under that gorgeous suit. He was a man of contrasts. Frustrating to be sure, but oh, so intriguing. She wanted to dig into his core in the worst way and expose all his secrets…like, why was he so resistant to being open and passionate as he'd been in Vegas? It wasn't her—his body's reaction anytime they got within two feet of each other gave her all the assurance she needed.

If only he'd bridge that gap and take what he so clearly wanted. What she'd so readily asked for. If only the heat between them could be allowed to explode, she'd show him he could be that man again in an instant.

She shook her head and chastised herself silently. Was she never going to learn? This was a business relationship only. Time to get back to that…

"Why would Avery do something so mean? Especially to her own mother."

Jason's head rested against her stomach and his eyes fluttered closed. It was oddly the most intimate moment they'd experienced, as if they were a normal couple helping each other decompress at the end of a long day. It snagged a tender place inside.

For an eternity, she thought he'd fallen into the moment, too, and didn't hear her question.

"Bettina and Avery are like oil and water," he finally said. "Mom says black, Avery says white. Honestly, they were happy to go off to their respective corners when Lynhurst Enterprises split."

"Still." Meredith couldn't quite let go of Jason's broad, strong shoulders and he didn't seem to be in a hurry for her to stop touching him, so she kept up the pressure. "What's a tip-off that turns out to be a lie going to accomplish?"

A ghost of a smile lifted his lips briefly. "It's twofold. Keeps me busy combating the negative press so I'm distracted. And she knows they're not going to uncover anything, but the implications are enough to put Lyn in a bad light. So when she throws in her bid for CEO, she can play up how new management will smooth everything over. Out with the old and in with the new."

"That's…" *Kind of brilliant.* But Meredith didn't dare say it out loud.

"Diabolical and perfect. Plus it upset Mom and that was a great side benefit in Avery's mind."

"But this is only the first strike, right? She'll have more up her sleeve."

The dread Meredith's mother's article had first induced came flooding back. Ferretting out Avery's plans—and hopefully nipping them in the bud—was supposed to be Meredith's job. Fat lot of good she was doing.

"Oh, yeah. This is only the beginning. Now you see why I need you so badly." His voice had turned husky as his muscles relaxed.

She tried to ignore the way the sound tore through her. For a man who wasn't supposed to be her forever, he surely shouldn't cause such strong, involuntary reactions. Especially since he hadn't meant that he needed her the way she wished he had. And she was falling down on the thing he *did* need her for.

"I'm sorry, Jason. This sucks."

She had to do better. Maybe if she succeeded, it would lead to that reconnection she'd been dreaming of.

That thought alone spurred her brain into action, and a half-formed plan began spilling from her mouth. "Here's what we're going to do. Get into a meeting with your marketing department and start brainstorming everything Lyn's done well since the split and then cross-reference that with anything, no matter how small, that Hurst House has stumbled over."

And the subsequent news blast would be titled: Hurst House—Where Is It Now?

*Thanks for the article, Mom.* Meredith smiled for the first time since last night.

"I'm listening. Then what?"

Meredith massaged his shoulders absently as she worked it over in her mind.

"We're going to bury Hurst House with facts about how fantastic Lyn has done since the split and, by default, how poorly Hurst has fared. We'll pretend the sweatshop witch hunt doesn't exist and by contrast, your rebuttal will come off as a well-written piece of journalism. You and Bettina will be featured as doing a great job, and as a nice side benefit, Avery's going to come out of this looking stupid and petty."

Jason's eyes flew open and he peered up at her. "Whoa. Are you sure you're not a Lynhurst? That's pure genius. It's short only an evil cackle."

Warmth filled her cheeks. Meredith could talk dirty—and then follow through—with the best of them and never think twice about it, yet a *compliment* made her blush? What was the world coming to? "Well, I'll throw the evil cackle in for free."

Jason's appreciative laugh sent the surge of warmth much lower.

"A total bargain." The smile slipped off his face. "Hey. It didn't escape my notice that you said 'we.' You also didn't correct me when I barged in and said we have a problem. You could have easily told me it was *my* problem. Thanks."

Their gazes fused and electricity rippled the atmosphere.

*There you are.* Wonderment filled her. *This* was the open, sensitive man she'd left behind in Vegas. Her breath caught. He hadn't vanished and she didn't misremember. Stupid tears of relief pricked at her eyelids and she blinked them away before he noticed.

"Yeah, yeah," she murmured. "We're on the same team. Don't forget it."

"I won't." He reached up and grabbed her hand, bringing it to his lips for a quick kiss. "I wish you could be in the meeting with Marketing. I'd love your insight."

She yanked her tingling hand away from his lips before she forgot about caution and jumped him in hopes of keeping that conduit to his soul open. "Take good notes. Then come back tomorrow night with more takeout and we'll talk."

He grinned. "I've never met a woman who likes to eat as much as you do. It's sexy."

"Shut up and finish your dinner. Serves you right for flirting with me that it's cold," she grumbled and slid into her own chair to finish her own cold dinner.

But it tasted a lot better than it had when it was hot. Because she'd finally seen a glimpse of what she'd hoped for—the man she'd never forgotten.

Now that she'd finally established he was still in there somewhere, how did she keep him around?

# Six

Unless the building caved in, Jason's morning couldn't get much worse.

The labor allegations, while complete bunk, grew legs and promised to keep Lyn's entire legal department hopping for the foreseeable future. The fact that the allegations were false didn't seem to matter to Lyn's factory workers, who must have viewed the new development as an opportunity to bring a few choice grievances to upper management. Jason had been funneling complaints to appropriate departments for hours.

Then, his assistant gave her two-week notice. It always sucked to lose critical staff, but she ran his life. He would have doubled her salary if it would have made a difference, but she was marrying her fiancé and moving to Germany.

The meeting with Marketing was nothing short of grueling, but three hours of brainstorming later, the team had an actionable plan. Meredith's idea had put smiles on the faces of his executive staff for the first time today and the press release was nothing short of brilliant.

It was chock-full of shiny highlights about Lyn's progressive fashion lines, one of which was favored by a couple of hot young actresses. Sadly—the release went on to point out—this success sharply contrasted with Hurst's lone lowlight of an evening-wear line that had failed to garner much interest outside of prom shoppers. All of which was true, but the release intentionally left out that the average price tag of a prom dress was fifteen hundred dollars, which contributed greatly to Hurst's bottom line.

A few more carefully selected Lyn Couture hits rounded out the piece, commenting carefully about how the two companies had fared since the split, and the last line contained a pointed message about Lyn's commitment to its workers, particularly those in the Manhattan factory.

Meredith had hit this one out of the park.

By five o'clock, Jason had been at work for over ten hours and fog took over his brain. It was the only reason he couldn't seem to focus on anything except how good Meredith's hands had felt on his tense shoulders last night. Or at least fatigue was his excuse and he was sticking to it.

It had been a nice evening. Casual and expectation free, as it should be. They were basically just friends who'd had a brief affair in the past.

He could get some takeout and drop by her hotel. She'd mentioned as much, so he had the perfect excuse. They could discuss the press release and eat. He didn't have to admit he'd thought about her all day. Or that in unguarded moments, the vivid memories of her body and the way she responded to his touch sneaked into his mind, lacing it with sensual images better suited for a triple-X flick than a boardroom.

Definitely not the thoughts of a friend.

By six, he figured it was late enough that it wouldn't seem as if he was so eager to see her, he'd left work early. He wasn't getting any work done anyway. Traffic wasn't too bad and he arrived at Meredith's hotel quickly.

Meredith swung open the door wearing a button-down oxford with a feminine cut and a pencil skirt. It should have made her look like a schoolteacher but she'd unbuttoned the shirt to the middle of her breasts, allowing the rounded globes to peek out, and the skirt's front-and-center split rose all the way to the juncture of her thighs. One wrong move and she'd show her secrets to the world.

He swallowed as the hard-on he'd been fighting all day raged to life again. The outfit hadn't looked like that on the runway model who'd last worn it at Fashion Week.

Finally his gaze wandered up to Meredith's face, but it was far too late to pretend he hadn't been checking her out. He couldn't have hidden the tenting going on down south, either.

She arched a brow. "You seem to be missing a couple of take-out boxes."

He cursed and fisted his empty hands. "I, uh…forgot."

Her wicked smile punched him in the groin. "Got something else on your mind, then?"

"What makes you say that?" His palms started to sweat. Could she read his thoughts now?

"Oh, I don't know. Because you're here. At my hotel. With no dinner. Kind of made me think you had an interest in an altogether different activity than eating."

Groaning, he scrambled for a response that did not include dipping his tongue into the crevice of her breasts, sliding a hand up the creamy thigh visible beyond the slit of her skirt or silencing her smart mouth with a thorough kiss, which would leave her too breathless to bait him.

He should have left the office at five. At least then he might've still had enough brain cells to remember a simple thing like bringing dinner.

"We should go out." Improvisation at its finest. "That's what I had in mind."

Her laugh tore through the rest of his defenses, weakening his knees.

"Nice recovery," she allowed with a nod. "You and I both know that's not what you were thinking about, but I'll let it slide for now."

Of course she'd realized he was making this up as he

went along. How could he have forgotten how easily she read him? "You're too kind."

Airily, she waved it away. "The sweatshop nastiness was the major topic of conversation at Hurst from morning coffee until quitting time. I'm sure you're exhausted."

"Yeah." He latched on to the handy excuse, which he'd have thought of all by himself if his head was where it should be—on his shoulders and not imagining itself between her thighs. "That's why I'm so absentminded. Work was hellacious."

"Then let's go." She ducked into the room to grab her bag and sling it over her forearm. "I'm dying to hear about the Marketing meeting and anyway, I'm starving. So where are you taking me?"

His response was cut off by a vaguely familiar ringtone emanating from the depths of Meredith's handbag. She fished out her phone and all traces of merriment drained from her face.

"It's Avery," she whispered. "Should I answer?"

"Of course." He crossed his arms as she said hello and listened for a beat.

"Sure. No problem. I'll be there in a few minutes." Meredith stabbed the phone to end the call. "She wants me to come back to the office. It's about her hushity-hush after-hours thingy."

Jason willed back the flood of disappointment. "That's great. Perfect timing."

He'd actually been looking forward to taking Meredith to dinner, never mind that it had originated as a way to save face.

He'd thought seriously about finding some out-of-the-way place and asking for a booth in the back with low lighting, ordering a bottle of wine and spending a couple of hours not thinking about the media circus of Lyn Couture. They'd laugh and flirt and enjoy each other's company. Which sounded an awful lot like a date. That was a bad, bad idea. Avery's timing *was* perfect.

Meredith made a face. "But what about eating?"

"This is more important." *And a far better use of her time.* Lyn and Hurst House were not going to spontaneously regroup, and he'd worked too hard to let what little gains he'd made slip away now. "I'll tell you what. I'll drive you and wait in the car. It can't take more than an hour or so. Then, when you're done, we'll go to a late dinner."

Where had that come from? He should tell her good-night. But she'd looked so crestfallen, as if she'd experienced a bout of disappointment over Avery's call, as well. He couldn't help himself.

And he was too tired to pretend he didn't want to lose himself in her.

She cocked her head and contemplated him with a small smile. "You'd do that? And here I thought going out was simply an excuse to get us into a public place so I couldn't take advantage of you. If I didn't know better, I'd think you meant the dinner invitation as a date."

"It's not a date," he growled. She definitely had some insight that allowed her to read his thoughts like a book and he did not like it. "And yes, I'll wait for you because I will want you to repeat every word Avery says verbatim. The sooner, the better."

"Of course." She hooked arms with him as they walked to the elevator and bent her head to breathe directly into his ear. "And I'm just here for the clothes."

Jason glanced at his watch, but only three minutes had passed since the last time he'd checked.

What was *taking* so long? Meredith had climbed from his car an hour and a half ago, with a parting squeeze to his thigh that still tingled. He'd tried to work on a strategy brief that needed to go out to the executive staff on Monday, but the only strategy on his mind was Avery's.

His cell phone beeped and he turned it over to see a text from Meredith. With a frown, he tapped it: Avery left and the place is deserted. You've got to come up here and see this.

Craning his neck, he searched the teeming sidewalk for his sister's profile, but he couldn't spot her amid all the foot traffic typical for 9th Street at this time of night. She must have already caught a cab.

What was so important for him to see that Meredith couldn't either tell him about it or take a picture?

He texted her back: What is it?

Meredith: I'm not sure. That's why I need you to look at it.

Jason: You can't just tell me?

Meredith: No, I need you. And I can't disturb the evidence.

And now she'd piqued his curiosity, which probably wasn't an accident.

Did he dare enter the sanctum of his father and Avery? He'd been inside Hurst one time, to attend a meeting nailing down the final details of the split. It had been upsetting to see former Lynhurst employees walking the halls, chatting and laughing as if nothing catastrophic had happened. Then he and Bettina had run into Caozinha Carvalho, the famed photographer who was also his father's new wife, on the way out. His mother had cried in the car on the way back to Lyn.

Before the sun had set, Jason had purchased a plane ticket to Vegas, desperate to get away from the crumbling foundation of his world. Never in a million years would he have guessed the next time he'd contemplate setting foot inside Hurst would be at the invitation of a woman he'd met and married on that trip.

But he was in a different place now, thanks to that woman. And he couldn't resist the opportunity to see inside the company that would be under his command soon. They'd have to avoid the security cameras, but it might be worth the extra care to see what was so important.

Quickly, he texted her back: Meet me at the elevator. I don't have a badge to get past the front doors.

Meredith was waiting for him when the elevator doors split, wearing a cryptic smile. "Thought you'd never get here. Come on."

"Do you know where all the security cameras are?"

"I never paid any attention." Dismay pulled at her expression. "Is it too risky?"

Probably. But he couldn't go back now, not with the dual promise of critical information at his fingertips and a chance to check out his father's company. "I'll keep my face behind my jacket. As long as you're sure no one else is around."

Half-blind, he laced fingers with Meredith, and let her lead him through the quiet office.

When he completed the merger, he planned to let Hurst's space go and rent the floor above Lyn, which would be vacated at the end of the month. He'd already put a deposit down on it in the name of a holding company.

"You and Avery were up here for a long time," he murmured as they passed the door marked *Paul Lynhurst, CEO*.

"Would have been longer if she hadn't gotten another call and hightailed it out of here." Meredith's fingers nested deeper inside his as she turned a corner and pulled him into the office marked *Avery Lynhurst, Vice President of Marketing.*

*This* was Avery's office? The antique desk and old-world decor did not mesh with the sister he knew, nor did it give the impression cutting-edge fashion happened here. It reminded him of something an eighty-year-old lawyer would prefer.

"So she left you here?" Seemed highly suspicious that Avery would jet with Meredith still in her office, with access to her stuff.

"Oh, no. I walked with her to the elevator, but I'd accidentally-on-purpose forgotten my phone so I shooed her out, insisting I'd be right behind her as soon as I retrieved it." Meredith shrugged mischievously. "It just took a little longer to find my poor lost phone than I expected. Fortunately, she was very eager to get to her next appointment, whatever it was."

When he'd first proposed this plan of planting Meredith in his sister's camp, he'd hoped for a bit of creativity, but this was beyond anything he could have devised. He really owed her.

"I'm very intrigued by the way your mind works." And who would have thought that would be so sexy? He'd long recognized that she had a potent combination of brains and beauty, but this was something else. "Were you always this good at fashion espionage or is this is a new development?"

"Totally new. You've inspired me."

Her smile teased one out of him and he enjoyed it so much, he didn't even care that they were standing there in his sister's office, grinning at each other like idiots—and still holding hands.

"Did you have something to show me?" he prompted.

"Oh, yeah." She dropped his hand and rummaged through some stencils on Avery's desk. "Designs for the new line she's working on. Very secret. Very hot. Very haute couture."

She handed him one and he glanced at it. Instantly, his good humor drained away. "Very stolen, as well."

To his shock, Meredith didn't even blink. She nodded grimly. "I was afraid of that. I didn't think Hurst designed anything like this. It's too high concept. When you first launched Hurst House, what was that, like eight years ago?

Anyway, the line was intended for the rack from the get-go. Accessible designs for real women."

"Yeah, that was the idea. How did you know that?"

"I do my research. When you hooked me up with this job, I wanted to fit in."

"You do," he said shortly. *Too much.* She'd filled a gap he hadn't known existed.

He stared at her with new appreciation. This was why she was so dangerous—he couldn't stay even one step ahead of her.

But all at once, he couldn't remember exactly why that mattered. She felt an awful lot like the solution, not the problem. She'd felt like that in Vegas, too. They'd connected then in a way he'd never connected with anyone. Why had he fought so hard to keep from repeating something so amazing?

"I was right to show these designs to you?" she asked, oblivious to the odd shift going on inside him. "The lines seemed too similar to some of the designs I saw on the walls at Lyn."

"You noticed the *lines* were similar?"

"It's like artwork," she said a touch defensively. "No one would confuse a Van Gogh with a Picasso, right? I thought the designs were suspect."

Captivated, he nodded. She knew style, he'd give her that.

"No, you're right. Hurst doesn't have any designers on staff capable of this kind of work." They certainly didn't have any who were paid to design haute couture. "But it doesn't matter. They were lifted from Lyn's vaults, no question. It's part of our Paris Fashion Week collection. How did Avery get her hands on it?"

*They had a spy at Lyn.*

He cursed. Avery had stolen his idea to plant a spy *and* stolen Lyn's design.

This was over the top. Sure, Meredith was at Hurst to

gather intel on Avery's CEO plans, but he'd *never* have asked her to steal designs. It was an all-out declaration of war.

*Squeal.*

Jason froze and Meredith's eyes widened.

Someone was in the hall.

*Squeal. Thump.*

They were about to get caught in Avery's office.

"It's the janitor," Meredith mouthed. "Quick, get behind the desk."

Pulse thundering, he raised his eyebrows in question.

"Do it," she whispered fiercely and yanked on his arm until he complied.

Kneeling down—and feeling ridiculous—he eyed the crack between Avery's horrendous wooden desk and the floor. The full skirt completely obscured him from view, the only benefit to the heavy furniture. How exactly did it matter if he hid behind the desk while Meredith lounged around plainly in the open?

More squealing emanated from directly outside the office door.

"Good evening," Meredith chirped. "Working late. Do you mind cleaning this office last today? It would be really helpful."

"Sure, miss," a masculine voice responded. The squeals faded into the distance.

Meredith popped around the desk and dusted off her hands. "Piece of cake."

"But he saw you," Jason said over the sudden hum of a vacuum cleaner down the hall.

It should feel even more ridiculous to still be kneeling behind the desk when the imminent danger had passed, but the slit in Meredith's skirt was at eye level and her silky smooth legs kept peeking out, begging for his attention.

And then she shifted and a flash of lacy white seared his vision. His groin went tight and he nearly groaned.

"So?" she asked. "I'm supposed to be here, retrieving my lost phone, remember? If the janitor says anything to anyone, which I doubt he will, that's my excuse. Let's get out of here before he comes back."

That was enough of a reason to stand.

"Good idea." When Meredith picked up the sketches, he shook his head. "Leave them. We don't want her to know we're on to her."

"Okay. But we have to get them back at some point. She can't get away with this."

Meredith's fierce tone made him smile. "If Lyn and Hurst merge, it doesn't matter. I get the designs back by default. No harm, no foul."

It was a lie strictly to soothe her. Avery's treachery hit below the belt and hurt much more than he dared let on.

They sprinted for the elevator and it wasn't until the doors closed that Jason turned to his coconspirator. "That was…"

One glimpse of her made him lose his train of thought.

Meredith's chest rose and fell from the slight exertion, drawing attention to her barely concealed cleavage. Her hair twined around her face in a mess of waves. She was amazing and gorgeous and her quick thinking had saved their hides.

His heart pounded and adrenaline coursed through his veins, waking up his nerves…and drawing the attention of the erection he'd been trying to ignore since the peek at her underwear.

The combination swept over him in a dark surge of awareness, along with a heady dose of her exotic perfume.

Breathing her in, he relaxed and reveled in the wild rush she never failed to evoke. Avery's plans, his plans, mergers, corporate politics—all of it was too much to resolve tonight and he didn't want to think about any of it. Once, he'd fallen into this woman's arms to escape the pain of his real life, and she'd restored him in a way he'd never anticipated.

He craved the connection they'd once had, the one that made him feel as if she understood him in a way no one else could. Why didn't he deserve to have some heat in his otherwise cold life? Why didn't she deserve the same?

Answering awareness sprang into her gaze and her lashes lowered as she focused on his mouth. An instant later, she swayed toward him and their lips fused.

Meredith's essence swept through his senses like a bright white light, clearing away everything but her. She opened under his mouth, her tongue slick against his, so hot and wet and tasting of erotic pleasures. She kissed like she did everything else—with abandon, purpose and raw sensuality. He could not get enough.

Her fingers danced along his spine and threaded through his hair, electrifying his skin wherever she touched. *Meredith.* She made him feel like nothing else ever had or would, as if only he could sate her carnal thirst, as if no other man existed for her.

It was powerful to know a woman like Meredith wanted him. So hot and exciting. Always had been.

*Deeper.* He plunged his tongue harder, mating with hers, bodies aligned tight. Those magnificent breasts brushed him and he wanted more. He snaked both hands to the small of her back and smashed her breasts against his chest, rubbing against the hardened tips he could feel through their clothes.

He dipped a hand in her skirt, desperate to feel her heated flesh. As he palmed her smooth, taut rear, the elevator doors opened.

Cursing, he tore his mouth from hers and guided her out of the elevator. "Hurry. We're picking up right where we left off."

The faster they reached the car, the less he could question himself about what he was doing. Hell, he already knew where this was going, but he lacked the incentive to stop it. His body screamed for her touch and he wasn't going to say no. Not this time.

He'd worry about angles and leverage and Meredith's odd hold over him tomorrow. Tonight, he wanted to live in the moment and forget about everything else.

# Seven

Jason's hand never left Meredith's waist, burning through her clothes with delicious heat. She shivered, nearly stumbling over the curb as he ushered her into the car.

What in the world had gotten into him? If she'd have known a few stolen sketches would bring out his inner Vegas, she'd have scrounged up some long ago.

That kiss had been hot. Like she remembered. Dare she hope this was the start of Amazing, Part II?

"Don't tease me, Jason." She scooted across the backseat of the black town car. "If we're on our way to eat and not my hotel, I'm going to push you out of the car at a very high speed."

The moment he took his seat next to her, he hit the button to raise the panel between the driver and the backseat. The panel whirred, but before it fully nested into place, Jason's mouth was on hers again.

Tipping her head back, he drank from her, tongue tasting her again with the same heat and fervor as he had in the elevator. Well, then. Hotel it was.

She moaned as his mouth rediscovered hers, waves and waves of hot pleasure soaking her with need. Never one to let a man lead, she hiked her skirt up so she could climb into his lap, her lips never leaving his.

Their hips aligned and his hard length rubbed against her core. A long spike of desire tore through her. *Oh, yes, exactly.* She needed this man right now. She rolled her hips, grinding faster, and they groaned in unison.

"Jason," she breathed and nearly came apart at the simple taste of his name on her tongue. A sob rose in her throat and he caught it with another long kiss.

"Right here, baby," he murmured and two fingers slid past the barrier of her panties to explore her damp heat.

Forcefully, he twisted into her, letting her ride his hand as a frisson of white-hot heat flushed over her. Rocking against him faster and faster, she writhed and sparks gathered at the pressure point.

*More.* Popping the button on her shirt, she palmed her breast and yanked her bra's cup down, offering her nipple to his already-questing mouth. As he sucked it between his teeth and laved the tip with his firm tongue, his thumb circled her nub and that was it.

She came on a thick flood of release, moaning his name and riding the ripples to a finale the likes of which she hadn't experienced in two long years. Slumping against him, she locked her lips against his neck as he stroked two more echoes from her core long past the time she'd expected the climax to end.

"We're here," Jason murmured and withdrew his fingers so sensuously and slowly, her muscles involuntarily clamped down again. "We have to get out."

"Then…stop making me…come."

His wicked laugh put a smile on her face as she reset her clothes. Which didn't take long; Jason was very skilled at finding her sweet spots. Was it any wonder she couldn't move on from a man who made her climax prior to the end of a seven-minute car trip?

He held her hand as he hustled her to the elevator bank. Once in the elevator, he nuzzled her neck, murmuring a few choice phrases about what else he planned to do to her when they got to her room.

Delicious. She just wished she knew what had burst his dam.

It took way too long to reach her floor. They flew from the elevator the moment the doors slid open.

Card key already in hand, he backed her against the door and kissed her thoroughly. She fell into it and into the sensations of the hard planes of his body pressing hers, the wood at her back, the urgency in his hands. All of it stoked a hot flame inside her.

And yet, she hesitated.

She wanted him so badly, but a little worm of doubt wouldn't let her continue until she got some answers, especially the most important one—was all this going to disappear if she blinked?

Pulling back, she put a finger to his beautiful mouth.

"I have to know," she murmured. "What's tonight all about? You've been resistant to this since the moment I walked into your office."

Her hands ached to touch his sculpted abs and her mouth salivated to taste the hard flesh she'd felt pressing into her abdomen. But she didn't move, waiting for his response with bated breath. If he claimed to be acting on the heat of the moment, she'd bid him good-night in a heartbeat. They weren't drunk, and neither of them had a life crisis to blame this on.

This was nothing but two adults coming together because they desperately wanted to be with each other. She needed to know he was choosing this.

"Yes," he acknowledged. "But not because I didn't want you."

"Then why?"

He swayed backward a fraction, but it was enough to alert her she'd hit a nerve. Running a hand through his spiky hair, he released her waist, letting his arm hang at his side. "You've got our experience in Vegas built up in your head as something legendary. I can't maintain that myth for you. I'm just me and you've already expressed disappointment over that."

"Oh, honey." She bit her lip before she spilled too hasty a denial. Because she had said that. "The only reason I have that experience built up in my head is because you're the man who made it legendary. Are you worried it'll only be mediocre?"

Patently ridiculous, if so.

He shook his head. "I'm saying I'm not like I was in Vegas in real life. I don't want to be wild and crazy on a regular basis. I can't. It leads to poor judgment."

As her heart twisted with disappointment, he shifted and pulled her close, wrapping his arms around her so that all the good parts of their bodies aligned. "But you seem to drag my wild side into the light whether I like it or not. I decided to let you, just for tonight."

Had *that* been the golden ticket all along? If she'd seduced him from the get-go, they could have avoided all this drama.

She smiled as her body relaxed in the knowledge that he wasn't about to deny himself what he clearly wanted. Which meant she won, as well. "I see. This is a relationship with an expiration date."

Guess that made it easier for him to let his guard down, as long as he could put it back up in the morning. Or at least that was what he was telling himself. She'd let him think that all he wanted, but that wasn't how it was going to happen.

She stepped aside so he could open the door. Then he picked her up in his strong arms to carry her to the bed, where he laid her out carefully and began unbuckling one stiletto while treating her ankle to butterfly kisses.

She sighed a little. "I thought you didn't believe in romance."

The shoe hit the floor. Eyes half-shut, he rubbed his stubbly jaw over the arch of her foot and murmured, "I said romance was for losers who couldn't get a woman into bed. I didn't need it to get you here. But that doesn't mean I don't think you deserve it."

The back of her throat burned with sudden, unshed tears and she couldn't speak. This was the Jason of two years ago and yet not. He was still gorgeous and pushed all the right buttons, but she didn't remember him being sweet. She couldn't quite get a grip on him.

"Meredith," he said, almost reverently. With extreme care, he took off her other shoe. "You're the most exquisite woman I've ever seen. Bar none. I want to taste you. All over."

"Sounds like a plan to me," she choked out.

"Hope you don't mind if I start here." He slid a hand up her thigh and hooked her panties, drawing them off. Then he parted her skirt at the slit and let his gaze travel over her flesh. He murmured near poetic words of appreciation.

Fevered desire swept along her skin.

He knelt on the bed, gripped her thighs and lowered his head. And then his tongue touched her intimately. Pressing harder, he explored her with the tip and then the broad, rough part laved her. Her eyelids fluttered closed as he pleasured her thoroughly, yanking another climax out of her almost immediately.

She let it wash over her, murmuring his name.

When she recovered, she popped one eye open. "Are you planning to join me at some point? Never mind. You don't have a choice."

While he was busy trying to romance her, she just wanted to put her hands on his naked chest, straddle him and ride into oblivion until they were both spent.

Before he could think of another way to prolong the agony, she jackknifed up from the bed and drew off his suit jacket, tossing it to the floor. Their gazes met and held as she unbuttoned his shirt. A powerful unspoken sense of awareness and electricity passed between them, darkening his expression.

She let the shirt fall from her fingers as his hands tangled in her hair, drawing her head backward so he could nibble at her throat. After what was surely an eternity, she spread her hands on his bare chest, fingertips memorizing the hard muscles.

"I want all of you," she murmured and quickly divested him of the remainder of his clothes, while he peeled her out of the outfit he'd given her.

When he was gloriously bare, she indulged herself in a good, long perusal. Mouth slightly quirked up, he stood still as she soaked in the perfection of Jason's body, especially the jutting arousal that signified how much he wanted her.

It was a thing of beauty.

And she wanted to make him feel as good as he'd made her feel. Kneeling before him, she ran her tongue along his hard shaft until she felt his fingers grip the back of her head. Instantly, she remembered that meant he was ready for more. So she drew him into her mouth and sucked until he pulsed against her tongue.

Harder and harder she sucked until he groaned and locked his knees, then came in a rush that left her feeling wickedly powerful.

"And now for the main course," she announced and backed him up to the bed where he collapsed in a heap, groaning her name. "Wait here."

She dashed to the bathroom to clean up and retrieve a dozen condoms—because if history was any indication, they'd need them all.

When she returned to the bed, he hadn't moved, as instructed. He lay there, arm over his eyes, clearly recovering from the massive orgasm she'd given him.

Shamelessly, she climbed up the length of his body to kiss him soundly. "Miss me?"

The arm moved and his dark gaze fastened on hers.

"Much more than I should have. You weren't gone that long."

Oh, my. There he went being sweet again. She'd mostly been kidding. What was he trying to do to her? "Here I am."

She squealed when he flipped her under him, and then his tongue was in her mouth, so she wisely let him kiss her senseless. All vestiges of humor drained away as his hands caressed her, taking her deep under his spell. The world fell away and became nothing more than a sea of sensation. When he lifted his head, breaking the long kiss, she whimpered.

"Just a sec," he whispered and sheathed himself one-handed, then parted her thighs.

*Yes, oh, yes.* She thrust upward as he entered her and they joined completely, inch by delicious inch.

Wrapping her legs around him so he couldn't move, she cupped his jaw and just looked at him for a moment. His heated gaze locked with hers. The moment stretched, filling her with the strangest sense of awe.

Jason was here. He was with her, inside her, surrounding her. Her heart shifted and resettled and finally felt as if it was in the right place. She almost cried out with the perfection of it. Only at that moment did she realize the sharp pieces of her fractured soul had been digging into her for two years. And in one instant, Jason had healed her.

"Make love to me," she whispered.

Oh, no. She'd said that out loud.

They'd never made love before. They'd had plenty of hot, dirty sex. But that had been before she went without him for two years.

She liked hot, dirty sex, like the fully clothed orgasm she'd had in the car while throngs of people raced around them, oblivious to the couple getting it on inside. Sex was part of her due as a human being, and she'd always made sure to get plenty of it. All at once, she wanted something more.

And it scared her. Making love wasn't what she and Jason did. He wanted wild and crazy, like they'd had in Vegas, for one night. He liked that she brought out that side of him, which wouldn't happen if she got all maudlin.

Besides, this was a relationship with an expiration date and they'd both agreed to that. For crying out loud, they were days away from signing divorce papers. What had gotten into her?

Clamping down on all the emotions, she smiled wickedly as he stared down at her, clearly at a loss about what she was asking for.

"But not like this," she said and flexed one hip to roll him off her. Fortunately, he let her because there was no way she could have moved a man his size with her own strength alone. Then she slung a leg over his waist.

Astride his muscular frame now, she placed both palms on his chest, like she'd been fantasizing about for days. Years. "Much better."

She began to move and flung her head back to keep him from seeing anything extra in her eyes that she didn't want to reveal.

Pure pleasure. Nothing wrong with that.

And pleasure her he did. Jason reached up to cup her breasts as she found her rhythm, tweaking her nipples expertly. Losing herself in him wasn't hard.

He groaned. "I love your body. It's the hottest I've ever seen, even in airbrushed magazines."

"And it's all yours, for now," she teased and pretended the catch in her throat was due to the physical pleasure instead of how sad "for now" had suddenly made her. What was *wrong* with her?

Hot. Dirty. Wild. Crazy. These were the things she should be focusing on. She threw herself into it, abandoning her thoughts to the heat Jason had created. His hips matched her thrusts, spiraling her into the heavens in another climax.

She slumped onto his chest, resting her cheek against his thundering heart. His arms held her tight and she shut her eyes. But she couldn't go to sleep cradled by this man like she desperately wanted to. It meant something different now than it had in Vegas.

She'd made the monumentally earth-shattering discovery that when she'd dreamed of reconnecting with Jason Lynhurst, it hadn't been about sex. Not solely. Maybe it hadn't even been just sex in Vegas, but she'd never stopped to examine it.

Her heart hurt and not in a good way. Was all this why she'd gotten so teary over his simple romantic gestures earlier? Why she couldn't forget him? All she'd wanted was a taste of his magic again, the feel of his body and the rush of a release only he seemed capable of giving her.

And he had. What else could she possibly ask for? Once she had the divorce, she could move on, go home and become a successful businesswoman. That's what the Grown-Up Pact was about, what she wanted. Didn't she? Frustrated, she bit her lip. This emotional muddle was not on the agenda.

After a few minutes of struggling to hold back the flood of confusion inside, she finally thought she could speak without tipping him off that she'd experienced a total freakout. "You've still got the moves, sugar. Anytime you want wild and crazy, you let me know. I'm your girl."

"I'll keep that in mind." He kissed her on the temple and spooned her against him. "Do you want me to stay?"

Of course she did. But coupled with the swirl of uncertainty and the fact that he'd actually asked made her blurt out, "You don't have to."

And then she hoped he'd see right through her words and insist that he wanted to stay. But he nodded and rolled away, taking his heat with him. "I do have an early meeting."

She smiled and faked being okay with him jetting off in the middle of her crisis. After all, she'd given him permission to leave. This wasn't a vacation where they could lounge around in bed for a whole weekend. He was busy. So was she. "See you later."

Actually it was better if he went, for both of them. This is what adults did when having a short-term affair. It was what *she* did. Always.

She didn't watch him get dressed and didn't glance up when she heard him turn the doorknob to leave. It was cold in this icebox of a hotel room. She pulled the blanket up to cover herself.

Long after he left, she stared at the wall, wondering how in the world they'd managed to get naked and have cataclysmic orgasms and yet she hadn't gotten what she wanted at all.

# Eight

With something akin to a herculean effort, Jason managed to hit the threshold of his office by eight o'clock. How, he had no idea. He'd tossed and turned all night, only to fall asleep at 5:00 a.m., thirty minutes before his alarm.

If only he could blame the inability to sleep on Avery's thievery or the merger plans or the damaging press he had been combating. As bad as all that was, it couldn't hold a candle to the vision of Meredith on permanent repeat in his head.

Oddly, the memory wasn't of her naked—though she had the body of any breathing man's wet dream. No, the image haunting him was of her in the car, when she'd mounted him with that little skirt hiked up and her breasts half spilling from her clothing.

The look on her face…rapturous. He couldn't stop watching her as he pleasured her. Sure, he'd been touching her intimately while in public, which was the very definition of the kind of crazy she induced. He should have been appalled at himself. Instead, he'd felt alive, invigorated. Powerful in the knowledge that he could make her come as many times as he wanted and she'd cry out *his* name.

That's why he hadn't stayed. Because he'd liked reconnecting with her far too much.

He groaned and groped blindly for the fresh cup of coffee on his desk, gulping it in hopes of banishing his wicked vixen of a wife from his mind. The coffee scalded his tongue and he swore. Colorfully.

There was not enough coffee in all of Midtown Manhattan to caffeinate him well enough to face the day anyway. He dumped the whole cup in the trash. Might as well make his morning complete by calling Avery.

Anyone who would steal a company's bread and butter deserved a special place in hell.

When Avery answered on the first ring, he knew something was up and the back of his neck tingled. "Hey. We need to talk."

How to bring up the designs? If he dove right into an accusation, Avery would figure out how to weasel out of admitting anything. Maybe he'd get the lay of the land first and then work his way up to it.

"I agree," she said smoothly. "I've been talking to Paul about the points made in the oh-so-clever article you released. By the way, nice job with that, little brother."

The sarcasm was so thick, he grinned. Meredith's strategy had worked. That article must have really pissed off Avery for her to be so nasty right out of the gate. "Marketing, plain and simple. Surely you of all people appreciate the value of truth in advertising."

She paused long enough for Jason to wonder if the connection had been lost.

"I'm a fan of the truth, actually," she returned cryptically. "So I mentioned to Paul that you weren't off the mark. Hurst doesn't have the heavy hitting haute couture reputation of Lyn. It's not in our DNA, nor our strategy. If we want to run with the big dogs, we have to consider our weaknesses."

*Ah.* So that was the reason behind the stolen designs. She planned to use them to launch a line that would compete with Lyn. But surely she realized that at least twenty people could attest under oath that those designs had originated inside Lyn's walls, not to mention the digital footprint of the saved files with date/time stamps. Hurst's reputation wouldn't be haute couture *or* prom dresses—it would become famous for being a company full of convicted felons.

The whole concept made him a little sick.

"What did Paul say?" Uttering his father's name didn't help the queasiness.

"This and that," she hedged. "The important thing is that I laid the foundation for the merger. So in reality, our dueling media blitz only helped that cause." And that would be the only admission he'd ever get that she'd orchestrated the sweatshop allegations. "In a few days, I'm going to mention the need for a new strategy. Then I'll casually drop the hint—have you thought about the benefits of bringing the company back under one roof?"

God, she was good. If he hadn't known about the stolen designs, he might have actually bought that song and dance. Avery didn't have a problem playing both sides of the table, obviously. And neither did he.

Suddenly, he didn't see the value in mentioning the designs. He'd rather wait to see how that played out. Though he'd still have to find a way to deal with the spy in his company.

"Fantastic. I'll do the same with Bettina, though I'll focus on revenue. She's interested in launching a swimsuit line." Normally, he wouldn't mention detail, but with it on the table, Avery couldn't steal it out from under Bettina now. "It would be a good time to talk financing and how expensive new lines are. Hurst's numbers are better than they've ever been, according to what you've told me. That's still true, right?"

"Of course." She sniffed. "Hurst House is and always will be the cash cow of the Lynhurst empire."

"This is great," he said heartily. "It's progress, which is sorely needed. Now we have to work on how to convince Paul and Bettina to relinquish their CEO roles to us."

The hope was that they could figure out a way to make

it seem attractive to retire or find other projects. Paul was going to be difficult as he'd been on the business side since the inception of Lynhurst Enterprises, whereas Bettina was a designer at heart. It might be possible to get her interested in stepping aside.

As always, Jason cared more about Bettina's feelings than Paul's. Honestly, if Jason and Avery ended up doing a hostile takeover of Hurst, it would be exactly what his father deserved.

After all, it was Paul's fault the company had split. And Paul's fault Hurst and Lyn weren't doing as well separately as they'd done together. But a hostile takeover would be difficult and costly and would breed ill will. It would be better to avoid it if possible.

"It's a problem," Avery conceded. "We'll have to brainstorm on how to solve it."

Inspiration hit, brought on solely by the combination of Meredith calling him up to Hurst's office and the night of passion following. "When you're hinting around about the merger, mention to Paul that he might want to take a backseat role in order to spend more time with Caozinha."

It was the first time he'd ever called his father's wife by her name. Since he didn't immediately feel like rinsing out his mouth with Jack Daniel's, he'd call that a victory.

"That'll work." Faint praise, but from Avery, it was practically the same thing as a gold medal.

They talked a few more minutes about some of the merger's legal details and when Jason hung up, he had to chalk it up to one of the more pleasant conversations he'd had with his sister in quite some time.

Either knowing about her secret plans had mellowed him or Meredith had. Maybe each had had an effect. And his wife was responsible for both. Who would have thought he'd gain such a valuable asset when he'd come to Meredith with the idea of not signing the divorce papers right away?

Mood vastly improved, Jason put the hammer down on

his to-do list and, by eleven, managed to accomplish more than he'd have expected. Which was fortunate because two minutes later, Meredith texted him: Meet me at the hotel for lunch. I have an idea.

Instantly, his mind filled in that blank. He had an idea, too. Several, in fact. Already happily anticipating another skipped meal, he texted her back: I'm walking out the door.

He canceled his one o'clock meeting and caught himself humming by the time he hit the elevator. Looked as if he wasn't against wild and crazy in the middle of the day, either.

Meredith was already in the room when he pushed the door open. God, she was exquisite, with silky hair halfway down her back. Her beautiful face—he could stare at it for hours.

"That was fast," she commented over her shoulder as she bent over the desk scribbling something on the phone pad. "Give me a minute."

"You take all the time you need." Because she was precisely where he wanted her.

He came up behind her and put both hands at her waist, fitting that shapely rear against his already-aching groin. The filmy sundress she wore scarcely provided a barrier and he could feel the folds of her sex. Hard as steel, he rubbed her intimately, pleasuring them both.

She stilled and then shifted, deliberately sliding against his erection.

"Oh, so that's how it's going to be?" she asked, her voice hitching.

"Uh-huh," he murmured and gathered her hair in one hand, holding it away from her neck. He nibbled at the creamy flesh revealed, grinding into her deeper.

*Oh, yeah. So sweet.*

She reached back and yanked the hem of her dress up to her waist, then guided his free hand to one breast. "If you're going to do it, do it right, honey." She arched backward, thrusting her hips in powerful bursts.

He nearly came then, still fully clothed, but he fought it long enough to thumb down the neckline of her dress, spilling her breast into his palm. Groaning, he took the nipple between his fingertips and the hot flesh pebbled instantly.

"I want to be inside you," he mouthed against her neck as he kissed it from behind.

"Condoms are in the bathroom. I'm not going anywhere."

He peeled away from her with no small effort and dashed to grab the string of foil packets lying on the vanity.

When he returned to the main area, Meredith stood palms-down at the desk, skirt still flipped up over her back. But she'd kicked off her panties and spread her legs in invitation. She turned her head a fraction and peered up at him through a curtain of hair. Her expression said he better hurry because she was impatient.

It was the single most erotic thing he'd ever seen. Dark, wicked lust zigzagged through his midsection.

His fingers shook as he tore off his pants and rolled on a condom over the fiercest erection he'd ever experienced. In seconds, he was back in place against her, gripping her hips and sliding into her heat.

She closed around him and the exquisite pressure heightened the urgency. He needed her. He reached for her nub, cradling her against his torso as he fingered her, driving them together again and again until she cried out. Her release squeezed him so perfectly that he followed her instantly. Eyes closed and lips against her neck, he let the orgasm blast through him.

Chest heaving with the exertion, he slapped a hand next to hers on the desk, bracing himself so he didn't collapse on her. "That was…"

*Amazing. Unbelievable.* But those words were so cliché for what she made him feel.

"Hot and dirty?" she suggested.

"And then some." They'd had sex in many inventive locations and positions before, but never in the middle of a workday when they both had to go back to an office. Somehow, the spontaneity had heightened the pleasure. And now he wanted her all over again.

He separated their bodies and turned her in his arms to lay a kiss on her lips. But as he started to lower his head, their gazes caught, freezing him. Vulnerability and tenderness flickered through her expression and he couldn't look away. One strap of her sundress fell off her shoulder and he slid it back into place, resting his hand on her still-hot flesh in a moment of perfect harmony that rocked him to the core.

All at once, he remembered similar moments from Vegas. After coming down from the height of their climaxes, they'd roll together and hold each other. Then they'd whisper things in the dark, secret things, fears. Hopes. Dreams. It had made the whole experience of sex something otherworldly. It was in those moments that she'd given him peace.

And nothing had changed.

When he'd given in to his desire for Meredith, he hadn't gotten just the wild and crazy he'd asked for. Maybe that wasn't all he'd been looking for, either, despite the lies he seemed willing to tell himself. He needed *her*, if only to remind himself that he wasn't cold-blooded. With her, he could be a man he actually liked.

"Meredith," he murmured and drew her forward into the kiss he suddenly ached for. Her lips molded to his, and she snugged into his embrace. It was comfortable and sexy and right.

As he angled her head to take them both deeper, she pulled away and cleared her throat. "You know, normally a guy starts out with the kiss, but it's fine if you want to do it the other way around."

Gaze on the floor, she located her panties and disappeared into the bathroom as if he wasn't standing there. At a loss, he drew his own clothes back on and pulled out his phone to check his email because it felt less pathetic than following her into the bathroom to demand an explanation for why she'd cooled down so fast.

She didn't owe him peace. He certainly hadn't given her any.

When she returned, the temperature hadn't risen much.

"So about my idea," she began and perched on the edge of the desk where they'd just had hot and dirty sex, as she'd dubbed it.

"That wasn't your idea?" He nodded to the scene of the crime.

"Uh, no. That was totally your idea."

Frowning, he searched her blank expression. "You seemed pretty on board with it."

"Of course I was." Impatiently, she flipped a lock of hair behind her back. "You're the sexiest man I've ever met. You pretty much just have to breathe on me to get me hot. But it wasn't what I had in mind when I texted you. The condoms were in the bathroom after all, not on the desk."

The compliment sounded decidedly uncomplimentary somehow. "Funny, I've been thinking about you all day."

"You wanna know what I've been thinking about? How to get the designs back from Avery." The fierce scowl on her face piqued his ire in kind because he had no idea what had set her off. "And I have an idea how to accomplish that. If you'll get your brain out of my panties, we can talk about it."

"That's rich, Meredith. You've been very free with the invitations into your panties, starting from second one in my office. Don't act like I'm the only horny one."

The oasis of peace vanished so fast, he wondered if he'd imagined it.

"What should I act like, then? Your wife?" She sneered.

"Because that's what I'm trying to do here. Give you what you want out of this marriage so we can both be done with it."

His hands fisted at his sides as pure frustration threatened the careful grip he held on his temper. "Why are you picking a fight with me?"

"Because! I…" She deflated all at once and sank into one of the chairs at the table, her head down. After a beat, she said, "I'm not trying to pick a fight. I just want to do my job and go home. Can you give me a break, here? I need you to understand. I have to go home."

Her gaze met his and all his mad drained away, as well. This conversation was upsetting her. But why? Did she want to get away from him that badly?

Clearly. And could he blame her? He'd held her up for an extra week already. She had a real life to get back to, just like he did. Obviously she didn't crave a warm place at his side, where together they could combat the cold, harsh business of daily life.

"Tell me your idea," he said, crossing to her and taking her hand so she could sense his sincerity. And because he wanted to touch her. "Really. If it works and I get the designs back, I'll call it even."

"Even?"

Her fingers curled around his. It was enough of a truce to force him to spit out the clarification—even though he didn't want to. He owed her and she deserved what she'd earned.

"I'll sign the papers." He swallowed against the sudden burn in his throat. Too late to take it back now. "I'll get my lawyer to expedite the divorce, and you can be on a plane before you know it. First class, my treat. How's that for understanding?"

It was yet another lie. In reality, he didn't understand at all. Because he didn't want to let her go and it had nothing to do with leverage or sex or anything he could name.

\* \* \*

Meredith blinked. "Just like that?"

It was almost over. She could go back to Houston, divorce in hand, and start figuring out how to scrub Jason from her soul. The faster she got away, the easier it would be to sort out all the confused feelings she couldn't seem to untangle.

Obviously, he was just as eager to get rid of her. Last night he'd insisted this relationship had an expiration date, which she'd conveniently ignored.

That had been before she'd realized sex and their affinity and all the things she'd dreamed about for two years were somehow connected via her heart.

"Sure." He shrugged nonchalantly as if it didn't matter either way. "Once I have the designs back, what else could you do? You've succeeded at exactly what I asked for. I've got intel on Avery's plans, and the information is stellar. Better than I could have hoped."

Jason was conceding. He'd given her high praise and told her she'd nearly fulfilled the terms he'd laid out. The elation should be so great, she shouldn't be able to hold it back. Instead, she felt as if she couldn't breathe.

"So you want me to do this one last thing and then I'm done?"

He nodded. "Seems like that's what I'm saying."

Fantastic. The timing couldn't be better. She didn't know how much longer she could keep being Jason's wild and crazy go-to girl. Not when the entire time he'd been blowing her mind against the desk she'd been so very aware that she wanted more, wanted him like he was during their stolen moments, but permanently. And she had a hard time not demanding it from him.

For once in her life, she was going to act like an adult and sleep in the bed she'd made. Which wasn't Jason's. He didn't want anything more than sex and honestly, that's all he'd wanted in Vegas, too. It was all *she'd* wanted...until she didn't.

How was she supposed to know that sex would create a deluge of emotions? Or that she'd have no idea how to handle them? That was her own fault, not his, and it wasn't fair to demand anything of him other than a divorce, especially when she was clueless about what she'd even demand.

Squaring her shoulders, she nodded once. "Awesome. So Avery has a meeting next week with some people about the after-hours project. I don't know what it's about, but I do know that Paul is on her case about the bad juju you created with the press release."

It had given her a thrill to know she'd had a hand in the tightness around Avery's mouth. The whole office had been walking on eggshells all morning and doing their level best to stay out of Avery's way. Except Meredith. She'd walked straight into the lion's den and volunteered to help.

No one had to know she'd done it for Jason as much as she'd done it for the divorce.

"She told me," Jason offered. "They're trying to do damage control with a strategic move. I think the stolen designs became a part of it."

Avery hadn't shared anything that detailed with Meredith. "I didn't realize you'd spoken to her."

He raised his eyebrows endearingly. "Didn't I mention it? Oh, that's right. I was a little busy with the desk gymnastics and then wading through the fight that wasn't a fight."

The eye roll she shot him wasn't nearly sarcastic enough. "*I've* been trying to have this conversation for forty-five minutes now. *You* started the desk gymnastics."

"You were the one bent over the desk wearing that sexy little dress. Next time, sit down. Or wear a potato sack."

His teasing tone saddened her a little.

If only things hadn't gotten so complicated, she'd probably have flashed her nipples in deliberate provocation, hoping he'd get her naked again. But the fact that he saw

nothing wrong with flirting in the same breath as inform-
ing her she could go home told her everything she needed
to know. She'd made the right decision to keep her mouth
shut about what was going on inside her.

"So anyway." She drew the last word out lightly, but
they needed to get back on topic before she fell apart. "A
drumroll would be a little anticlimactic at this point, but
I'm going to ask Avery to let me take her place at this
meeting about the after-hours project so she can focus on
Paul's strategy concerns. She might say no, but it's worth
it to ask."

"I'm impressed." Jason crossed his arms and leaned
against the wall, the same spot he'd been in since she returned from the bathroom. "It's a good idea and I like it.
When is the meeting?"

"I think it's Monday." Which meant she had the rest of
the afternoon to work out how she'd get Avery to agree.
It was all in the timing, especially if she could corner the
busy woman right after the two-hour meeting Avery had
booked with Paul Lynhurst later today.

Surely that meeting would end with a number of action
items assigned to Avery with no relief in sight. Meredith,
to the rescue.

And if Avery didn't want Meredith to know her schedule, she shouldn't leave her calendar open on her phone in
plain sight.

"Will she go for it?" Jason asked. "Avery doesn't trust
anyone. Have you gotten close enough to her that she'd give
you such an important task?"

Meredith shrugged. "Can't hurt to try. But it's the only
shot I'll have to get the designs into my possession without
raising her suspicions and then oops. Maybe I accidentally
set them on fire. You have backup files, right?"

"You bet."

"And if I get lucky, she'll fire me. I'll be going home
soon anyway, so it's a chance to tell her what I really think

of her. It will probably include swearing." Judging by the way Jason's grin widened, her plan met with his approval. "So you're cool with all this? Without the designs, she has no strategy left and you'll be able to expose her as a thief. We're talking about ruining Hurst. A company run by your father and your sister. No second thoughts?"

"My father ruined Hurst all on his own when he split it apart," Jason countered fiercely. "Whatever he gets is no less than he deserves."

His entire demeanor changed in a snap. Distress warred with passion, and his body fairly vibrated with it. His vitality bled through the atmosphere to ping around inside her.

Open, vulnerable Jason from Vegas hadn't grown up and grown cold—he'd transferred his angst and helplessness into his merger plans. How had she missed that? He'd talked about his plans before—a lot—but always in a factual kind of way.

This was different. He'd never revealed so much in so few words, especially not about his feelings toward his father.

"Tell me about it," she commanded softly, terrified she'd shove him back behind his walls if she pushed too hard. But if she could bring out the wild and crazy in him, surely she could coax out more of the sensitive and passionate, as well. She had to try.

Intimacy and soul-baring conversations—it was the stuff of her fantasies. If she'd begged him to stay last night, could they have gotten there then?

He took a deep breath, clearly struggling to maintain his composure.

"That's why it's so important for me to reunite Lyn. I'm going to fix it. Paul failed, as a father, as a husband, as a CEO." Jason's hands fisted at his sides, his mouth twisting into a frown. "My mom never wanted to be in management. But he forced her into it when he left."

His ravaged expression nearly undid her.

She ached for him and for his mother. Avery, too, as at least some of her abrasive personality probably stemmed from her hurt over the events of two years ago. Meredith had a lot of sympathy for them all. "I'm sorry, honey."

"Don't be. I'm going to step up and be the man he wasn't. I'm going to make the company whole again, and if I'm CEO, then he can't be. It's the perfect payback for what he did to Lynhurst Enterprises because running things was always his role."

"Oh, honey." She shook her head and let a small smile bloom. "You might be telling yourself that this is all about revenge, but admit it. You're working so hard on this merger for your mom."

Surprise flitted across his expression. Had he not realized that until this moment?

"I'll give you that one. It's partially true. I forget how easily you read me," he groused but didn't seem too upset about it.

He'd designed his dastardly plans to right the wrongs his father had done to his mother. It was somehow sweet and her heart squeezed with raw emotion. Unable to stop herself, she slid from the chair and wrapped him in a tender embrace.

"You look like you need a hug," she offered in explanation, though he hadn't asked and it wasn't exactly true.

*She* needed the contact, needed to touch this complex, wonderful man buried underneath the fashion-espionage mastermind.

His arms encircled her, holding her tight, and he rested his head on top of hers.

They stood there wrapped in each other and it was every bit the connection she'd yearned for. And they were both fully dressed. Who would have seen that coming?

"I have to get back to work," Jason said gruffly. "It's really late."

"Yeah."

Lots of work to do this afternoon. Lots of Allo to endure and lots of Avery to outwit. The thought exhausted
her all of a sudden. All she really wanted to do was stay
in the circle of Jason's arms for the next week or two and
forget about real life.

Since that wasn't in the master plan, she stepped back
and shoved him lightly. "Go. But come back. Bring dinner and I'll tell you about my conversation with Avery."

They weren't divorced yet. Until then, she'd keep pushing for that connection.

# Nine

There was literally no point in Jason going back to work if he intended to get anything done. Apparently, taking a two-hour lunch meant an afternoon of interruptions.

An interview had surfaced in the press sometime in the past few hours with more sweatshop allegations, this time from an unnamed source who claimed to be a current Lyn employee. It was not pretty. And he had the worst feeling Avery wasn't behind this one, which meant he had bigger problems.

When Bettina pinged Jason via instant message asking him to come to her office, he groaned. He could not deal with another round of his mother's teary, mournful snuffling over the continued media onslaught. Yes, they were maligning the company with her name on it, but it was his name, too, and if she wanted him to fix it, she needed to give him a break.

It was shaping up to be a late night at the office. There went his plans for takeout with Meredith, which he'd been actively anticipating.

"This is the last time, Mom," he muttered to his laptop screen and grabbed a Red Bull from the small refrigerator by his desk for fortification.

When had he turned into such a liar? He'd be there for his mother forty-seven more times today if that's what she needed. When Paul moved out two years ago, Jason had been his mother's only ally. Gladly. After all she'd done for Jason, it was the least he could do for her. Plus, she was his mom.

Chugging the energy drink, he poked his head into Bettina's office and she was smiling.

"There you are. Come in," she invited and leaped up from behind her desk, rounding it more quickly than a sixty-year-old woman should be able to.

Before Jason could blink, she'd thrown her arms around him in a totally out-of-character motherly hug. He hugged her back, mystified by what had prompted such a turnabout.

"Avery told me," his mother said when she stepped back to look at him with a misty smile. "Though why you didn't, I'll never understand."

"Told you what?" Baffled, he searched his mother's expression for some clue as to what had elevated her mood.

"About the wife you've been hiding from everyone."

"About the...*what*?" Jason's stomach tensed as his mother came in for another round of hugs.

Should he brazen it out or come clean? Well, obviously it was too late to pretend he didn't know what Bettina was talking about.

*Avery.* He swore. He'd underestimated her yet again. How had she found out? God, this was so much worse than labor allegations. He should have seen this coming.

"Why didn't you tell me you'd gotten married?" his mother scolded, but the thrill in her voice belied the reprimand.

"Uh...I thought you'd be upset." Since that clearly wasn't the case, he scrambled for how to spin this new development, while simultaneously trying to figure out why Avery had struck at him in this particular way.

"On the contrary. It's the best news I've had in a long time." Her voice lowered. "I would never have said anything, but I didn't like the idea of you marrying Meiling in some kind of loveless arrangement. But a whirlwind romance and quick wedding? That's wonderful."

"I'm glad someone thinks so," he mumbled darkly.

He'd assumed Bettina would see the business benefits of his "arrangement" with Meiling. Fine time to find out differently.

His mother clapped her hands. "You must let me take you and your wife to dinner so I can meet her. Avery said she's working at Hurst? Which I don't understand, but I'm sure you can explain."

He muttered another curse under his breath and shut his eyes. Bettina's feelings were hurt that he'd let his wife work for The Enemy.

Jason was going to kill Avery. Slowly. "It's complicated."

She nodded, growing serious. "With your father and I on such bad terms, how could it be anything but? The divorce was hard on all of us. But you don't have to hide the most important relationship of your life from me. Sure I'm lonely occasionally, but that doesn't mean I don't wish great things for you. I'm genuinely happy that you've found someone."

Oh, man. Bettina thought he hadn't told her out of fear she'd be *jealous*? That wasn't precisely the sort of "upset" he'd assumed she'd be if she discovered he'd married Meredith in front of an Elvis impersonator in Vegas, while intoxicated. Two years ago, no less.

The Lyn and Hurst executive staffs wouldn't see his Vegas wedding as a plus, and Avery probably had more fun surprises in store for him regarding when and how she'd drop this marriage bombshell to others.

Damage control needed, ASAP.

"Thanks, Mom," he interjected smoothly. "And for the record, Meredith is only working at Hurst temporarily. I'm sorry I didn't tell you she was my wife when I asked you for the recommendation."

At least he didn't have to lie to preserve his mother's feelings. He wasn't hiding Meredith from Bettina by placing her at Hurst. But she needed to understand that his marriage wasn't going to last much longer. *Before* she started naming her imaginary grandchildren.

He had a feeling this news was not going to go over well. Bettina would be very disappointed that her son wasn't happily married after all. How had he gotten to this place?

"Mom, Meredith and I, we're not—"

"Oh, don't say you're not interested in dinner. I'm dying to meet my new daughter-in-law. I want to hear all the wedding details. And you're really horrible for not taking her on an extended honeymoon. Be sure you make that up to her."

*New* daughter-in-law? Was it possible Avery didn't actually spill the whole story? Or even better, perhaps Avery didn't actually know the full story. There was still a possibility of salvaging this situation. "Please, Mom. I do not now, nor do I ever, want you to explain what you think I should do to make it up to her."

Bettina laughed. "Let me take you to dinner. Are you free tonight?"

"We had plans to get takeout."

"Then it's settled." She leaned in and took Jason's hand in hers. His mother's skin felt paper-thin and prominent veins stood out against her wrinkles. When had she aged so much? "I worry about you. I'm glad you decided to settle down and spend your life with someone. It makes it so much easier to think about retiring."

"Retiring?"

That word had never come out of Bettina's mouth. His mother was one of the biggest obstacles to his plans because she'd never approve of merging with Hurst. He'd been racking his brain for a way to convince her to focus on her new swimsuit line and let him take care of the company.

But if Bettina retired…it was a whole new game.

Bettina patted his hand. "Not today. But maybe soon. I

didn't want to consider retiring, but now that you're settled, I can leave Lyn in your hands with confidence."

*Settled.* It had a much nicer ring than he'd have anticipated. Jason's gut spasmed at the same moment his mind spun in a billion directions. *What if he didn't have to end things with Meredith so quickly?*

Instantly, Jason's vision of the future shifted. He could stay married. And he had the perfect excuse to avoid examining why that was such a great thing.

"You'll be a fantastic CEO," Bettina finished with a nod.

Right. That's what he should be focusing on, not Meredith and her special ability to drive him insane. His mother was talking about retiring and naming him as the next CEO, a huge win for his plans.

If he was already the CEO of Lyn, the merger would go a lot more smoothly, and no one would question whether he should continue to be the head of the newly reformed company.

Because he would be *married.* To Meredith.

Who wanted a divorce, which he'd conveniently forgotten.

In the mixed-up, crazy place Jason's life had become, the wife he'd been working to get rid of was now the wife he apparently needed to keep. His marriage had just become very valuable.

Marriage was a tool. He'd always thought so. This was nothing new, nothing different. Meredith knew this and all he needed to do was have a conversation with her about the change of plans. She'd handle the curveball, despite the fact that he'd told her a few hours ago he'd sign the papers.

His palms started to sweat. "I have to get back to work. I'll let you know about dinner."

Bettina's glowing smile stuck with him the rest of the afternoon. As did the cramp in his stomach. He couldn't sign the papers, not even if Meredith got the designs back. And he had the worst feeling she'd hear the phrase "no divorce" and it would paint him as ruthless and cold-blooded...and exactly like Avery.

At which point she'd likely express her disappointment again over who he'd become. And then he'd have to think about how he longed to be a better man, the one she encouraged him to be.

Actually, as soon as he mentioned staying married a little while longer, she'd probably smile and say something provocative about him using this as an excuse to get her into his bed.

God, he hadn't thought that far ahead. But it only made sense that she had to move into his house, didn't it? That's what married people did. And how dumb would it be to suggest she stay in his guest room? But if he suggested she sleep with him, what did that imply?

Obviously, it implied he was asking her to move in with him and be his wife. In every sense. Because he wanted to be around her, live with her, sleep with her, like they were in a relationship. Something hitched in his chest as he imagined waking up next to Meredith every morning, her gaze sleepy and full of promise.

*Yes.* That's what he wanted.

No. He couldn't let her think that. There was no way he'd ever have a marriage based on anything other than how it could help him further his merger plans. People who fell in love eventually fell out of love and damaged everything around them, and he'd never willingly do that to anyone.

Nor could he give her the impression this was a desperate ploy to get a few more days with her, though he liked that aspect of it more than he should. If only this had happened before they'd started sleeping together again, the complications would be far fewer. And he'd never have to admit, not even to himself, that he wanted to seize this opportunity to keep her around.

Fortunately, he and Meredith saw eye to eye on the purpose of their marriage.

Meredith was starving and Jason had taken his sweet time getting to her hotel after work.

He finally knocked at ten after seven.

The darkness in Jason's gaze had her immediately itching to smooth the line from between his eyes. Tension was evident in the rigid set of his shoulders.

"Is this going to be a running theme, then?" She nodded to his empty hands. "I can start being in charge of dinner. Unless you wanted to skip eating again? Because I'm okay with that."

He didn't laugh.

"We're going out," he said shortly.

She glanced down at her yoga pants and off-the-shoulder T-shirt, which she'd changed into an hour ago. "I'm dressed for takeout."

"It doesn't matter. Avery knows we're married. And she told Bettina. The secret will probably be public knowledge by midnight. If it takes that long."

Meredith cursed. That explained his snippy mood.

The news probably wouldn't take very long to filter down to Texas, either, and then where would she be? Her father's lawyer had given her a very short time frame to settle this divorce, and he'd been clear—tell her father or he'd do it for her.

Now the press might beat him to it. She cursed again.

"Yeah." Jason's smile was grim. "That's exactly what I said."

"How did Avery find out? Oh, *no*. Not the—"

"Security camera." He nodded and pressed the spot between his brows, hard. "My best guess is we weren't as careful as we thought. Or if not that, she wasn't out of sight when I got out of the car at Hurst the other night. Somehow she saw us together and started poking her nose into my business."

"What does that mean? I can't be your spy anymore. Right?"

And if she couldn't be his spy, that meant he had to sign the divorce papers whether she got the designs or not.

Fabulous. Though she was a little sad to have no excuse to go in Avery's place to her meeting tomorrow. Despite the stolen nature of the designs, Meredith had been looking forward to seeing what happened in a fashion-house deal.

Was that why Avery had agreed to let Meredith go— because she already knew that Meredith was Jason's wife?

The back of her throat soured. So much for her stellar espionage skills. She'd looked forward to crowing over her victory with Jason tonight.

He sighed and propped a shoulder against the door frame as if his legs couldn't hold him up any longer. "It means my mother's freaking thrilled that I got married. She wants to take us to dinner tonight. I couldn't say no."

Dinner with Bettina Lynhurst? As what, a *couple*?

"Uh…it's not hard. *No*. See? Easy." Jason glared at her so hotly she shoved the door wide. "You better come in."

How had everything become so complicated?

He brushed past her as if she wasn't even standing there and flung open the closet to sift through her clothes. "Where's that gold top I brought you? Bettina likes it. You should wear it with the white cropped pants and your Stuart Weitzman sandals."

She put a palm on his arm to still his near-frantic rooting through her stuff. "As sexy as it is for a guy to expend so much effort to put clothes *on* me, chill out for a second. I don't want to go to dinner with your mom, like we're a happily married couple. There's no point in it. We're about to sign divorce papers. I'm going back to Houston."

"About that." He turned to face her and in the close

confines of the closet, the smell of his soap and his skin melded into something wholly Jason and wholly delicious.

She didn't want to notice the way he smelled, not with the calculating glint she caught in his gaze. "What about it? Don't you dare tell me I have more stuff to do before you divorce me after all. If the secret is out, my job is over. I'm not of any use to you any longer."

"Not true. I can't divorce you. Not yet."

She shook her head before he'd stopped talking. "You have to. It's over. Avery messed up your plans, and while I'm sad I don't get to tell her off, what else can I do here?"

"Bettina likes that I'm married. She actually said she can consider retiring now and would gladly turn over the reins to me since I've settled down." In a totally surprising move, he took her hand and curled her fingers around his, as if they often held hands while talking. "Avery's plan, whatever it was, backfired. Don't you see?"

It dawned on her, though how her brain still functioned with Jason's fingers brushing hers was mystifying. "You mean she did it to make you look bad. She thought Bettina would take it as an act of irresponsibility."

"Exactly. But she didn't. The opposite, in fact."

The unsettled feeling in her stomach turned into one big knot of foreboding as she connected the dots. "Let me get this straight. Your mom is all set to retire and name you as the new Lyn CEO because you got married. So you're not going to sign the divorce papers. Because it benefits you to stay married."

"In a nutshell." He dropped her hand. "I'm asking you to be my wife, out in the open. We'll make an announcement and everything, and you'll move into my condo. Once Bettina follows through with handing me the CEO job, then I'll divorce you."

"No. No way." She couldn't spit it out fast enough, especially since her heart was screaming "Yes, yes, yes" to being Jason's wife for real, for as long as it lasted. "Not for anything could you convince me this is a good idea."

It was too open-ended, too real, too rife with possibilities for her to get used to the arrangement, and then where would she be? Trying to forget Jason after a whole new level of intimacy.

He smiled and it did dangerous things to her pulse. "I'll give you whatever amount of money you were going to get as a loan from your father. Name it."

She didn't hesitate. "A hundred thousand dollars."

"Done. And now you don't have to tell your family that you messed up in Vegas. Think about it. No loan. All you have to do is fake this marriage well enough so my mother feels warm and squishy about retiring."

*Crap.* She'd thought he'd say no to such an outrageous sum and now she was stuck. "I can't… You want me to *live* with you? What are you saying, that we'll sleep in the same bed and stuff? Pretend we're in love?"

Her throat tightened. How long could she keep that up before it became a reality?

*Forever.* She'd have to keep it up forever because she was *not* falling in love with Jason. It was too dangerous.

"No to the first, yes to the second. I have a spare room."

"Of course. Sleeping with your wife is way over the line." She hadn't meant for that to come out so sarcastically.

Was she actually disappointed that he wasn't using their marriage as an excuse to play husband and wife to the fullest? Separate bedrooms actually made a sick sort of sense. It was tawdry to trade sex for a hundred thousand dollars and she'd deck him if he had suggested it.

But what if he'd suggested something totally different? Like the two of them having some kind of normal relationship full of making love and fun and togetherness. Falling asleep wrapped in each other's arms and sharing secrets in the dark. That she would have agreed to in a heartbeat because it meant he felt all the same confusing, scary things she felt.

Her mind buzzed dully with all the implications of that one crystalline realization. Maybe she wasn't so confused after all because there it was. She wanted something special and real and lasting with Jason. He didn't.

He cocked his head and contemplated her. "Sharing a bedroom complicates our interaction unnecessarily. This is a business proposition. Same as the first one."

Right, how could she forget? She wanted something he would never give her—the man buried beneath his strategy. "I know. Marriage is still your weapon of choice."

This new deal was far more difficult to agree to. She'd be insane to say no. This would solve all her problems in one, easy shot. Except for the one where she'd be acting like Jason's wife without any of the benefits, like a supportive husband who cared about her and thought she was the best thing that ever happened to him.

She'd be insane to say yes.

"I need you, Meredith." His blue eyes filled with vulnerability and her breath hitched. Not the puppy-dog eyes. She could stand anything but that. It threw her back to that time two years ago when he'd needed her. And she'd needed him.

God help her, she still did. She couldn't resist him when he morphed into that man she'd spent so many blissful hours with. It was stupid to even pretend she didn't want to stay a few more days. Stupid to pretend she'd snatched back that piece of her soul she'd given him in Vegas.

This was her chance, her very last chance, to find out if she'd made a mistake walking away from him in Vegas. And the last chance to find out if she was making a mistake wishing for something more this time.

If living in the same house couldn't afford her an opportunity to get there, nothing could. She could go back to

Houston with the knowledge that Jason wasn't the man for her and get over him, once and for all. Somehow.

"How long?" she croaked. "I do have another job, my real job, to get back to."

Which was less and less attractive the longer she stayed smack-dab in the middle of the New York fashion industry. Wedding dresses was Cara's forte, Cara's love. Meredith only worked with Cara because they were family, and her sister didn't care that Meredith brought nothing to the table other than money.

"I don't know. Maybe a couple of weeks. Is that a yes?" The hopefulness in his voice coupled with vulnerability pretty much made her choice for her.

She held up a hand before his smile grew any wider. "How can this possibly work? I don't understand what your mother thinks we've been doing for two years with no contact."

He shook his head. "She thinks we got married recently. She's all gushy over the romance of it."

"Wait a minute. So now we're going to take our marriage, pretend it's fake with each other but real to everyone else *and* lie about the timing? How does that make sense? Avery figured out we were married from somewhere and might actually know the whole story. Do you really want to give her that much leverage?"

Jason grinned instead of getting huffy about her contradicting him, like she'd expected. "I love the way your mind works. Please, my beautiful wife, tell me what we should do instead."

Rolling her eyes, she crossed her arms before she punched him. "We tell everyone we got married in Vegas and intended to get it annulled, but neither one of us could bear to go through with it. Then we reconnected because you had to get the divorce to marry Meiling. It was obvious to both of us we never stopped loving each other and you knew you could never go through with your arranged marriage and here we are."

"That's—"

"Brilliant. Duh. Always ask a woman to give you a romantic cover story."

*Cover story.* Because it wasn't true. There was no romance to their practical union and they weren't in love. But she couldn't stop herself from thinking about what might happen while they were living under the same roof. If she could only get him to let his guard down, like when he'd gotten so emotional about his father, she could say *Adios* to the corporate Jason Lynhurst. The man she wanted was in there and she'd entice him into making a more permanent appearance. Then, all bets were off.

His expression veered between amusement and admiration. "Great. It's all settled, then. Right?"

She sighed. "I'm the least settled I think I've ever been in my life."

"You'll be great." He waved it off as if he had the slightest clue what she was feeling, but he couldn't possibly. "And we're late for dinner. Mess up your hair and we'll act like we had a really good reason for our tardiness."

"Careful, or you'll find yourself putting your money where your mouth is."

He grinned as if she was kidding and glanced at his watch. "Gold top. White pants. Get a move on, Mrs. Lynhurst."

*Mrs. Lynhurst.* Why did that make her shiver with a strange combination of apprehension and wonderment? She'd come to New York for a divorce. And yet she'd agreed to tell the world she and Jason were married in hopes of turning their relationship into something more than an advantage.

She handed him the remote. "Make yourself comfortable. I plan to take a while getting ready while I practice how I'm going to tell Hurst I quit."

"But we're already late," he protested.

"You asked for a wife. You got one. And all the idiosyncrasies that come with it. Welcome to married life."

She flounced to the bathroom and the only reason she slipped into the gold top was because she never had to see Allo again. She'd throw Jason a bone for that one.

# Ten

Fortunately, Bettina was still waiting patiently at the restaurant, despite the fact that Jason and Meredith walked in almost an hour past the time she'd specified. Grinning like a loon, Bettina's gaze skittered right over Jason and fastened on the woman he'd brought.

"Sorry, Mom." Jason bent to kiss her cheek and opted not to offer a lame excuse for why it had taken him nearly sixty minutes to convince his wife to let her mother-in-law buy them dinner. "This is Meredith."

"Ms. Lynhurst, it's a pleasure." Meredith held out her hand and after a perfunctory shake, she slid into the chair opposite his mother and leaned in, elbows on the table. "Your jeans are my favorite. The fit is divine. You're one of the reasons I learned to sew when I was a teenager."

Jason did a double take. That was laying it on a bit thick, wasn't it? But Meredith's face exuded sincerity and his mother was eating it up.

Bettina beamed. "Call me Bettina. I'm so happy to meet you at last. Jason is off my Christmas list for not introducing us at the Garment Center gala the other day."

"Geez, Mom."

"Oh, I know," Meredith said on top of his protest and shushed him. "I was disappointed when he hustled me out the door so soon after we'd arrived. He couldn't wait to get me alone."

With a curse, Jason took his own chair and signaled the waiter. It did not distract either woman from their conversation…which apparently didn't include him.

Bettina laughed. "I'll bet. He couldn't keep his eyes off you the entire time I was talking to him. Obviously, he was thinking about taking you home then."

"Really?" Meredith's hand found its way onto his thigh and she shot him a sideways glance that he had no trouble interpreting. It was hot and wicked and set his blood on a low simmer.

This was not exactly how he'd envisioned dinner going. Or their marriage, for that matter. This was the problem with Meredith; she had her own vision of how things should go and it rarely coincided with his.

"That's enough about the gala," Jason interjected before his mother could say something else risqué that gave Meredith the wrong idea. He wasn't hung up on Meredith like his mother had made it sound. He'd only been watching her so closely because she'd been talking to Avery.

Mostly. You couldn't blame a guy for noticing how beautiful Meredith was. Or how smart and funny and…good for his plans. *That* was her best quality, he reminded himself.

"Well, you should have told me Meredith was your wife when I mentioned her." His mother ordered an obscenely expensive bottle of wine from the waiter and waved him off to focus on Meredith again. "How do you like working for Hurst?"

Meredith wrinkled her nose. "It's got no soul. The designs are good, but not great. All the people are in it for the money, you can tell."

"I couldn't agree more." The woman *Vogue* had once dubbed the First Lady of Fashion contemplated the composed younger woman across the table. "Where did you study?"

"Meredith didn't go to college," Jason said, a little miffed that he'd been excluded from the conversation thus far.

The temperature from his wife's glare nearly gave him a sunburn and her hand slipped away from his thigh. And now that it was gone, he wished she'd put it back.

"She was talking to me." Meredith flicked a fingernail at his arm, her tone mild, but he could tell she was not happy with him. "You've had her attention for thirty-some-odd years. Now it's my turn." She refocused on Bettina. "My sister is a designer and I've been working with her for a couple of years. Other than that, I'm self-taught."

Meredith and his mother descended into a lengthy back and forth about the merits of formal education versus finding a mentor, leaving him to stew over his wine.

Why was his temper flaring? This was exactly what he'd asked for—Meredith playing up the part of his wife.

He just hadn't expected her to do it so well.

Or for his mother to like her so much. How was he going to break it to Bettina when he signed the divorce papers? He hated it when he couldn't see all the angles, hated it when he hadn't anticipated the direction a situation was going to go.

He dug into his filet mignon and asparagus tips, determined to get through this dinner so he could take Meredith back to her hotel and get her stuff. They needed to strategize on the announcement and settle her into his condo.

Letting her into his space was going to be a trick and a half. He'd never lived with a woman and had spent the past six months working through the idea of sharing his condo with Meiling. She would have respected his personal territory. She would never have barged into the bathroom with him, curling iron in one hand and a raspberry-filled donut in the other, wearing nothing but a loosely-tied robe.

When Meredith had done that, he'd ended up licking the raspberry filling from the tips of her breasts. Of course, he'd been the one to swirl it there, much to her dark-eyed delight and moans of pleasure.

Maybe she'd let him do it again.

"Isn't that right, Jason?" his mother prompted.

What had he missed during his donut-induced fantasy? "Uh… What?"

"She was telling me about the innovative partnership you spearheaded with the Style Channel." Meredith's eyebrows rose as she silently shot him get-your-crap-together vibes. "Clearly you get your fashion and business sense from your mother. And your ability to pay attention from your father."

His mother dissolved into a good, long laugh. Jason couldn't remember the last time he'd heard her laugh like that. An answering smile tugged at his mouth.

"Sweetie, we're going to get along fine," Bettina told Meredith. "And you," she said to Jason, "are back on my Christmas list for having the foresight to marry such a great woman."

*Mission accomplished*, he thought sourly and decided to keep his mouth shut the rest of the evening. Which he almost succeeded in doing, at least until he and Meredith slid into the car to go back to her hotel.

"Let me check you out and then I'll help you pack," he said. "You can take the weekend to get settled in."

She crossed her white-cropped-pants-clad legs and grinned. "You sure you know what you're signing up for? I am a girl. With lots of girl stuff."

"It's the least I can do." He tore his gaze from her shapely legs, but it didn't erase the sharp desire to feel them wrapped around his waist. "Thanks, by the way. For wearing the outfit I picked out and for being nice to my mother. You were great."

"You say that like your mom is a witch and I had to suffer through dinner. She's amazing. Such an inspiration. I had a hard time keeping my inner fangirl in check."

News to him. But then, they never really talked about Meredith's interests. It never occurred to him until that moment that she'd yet to share thought one about her long-term plans after buying into the wedding-dress business.

And now he was intrigued anew by this woman he'd married. "I thought you were just being nice."

She twirled a lock of mahogany hair and batted her eyes. "In that case, I expect to be well compensated for my time."

"What, a divorce and a hundred grand isn't enough for you?" he teased.

"It's a start." Her wicked smile said the compensation should also include several orgasms in a row.

Despite that, he couldn't help but ask, "Seriously, what would be enough? If you could have anything in my power to give you, what would you ask for?"

The car had almost reached her hotel, but oddly, he didn't want to end the conversation. She was a woman of deep passion and convictions and he had the strangest urge to know her better. Not because of any paranoid need to pretend their marriage was real; ten minutes into dinner with his mother, it was obvious there was no danger of anyone questioning the authenticity of it.

But because after a long day of strategy and worrying about all the angles, he just wanted to be with Meredith. Connecting. She relaxed him and he liked it. Probably too much.

"You mean besides sex?" Her gaze softened as she glanced at him. "Oh, so we're done flirting. You don't have to give me anything. This has been fun. I'm working for a top-notch designer and I'm learning a lot. Allo's horrible, but he's as much a legend as your mom. Sometimes, I feel like I was dropped into the middle of a fairy tale."

"Really?" He glanced at her, but she seemed sincere. "You never said anything about wanting to be a designer. Is that part of your dream alongside wedding dresses?"

Her brow furrowed and she hesitated.

The sign for her hotel popped into his peripheral vision and he motioned to the driver to circle the block. There was no way they were cutting this conversation short, not when he'd just realized Meredith had a hidden layer he'd yet to discover. In all their many conversations, how had this never come up? The mystery fascinated him.

"Come on," he prompted. "You know all about my stuff with my father and the split. And that was all pre-Vegas anyway, so you heard about it back then. Wedding dresses are new. Tell me what's going to happen when you get back to Houston."

They were married and he wanted to know his wife's every last secret.

Meredith curled her hands into a tight knot high in her lap and thought seriously about blowing off Jason's question with a flip comment. But she'd never talked to anyone about her plan except Cara, and her sister hadn't asked any questions. She'd hugged her and murmured something about welcoming her with open arms.

It wasn't exactly the same as a glowing endorsement of her skill set or as if she'd earned a spot because she'd busted her butt. She'd actually never even interviewed for a job in her life. How could anyone take her seriously?

Was it so wrong to want validation? To ask someone who got what she was trying to do to acknowledge her plan and say it didn't suck?

She glanced at Jason sideways. This man she'd married had design and business expertise bred into his genes. He'd grown up immersed in the world of couture. And he'd seen her naked. Who better to bare her soul to? She'd done the same in Vegas and it had been a part of their connection.

"I'll become a partner in a successful business," she stated firmly. "Like a real grown-up."

"What are you now?" Jason's blue eyes glinted with amusement. "A fake one?"

Yeah, so that was why she should have kept her mouth shut. For a moment, she'd forgotten all the soul-baring in

Vegas had centered on their mutual lack of direction. He'd found his and apparently thought it was funny that she hadn't.

She glared at him. "I'm not anything right now. Former beauty queen. Allo's lackey. Wife to Jason Lynhurst. Soon-to-be wedding-dress-business owner. That's the extent of my identity."

He sobered and took her hand to kiss the knuckles. "That's a pretty good list of things to be proud of. How many other wives do I have? You're one of a kind."

She rolled her eyes. *Men.* Or maybe it was just Jason who was that full of himself. "So, I'm supposed to think it's some honor that we're still married? Marriage is one of the many weapons in your arsenal, right?"

"Yeah, and I don't wield my rocket launcher indiscriminately," he pointed out quietly. "If you weren't valuable to me, I'd have signed the papers on day one and found another strategic marriage. Why do you think I've fought so hard to keep you?"

That set her back. How had he managed to make that sound so romantic? Her stomach fluttered and she rubbed the spot as she flailed for something to say.

"Because I rock your socks, obviously. That's the only reason I can think of," she mumbled.

"Don't sell yourself short, Meredith." He stroked her hand until she glanced at him. "You'd be an amazing asset to anyone. Your sister is lucky to have you as a partner, especially if you're as good at designing wedding dresses as you are at understanding the business angles."

"Now you're just humoring me." She smiled to dispel the contradiction. "And I'm probably equally good at both, which is not very. Honestly, I don't know the first thing about designing wedding dresses. I can sew and cut patterns, which is why Cara keeps me around."

The thought sent a frisson of fear up her spine. Actually, she hadn't gotten as far in the plan as to what would happen once she returned to Houston and handed over money to her sister. She'd kind of thought that would be it and then she'd magically feel like an adult.

But what would happen the next day? Would Cara expect Meredith to start doing *her* job and design something? Was that part of the partnership deal?

Seemed like a phone call to her sister was in order, pronto. All this needed to be ironed out or she would fail.

"You can learn design if that's your goal," Jason said mildly. "Or you can work the business side. Make it what you want."

"You say that like I have all this flexibility." In reality, she was doing the one thing available to her. It wasn't like she could start her *own* business.

Or could she?

Her brain turned that over from all angles. If Jason gave her the money and she didn't have a loan, the possibilities were endless. When she'd left Houston, Cara Chandler-Harris Designs had been the be-all and end-all. But Jason had expanded her worldview enormously. Maybe wedding dresses wasn't the only thing she could do. Or the only thing that would work to get her where she wanted to be.

"Don't you have flexibility? This is your dream, sweetheart." He tipped her chin up and sucked her into his gaze, holding her attention like a hypnotist. "Don't spend your life doing something that doesn't speak to you. Lynhurst Enterprises is my heritage, built from the ground up by people who gave me life and share my blood. I'd do anything, sacrifice everything, to keep it afloat. What are you that passionate about?"

The fire in his expression and conviction in his voice mesmerized her. She loved it when he forgot to be the mastermind and spilled what was in his soul.

"I...don't know." But she wanted to name something in the worst way, especially if it kept them in this place of connection. Random thoughts, snippets of ideas formed on her tongue. "I love clothes, love the feel of fabrics, the art of fit and color. I've dabbled in design, but I think I'm better at seeing what doesn't work than at creating something from scratch."

"Good. What else? Talk to me more about your impressions of Hurst, like you did with Bettina."

"Hurst is *interesting*." The most politically correct word she could use to describe an environment slightly less welcoming than a room full of Miss Texas contenders when they realized you were a Chandler. "But Lyn is something else. Like Disney World for lovers of fashion. I know I was only there for a few minutes, but as soon as I walked through the doors, it hit me here."

She touched the center of her chest with a finger, but his intent gaze didn't leave her face.

"Why?" he prompted.

"Because the ambience was, I don't know, alive." Bit by bit, his attentiveness and genuine interest spurred her to articulate things she'd hardly recognized prior to this. "Like the creative spirit had soaked into the walls. I had the strangest physical reaction. Giddiness. Expectation. You probably think I'm crazy."

"No, I think you're speaking like a woman who has couture in her soul. Keep it up and I might throw in an executive job at Lyn along with the 100K," he advised with a brow lift.

With a sharp inhale, she searched his expression. "An executive job? At Lyn? Where in the world did that come from? We were talking about me owning half a wedding-dress business. I'm not executive material."

He shrugged. "I say differently, and I'm pretty sure I qualify as an expert at what it takes since I've hired a few executives in my life. Is it really that much of a surprise that I think you're incredible? You naturally think strategically and you honor your commitments. You show up and work hard. Those are all qualities of successful executives. Your love of fashion is a bonus."

"I can't work at Lyn," she protested and bit her lip as the image of an office with *Meredith Chandler-Harris* on the door materialized in her mind. And wouldn't dissolve. "I have a job. With my sister. Besides, I live in Houston."

But in New York, no one knew her. If she made it here, she could say indisputably that she'd done it on her own—without Cara, without her father's money and influence, without her mother's social connections, without the title of Former Miss Texas.

She'd never thought that would feel so necessary and important until this conversation with Jason.

"People move for jobs all the time."

Never in a million years would she have thought she might be in a position to accept...because she'd elected to stay in New York. If she did, she'd see Jason every day. *Every day.*

That thought gave her a physical reaction that far eclipsed the one she'd experienced when walking into Lyn. Hope and anticipation uncurled in her chest. And then she had to squash it before it rooted too deeply. "More importantly, we're about to get divorced."

"What's that got to do with anything? Divorced people can work together, if they're both mature about it."

"Your parents couldn't," she pointed out before she thought about how it would come across.

His gaze darkened. "Yeah, but they were in love once. We won't have that problem."

"Right." That somehow didn't make it any better. Because all at once, she wanted Jason to be as passionate about her as he was about Lyn.

Once, he had been. And the taste of it had stuck with her for two years.

She was still in New York due to that as much as or more than the opportunity to work at a genuine fashion house, if she was being honest. The divorce wasn't even a factor. Maybe it hadn't been for quite some time.

"Think about it. It was a sincere offer." He glanced away as the car rolled to a stop at the curbside of her hotel. "Let's get your stuff. It's been a long day already."

Meredith took his hand to allow him to help her from the car, her mind in a whirl of confused emotions and trepidation and a strange sense of determination. Because she got it now. At the same time she pulled passion out of Jason, he pulled it out of her. It just revealed itself in different ways.

She wouldn't be executive material in Houston. She probably wouldn't even be a good wedding-dress-business partner. And she definitely wouldn't make that leap from Former Miss Texas to Full-Fledged Adult because only with Jason's guiding influence and help and support could she truly succeed. She needed him, needed his belief in her, needed him to goad her into stretching and growing her skill set.

Most of all, she needed him because, despite her confusion and protests to the contrary, she was pretty sure she was falling in love with this man she'd accidentally married, who'd slowly let her peel back his layers, exactly as she'd hoped. Who also wanted to use their marriage to get himself into the CEO's office and then divorce her.

What was she going to do?

# Eleven

Jason's loft condo on 12th Avenue was the most gorgeous piece of real estate Meredith had ever seen. And that was including the mayor of Houston's house, her parents' house and Lyn Couture's office.

"Oh, my God, Jason," she breathed when she walked through the door to take in the floor-to-ceiling glass on three sides that displayed the illuminated New York skyline like a photograph.

But it wasn't a still life; the vibrant city zipped by in a string of lights, people and vehicles. To the west, the Hudson flowed to the Atlantic, while high above, she and Jason watched from the hushed, darkened atmosphere of his home.

Ebony hardwood floors polished to a high sheen reflected the city's movements, and when Jason snapped on the lights, she gasped again as the open floor plan spread out around her. The stainless-steel and grey granite kitchen looked like something out of a magazine, and the masculine furnishings accented the huge living area creatively to block out individual rooms despite the lack of walls.

An angular staircase zigzagged from the hardwood to the second floor, where she could see another sitting area beyond the glass divider, as well as two doors leading to what were probably the bedrooms.

And this was where she would stay for however long she could finagle it. With Jason. It made her a little faint.

Dropping her shoulder bag, she put a hand on his arm and leaned in with as grave an expression as she could muster. "I mean this in all seriousness. Can I have the condo in the divorce?"

"Not unless you have a really good lawyer," he dead-panned with a wry twist of his lips. "I take it that means you like it."

"It's breathtaking. I had no idea something like this existed. I mean, you see the pictures in magazines and you think they used Photoshop or something to make the views so spectacular."

With a grin, he picked up the bag she'd dropped and hefted the other one, then nodded for her to precede him toward the stairs. "It's smaller than some places and not in a trendy neighborhood. But I like it."

She could tell. The furnishings and decor had Jason Lynhurst stamped all over them. This place was clearly something he took pride in, and inside these walls, she'd bet he forgot all about his suits and business deals. She was dying to find out.

He bid her good-night at the door of her room and she let him go with no small amount of regret. It was appropriate to sleep apart. Sleeping in the same bed had implications. Hell if she could remember what they were right this minute, but she'd make the best of it.

Well, this was no different than sleeping alone in a hotel room. But that was before she'd realized how strong her feelings for Jason were becoming.

Her room was small but functional, with a tiny window that let in almost no moonlight, but the room was along the interior of the building. At least the bedroom had an en suite bathroom so she didn't have to parade through the upstairs sitting area to get to the other one.

She turned on all the lights and got ready for bed, but sleep didn't come easily. Jason's surprise job offer churned through her mind. Being Cara's assistant was more her speed, but it was safe and familiar. Was that what she wanted? What was New York if it wasn't a place to take a leap?

Of course, Jason could very well recant in the cold light of morning. After all, he had a history of making rash decisions and then taking them back the next day.

At some point, she fell asleep. A vivid dream took her down a rabbit hole of confusion. Jason was gone. She had a sense of being alone…and frightened…

She awoke in a cold sweat, startled and with no clue where she was. All at once, reality settled over her. She was in New York, in Jason's loft.

Chest heaving, she tried to calm her racing heart. Nothing she did worked. Her heart beat erratically and painfully in her chest and she couldn't catch her breath.

Whose stupid idea was it to sleep in separate bedrooms? Meredith was flesh and blood and wanted Jason's comforting arms around her. Right now.

Slipping from the bed, she padded out of her room and across the sitting area before her screaming conscience could remind her that they'd agreed it was better not to sleep together.

Jason's door was ajar. She let herself in, pausing for a moment to let her eyes adjust. The bed took shape and then she just barely made out the sleeping form in it.

*Jason.* Her heart sighed in relief.

She slipped beneath the sheet and rolled into his warm body. Pulse settling, she breathed in his scent, and it triggered something incredibly relaxing. It came back to her on a flash of memory—sleeping with him like this in Vegas. Sheer bliss. She loved curling up against his back.

But then he sighed and flipped over, disrupting her position.

"Uh, sleeping here," he muttered and said something else unintelligible.

"I had a bad dream," she whispered. Out of nowhere, her voice broke on a sob.

"Hey," he said softly and his fingers slid through her hair, his thumb featherlight against her jaw. "God, Meredith. You're shaking."

He shifted, reaching behind him to what had to be a bedside table. With a snick and a whir, a dark curtain behind the bed rose, spilling light over them. The whole wall behind the head of the bed was glass, and the skyline he'd revealed was almost as gorgeous as her husband. Jason lay spread out in his bed, sheet at his waist and one hand under the pillow as he faced her.

Not so much of a cure for her racing heart, then.

He tilted her chin to look her in the eye, evaluating. "Come here," he instructed and lifted an arm in invitation. "You're freezing."

Yes, she was. On the inside, where she couldn't reach it. Ice ran through her veins, overwhelming her all at once.

Unable to stop shaking, she nestled her backside into his torso and when the heavy weight of his arm dropped against her waist, she closed her eyes, fully at peace for the first time in…forever.

Lacing her fingers through his, she absorbed his body heat and let it soak into her bones, liquefying them. "This wasn't a cheap ploy to get into your bed. I swear. This isn't about sex."

He was silent for a moment, nestling her a little tighter against him. "I could see for myself that it wasn't. Better now?"

"Yeah. Thanks."

His thumb absently stroked hers. She wondered if he even realized how comforting it was. How greatly she'd needed him. But he couldn't possibly know because she hadn't told him. Regardless, he'd instinctively guessed the exact right thing to do to make her feel better.

And this was not like Vegas at all. It was far, far better than she could have ever imagined.

"What was your dream about?" he asked softly.

Bits and pieces of it floated back to her. "I was looking for…something."

It had been on the tip of her tongue to spill all the images and emotions from her dream. How she'd dashed out to the street in her lacy pajama top and shorts, searching for any sign of Jason's familiar form. How she couldn't find him.

But she didn't say any of that. Interpreting the dream wasn't difficult. She was scared of losing him and had no idea how to hold on to him.

"Something important?" Jason prompted.

"Critically. But I couldn't find it and it scared me." She sighed. "Sounds stupid to be so scared over that."

Especially since her real fear was the exact opposite—that she'd continue to have daily contact with Jason for the foreseeable future and it would be torturous because it wouldn't unfold like she'd desperately come to want. She wished for their relationship to be like *this*. Holding each other in the dark. Whispering about their dreams and failures and uncertainties. Being there for each other. Loving each other.

And that wasn't the marriage she'd signed up for. She couldn't even open her mouth and tell him her secrets.

"Fear isn't something we can rationalize." His voice drifted and she realized he was tired but fighting to stay awake. For her sake.

"Sorry I woke you up. I just needed to feel safe. Don't kick me out."

"'Kay."

His arm grew heavier and his breathing even. And he didn't so much as roll away from her even a little. He cared about her; there was no mistaking it. It just wasn't enough.

Maybe it was time to figure out what could be enough.

Jason woke all at once, extremely aware of two things: one, the raised curtain let in a hell of a lot of sunlight for 6:00 a.m. Two, Meredith was in his bed, snugged up against him, spoon-style, despite an ocean of bed on the other side of her.

And he liked her exactly where she was. His lower half firmly approved and raised the flag in joyful salute.

That was bad. She'd come to him in the middle of the night looking for a security blanket, not a lover. He couldn't take advantage of her. They'd agreed to a civil relationship conducted in separate bedrooms. Like what he would have had with Meiling.

She made a noise in her throat and arched, presumably in a just-waking-up stretch. Her bottom grazed his groin and her noise transformed into a sexy moan. She murmured his name and snuggled closer.

He groaned. Who was he kidding? He hadn't married Meiling. He'd married Meredith and he couldn't resist her. Not now, not ever. She was in his bed, in his head, drugging him with her seductive lure. Fisting his hands in the fabric at her hips, he hauled her closer, as she twisted against his erection in a slow, sensuous, deliberate slide.

Need exploded in his midsection, urging him to slake his thirst in his wife's sweet center.

"Meredith," he growled. She had four seconds to vacate his bed or reap the consequences. Which would be a very delicious and well-deserved punishment indeed.

"Yeah, hon?"

"*Now* it's about sex."

"You better believe it."

That was all the encouragement he needed. His boxer shorts hit the floor.

In seconds, he peeled the lacy top and shorts off her killer body and threw them over his shoulder, then spooned her back into place. He nipped at her throat at the same moment she reached back to guide his hands to her breasts. Hot and firm, they filled his palms, and he explored her peaked nipples at his leisure until she pushed deeper into his hands, silently begging for more.

"I need you now," she murmured thickly and her desire zinged through him.

He had a goddess in his bed, in his arms, and he wanted to be inside her, pleasuring her, completing her, while she filled him from the inside out with her unique power.

Groaning with the effort, he rolled away and fumbled in his nightstand for the condoms that he was pretty sure were still there from his last relationship…which had ended six or eight months ago if he recalled. His fingers closed around one and miraculously, he got it into place without losing it altogether.

He slid into heaven a moment later. She gasped and tilted her hips, drawing him deeper. The perfection sent him into an upward spiral, nearly initiating a premature explosion he wasn't ready for.

"Wait," he gasped and stilled her writhing body with a flat hand to her stomach.

"Uh, no." She thrust backward, and his eyes crossed as the pressure built. "You feel amazing. I can't wait. Touch me."

With no clue how he'd held back, he complied, fingering her center with quick, firm circles and letting her set the frantic pace until she stiffened and cried out. Ripples of her fierce climax set off his and he buried himself to the hilt with a hoarse cry.

Spent, he held her close, reveling in the heat and sensation bleeding through his body.

"You feel free to have a nightmare any night you choose," he muttered into her hair.

She didn't respond for so long, he wondered if maybe she hadn't heard him. Or maybe he'd said the wrong thing. "You okay?"

She rolled to face him and he missed the feel of her body against his.

"What are we doing here?"

*Connecting.* Exactly like he'd imagined, except better. She belonged in his bed. "I was taking advantage of the fact that it's Saturday. What were you doing?"

Her brows drew together. "I mean with us. I didn't climb into your bed with the intent of seducing you."

He hid a smile. "Is that what you did? Oh, no. I feel all compromised and stuff."

"Stop making jokes and listen. This is serious. We're married. We're living in the same house. We slept together last night and you held me through the remnants of a nightmare. Then we woke up to indulge in wicked, hot morning sex. All things real couples do. What part of this marriage is fake?"

All vestiges of good humor fled as her meaning sank in. "I guess… Well, when you put it that way, none of it is."

"Yeah. This is as real as it gets. And I don't think I can do it any other way."

"You mean you want to share a bedroom and be a couple?" How he got that out with a straight face was beyond him. Because that cart was already a mile down the road ahead of the horse. All they were doing now was chasing it down so the cart and horse could have a conversation about how they'd be hooked together.

Her gaze fastened on to his and wouldn't let him shake loose. "Is that what you want?"

He waited to feel a sense of panic or dread, but nothing materialized. Why not have a 100-percent real marriage, at least until they signed the papers? The benefits suited him pretty well and the more lovey-dovey they came across to his mother, the better.

He could sleep with Meredith every night. The thought made him downright light-headed with glee.

"It's not what I thought would happen," he said slowly. This was the core of his problem with Meredith; she messed up his vision. Instead of balking against it, maybe it was time to embrace it. "But I'm not opposed to it. If you're not."

As long as they both understood this was still a marriage with a purpose, all would be well. Under no circumstances could he allow any sort of emotion to be tied to this marriage. That's when all the problems happened. The second he gave her any leverage over him—or worse, fell for her—she'd mess him up. Jason refused to be the kind of leader who let emotional distractions ruin a company. One Lynhurst with that track record was enough.

"I'm not." Her smile grew tremulous. "It just scares me."

"What, the idea of having a non-fake marriage?" He shrugged. "It's not so different than what we've been doing."

That was the key. Everything should—and could—stay the same.

She sat up, clutching the sheet to her chest, but not very well, and one nipple peeked out over the top. She couldn't have struck a more erotic pose if a men's magazine photographer had positioned her. Somehow, he didn't think she'd appreciate knowing she'd turned him on all over again in the middle of her serious discussion.

"Jason, we've never dated. Never had that getting-to-know-you period. It's not like we can go backward. This is all too real, too fast. It doesn't terrify you?"

"The only thing that scares me is the thought of doing anything that jeopardizes my merger plans. As long as you're not in the way of that, what's the problem? We live together for a few weeks, get my mother comfortable with retiring and file the divorce papers. I'll take you out on as many dates as you want."

She stared at him as if he'd lost all of his marbles and then tried to take some of hers. "Why would we still get a divorce?"

All the air left the room. "Wait, when did we start talking about not getting a divorce?"

He couldn't be married to Meredith long-term, letting her influence him and coerce him into losing his brain on a regular basis. The promise of divorce gave him a time box. He couldn't lose that out.

"That's the crux of this whole conversation." She shook her head. "Neither one of us *needs* a divorce any longer. This is a matter of what we want now. You weren't going to divorce Meiling after a few weeks, were you? Why is our relationship different?"

"Because it is," he sputtered, scrambling to figure out why this part of the conversation *did* scare him. "Her culture frowns on divorce, and the textile agreements would have been long-term anyway."

The atmosphere turned frigid as she watched him.

The fear uncoiling in his belly actually felt an awful lot like denial. He couldn't have married Meiling. He was *glad* he hadn't married Meiling. It probably would have been exactly the marriage he envisioned and he'd be unaware the entire time how unhappy he was.

But what would make him happy? Meredith? How could he possibly know that before making a mistake that couldn't be easily undone? Or worse, before letting her into his heart where she might become more important than Lynhurst Enterprises?

This was backward and inside out. He *should* be telling her whatever she wanted to hear so he could keep her in place by his side. He needed to stay married. What Meredith suggested suited his plans to a T.

*Why* wasn't he saying yes and worrying about the fallout later? "You and Meiling are different. Leave it at that."

"So you're okay with landing your CEO job under false pretenses and then telling your mom you're getting a divorce within a few days? She's giving you that job in good faith." Her gaze tried and convicted him. "Is that really the kind of man you want me to believe you are?"

*No.* He wanted to scream it. But he couldn't speak,

couldn't think around the roaring in his head. The question was too big to answer and too big to not answer.

She didn't wait for him to figure it out.

"So as long as I'm convenient, I'm allowed to stick around and sleep in your bed. I get it." Her mouth firmed into a flat line that conveyed exactly how disappointing she found this whole conversation. "This is still about how your marriage affects your merger plans. If I outlive my usefulness, then I get the ax. Even after last night…and this morning."

Last night, when he'd held her close and breathed in her scent and it was every bit as wonderful as he'd remembered.

Something hitched in his chest as he saw very clearly what she'd hoped they were discussing. That their marriage could become real in every sense. Emotionally *and* physically. Her feelings were all over her face and glinting from her gaze. It sucked at him, encouraging him to spill things from his own heart. Things that shouldn't be there because they led to bad decisions.

The pain behind his rib cage intensified. He had to shut down her hopes for anything more than the business arrangement they'd agreed to. "What else would you expect our marriage to be about?"

A shutter dropped over her expression and she looked away. "Nothing. Sounds great. Glad we talked. Let me know when you decide what's happening with our marriage. I'm going to take a shower."

Wordlessly, he watched her flee the bed. He knew he'd upset her, but he lacked the ability to fix it. And it hurt. He didn't like disappointing her and he didn't like not knowing what she might do about it. Would she leave him? That thought scared him more than the idea of staying married forever.

Yep. This was definitely a real marriage now, for better or worse.

* * *

Meredith didn't bring up the subject of marriage again. Neither did she speak to him in more than monosyllables for the remainder of the weekend. She didn't even say good-bye when he left for the office Monday morning.

Three days into this marriage that never should have happened and it was already a disaster. Twice during the course of the morning, he reached for the phone to call her and broach the subject of their divorce and stopped.

What would he say? He definitely didn't want a divorce. But he wasn't prepared to articulate why, even to himself. Though his brain had no problem reminding him constantly that if they got divorced, she might find someone else, and he couldn't stomach the image of another man's hands on Meredith.

On the flip side, he was equally unprepared to hear all of Meredith's terms for a real marriage. How was he supposed to have a normal relationship? Lynhurst DNA laced his chromosomes, which apparently rendered males senseless when they got around a woman who was hot for them.

But he and Meredith couldn't stay in limbo forever. They'd have to talk about it eventually.

It took the company grapevine about thirty minutes to send the news around that Jason Lynhurst had gotten married and his new wife had been working for Hurst. People dropped by all day to congratulate him, which he accepted with sincere thanks.

They didn't have to know there might be a divorce on the horizon. Or there might not be.

The one person he didn't talk to was Meredith.

He kept expecting her name to pop up on his phone, maybe with a sexy text message or a suggestion that he come home for lunch. Not that he'd been fantasizing about that or anything.

He watched the clock until after one and cursed when he realized he'd been hoping she'd at least take two minutes to let him know she was okay. Or what she'd done all day to keep herself occupied while he was at work.

She didn't. He tried not to think about her during the interminably long day, but failed. Miserably. Her feelings were probably still hurt, and being responsible for that dug at him worse than not talking to her.

At five after five, he couldn't stand the silence and he couldn't stand any more brooding about it. This was ridiculous. At the very least, he and Meredith were going to be married for a few more weeks. They couldn't go on like this.

He went straight home, irritation just this side of boiling over, and it made him even angrier that he had no good reason to be mad. When he stormed into the loft, she was standing in the foyer, filling his house with her presence, and it hit him in the gut. His temper drained away.

"Hey," he croaked and cleared his throat.

She was so lush and beautiful and he loved that he could come home to her. She lived with him because she'd chosen to. Why that mattered, he had no clue. But it did.

"Hey," she returned coolly, her smile strained. "I was going out. Hope you don't mind."

Enough was enough. He slammed the door with one hand and with the other, he yanked her into his embrace and growled, "I do mind."

Then he poured all his frustration and longing into a scorching kiss. He hadn't planned it, but he couldn't go one more second without her in his arms. She was his wife and right now, he wanted her to know it.

She softened under his mouth and her hands clutched his shoulders weakly as he backed her against the door.

God, he'd missed her. They'd only been apart a few hours, but that was long enough for him to go numb. The taste of her zinged along his nerve endings, waking him up. And he wanted more, wanted her raw and open to him.

Wanted to take her, right here, right now, so there was no question that she belonged to him.

Clearly of the same mind, she moaned, and one leg slid along his sensuously, electrifying his senses. Their tongues melded as he yanked her silk blouse from the waistband of her skirt and snaked a hand inside, running a palm down the globe of her gorgeous rear end.

She wiggled out of her panties in a flash. His eyelids flew shut as he dipped a finger in her accessible, wet center. *Perfection.* The feel of her slick readiness went straight to his head, sensitizing him, and he craved possession. Fully. Irreversibly. Before he knew it, she'd unzipped his pants, releasing him into her eager fingers. Stroking him with a throaty moan, she lifted a leg and hooked it behind his waist, grinding her damp sex against his bare flesh.

"Now. Make me come," she commanded.

As if he could wait.

He slid into her with a groan and they joined. A flash of heat and something wholly amazing encompassed him as he made love to his wife against the door of their home. No condom, no pretending, nothing other than two people who completed each other.

His chest hurt as something inside him swelled.

He couldn't possibly possess her because it was the other way around. She owned him. Wholly. And had for some time. That's what he'd been trying to avoid, but it was too late to pretend he didn't feel anything for Meredith.

She shuddered and climaxed in three hard thrusts, finishing him off, as well.

They slumped together, and he was physically unable to separate from her. "I'm not going to apologize. I had to have you. I couldn't wait."

Sated and glowing, she glanced up at him through her lashes and smiled. "I wasn't confused. You've made quite a habit out of seducing me."

"Me? *You're* the one who comes on to me every waking

moment." He grinned back because he didn't hate it. It was a huge turn-on to be the object of her lust.

She blinked. "You realize that every time we've had sex, you've initiated it. Right?"

No, he hadn't. *She* was the sex goddess, enticing him to sample her gorgeous wares like a mythical Athena. "You're…"

And then he thought back. In the car. On the desk. Saturday morning, in bed. This afternoon, against the door. It was the sexual equivalent of the board game Clue and all the cards pointed to Jason.

"Not complaining," she finished for him. "But since you can't keep your hands off me, I'll start carrying condoms on my person at all times. The last thing we need is an accidental pregnancy to make our divorce complete."

Yes, that would put the icing on his upside-down cake of a life.

"Let me take you to dinner. No more divorce talk," he murmured. "Not now."

Not while he was still sorting through what in the hell Meredith had done to his careful plans to stay completely disentangled from his wife.

# Twelve

Dinner was less strained than Meredith had expected. Of course she'd been thoroughly mellowed by the hot and quick orgasm courtesy of Lyn's chief operating officer.

He'd taken her against the door and then taken her to an outrageously expensive restaurant, flirting with her over lobster and crisp sauvignon blanc. Then he'd held her hand in the car and chatted all the way home about various topics like what he should give his mom for her birthday next week and whether Meredith would like to update the decor in his loft. Because he wanted her to feel at home.

She took it all in with a dollop of suspicion. Just a few days ago, he'd hemmed and hawed about the kind of marriage he really wanted: short-term vs. long-term, real vs. fake, same bed vs. separate beds. It was madness and she was thoroughly sick of being confused and scared that he'd never let himself be the caring, sensitive man she only got to experience when he forgot about being the mastermind, usually in the dark. That man would have no problem believing they could have a relationship based on something other than what was advantageous for Lyn.

That Jason was the one she loved and the one she wanted. She hadn't given up hope that he'd eventually be that man permanently. *That* Jason might actually admit it if he developed feelings for her in return.

Was she crazy to hang around waiting for that miracle to happen?

At quarter till nine, Jason's cell phone rang as they were walking through the door of his loft after dinner. He glanced at it and mouthed, "Avery," and answered. After a couple of "Uh-huhs" and a "We'll be here," he hung up and raised an eyebrow. "She wants to talk to us. Both of us."

Foreboding flooded Meredith's chest. "About what?"

"She didn't say. But she mentioned it was important. Do you mind?"

Avery with a secret mission sounded like the opposite of fun. Meredith sighed. She'd been fantasizing about taking a long, hot bath in Jason's enormous garden tub that overlooked the skyline. "It's fine. I'll open a bottle of wine. Unless you think it's not a social visit?"

He shrugged. "Avery is about as social as a black widow. Open the wine for us. So we can tolerate her."

Somehow that got a smile out of her. She selected a Merlot from Jason's well-stocked wine rack and pulled the cork. The pop coincided with the doorbell. Avery must have been in the lobby when she called.

Jason answered the door while Meredith poured three big glasses. Then added another quarter inch of wine to hers. For fortification. Either this surprise visit would be her second "real marriage" test at the hands of Jason's family or Avery planned to litter the loft with the shrapnel of whatever new bomb she had in store in her campaign to become CEO of Lynhurst Enterprises.

What else could she possibly be here for?

Avery swept into the room, not one blond hair out of place. Her chic Hurst House suit outclassed all of the women's outfits in a five-block radius, as always, because Avery wore clothes like everyone else wore skin—effortlessly and as if everything she put on had been created specifically for her. Meredith had never seen the woman miss a trick when it came to dressing for the occasion.

It was a talent Meredith envied despite her personal feelings for Jason's sister.

"Avery," Meredith greeted smoothly. "How nice of you to drop by. That suit is divine. Wine?"

Jason glanced at her sideways, but she ignored him. Southern manners had been bred into her since she was old enough to tell the difference between a teaspoon and a soupspoon, and sibling rivalry couldn't pry graciousness from her. At least not right out of the gate. When Avery got to the point of this visit, all bets were off.

"Thank you." Avery nodded and took the long-stemmed glass from Meredith's hand. "Sorry for the short notice. I'm glad you were free."

"Of course," she allowed. If nothing else, Avery had piqued their curiosity. Deliberately, she was sure.

Meredith indicated the sofa facing the Hudson in an invitation to Avery to take a seat, and then sank onto the other sofa next to Jason and handed him his glass of wine. Wasn't this cozy?

She gulped a third of her wine in thirty seconds as Jason put an arm around her. It was a clear message to both her and Avery. Meredith and Jason were a team, regardless of the blood flowing through the Lynhurst veins.

The show of solidarity touched her and she had to school her expression before she melted into a mushy puddle. His thumb stroked her waist and she managed to shoot him a small smile that conveyed none of her surprise at how normal it felt to sit with him in the home they shared, entertaining.

Avery's gaze cut between the two of them. "I have to confess, part of me wanted to see for myself that you were really a couple."

"You mean you didn't already know that we've been married for two years?" Jason asked in a flat tone that said if she denied it, he'd call her a liar.

"I knew," she conceded readily. "I thought it was a much more scandalous story than it apparently is."

More scandalous than a drunken, accidental Vegas

wedding that shouldn't have happened? What in the world would have qualified for *that* honor?

"Sorry to disappoint you," Jason shot back with a glower. "If you only came here to check up on me, you can leave."

Meredith put a calming hand on his arm, a little amused that playing the composed half of their couple had fallen to her. "It's okay, honey. It's natural for people to be curious, especially your family."

With an evaluating once-over, Avery zeroed in on her. "That's not the only reason I'm here. I actually came to congratulate you on your marriage. And on getting one up on me. I wasn't going to use the stolen designs, or at least not the way I led you to believe. I was dead sure I had a Lyn spy at Hurst and I planted them in hopes of flushing out the culprit."

*I knew it!* The after-hours project wasn't real.

"Guess it worked," Meredith responded mildly, but it took every ounce of Miss Texas in her blood to keep the shock off her face.

It had been a trap. The whole time. Normally Meredith prided herself on reading people, especially women, but this was something else. If she wasn't so furious, she might be impressed.

Avery's smile chilled the air. "I left Meredith alone that night on purpose, hoping to catch her. Imagine my surprise when I reviewed the security tapes and saw my brother in cahoots with the spy."

"Called it," Jason murmured. "So you felt compelled to figure out our association. Nice."

"For all the good it did. Mom flipped and not the way I intended." Avery made a big show of sipping her wine and then commented, "You certainly managed to come out of this the winner, didn't you?"

Clutching his chest in a mock heart attack, Jason smirked. "Hurt much to admit that?"

"Not as much as what I'm about to admit." With a Gallic

shrug, Avery focused on Meredith again. "When you called me this morning to resign, I wasn't surprised. I wouldn't have welcomed you back. Until Allo stormed into my office and threatened to quit unless I hired you back. Apparently HR quite gleefully informed him it was my fault you left."

"What?" The wineglass tilted in Meredith's suddenly numb hand and only Jason's quick reflexes kept it off the pristine white throw rug. "Allo hates me."

"Allo hates everyone," Jason and Avery both said at the same time.

"Be that as it may," Avery continued with a wry twist of her lips, "he was quite adamant that you are the best assistant he's ever had and will not cross the threshold of Hurst again until you agree to come back."

Meredith was already shaking her head. "Not interested."

She had job offers coming out of the woodwork: a yet-to-be-defined executive's job from Jason and now this. And half a wedding-dress business that she could still buy into if New York dropped off the face of the map. Or she could take the money Jason was paying her to hold off on the divorce and live in Timbuktu as a basket weaver.

"I don't think you understand," Avery broke into the swirl of Meredith's thoughts impatiently. "I cannot lose Allo. He is Hurst's premier designer and without him, we'd fold in six months. I'd pay you two-fifty in a heartbeat if that's what it took."

Confused, Meredith stared at her. "Two-fifty what? Dollars?"

"Two hundred-and-fifty *thousand*. A year. I'd pay you a quarter of a million dollars annually to ensure my company doesn't go under."

*Oh, my God.* The sum made her vision black out for a moment.

The number of choices suddenly open to her pounded through her head. She had choices…and *Avery's offer didn't require her to stay married to Jason.* There was absolutely nothing holding her to him any longer. If she accepted, she didn't need Jason's money. New York was wide-open to her.

She had no reason to stay in this marriage other than the obvious one—she'd still be married to Jason.

"Allo's a pain in the ass. He treated Meredith like dirt, and even if he apologized on his hands and knees, she's too good to waste her talent on him," Jason countered fiercely. "But I'll shut up now because it's her decision."

Okay, *that* was the most romantic thing he'd ever said. The warmth of his hand against her waist bled through her, arrowing straight to her heart and swelling it tenderly.

Did he realize that she alone held the power to end this rivalry between Jason and Avery by simply declining Avery's offer?

Avery would be publicly humiliated, Hurst would be in trouble and Jason could save the day with his merger plans. No one would ever consider making Avery CEO of the newly merged company, not when she had driven off the jewel in Hurst's crown.

But if Meredith did that, she'd be feeding the mastermind, not nurturing the man she loved.

It was all too much.

Shooting to her feet, she set down her empty wineglass. "I appreciate the offer, but it's been a long day. I'll have to let you know."

Avery stood, as well, obviously recognizing that she was being dismissed. "I won't take no for an answer. I can make your life very difficult if you refuse. You know where to find me."

It must be killing her that Meredith's hand held all the aces. And that was the only reason she didn't bust Avery in the mouth and spill blood all over that gorgeous suit. "I do know where to find you. Which means you might want to reconsider threatening me."

Despite her show of bravado, Meredith's hands started

to shake. Houston sounded mighty nice, and all at once, she longed to escape the politics and threats and manipulation.

Jason escorted his sister out and immediately came back to engulf Meredith in his embrace, murmuring reassuring phrases into her hair. Burying her head in his shoulder, she let his touch wash through her, calming her, warming her. And now *he* was the composed one. Apparently they were going to tag-team.

She sniffed and choked off a flood of emotionally laden words that she wouldn't be able to take back.

"You okay?" he said softly and pulled back to caress her cheek. "I'm sorry she upset you. Avery doesn't pull punches."

Normally, Meredith didn't pull punches, either, but Jason had her all messed up and emotional over every little thing. "That's the reason I'm still here. You can't take her on by yourself."

His smile settled her in a way she'd never have expected. "Maybe not, but I can take *you* on by myself."

With that, he swept her into his arms and carried her upstairs to his bed, where he undressed her so carefully and reverently, she couldn't speak. Once she was naked, he palmed the remote and clicked open the curtain. It whirred up to let in the neon night and he stared at her, worshipping her with his gaze.

"Jason, I—"

"Want me to make love to you? That was the plan."

And then he did exactly that, silently ministering to her pleasure with such exquisite care that genuine tears rolled from her eyes when he finally pushed into her. As before dinner earlier, he didn't bother with a condom and it took on new significance. Real marriages—ones with no divorce on the horizon—didn't require condoms.

Was this his way of communicating with her? Of proclaiming his feelings about her and their marriage?

Afterward, he spooned her against him, murmured her

name and he fell asleep as she stroked his leg. And that was when she realized she didn't have a choice. She loved Jason Lynhurst and wanted to be his wife forever. All of the confusion over her feelings and the job offers and everything else blew away.

She loved him. Nothing else mattered. Except for the fact that she still had to figure out how to tell him.

In only a matter of days, Meredith had taken over Jason's condo.

It was the only phrase for it. She had almost no stuff. Basically just the clothes she'd packed from home and the new wardrobe he'd given her. But a simple pair of stilettos in his living room felt more invasive than a military coup.

Her perfume lingered in the air, even after she left.

Their relationship had evolved into something he didn't understand. Somehow. It didn't seem to matter that he'd been trying to keep to the status quo; Meredith did her own thing. The shoes proved the point and he didn't like it.

The front door opened, startling him out of his dead stare at her sandals on the floor.

And there she was in the entry of his condo, hair wild and windblown around her shoulders and a bag of groceries in the crook of one elbow. His heart lurched, a live thing attempting to break free. How had he gotten to the point where simply gazing at Meredith caused all these *things* to happen inside?

"Hey," she called. "I thought you were going to the office."

"It's Saturday," he reminded her needlessly, since they'd had a conversation about that very fact forty-five minutes ago as she'd sailed out the door to pick up a few things. "And you left your shoes in the living room again."

This was the kind of stuff he'd imagined going over with Meiling and reaching a civil agreement about how their life would go. The less change, the better. Meredith ignored him when he tried to explain that the vanity wasn't a catchall for her cosmetics. Actually, that conversation hadn't even made it past the opening argument because she'd dropped her towel with a provocative arch of her eyebrow.

"So?"

Meredith swished into the black granite and stainless-steel kitchen that he'd have sworn was masculine two weeks ago. With his wife in it, the sharp angles softened and the hard glass took on a feminine sheen he'd never noticed before. It was like everything else in the condo; Meredith changed whatever she touched, looked at, breathed on.

Including him. He couldn't keep letting that happen or he'd wake up one day and realize he'd turned into his father overnight. "Someone might trip over them."

She shot him a look over her shoulder as she put some kind of wrapped meat in the refrigerator. "Like the elves that come in during the night?"

He bit back a smile. He didn't want to laugh. This was serious.

"Yeah, that's what I was thinking about. The elven OSHA union," he shot back before he could stop himself.

She giggled and the sound washed over him. He loved her laugh. The condo had been hushed and quiet before she moved in. He'd assumed that was best. Now he wasn't so sure.

Before he could move, she flowed into the living room and climbed into his lap, straddling him like she'd done in the car and his pulse scattered. This was his favorite position, his favorite way to watch her, his favorite way to lose himself in her.

"You should probably punish me, then," she murmured and her hands slipped under his shirt to drive him insane with her touch.

"Meredith." Somehow he had the presence of mind to grab her hands and drag them away from his skin. And then he forgot why he'd been so certain he needed her to stop.

"Yeah, baby?" Then she twisted and crossed her arms behind her back, taking his with them. Her breasts were flush against his chest, exciting them both if the hardness of her nipples was any indication, and his arms were holding her captive. With her mouth inches apart from his, her energy and vibrancy spilled down his throat, and all he could think about was kissing her.

"So is this how it's going to be from now on?" he muttered and sucked in a breath as she shifted deeper into his lap. "I try to have a serious conversation and you distract me with sex?"

"Only if you're saying the shoes are serious." She fluttered her lashes. "Otherwise, I'm just angling for sex. No distraction involved."

Something about her cavalier attitude or the shoes or the swirling mass of uncertainty in the pit of his stomach over the state of their marriage triggered his temper. "Maybe we should have a conversation once in a while."

She hummed happily in her throat. "Mmm. That's my favorite. Talking *and* sex at the same time."

Her hands slipped from his grip and snaked back under his shirt.

He groaned. "That's not what I meant. The merger is at a critical stage. You've got Avery's job offer to consider. We're both at the cusp of our plans coming to fruition and we can't afford to make any missteps."

Saucily, she cocked her head and smiled. "Sounds like a reason to celebrate naked to me."

Then she wiggled expertly against his groin, and nuzzled his neck, working her way up to his lips, where she sucked him into a hot kiss.

He almost lost his train of thought as her tongue found his and deepened the kiss. This couldn't go on. He wrenched away, while his body screamed to dive back in.

"Is sex all you think about?" Frustrated, he pulled her

hands out of his clothes again. He couldn't think when he got wrapped up in her seductive web.

Clueing in finally, she drew back to scowl at him. "No, sugar. Sometimes I do quadratic equations in my head when you're inside me. What would you like me to be thinking about when you're kissing me?"

"I'm sorry." He blew out a breath and tilted his head to touch his forehead to hers. "I'm on edge."

"It's okay." She threaded her fingers through his hair, but instead of turning him volcanic instantly, she caressed him with unveiled tenderness and it split something open inside him. "I'm here for whatever you've got in mind. It doesn't have to be sex."

He shrugged and spit out the first thing he could think of to divert attention from the affectionate moment. "Seems to be the only thing we're good at. Which I guess is appropriate for a relationship based on sex."

Her fingers found his chin and lifted his gaze to hers. Her expression blazed with denial and anger and something else he couldn't begin to understand.

"That's a crock and you know it. We're not just screwing each other. We have an amazing connection and don't you dare devalue what's going on here."

Taken aback at her forcefulness, he stared at her for a moment. "What's going on here?"

She thumped him lightly on the head. "I'm in love with you, you big dolt. Why else would I put up with your horrible sister and your bad attitude and obvious lack of reverence for Jimmy Choos?"

"You're in love with me?" His pulse kicked up, rushing blood from his head. "You can't be."

Shaking her head, she frowned. "Don't tell me how to feel. And I guess that answers my question about whether you feel the same."

No, it didn't. Not at *all*. Because she hadn't asked that and thank God she hadn't because then he'd have to tell

her the truth, which was that he didn't know, didn't want
to think about it. "Our marriage is advantageous. Period."

True statement. Or at least it used to be. Somewhere
along the way, things had changed. And he didn't like that,
either. She'd mixed up his plans with her unwanted decla-
rations and sweet personality and amazing insight into...
everything.

"Jason." She paused, her chest heaving. "Being in love
has far more advantages than your 'marriage is a tool'
spiel."

"Not for me," he countered. "Love destroyed everything
I've ever worked for. I don't believe in it. Don't believe it
can last, don't believe someone can make a lifelong decision so quickly about whether a person will stick with you
forever."

That went for both of them—how could she possibly
trust him with her heart after all of this? He wasn't a good
bet for a relationship.

Disappointment pulled at her mouth. "Nothing that's
happened in the last couple of weeks challenges that?"

*Everything* that had happened in the past couple of
weeks challenged him. He'd tried avoiding it, tried keeping things on an even keel, bargained, flung out off-the-cuff
counteroffers. None of it had worked to keep this woman
out of his arms or out of his heart.

And it kind of made him wonder whether that had actually been his goal. "I've never made a secret out of what
I hoped to achieve from this marriage."

"Well, guess what? Sometimes you don't get what you
pay for. And sometimes you do," she countered cryptically. "Do you want to know what I wanted to get out of
this marriage?"

"A divorce. You've been very clear."

And he'd done everything in his power to stop that from
happening. He didn't want to let her go and he pretended it
was about the merger, when in reality, it was about avoid-

ing what was happening between them so he didn't have to face his shortcomings. If this marriage morphed into a love affair, he'd have to be a better, different man than his father. What if he couldn't do it?

"No. I hoped to find out who I'm going to be when I grow up."

The memory blazed through him instantly—that first night together, in his hotel room. After she'd turned his world into a wicked den of hedonistic pleasure, they'd lain draped across his bed. The scent of her perfume had emanated from his sheets and lingered on his skin. She'd pillowed her head on his stomach, gloriously, unashamedly naked, and told him being a grown-up scared her because she didn't know who she was going to be.

But that had been two years ago.

Puzzled at her deliberate reference to Las Vegas, he asked, "That was what the Grown-Up Pact was about. Don't you already know?"

"I didn't. Not for a long time. But I finally figured it out." She contemplated him for a long moment. "I'm curious about something. You cooked up this plan to fix the broken company in Vegas, right?" When he nodded, she continued. "Say you become the CEO like you've envisioned and you start your merger plans. Voilà! Lynhurst Enterprises is reunited. Then what?"

What did this have to do with what she wanted to be when she grew up? "What do you mean, then what? Everything will be like it was."

"What's so great about that? Did the two halves complement each other? Have they struggled apart? What are you going to do with the reunited halves to prove to everyone that you had the right idea all along?"

Speechless, he stared at her. Because he had no answer. He and Avery had talked about launching a new line, but the intent was to drum up buzz and goodwill for the newly formed company. Past that, he'd done nothing to strategize or determine the best path forward.

Because he'd been too busy strategizing how to best use his marriage to keep Meredith in his arms. She'd messed him up more than he'd realized.

Her smile softened his shock. "See? You haven't figured it out, either. These are the same kinds of questions you asked me about why wedding dresses and it helped me think through what I'm doing with my life. We need each other. I love you, but I have no idea how to be married. No idea what it means for either of us or the dreams we've talked about. Let's figure out what being a grown-up means. Together. Don't walk away this time."

There was that word again. *Love.* It was no longer a nebulous concept he'd grown to hate because it had been Paul's excuse for all his selfish moves two years ago. But what was it, if not that?

Confusion kicked up his temper, burning at the base of his throat. Everything had come to a head in an instant. There was no more leverage, no more excuses, just a woman freely offering her love. What if he accepted it? Would he be like his father, eventually sacrificing the good of Lynhurst Enterprises for his wife?

But how did he know what would be good for Lynhurst Enterprises? He couldn't even answer a simple question about his post-merger plans, and his track record for earning a promotion to CEO started and ended with accidentally marrying a woman his mother approved of.

Which he'd then turned around and used as leverage to keep Meredith around. It was far worse than anything Avery had done in the pursuit of winning. A sick sense of dread heated his chest.

He couldn't think with Meredith in his lap. Carefully, he set her on the couch and turned away, unable to look at her for fear she'd read something in his expression he didn't want to reveal.

"I can't—" He swallowed. He couldn't even say it.

He didn't deserve her. She didn't deserve to be married to him, a manipulative SOB who'd suddenly realized he didn't want to be handed anything because of how he'd spun the situation. They weren't even married because he'd earned Meredith's love. It was an accident.

She was right. He hadn't figured out how to grow up in Vegas.

"Why can't we go back to the way things were?" he asked, desperation pulling things out of his mouth without his consent. "Why does love have to be a part of this?"

But it was too late to go back. He knew that. Two years too late.

"Because that's what I want," she suggested quietly. "I won't settle for less than everything. I spent two years trying to forget you and it didn't work. Because I fell in love with you in Vegas and was too stupid to realize it. I want what we started back then."

"Vegas wasn't real."

It had been a mirage, guiding him down the wrong path. Guiding him toward a goal he could never achieve. The broken company wasn't going to magically come back together because he'd written a few documents describing the new corporate structure. Even if he and Avery pulled off the merger, it wouldn't magically fix all the problems he had with his sister or with his father, both of whom he would be working with again.

And he'd become CEO because he'd gotten *married*. Not because he'd created a vision for the company's future. Not because he'd earned it.

If Vegas wasn't real, then neither was anything in his relationship with Meredith.

"Yes. It was real," she insisted. "As real as what's happening in our marriage. Can't you see that what happened in Vegas wasn't ever meant to stay there?"

"Vegas was about sex," he said flatly. "You can't sit

there and tell me you were waxing philosophical when you were screaming my name that second time in the shower."

Harsh. But he needed to distance her. For once. He didn't trust himself one iota at this point.

Coolly, she blinked. "But afterward, I didn't get dressed and leave. I'm glad I didn't because that's when we connected. It may have started out as two people with a mutual need for an anonymous release, but that's not how it ended. The whole time, we were taking baby steps toward the future, but it's a future where we're together forever. That's the point. It still hasn't ended because neither of us wants it to end."

As always, she read him easily. "You're right. I could have ended this many times and I didn't."

Because he was incredibly selfish. *That* was how he was like his father, a danger he'd ignored, assuming love was the problem when all along it was something else entirely. Something he had no idea how to guard against.

He'd been turning their relationship to his advantage from second one, ensuring he alone had all the leverage and peeking under every rock to uncover her motives so she didn't get the drop on him.

The whole time he'd been wondering what she was doing to him, it never occurred to him to pay attention to what he was doing to her. He'd been leading her to expectationville by inviting her into his home, and into his bed.

He owed it to her to give her the divorce she'd come for so she could get started on being a grown-up. Without him there to screw it up for her again.

"We can't have a real marriage and I can't be in love with you," he told her dully.

Not yet. Maybe not ever, but he couldn't ask her to stick around until he learned to be selfless. He owed her for everything she'd done for him. Letting her go was the right thing. The grown-up thing.

The stark emotion in her expression clawed at his windpipe and he shut his eyes for a beat. When he opened them, tears had gathered in her eyes and she shook her head in disbelief.

"That's it? You're giving up what we have?"

"I have to." Let her interpret that in whatever way she chose. "I'll sign the papers. It's the least I can do."

She stood and locked her knees. "This is your chance to have everything, to take what you want, like you did two years ago, like you do every time we're together. Stop letting your head rule your heart."

Mute, he stared at her, unable to conceive of anything else he could say that would make a difference. Besides, he was afraid if he started talking, the truth would pour out. That he'd like nothing better than to do exactly as she suggested and chuck it all in favor of a blistering love affair with his wife.

But he couldn't. She deserved a grown-up husband.

Nodding, she firmed her mouth. "I'll be out of the loft by five."

"You're leaving?" *What else would she do, moron?* It hadn't quite hit him that he was letting her go forever until that moment.

"Yeah. Me and my broken heart will go somewhere you're not, but this time, I won't come back." She reached into her purse and pulled out a slip of paper, then scribbled something on it. "Send the divorce papers to this address."

He glanced at it. *Houston.* So she was going home. That was best for her. "For what it's worth, I'm sorry it had to end this way."

She nodded and fled to the bedroom.

He got his bag and went to the office after all, without saying goodbye. There was no way he could watch her pack.

Once at his desk, he didn't turn on his laptop. Instead, he rested his aching head on the cool cover and wondered if Meredith even realized he'd sacrificed his CEO position and put the merger in jeopardy by giving her the divorce she no longer wanted.

If she went home, Avery would lose Allo for sure, and Hurst would crumble. No one on Lyn's executive team would approve a merger with a failing company. And Bettina would yank back her support for his promotion without a wife by his side.

And the only part he cared about was that he'd hurt Meredith, which he would never forgive himself for. Somehow, he had to find a way to make it up to her.

# Thirteen

The white sand of Barbados stretched out as far as the eye could see and a balmy breeze played with Meredith's hair. The sun shone, she was relaxing in a bikini and the resort hadn't opened yet, so it wasn't crowded. Paradise—except for the part where she was miserable.

She'd walked away from Jason again, but this time, he'd kicked her out the door. It was over and she'd lost the only man she'd ever loved. Probably the only man she ever *would* love.

And with absolutely no emotion on his face, he'd stared her dead in the eye and chosen divorce instead of love. It was a flat-out declaration of the temperature of his blood—cold. Obviously she was as empty-headed as she'd always feared if she hadn't seen that coming.

Meredith sucked the bottom out of her piña colada and wished it had deadened even a tenth of the pain a shattered heart caused. If the past two years were any indication, she had a long, difficult ride ahead full of painful memories.

Her sister, Cara, who was stretched out in the next lounge chair sewing the bodice piece of what would become some bride's happily-ever-after dress, glanced at Meredith's glass longingly. "Can you drink another one and let me watch?"

"Alcohol envy?" Meredith suggested with raised brows. When Meredith had shown up in Barbados without call-

ing and without explanation, Cara had simply hugged her
and said she was so glad to see her. Because she hadn't
wanted to tell Meredith over the phone that she was pregnant.

Everything else ceased to matter in that moment as Meredith had smiled and laughed with her sister over the joyous
news. Cara had survived an emotionally painful miscar-
riage with her first pregnancy and Meredith prayed this
time it would stick.

"And how." Cara patted her bare stomach. "I won't be
able to drink for like another year and a half because I'm
planning to breastfeed."

That was enough to start the tears again. Why, Meredith had no clue. It wasn't as if she'd gotten to the point
of thinking about having Jason's baby. She wasn't mother
material—at least not yet. But it was hard to be around
someone so blissfully happy, who'd figured out how to
navigate choppy relationship waters.

It was a skill and Meredith lacked it. Obviously.

"Honey, that's the third time." Cara rubbed her shoulder. "Maybe one of these days you'll tell me what happened in New York?"

Meredith had arrived in Barbados a week and a half ago
and somehow, after the baby news and diving right into
being Cara's assistant again and the slightly numb feeling
that never eased, well…talking about Jason had gone from
hard to impossible.

"Guy trouble," she mumbled and adjusted the strap on
her bikini.

God Almighty, what else could she possibly say? *I went
to New York for a divorce, fell in love with my husband
all over again and got dumped like yesterday's trash. Oh,
that's right, you didn't know I got married. See, there was
this trip to Vegas…*

Cara rolled her eyes. "Duh. I've just never seen you cry

over a guy before. Find another one. You've always got some man on a string."

"You say that like it's a bad thing," Meredith sniffed. "And I've tried finding another one. It's useless."

"Honey, you've only been here less than two weeks. Give it time."

"I've been trying for two years," Meredith muttered under her breath.

Plus three weeks, which was how long ago she'd left New York, broken and bleeding and too proud to admit to anyone what a mess she'd made of her life because she was flat dumb enough to think an accidental marriage to a man she'd met in *Las Vegas* would work out.

Cara, cheer-up speech in full swing, waved the needle in her fingers at the interior of the resort beyond the beach. "Find another pool boy, like Paolo, and let him talk your clothes off. Paolo seemed pretty good at making you smile."

Meredith searched her memory. "Paolo? Oh, from the Grace Bay resort."

She and Cara had attended a bridal expo in Turks and Caicos last fall, where Cara had reconnected with Keith, the man responsible for her current blissful condition. Meredith had chased yet another set of gorgeous abs while trying to forget Jason.

"I was faking it," she informed her sister. "Paolo is obviously very forgettable."

"Obviously." Cara fell silent for a moment and then cocked her head. "Can you at least tell me if you're planning to stay? Because if you're going home, I have a couple of things lined up for you to take care of. You know, if you're still interested in being partners."

It was the perfect segue into a difficult subject, but it was one Meredith needed to address. That was what grown-ups did—tell people the truth, even when it was hard. "I have to be honest. I'm not sure what I want to do, but I know that wedding dresses is your dream, not mine. Would you hate me forever if I backed out?"

Meredith wasn't willing to settle for a job unless she could be passionate about it, and it wasn't fair to Cara for Meredith to go into a partnership unless she could give her whole heart.

With a smile, Cara shook her head. "Not at all. I was hoping you'd eventually figure out that it wasn't what you really wanted. But I would have welcomed you regardless."

How had she gotten lucky enough to be related to such a wise woman?

Cara stretched and motioned at the dress she'd been stitching. "I'm at a stopping place and I need to get out of the sun."

Meredith nodded and helped her sister carry her sewing supplies so she wouldn't get sand in the dress pieces. They walked through the pool area to the main building and not one pool boy caught Meredith's eye.

The mention of Grace Bay also reminded her that Cara had walked a similar path as Meredith. Albeit much more successfully, as she was currently carrying the baby of the man she'd married, despite a rocky beginning to their relationship, which had included Keith leaving Cara at the altar the first time they'd planned to get married.

"You and Keith got back together after two years. How did you make it work the second time around?"

Cara shrugged and paused at the front desk to situate the fabric over her arm. "We didn't know each other well the first time. When I ran into him again in Grace Bay, I swore I wasn't falling for him again. But I was so jealous of you and how easily you seemed to love 'em and leave 'em. I wanted to try that. Keith was supposed to be my tropical island fling. I clearly missed the memo about how a fling works."

Her sister laughed as Meredith shook her head. "I'm the last person you should be jealous of. I suck at everything."

"The only thing you suck at, sweetheart, is paperwork."

The familiar masculine voice washed over her as she and Cara jerked their heads simultaneously to view the speaker.

And there stood the man of her fantasies, in the flesh. Jason—with one hand stuck in his khaki pants pocket and an intense smile deepening his delicious cheekbones.

*He'd come for her.* He missed her. He was sorry and wanted to try again.

"Jason," Meredith croaked. "What—"

"Well, *hello* there," Cara interrupted with an inquisitive brow lift and an extended hand, dress pieces forgotten on the front desk. "Cara Mitchell. You must be the reason my sister is visiting me in Barbados?"

"Yeah, seems like." Jason held out his hand to shake Cara's. "Jason Lynhurst. Meredith's husband."

*Crap.* That had *not* just come out of his mouth. That was so like a man. As if he could fly in here and she'd fall into his arms, as if everything was fine and they were a married couple meeting in Barbados, as planned. All is forgiven. *Let's get it on, little wife.* Jerk.

"Oh, my." Cara tsked as she barged on past Meredith's squeak of denial. "This is a far better story than I was hoping. Do tell."

Meredith unstuck her tongue from the roof of her mouth and elbowed her sister in the ribs. "I'm standing right here."

"Uh-huh," Cara agreed. "And yet you've never breathed the word 'husband' to me one single time, so maybe you should hush up and let me talk to my brother-in-law."

"As if." Meredith tossed her head and zeroed in on Jason with equal parts attitude and scorn. Just to cover the nervous flutter of her pulse at the sight of his gorgeous self not three feet from her. "You shouldn't go around sneaking up on people who deliberately flew thousands of miles away to hide. And you definitely shouldn't introduce yourself as my husband."

"Then you definitely shouldn't have married me," he countered brightly.

Too brightly, especially for a man who—if life was fair—was miserable without her and had tracked her down in the Caribbean because he wanted to throw himself at her feet, begging for mercy.

She might even forgive him after a fair amount of groveling. Or she might not. Too early to tell.

That's when she noticed the manila folder in his hand, like the kind used to hold important papers. Her pulse dropped. He'd tracked her down all right. To finally divorce her, once and for all.

Her stupidity knew no bounds.

"What are you doing here?" She crossed her arms before he noticed her shaking hands. "You were supposed to mail me the divorce papers, not deliver them personally."

"I did mail them. Three weeks ago. But funny thing—I never got my copy of the filed papers back."

Neither of them broke the staring contest they had going on as Cara murmured that she had something else to do and slipped away.

"I didn't get the papers." Because she'd gotten on a plane to Barbados, too numb to even think of mentioning to her mother that she was expecting divorce papers in the mail. Guess she'd proven beyond a shadow of a doubt that she couldn't be trusted to resolve adult problems like filing for a divorce.

She glared at him. "If you came here to rub it in how much of a dingbat I am about paperwork, you're two years too late."

His expression softened. "I'm here because I finally figured out what I want to be when I grow up. But I can't do it without you."

The words lanced through her. Why would he deliberately throw that into the mix now, when she'd already tried to have this conversation back in New York? It was too little, too late.

"You want to be CEO," Meredith reminded him. "You made it really clear you don't need me for that."

She'd laid everything on the line: her heart, her future, her happiness, her marriage. Even her job prospects. All with the belief that he'd been warming up to the possibility of forever, only to be crushed with the truth. He wasn't willing to give her the one thing she wanted from their marriage—love.

"Maybe this will help explain." He handed her the folder. "Go ahead. Read it."

The manila folder scalded her hand and she nearly dropped it. "I know what the divorce papers say. My father's lawyer drew them up."

With an intense once-over she didn't dare interpret, he shook his head. "It's not what you think. Inside is the manifesto for revamping Lynhurst Enterprises. Bettina, Paul, Avery and I worked on it together."

Meredith's eyes narrowed even as her fingers curled around the folder, itching to open it and verify what he was telling her. "The four of you were in the same room? And no homicide detectives had to be called?"

His smile melted her and she forgot to breathe. Apparently her body hadn't gotten the message that this man wasn't hers anymore.

"It was touch and go for the first couple of meetings. But I remembered what we talked about. How Lynhurst Enterprises is my passion and I'd sacrifice anything for it because it was built by people with my blood. Figured it was time to put it to the test."

A little off balance, she opened the folder. Page after page of black type detailed a mind-numbingly comprehensive business plan. Like he'd said. "I don't understand. What happened to the merger plans you worked on with Avery?"

Jason's need for vengeance against his father couldn't have vanished so easily. Neither could his rivalry with Avery. They'd both been his sole focus for too long.

"Some of it is still in there, but it's better now. The manifesto details the restructuring of Lyn and Hurst under one umbrella using Hurst's capital and incorporating Lyn's soul." He reached for her hand and held it to his heart, a bold move that she appreciated enough to keep from snatching her hand back. "It's nearly complete, but it's missing one important stamp of approval. Yours. The only Lynhurst who hasn't reviewed it yet."

"Um…what?" Meredith's cheeks went hot at the same moment her spine went cold. "You want me to be involved in this? Why? I'm not a Lynhurst."

But she wanted to be and for more reasons than solely to be Jason's wife. She'd found a place in the world where she truly fit, where her mind mattered far more than her body and he'd ripped it away from her.

Only to appear out of thin air and offer her…what?

His gaze grew heavy with significance and she couldn't look away.

"You were the inspiration for the whole thing, Meredith. Avery quoted you. Bettina quoted you. I don't think I had an original thought the entire time. It was all you. We used everything the marketing department came up with to refute Avery's sweatshop allegations and it all took off from there." He gripped her hand tighter. "You are a Lynhurst. At heart, where it's most important. It's one of the many things I learned from you. Leading with my heart is not easy for me and I needed to get better at it. Unfortunately, it came at a terrible price—it cost me you."

Her eyes burned as she registered the sweet vulnerability in his gaze, the same way he looked at her when they were connecting. That nearly undid her. "It didn't have to cost anything. I loved you for free."

It was a vicious reminder that she didn't want his money,

or his loft, or a job offer from anyone named Lynhurst. Just Jason's love, and he'd handed her heart back to her. She didn't know if she could trust him with it again.

*I loved you.* Past tense. *God, please don't let me be too late.*

When Jason had left New York for Houston, he'd hoped she hadn't filed the papers yet because she didn't want to. Because she wanted to try again, like he did. Never had it crossed his mind that he'd get to Houston and discover his wife had fled to the Caribbean. And that he'd have to scrap his entire rehearsed speech since he had no idea *what* her state of mind would be when he found her.

Jason swallowed the lump in his throat and flexed the muscles in his hand, which ached to pull Meredith into his embrace.

But her steely expression hadn't given an inch since he'd started talking and she wouldn't welcome him with open arms. Not yet. But maybe soon, if he could somehow explain the decisions he'd made, and the path he'd forced himself to walk the past few weeks. He'd let her storm out of his life, convinced she would be better off without him, only to discover that he yearned to be the man she deserved…and worked tirelessly fourteen hours a day until he felt closer to it than he ever had before.

Now he needed to know if she agreed that he'd become worthy of her.

"You gave me your heart freely, Meredith." Greedily, he searched her face for some sign she still had those feelings, but her guarded expression gave him few clues. "But I hadn't done anything to earn your love. Letting you go was the hardest thing I've ever done. I didn't want to."

Growing up sucked. But if Meredith forgave him for taking so long to figure out what that looked like, it would all be worth it. Assuming she didn't tell him to take a hike, which she would be well within her rights to do.

"Why *did* you let me go, then?" Meredith demanded. "I would have stayed and worked through the manifesto with you. I would have helped you figure out how to lead with your heart. I wanted to."

"I know." God, did he ever. The look on her face when he'd told her he couldn't love her…awake or asleep, it had haunted him. "I'm sorry, honey. So sorry that I hurt you, but I wasn't good enough for you. Hell, I couldn't even give you what you needed. What did I know about love? Staying wouldn't have worked. Or been fair to you."

The shadows in her eyes didn't magically fade. "So you sent me away for my own good. Forgive me for not thanking you. You did it so you could focus on Lynhurst Enterprises. That's always been more important than me."

The hurt in her voice cut through him and he cursed under his breath. He was screwing this up, which was what happened when you went into a potentially volatile situation with no plan and no backup. But he'd come unprepared on purpose, carrying with him the only thing he could possibly offer—his love.

He'd hoped it would be enough.

"Sweetheart, my plans for Lynhurst Enterprises are over. That's what the manifesto is all about. I needed to grow up and you helped me not only see that, but do it. You were my inspiration for walking into that room full of Lynhursts with the intent of working together on a common goal. And I did it because nothing is more important to me than you."

With her at the top of the list—even above Lynhurst Enterprises—his vision cleared and allowed him to see what needed to happen with the company in a way he'd never have imagined. Who would have thought that falling in love would actually make him a better executive?

"What are you saying?" she whispered. "That you want to try again?"

She was killing him. This was the most painful conversation he'd ever had, but he wouldn't get better at being honest with his feelings by keeping them to himself. Or by hiding behind a ridiculous marriage philosophy that only facilitated selfishness.

"There's no trying this time." He flipped open the folder again and pulled out the divorce papers, which he'd tucked behind the manifesto. "Only choices. Here's the signed divorce decree. If you want to file it, file it. I hope you don't because that's not what I want. But it's your choice to make."

His pulse raced with uncertainty and genuine fear at giving up his edge with Meredith, but he'd left New York bent on ensuring she knew exactly what she meant to him.

Standing before her wasn't good enough. He sank to one knee, still clutching her hand like a lifeline. Because in many ways, she was. She'd breathed life into his cold heart and he couldn't imagine it beating properly without her.

"Meredith, I love you. No leverage. No deal. I never want you to question if I'm married to you because it's advantageous. I'm choosing to be with you because I love you. Choose to be with me because you love me, too. No other reason."

Stricken, she stared down at him. "What about trouncing Avery for the CEO position? Did you just hand it to her? Tell me you didn't do that."

His heart went heavy. Of course she'd ask about that. What had he done to convince her he truly didn't care who won?

"Page fifteen," he told her softly. The verbiage was etched on his soul since he was the one who'd written the clause. "Paul will assume the CEO's office until he retires, at which point the job will go to whomever the executive committee appoints." He shrugged, his pulse pounding in his throat. "That's the fairest way, right? If I earn the job, great. If not, I'll keep being the best COO I can."

And he'd be working for his father. A reality Jason couldn't have possibly envisioned without Meredith in his life. He needed her to keep him sane after a long day in the fashion-world trenches.

She didn't open the folder or even glance at it. "If you're not going to be CEO when you grow up, who are you going to be?"

"I want to be your husband." The phrase scratched at the back of his throat, and of all things, his eyes burned a little, too. "If you'll have me. I love you so much and I'm sorry it took me so long to become the man I should have been when you married me."

In a tangle of long hair and bikini and killer body, she launched into his arms, holding him as if she never wanted to let go. Which worked for him. His heart filled so fast, it was a wonder it didn't burst like a dropped watermelon.

"Is that a—"

"Yes," she finished for him. "It's a yes."

His smile was so wide, his cheeks hurt. "I love it when you finish my sentences."

That should have been his first clue they were made for each other. He'd lost track of the number of times they'd completed each other's thoughts. It was a natural progression to completing each other's lives.

"I love it when you chase after me."

Unable to stop touching her, he smoothed her hair back from her face. "So tell me. Who do you want to be when you grow up?"

She shot him an enigmatic smile and kicked the folder full of paperwork across the floor. "Mrs. Lynhurst."

The title blasted through him with a thrill. And a punch of agony. If only they'd gotten the answers to these questions right two years ago, they might have walked away from that weekend in Vegas with a totally different life. Because at the end of the day, Vegas wasn't about coming up with a plan for growing up. It was about finding someone worth growing up for.

"No divorce, then?" he asked, his heart aching in anticipation of the answer.

"I'm shredding the papers," she said decisively. "Isn't that what you do with something you don't want to fall into the wrong hands?"

Her gaze skittered down his body and left a whole lot of heat in its wake. "Yep. Credit card numbers, legal documents. Divorce decrees that you realize you never should have agreed to sign in the first place."

Someone cleared their throat and Jason glanced up to see Meredith's sister holding the hand of a dark-haired man with a look of authority about him.

The resort wasn't open to guests yet, as it was apparently undergoing some type of renovation. Meredith's name had gotten him past the front gate, but beyond finding his wife and settling their future, he hadn't thought about anyone witnessing his near-disastrous makeup session.

Jason climbed to his feet and pulled Meredith to hers.

The dark-haired man leaned forward to clasp Jason's hand. "Keith Mitchell. I've been waiting a long time to shake your hand."

With a small laugh, Jason shook his head. "I just got here."

"Yeah, but I've been dying to meet the man with the fortitude to fall in love with Meredith for ages. You bring your steel-plated armor?"

Meredith glared at her brother-in-law. "Shut it, Mitchell."

Jason grinned. "It's in my other suitcase."

It was a far different family dynamic than the one he was used to, but he liked it.

Keith nodded. "Good man. If you have any problems during your stay, you let me know so I can address them."

"Are we staying?" he asked Meredith.

"Uh, yeah. Unless you had another honeymoon getaway planned? You know, to make up for not taking me on one

the first time." The sizzling once-over she treated him to
said she'd like to get him behind locked doors quickly.

And he'd like to let her. He'd missed her fiercely.

"Some people would consider a weekend in Vegas a honeymoon," he suggested without an ounce of irony.

"And some people actually propose to their wives. With
like a ring and everything." Her arched brow made him
laugh. "It's a good thing for you that I'm the soul of forgiveness."

Yes, it was a good thing for him. Otherwise, he'd be
going back to New York without her and living the rest of
his life in misery.

Cara snapped her fingers. "Lynhurst! Of course. That's
why you look so familiar." She glared at Meredith. "I can
forgive you for getting married and not telling me, but
marrying Bettina Lynhurst's son and failing to mention
it is plain cruel."

With a sigh, Meredith waved at Jason. "Cara, meet the
heir to the Lynhurst couture empire, also known as the
man I can't seem to get rid of no matter how many times
I ask for a divorce."

Cara glanced between the two of them as if she was
watching a fascinating tennis match. "Really? How many
times have you asked?"

"Too many," Meredith muttered, as Jason said, "Never.
She mostly orders me to sign the papers. Except when she's
asking me not to."

"Geez, this is better than a soap opera," Cara said. "How
long have you been married?"

"Two years," Meredith admitted.

"But only because we didn't know," Jason added. "Meredith kindly informed me when she came to New York and
changed my entire life."

Two years ago, he'd been wandering around looking for
a plan, an idea—*something*—to make him feel whole. And
he'd found it. By some miracle, she'd fallen in love with

him and done it all over again. Meredith had turned him into a man he could be proud of.

"I don't get it," Keith interjected with a furrowed brow. "How did you get married two years ago?"

Jason glanced at Meredith to gauge whether or not she wanted to keep that a secret. But she nodded with a sigh. "Seems like the whole story is bound to come out anyway."

"Equal parts Las Vegas, tequila shots and an Elvis impersonator." Jason caught Meredith's hand and brought it to his lips. "Best mistake I've ever made."

Fingers over her mouth, Cara half laughed and half gasped. "You didn't."

"It wasn't supposed to be real," Meredith insisted. "We never intended for the papers to be filed. Somehow I messed up and here we are, thanks to my boneheaded mistake."

She shot him a smile that warmed him thoroughly. "Luckily, you were boneheaded enough to fall in love with me, too."

And then his wife kissed him.

# Epilogue

Meredith pushed open the door of the loft she shared with her husband, humming happily despite a ten-hour day that had included Allo dropping a bolt of fabric on her foot, Avery herding her into a two-hour marketing meeting and Jason not responding to the sexy text message she'd sent on the way home.

It was all good when you lived in the most exciting city in the world with a supportive husband who loved you.

Both Jason and Bettina had begged her to take jobs working for them at Lyn, but she turned them both down to go back to work for Allo. Maybe it was crazy, but Meredith wanted to prove she could make it in New York on her own terms.

Said supportive husband had beaten her home and she took a long minute to soak in the visual splendor waiting for her in the living room. The view of the New York skyline wasn't bad, either, but it couldn't hold a candle to the gorgeous man lounging on the couch, wearing a mischievous smile.

"About time you got home," Jason scolded without any heat. "I've been waiting very patiently."

Eyebrows raised, she surveyed the bottle of golden liquor and two shot glasses spread out on the coffee table. "Trying to get me drunk so you can take advantage of me? Because you know good and well you don't need alcohol for that."

"Figured you needed a break after working all day with the most horrible boss in the world."

Meredith grinned and climbed into Jason's lap—astride, her favorite way to talk to him. "But tequila shots?"

"For our anniversary." Settling his hands in place against her waist, he nestled her closer. "That's what we did on our wedding night. Figured we should keep the tradition."

It wasn't their anniversary. That wouldn't happen for another couple of months, but the thought was sweet. So sweet, she felt compelled to blurt out, "I have a confession. I didn't actually drink the shots in Vegas."

She'd poured them out when Jason wasn't looking, mostly because she didn't want to hurt his feelings, but also because tequila was vile.

"Um…neither did I. I don't like tequila straight." His blue eyes bored into hers as they shared a long glance heavy with dawning comprehension.

"So wait. How many drinks had actually made it down your throat when you came up with the brilliant idea to find the all-night wedding chapel?"

Guilt clouded Jason's expression. "Maybe two."

Figured. Meredith dissolved into a fit of giggles. "Guess we can't tell people we got drunk and got married anymore. What'll we say instead?"

Jason's chuckle warmed her from the inside out. "The truth. That we fell in love and got married but were too worried about what other people would think to claim our happiness."

"Whew. Glad we're not that young and stupid any longer."

He grinned. "What are we going to do to celebrate now that we've established we both hate tequila?"

"Guess we'll have to do something we both like." Shooting him a sultry smile, she plunked the remote into her hand. "Watch *Project Runway*."

With a growl, he knocked the remote to the carpet and

treated her to a scorching-hot kiss that communicated every bit of his love and desire for her. Who needed fashion on television when she'd already found the perfect fit?

\* \* \* \* \*

# THE BILLIONAIRE'S
# BEDSIDE MANNER

## ROBYN GRADY

For the gorgeous Jade Pocklington
for her input on all things French!

With thanks to my editor, Shana Smith,
for her unfailing support and advice
and belief in my stories.

# One

"Just shout if it's a bad time to drop in."

The instant the words left her mouth, Bailey Ross watched the man she had addressed—the man she knew must be Doctor Mateo Celeca—brace his wide shoulders and spin around on his Italian, leather-clad feet. Brow furrowed, he cocked his head and studied her eyes so intently the awareness made Bailey's cheeks warm and knees go a little weak. Mama Celeca had said her obstetrician grandson was handsome, but from memory the expression "super stud" was never discussed.

When Bailey had arrived at this exclusive Sydney address moments ago, she'd hitched her battered knapsack higher as she'd studied first the luggage, set neatly by that door, then the broad back of a masculine frame standing alongside. Busy checking his high-tech security system, Mateo Celeca had no idea he'd had company. Bailey wasn't normally one to show up unannounced, but today was an exception.

Remembering manners, Mateo's bemused expression eased into a smile…genial but also guarded.

"Forgive me," he said in a deep voice that hinted at his Mediterranean ancestry. "Do we know each other?"

"Not really, no. But your grandmother should have rung. I'm Bailey Ross." She drove down a breath and thrust out her hand. But when Dr. Celeca only narrowed his gaze, as if suspecting her of some offense, Bailey's smile dropped. "Mama Celeca did phone…didn't she?"

"I received no phone call." Sterner this time, that frown returned and his informal stance squared. "Is Mama all right?"

"She's great."

"As thin as ever?"

"I wouldn't say thin. After enjoying so much of her Pandoro, I'm not so thin anymore, either."

At her grin, Mateo's cagey expression lightened. A stranger lands on your elite North Shore doorstep with a half-baked story, looking a mess after fifteen hours in the air, who wouldn't dig a little deeper? But anyone who knew Mama Celeca knew her delicious creamy layer-cake.

Looking like a sentinel guarding his palace, Mateo patiently folded his arms over the white button-down shirt shielding his impressive chest. Bailey cleared her throat and explained.

"This past year I've backpacked around Europe. I spent the last months in Italy in Mama Celeca's town. We became close."

"She's a wonderful woman."

"She's very generous," Bailey murmured, remembering Mama's final charitable act. She'd as good as saved Bailey's life. Bailey would never be able to repay her, although she was determined to try.

When a shadow dimmed the light in the doctor's intelligent dark eyes, fearing she'd said too much, Bailey hurried on.

"She made me promise that when I arrived back in Australia, first thing, I'd drop by and say hello." She stole another glance at his luggage. "Like I said…not a good time."

No use delaying her own day, either. Now that she was home, she needed to decide what her next step in life would be. An hour ago she'd suffered a setback. Vicky Jackson, the friend she'd hoped to stay with for a couple of days, was out of town. Now she couldn't go forward without first finding a place to sleep—and finding a way to pay for it.

Mateo Celeca was still studying her. A pulse in his strong jaw began to beat before his focus lowered to his luggage.

Bailey straightened. *Time to go.*

Before she could take her leave, however, the doctor interjected. "I'm going overseas myself."

"To Italy?"

"Among other places."

Bailey frowned. "Mama didn't mention it."

"This time it'll be a surprise."

When he absently rotated the platinum band of his wristwatch, Bailey took her cue and slid one foot back.

"Well, give her my love," she said. "Hope you have a great trip."

But, turning to leave, a hand on her arm pulled her up, and in more ways than one. His grip wasn't overly firm, but it was certainly hot and naturally strong. The skin on skin contact was so intense, it didn't tingle so much as shoot a bright blue flame through her blood. The sensation left her fizzing and curiously warm all over. How potent might Mateo Celeca's touch be if they kissed?

"I've been rude," he said as his hand dropped away.

"Please. Come in. I don't expect my cab for a few minutes yet."

"I really shouldn't—"

"Of course you should."

Stepping aside, he nodded at the twelve-foot-high door at the same time she caught the scent of his aftershave...subtle, woodsy. Wonderfully male. Every one of her pheromones sat up and took note. But that was only one more reason to decline his invitation. After all she'd been through—given how narrowly she'd escaped—she'd vowed to stay clear of persuasive, good-looking men.

She shook her head. "I really can't."

"Mama would have my head if she knew I turned a friend away." He pretended to frown. "You wouldn't want her to be upset with me, would you?"

Pressing her lips together, she shifted her feet and, thinking of Mama, reluctantly surrendered. "I guess not."

"Then it's settled."

But then, suddenly doubtful again, he glanced around.

"You just flew in?" He asked and she nodded. He eyed her knapsack. "And this is all your luggage?"

Giving a lame smile, she eased past. "I travel light."

His questioning look said, *very.*

Mateo watched his unexpected guest enter his spacious foyer. *Sweet,* he noted, his gaze sweeping over her long untreated fair hair. Modestly spoken. Even more modestly dressed.

Arching a brow, Mateo closed the door.

He wasn't convinced.

The seemingly unrehearsed sway of hips in low-waisted jeans, no makeup, few possessions...Bailey Ross had described his grandmother as "very generous," and it was true. In her later years Mama had become an easy touch. He didn't doubt she might have fallen for this woman's lost-kitten look and his gut—as well as past experience—said Miss Ross had taken full advantage of that.

But Mama was also huge on matchmaking. Perhaps Bailey Ross was here simply because his grandmother had thought she and her grandson might hit it off. Given how she tried to set him up with a "nice Italian girl" whenever he visited, it was more than possible.

His first instinct had been to send this woman on her way... but he was curious, and had some time to spare. His cab wasn't due for ten minutes.

Taking in her surroundings, his visitor was turning a slow three-sixty beneath the authentic French chandelier that hung from the ornately molded second-story ceiling. The crystal beads cast moving prisms of light over her face as she admired the antiques and custom-made furnishings.

"Dr. Celeca, your home is amazing." She indicated the staircase. "I can imagine Cinderella in her big gown and glass slippers floating down those stairs."

Built in multicolored marble, the extravagant flight split midway into separate channels, which led to opposite wings of the house. The design mimicked the Paris Opera House, and while the French might lay claim to the Cinderella fable, he smiled and pointed out, "No glass-slippered maidens hiding upstairs, I'm afraid."

She didn't seem surprised. "Mama mentioned you were single."

"Mentioned or repeated often?" He said with a crooked, leading grin.

"Guess it's no secret she's proud of you," Bailey admitted. "And that she'd like a great-grandchild or two."

Be that as it may, he wouldn't be tying any matrimonial knots in the foreseeable future. He'd brought enough children into the world. His profession—and France—were enough for him.

She moved to join him. Her smile sunny enough to melt an iceberg, her eyes incredibly blue, Bailey and Mateo descended a half dozen marble steps and entered the main reception room. Standing among the French chateau classic decor, pausing before the twenty-foot-high Jacobean fireplace, his guest looked sorely out of place. But, he had to admit, not in a bad way. She radiated *fresh*—even as she suppressed a traveler's weary yawn.

Was there reason to doubt her character? Had she fleeced his grandmother or was he being overly suspicious? Mama could be "very generous" in other ways, after all.

"So, what's first on the itinerary?" She asked, lowering into a settee.

"West coast of Canada." Mateo took the single saloon seat. "A group of friends who've been skiing at the same resort for years put on an annual reunion." The numbers had slowly dwindled, however. Most of the guys were married now. Some divorced. The gathering didn't have the same feel as the old days, sadly. This year he wasn't looking forward to it. "Then on to New York to catch up with some professional acquaintances," he went on. "Next it's France."

"You have friends in Paris? My parents honeymooned there. It's supposed to be a gorgeous city."

"I sponsor a charitable institution in the north."

Her eyebrows lifted as she sat back. "What kind of charity?"

"Children without homes. Without parents." To lead into what he really wanted to know—to see if she'd rise to any bait—he added, "I like to give where I can." When she bowed her head to hide a smile, a ball of unease coiled low in his stomach. With some difficulty, he kept his manner merely interested. "Have I said something funny?"

"Just that Mama always said you were a good man."
Those glittering blue eyes lifted and met his again. "Not that
I doubted her."

Mateo's chest tightened and he fought the urge to tug an
ear or clear his throat. This woman was either a master of
flattery or as nice as Mama obviously believed her to be. So
which was it? Cute or on the take?

"Mama is my biggest fan as I am hers," he said easily.
"Seems she's always doing someone a good turn. Helping out
where she can."

"She also plays a mean game of Briscola."

He blinked. *Cards?* "Did you play for money?" He
manufactured a chuckle. "She probably let you win."

A line pinched between Bailey Ross's brows. "We played
because she enjoyed it."

She'd threaded her fingers around the worn denim knees of
her jeans. Her bracelet was expensive, however—yellow-gold
and heavy with charms. Had Mama's money helped purchase
that piece duty free? If he asked Bailey straight out, what
reply would she give?

As if she'd read his mind and wasn't comfortable, his guest
eased to her feet. "I've held you up long enough. You don't
want to miss your flight."

He stood too. She was right. She wasn't going to admit to
anything and his cab would be here any minute. Seemed his
curiosity with regard to Miss Ross's true nature would go
unsatisfied.

"Do you have family in Sydney?" He asked as they crossed
the parquet floor together and she covered another yawn.

"I was raised here."

"You'll be catching up with your parents then."

"My mother died a few years back."

"My condolences." He'd never known his mother but the

man he'd come to know as Father had passed away recently. "I'm sure your father's missed you."

But she only looked away.

Walking alongside, Mateo rolled back his shoulders. No mother. Estranged from her father. Few possessions. Hell, now *he* wanted to write her a check.

He changed the subject. "So, what are your broader plans, Miss Ross? Do you have a job here in town to return to?"

"I don't have any real concrete plans just yet."

"Perhaps more travel then?"

"There's more I'd like to see, but for now, I'm hanging around."

They stopped at the entrance. He fanned open the door, searched her flawless face and smiled. "Well, good luck."

"Same to you. Say hello to Paris for me."

As she turned to walk away, hitching that ratty knapsack higher on one slim shoulder, something thrust beneath Mateo's ribs and he took a halting step toward her. Of course, he should let it alone—should let her be on her way—but a stubborn niggling kept at him and he simply had to ask.

"Miss Ross," he called out. Looking surprised, she rotated back. He cut the distance separating them and, having danced around the question long enough, asked outright. "Did my grandmother give you money?"

Her slim nostrils flared and her eyebrows drew in. "She didn't give me money."

Relief fell through him in a warm welcomed rush. As she'd grown older, Mama had admitted many times that she wasn't overly wealthy by design; she had little use for money and therefore liked to help others where she could. There was nothing he could do to stop Mama's generosity—or gullibility as the case more often than not proved to be. But at least he could leave for his vacation knowing this particular young woman hadn't left his grandmother's house stuffing bills in her pocket.

But Bailey wasn't finished.

"Mama *loaned* me money."

As the stone swelled in his chest, Mateo could only stare. He'd been right about her from the start? She'd taken advantage of Mama like those before her. He took in her innocent looks and cringed. He wished he'd never asked.

"A…loan," he said, unconcerned that his tone was graveled. Mocking.

Her cheeks pinked up. "Don't say it like that."

"You say it's a loan," he shrugged, "it's a loan."

"I intend to pay back every cent."

"Really?" Intrigued, he crossed his arms. "And how do you intend to do that with no job, no plans?" From her reaction to his question about her father, there wouldn't be help coming from that source, either.

Her eyes hardened. "We can't all have charmed lives, Doctor."

"Don't presume to know anything about me," he said, his voice deep.

"I only know that I had no choice."

"We all have choices." *At least when we're adults.*

Her cheeks flushed more. "Then I chose escape."

He coughed out a laugh. This got better and better. "Now my grandmother was keeping you *prisoner?*"

"Not your grandmother."

His arms unraveled. Her voice held the slightest quiver. Her pupils had dilated until the blue was all but consumed by black. But she'd told him what he'd stupidly wanted to know. She'd accepted Mama's money. He didn't need or want excuses.

"Goodbye, Miss Ross." He headed inside.

"And thank you, Doctor," she called after him. "You've

killed whatever faith I had left in the male species." A pulse thudding at his temple, he angled back. Her expression was dry. Sad. *Infuriating.* "I honestly thought you were a gentleman," she finished.

"Only when in the presence of a lady."

Self-disgust hit his gut with a jolt.

"I apologize," he murmured. "That wasn't called for."

"Do you even want to know what I needed to escape?" She ground out. "Why I needed that money?"

He exhaled heavily. Fine. After that insult, he owed her one. "Why did you need the money?"

"Because of a man who wouldn't listen," she said pointedly, her gaze hot and moist. "He said we were getting married and, given the situation I was in, I *didn't* have a choice."

# Two

"You're engaged?" Mateo shook himself.

"No." In a tight voice, she added, "Not really."

"Call me old-fashioned, but I thought being betrothed was like being pregnant. You either are or you aren't."

"I...*was* engaged."

Slanting his head, he took another look. Her nose was more a button with a sprinkling of freckles but her unusual crystalline eyes were large and, as she stood her ground, her pupils dilated more, making her gaze appear even more pronounced. Or was that scared?

*I didn't have a choice.*

An image of the degrees decorating his office walls swam up in Mateo's mind. Time to take a more educated guess as to why Mama might have sent this woman. He set his voice at a different tone, the one he used for patients feeling uncertain.

"Bailey, are you having a baby?"

Her eyes flared, bright with indignation. *"No."*

"Are you sure? We can do tests—"

"Of *course* I'm sure."

Backing off, he held up his hands. "Okay. Fine. Given your circumstances, it seemed like a possibility."

"It really wasn't." Her voice dropped. "We didn't sleep together. Not even once."

She spun to leave, but, hurrying down the steps, she tripped on the toe of her sandal. The next second she was stumbling, keeling forward. Leaping, Mateo caught her before she went down all the way. Gripping her upper arms, he felt her shaking—from shock at almost breaking her neck? Or pique at him? Or was the trembling due to dredging up memories of this engagement business in Italy?

She was so taken aback, she didn't object when he helped her sit on a step. Lifting her chin, he set out to check that the dilation in her eyes was even, but with his palm cradling her cheek and his face so close to hers, the pad of his thumb instinctively moved to trace the sweep of her lower lip. Heat, dangerous and swift, flared low in his belly and his head angled a whisper closer.

But then she blinked. So did he. Spell broken, he cleared his throat and got to his feet while she caught her breath and gathered herself.

He might be uncertain about some things regarding Bailey Ross, but of one he was sure. The constant yawning, tripping over herself...

"You need sleep," he told her.

"I'll survive."

"No doubt you will."

But, dammit, he was having a hard time thinking of her walking off alone down that drive and Mama phoning to ask if he'd looked after her little friend who'd apparently had such a hard time in Casa Buona. Given her stumble, her jet lag, Mama would expect him to at least give Bailey time to recuperate before he truly sent her on her way. And that was the only reason he persisted. Why he asked now.

"So…who's this fiancé?"

Closing her eyes, she exhaled as if she was too tired to be defensive anymore.

"I was backpacking around Europe," she began. "By the time I got to Casa Buona, I'd run out of money. That's where I met Emilio. I picked up work at the taverna his parents own."

Mateo's muscles locked. "Emilio Conti is your fiancé?"

*"Was."* She quizzed his eyes. "Do you know him?"

"Casa Buona's a small town." Emilio's kind only made it feel smaller. Mateo nodded. "Go on."

Elbows finding her knees, she cupped her cheeks. "Over the weeks, Emilio and I became close. We spent a lot of time with his family. Time by ourselves. When he said he loved me, I was taken off guard. I didn't know about loving Emilio, but I'd certainly fallen in love with his parents. His sisters. They made me feel like one of the family." Her hands lowered and she brought up her legs to hug her knees. "One Saturday, in front of everyone, he proposed at the taverna. Seemed like the whole town was there, all smiling, holding their breath, waiting for my answer. I was stunned. Any words stuck like bricks in my throat. When I bowed my head, trying to figure out something tactful to do or say, someone cried out that I'd accepted. A huge cheer went up. Before I knew what had happened, Emilio slid a ring on my finger and…well…that was that."

Bailey ended by failing to smother a yawn at the same time the sound of an engine drew their attention. His ride—a yellow cab—was cruising up the drive.

"Wait here," he said, and when she opened her mouth to argue, he interrupted firmly. "One minute. Please." He crossed to the forecourt and spoke to the driver, who kept his motor idling while Mateo walked back and took a seat on the step alongside of her.

"Where do you plan to go now? Do you have anywhere to stay?"

"I'd hoped to stay with a friend for a few days but her neighbor said she's out of town. I'll get a room."

"Do you really want to waste Mama's money on a motel?"

"It's only temporary."

He studied the cab, thought of the dwindling group of guys doing their annual bachelor bash in Canada and, as Bailey pushed to her feet, made a decision.

"Come back inside."

Her look said, *you're crazy.* "You're ready to leave. The meter's running."

He eyed the driver. Best fix that.

He strode to the vehicle, left the cabbie smiling at the notes he passed over and heard the engine rev off behind him as he joined Bailey again.

Her jaw was hanging. "What did you do?"

"I'd thought about cancelling the first leg of my trip anyway. Now, inside." He tilted his head toward his still open front door.

"Flattering invitation." Her smile was thin. "But I don't do *fetch* or *roll over,* either."

Mateo's chin tucked in. She thought he was being bossy? Perhaps he was. He was used to people listening and accepting his advice. And there was a method to his madness. "You say the money Mama gave you is a loan. But you admit you have no income. No place to stay."

"I'll find something. I'm not afraid of work."

Another yawn gripped her, so consuming, she shuddered and her eyes watered.

"First you need a good rest," he told her. "I'll show you to a guest room."

Another *you're crazy* look. "I'm not staying."

"I'm not suggesting a lease, Bailey. Merely that you recharge here before you tackle a plan for tomorrow."

"No." But this time she sounded less certain.

"Mama would want you to." When she hesitated, he persisted. "A few hours rest. I won't pound on the door and get on your case."

She glared at him. "Promise?"

"On my life."

All the energy seemed to fall from her shoulders. He thought she might disarm him with a hint of that ice-melting smile, but she only nodded and grudgingly allowed him to escort her back inside.

After ascending that storybook staircase, Mateo Celeca showed her down the length of a wide paneled hallway to the entrance of a lavish room.

"The suite has an attached bath," he said as she edged in and looked around. "Make yourself at home. I'll be downstairs if you need anything."

Bailey watched the broad ledge of his shoulders roll away down the hall before she closed the heavy door and, feeling more displaced than she had in her life, gravitated toward the center of the vast room. Her own background was well to do. With a tennis court and five bedrooms, her lawyer father's house in Newport was considered grand to most. Her parents had driven fashionable cars. They'd gone on noteworthy vacations each year.

But, glancing around this lake of snowy carpet with so many matching white and gold draperies, Bailey could admit she'd never known *this* kind of opulence. Then again, who on earth needed this much? She wasn't one to covet riches.

Surely it was more important to know a sense of belonging…
of truly being where and with whom you needed to be. Despite
Emilio, irrespective of her father, one day she hoped to know
and keep that feeling.

After a long warm shower, she lay down and sleep
descended in a swift black cloud.

When she woke some hours later in the dark, her heart was
pounding with an impending sense of doom. In her dream,
she'd been back in Casa Buona, draped in a modest wedding
gown with Emilio beckoning her to join him at the end of a
long dark corridor. She shot a glance around the shadowy
unfamiliar surrounds and eased out a relieved breath. She was
in Sydney. Broke, starting over. In an obstinate near-stranger's
house.

She clapped a palm over her brow and groaned.

Mateo Celeca.

With refined movie-star looks and dark hypnotic eyes, he
did all kinds of unnerving things to her equilibrium. One
minute she was believing Mama, thinking her grandson was
some kind of prince. The next he was being a jerk, accusing
her of theft. Then, to really send her reeling, he'd offered her
a bed to shake off some of the jet lag. If she'd had anywhere
else to go—if she hadn't felt so suddenly drained—she would
never have stayed. She wasn't about to forgive or forget his
comment about her not being a lady.

She swung her legs over the edge of the bed at the same
time her stomach growled. She cast her thoughts away from
the judgmental doctor to a new priority. Food.

After slipping on her jeans, she tiptoed down that stunning
staircase and set off to find a kitchen. Inching through
someone else's broad shadow-filled halls in the middle of
the night hardly felt right but the alternative was finding a
takeout close by or dialing in. Mateo had said to make herself
at home. Surely that offer extended to a sandwich.

Soon she'd tracked down a massive room, gleaming with stainless steel and dark granite surfaces. Opening the fridge she found the interior near empty; that made sense given Mateo was meant to be on vacation. But there was a leftover roast, perhaps from his dinner earlier. A slab went between two slices of bread and, after enjoying her first mouthful, Bailey turned and discovered a series of floor-to-ceiling glass panes lining the eastern side of the attached room.

Outside, ghostly garden lights illuminated a divine courtyard where geometrically manicured hedges sectioned off individual classical statues. Beyond those panes, a scene from two thousand years ago beckoned…a passionate time when Rome dominated and emperors ruled half the world. Chewing, she hooked a glance around. No one about. Nothing to stop her. A little fresh air would be nice.

She eased back a door and moved out into the cool night, the soles of her bare feet padding over smooth sandstone paths as she wandered between hedges and those exquisite stone figures that seemed so lifelike. She was on her third bite of sandwich when a sound came from behind—a muted click that vibrated through the night and made the fine hairs on her nape stand up and quiver. Heart lodged in her throat, she angled carefully around. One of those figures was gliding toward her. Masculine. Tall. Naked from the waist up.

From behind a cloud, the full moon edged out and the definition of that outline sharpened…the captivating width of his chest, the subtle ruts of toned abs. Bailey's gaze inched higher and connected with inquiring onyx eyes as a low familiar voice rumbled out.

"You're up."

Bailey let out the breath she'd been holding.

Not a statue come to life, but Mateo Celeca standing before her, wearing nothing but a pair of long white drawstring pants. She'd been so absorbed she'd forgotten where she was, as well as the events that had brought her here. Now, in a hot rush, it all came back. Particularly how annoyingly attractive her host was, tonight, with the moonbeams playing over that hard human physique, dramatically so.

When a kernel of warmth ignited in the lowest point of her belly, Bailey swallowed and clasped her sandwich at her chest.

Mateo Celeca might be beyond hot, but, at this point in her life, she didn't care to even *think* about the opposite sex, particularly a critical one. Her only concern lay in getting back on her feet and repaying Mama as soon as possible, whether the doctor believed that or not.

"I didn't mean to wake you," she said in a surprisingly even voice that belied how churned up she felt.

"You tripped a silent alarm when you opened that door. The security company called to make sure there'd been no breach. I thought it'd be you, but I came down to check, just in case."

Bailey kicked herself. She'd seen him fiddling with a security pad when she'd arrived. Heaven knew what this place and its contents were insured for. Of course he'd have a state-of-the-art system switched on and jump when an alert went off.

"I was hungry," she explained then held up dinner. "I made a sandwich."

She wasn't sure, but in the shadows she thought he might have grinned—which was way better than a scowl. If he started on her again now, in the middle of the night, she'd simply grab her bag and find the door. But he seemed far more relaxed than this morning when he'd overreacted about the money Mama had loaned her.

"You usually enjoy a starry stroll with your midnight snack?" He asked as he sauntered nearer.

"It looked so nice out."

"It is pleasant."

He studied the topiaries and pristine hedges, and this time she was certain of the smile curving one corner of his mouth as he stretched his arms, one higher than the other, over his head. She wanted to fan herself. And she'd thought the *statues* were works of art.

"Are you a gardener?" She asked, telling herself to look away but not managing it. Bronzed muscles rippled in the moonlight whenever he moved.

"Not at all. But I appreciate the effort others put in."

"This kind of effort must be twenty-four seven."

"What about you?" He asked, meandering toward a trickling water feature displaying a god-like figure ready to sling a lightning bolt.

"No green thumbs here." Moving to join him, she tipped her head at the fountain. "Is that Zeus?" She remembered a recent movie about the Titans. "The god of war, right?"

"Zeus is the god of justice. The supreme protector. Perhaps because he could have lost his life at the very moment he entered the world."

"Really? How?" Moving to sit on the cool fountain ledge, she took another bite. She loved to hear about ancient legends.

"His father, Cronus, believed in a prophecy. He would be overthrown by his son as he had once overthrown his own father. To save her newborn, Rhea, Zeus's mother, gave him up at birth then tricked her husband into thinking a rock wrapped in swaddling clothes was the child, which Cronus promptly disposed of. He didn't know that his son, Zeus, was being reared by a nymph in Crete. When he was grown, Zeus joined forces with his other siblings to defeat the Titans, including his father."

She couldn't help but be drawn by Mateo's story, as well as the emotion simmering beneath his words. Had she imagined the shadow that had crossed his gaze when he spoke of that mother needing to give up her child?

"What happened to Zeus after the clash?" She asked.

"He ruled over Olympus as well as the mortals, and fathered many children."

"Sounds noble."

"The great majority of his offspring were conceived through adulterous affairs, I'm afraid."

*Oh.* "Not so good for the demigod kids."

"Not so good for any child."

Bailey studied his classic profile as he peered off into the night…the high forehead and proud, hawkish nose. She wanted to ask more. Not only about this adulterous yet protective Roman god but also about the narrator of his tale. Not that Mateo's life was any of her business. Although…

For the moment he seemed to have put aside his more paranoid feelings toward her, and this was an informal chat. In the morning she'd be well rested and on her way, so where was the harm in asking more?

Making a pretense of examining the gardens, she crossed her ankles and swung her feet out and back.

"Mama mentioned that you left Casa Buona when you were twelve."

His hesitation—a single beat—was barely enough to notice.

"My father was moving to Australia. He explained about the opportunities here. Ernesto was an accountant and wanted to look after my higher education."

"Have you lived in Sydney since?"

He nodded. "But I travel when I can."

"You must have built a lot of memories here after so long."

Who were his friends? All professionals like him? Did he have any other family Down Under?

But Mateo didn't respond. He merely looked over the gardens with those dark thoughtful eyes. From the firm set of his jaw, her host had divulged all he would tonight. Understandable. They were little more than strangers. And, despite this intimate atmosphere, they were destined to remain that way.

A statue caught Bailey's eye. After slipping off her perch, she crossed over and ran a hand across the cool stone.

"I like this one."

It was a mother, her head bowed over the baby she held. The tone conjured up memories of Bailey's own mother...how loving and devoted she'd been. Like Rhea. Both mothers had needed to leave their child, though neither woman had wanted to. If she lived to one hundred, Bailey would miss her till the day she died.

"Is this supposed to be Zeus as an infant?" She asked, her gaze on the baby now.

Mateo's deep voice came from behind. "No. More a signature to my profession, I suppose."

His profession. An obstetrician. One of the best in Australia, Mama had said, and more than once.

"How many babies have you brought into the world?" She asked, studying the soft loving smile adorning the statue's face.

When he didn't reply, she edged around and almost lost her breath. Mateo was standing close...close enough for her to inhale that undeniable masculine scent. Near enough to be drawn by its natural heady lure. As his intense gaze glittered down and searched hers, a lock of dark hair dropped over his brow and jumped in the breeze.

"...to count."

Coming to, Bailey gathered herself. He'd been speaking, but she'd only caught his last words.

"I'm sorry," she said. "To count what?"

His brows swooped together. "How many babies I've delivered. Too many to count."

Bailey withered as her cheeks heated up. How had she lost track of their conversation so completely?

But she knew how. Whether he was being polite or fiery and passionate, Mateo exuded an energy that drew her in.

Indisputable.

Unwelcome.

Heartbeat throbbing in her throat, she lowered her gaze and turned a little away. "Guess they all blur after a time."

"Not at all. Each safe delivery is an accomplishment I never take for granted."

The obvious remained unsaid. Even in this day and age, some deliveries wouldn't go as planned. No matter how skilled, every doctor suffered defeats. Just like criminal lawyers.

She remembered her parents speaking about one client her father had failed to see acquitted. The man's family had lost nearly all their possessions in a fire, and her father donated a sizable amount to get them sturdily on their feet again. She'd felt so very proud of him. But he seemed to lose those deeper feelings for compassion after her mother passed away.

As Mateo's gaze ran over the mother and child, Bailey wondered again about *his* direct family. He'd lived with his grandmother in Italy. Had come to Australia with his father. Where was his mother?

"I'm turning in," he said, rolling back one big bare shoulder. "There's a television and small library in your room if you can't get back to sleep." That dark gaze skimmed her face a final time and tingling warmth filtered over her before he rotated away. "*Sogni d'oro,* Bailey."

"*Sogni d'oro,*" she replied and then smiled.

*Sweet dreams.*

Mateo sauntered back inside, his gait relaxed yet purposeful.

He was a difficult one to work out. So professional and together most of the time, but there was a volatile side too, one she wondered if many people saw. More was going on beneath the sophisticated exterior…deep and private things Mateo Celeca wouldn't want to divulge. And certainly not divulge to a troublesome passerby like herself. Even if they had the time to get acquainted, he'd been clear. She wasn't the kind of woman the doctor wanted to get too close to.

Bailey thought of those shoulders—those eyes—and, holding the flutter in her tummy, concurred.

She didn't need to get that close either.

# Three

Early the next morning, Mateo strode out his back door and threw an annoyed glance around the hedges and their statues. Not a sign of her anywhere. Seemed Bailey Ross had flown the coop.

After knocking on her bedroom door—politely at first—thinking she must be hungry and might join him for breakfast, he'd found the room empty. The shabby knapsack vanished. No matter her consequences, she shouldn't have taken money from an elderly, obviously soft-hearted woman. Equally, she ought to have had the decency to at least stay long enough to say "thanks for the bed," and "so long."

He'd practically laughed in her face when she'd vowed to pay that "loan" back. After this disappearing act, he'd bet all he owned neither he nor Mama would hear from Miss Ross again. She was a woman without scruples. And yet, he couldn't deny it—he was attracted to her.

After her stumble yesterday, when he'd cupped, then

searched, her face, the urge to lean closer and slant his mouth over hers had been overwhelming. Last night while they'd spoken among the shadows of these gardens, he'd fought to keep a lid on that same impulse. Something deep and strong reacted whenever she was near. Something primordial and potentially dangerous.

He'd felt this kind of intense chemistry once before, Mateo recalled, looking over the statue of mother and child Bailey had found so interesting last night. Unfortunately, at twenty-three he'd been too wet behind the ears to see that particular woman for what she was: a beautiful, seductive leech. He'd fallen hard and had given Linda Webb everything she'd wanted. Or, rather, he'd *tried*. Expensive perfume, jewelry, even a car. She was an unquenchable well. Took twelve months and a ransacked savings account before he'd faced facts—unemployed Linda hadn't wanted a fiancé as much as a financier.

Unlike Mama, he had no problem with being wealthy. He'd worked hard to achieve this level of security and he wouldn't apologize for doing well. He also liked to be generous—but only where and when his gifts were put to good use and appreciated. That cancelled out the likes of Linda Webb and Bailey Ross.

Giving up the search, Mateo rotated away from a view of bordering pines at the same time he saw her.

Beyond the glass-paneled pool fence, a lithe figure lay on a sun lounge, floppy straw hat covering the back of her head and the teeniest of micro bikinis covering not much of the rest. An invisible band around Mateo's chest tightened while his clamoring heartbeat ratcheted up another notch. Last night in the moonlight she'd looked beyond tempting, but in an almost innocent way. There was nothing innocent about the way Miss Ross looked this morning.

Those bikini bottoms weren't technically a thong, but

far more was revealed by that sliver of bright pink fabric than was covered. Minus the jeans, her legs appeared even longer, naturally tanned. Smooth. His fingertips, and other extremities, tingled and grew warm. He couldn't deny that every male cell in his body wanted to reach out and touch her.

One of Bailey's tanned arms braced as she shifted on the lounge. The disturbed floppy hat fell to the ground. When she blindly felt around but couldn't find it, she shifted again, pushing up on both palms. A frown pinched her brow and, as if she'd sensed him standing nearby, her gaze tipped higher then wandered across the lawn.

When their eyes connected, hers popped and she sprang up to a sit while Mateo fought every impulse known to man to check out the twin pink triangles almost covering her perfect breasts. With difficulty, he forced his face into an unaffected mask.

*Get a grip. You're a medical doctor. An obstetrician who has tended hundreds of clients.*

But there was a distinction between "work" and this vastly different environment. Irrespective of profession, he was still a man, complete with a man's urges and desires. Under normal circumstances, being physically attracted to a member of the opposite sex was nothing immoral. Trouble was…he didn't *want* to be attracted to Bailey Ross. Whether she was a victim or a schemer, she was a drifter who seemed to court trouble.

As Bailey swiped her T-shirt off the back of the lounge, Mateo set his hands in his trouser pockets and cast an aimless glance around. When he was certain her top half was covered, he crossed over.

"I took an early morning dip," she said as he entered the pool area.

"When I couldn't find you inside, I thought you'd run off."

She frowned. "I wouldn't leave without saying goodbye."

"Unless I was your fiancé?"

"I'm grateful for the bed," she said, standing, "but not appreciative enough to listen to any more of your put-downs."

He moved to the rock waterfall, wedged his hands in his pockets again and, after debating with himself several moments, said calmly, "So tell me more about your situation."

"So you can scoff?"

"So I can understand."

Dammit, one minute he was wanting to help, offering her a bed, the next he was lumping her in the same class as Linda. Was Bailey genuine about paying that money back, or were her dealings with Mama merely a side issue for him? Was his interest more about that long fair hair, those blazing blue eyes?

That, after his last comment, seemed to have lost a little of their fire.

Folding back down again, she set that straw hat on her lap and explained.

"After that night…the night Emilio proposed," she said, "his sisters jumped into organizing the wedding. Emilio set the date two months from the day he shoved that ring on my finger. He wouldn't listen when I told him it was a mistake. He only smiled and tried to hug me when I said this had all happened too fast. Everyone kept saying what a great catch he was."

"Not in your opinion."

"Sure, we had fun," she admitted. "Up to that point. But after that night, whenever I got vocal and tried to return his ring, Emilio got upset. His face would turn red and beads of sweat would break on his brow. He'd proposed, he'd say, and I'd accepted. I'd taken his family's charity by working at the taverna and sleeping under their roof. We were getting married and he knew once I got over my nerves I'd be happy. I didn't have nearly enough money for a ticket home. I was trapped." Looking at her feet, she exhaled. "One day at Mama's place, I broke down. We were alone and when she asked what was wrong I told her I couldn't go through with the wedding. Everyone else might have been in love with Emilio but I wasn't."

"Why not call your father?"

Regardless of disagreements, family was family. His own father had been there through thick and thin. Or rather the man he knew as a father was.

"If I introduced you to Dad," she plopped her hat back on her head, "you'd understand why. I went overseas against his advice. The last thing he said to me was that if I was old enough not to listen, I was old enough to figure out my own problems." Her voice dropped. "Believe me, he wouldn't want to know."

"You've made a few mistakes in the past?" An insensitive question, perhaps, but he was determined to get to the bottom of this maze.

"Nothing monumental."

"Until this."

Screwing her eyes shut, she groaned. "I knew I could've said no to Emilio on the day of the wedding, but I couldn't bear to think of everyone's meltdown, particularly his. Or I could simply have packed up and stolen off in the middle of the night and moved on to the next town. But Emilio proved to me he wasn't the kind to let go what he believed was his. He'd come after me and do all he could to bring me back."

From what Mateo remembered of Emilio, he had to agree. Beneath the superficial charm lived a Neanderthal.

Moving to a garden crowded with spiky Pandanus palms, Mateo swept his foot to move stray white pebbles back into their proper bed.

"What makes you so sure he won't come here?"

"I'm *not* sure. I mailed him a package from the airport. The letter explained how I wished he'd listened and I wasn't coming back. I put his ring in, as well. Hopefully that will be enough."

Mateo grunted. "He's thick but not entirely stupid." When she glanced over, curious, he explained. "The summer before I left Italy, a twelve-year-old Emilio tried to call me out. Can't recall the reason now but certainly nothing to warrant a fistfight. When Emilio and a couple of friends cut me off in an alley, I defended myself. Emilio didn't bother me after that."

Surrounded by memories, Mateo absently brushed more pebbles into the garden bed. How different his life would have been if he'd stayed in Casa Buona. What if no one had come for him all those years ago in France? What would have become of him then? If Mama hadn't offered her help to this woman—if what she said was true—what would have happened to Bailey?

"I'm going to pay her back," Bailey insisted. "If it takes five years—"

"Mama may not *have* five years."

Her head went back as if she hadn't considered Mama's advanced age. But then one slender shoulder hitched up and she amended. "I'll get a loan."

A loan to pay a loan. "With no job?"

Sitting straighter, she crossed those long tanned legs. "I'm fixing that."

"Looks like it," he muttered, eyeing the pool sparkling with golden east coast sunshine. Linda was always on the verge of getting a job too.

Bailey's jaw tightened. "Accepting Mama's money wasn't any moral highlight—"

"And yet you did accept."

The frustration in her eyes hardened before the irritation evaporated into resignation. She slowly shook her head. "Someone like you…you could never understand what it's like to feel powerless."

Oh, but he *did* know. And he'd spent his entire adult life making certain he never felt powerless again. He'd done it through hard work, not lying around a pool. Although part of her plan had merit.

"Getting a loan is a good idea," he said, "but not from an institution. There's interest. If you get behind, there are fees."

"Maybe I should throw some cash at a roulette wheel," she groaned.

"I have a better idea. I'll pay Mama the money you owe—"

*"What?"* She shook her head. "Absolutely not!"

"—and you can pay me back."

"I don't want to owe *you* anything."

"So you're not serious about paying her back as soon as possible?"

She eyed him as Little Red Riding Hood might eye the big bad wolf.

"What are the terms?" She finally asked.

"A signed agreement. Regular repayments."

"Why would you do that for me?"

"Not for you. For my grandmother." The amount Bailey owed wouldn't make a dent in any of his accounts but he liked to think that, for once, Mama wouldn't be left out of pocket by virtue of her soft heart.

Bailey pushed to her feet, paced around the back of the sun lounge, studied him and then, defiant, crossed her arms. A few more seconds wound out before she announced, "Well, then, I'd better get cracking."

That floppy hat stuck on her head, she fished her jeans out of her knapsack and drove her legs through the denim pipes. When he realized he'd been staring while she wiggled and scooped her bottom into the seat of her jeans, he jerked his gaze away and heard her zip up. He'd already faced the fact Miss Ross wasn't the kind of woman with whom he wished to become more involved than he already was.

In time, he looked back to see her heading for the pool gate, that knapsack swinging over a shoulder. "Where are you going?"

"To get a job. I'll be back by five to sign that contract. And about those repayments…" She stopped at the gate and her glittering blue eyes meshed with his. "I want them as steep as possible."

His eyebrows jumped. "To get the debt paid off in record time?"

"To get you out of my life ASAP."

As she strode away, Mateo gave himself permission to drink in the sway of those slim hips and long hair. High on each thigh, his muscles hardened as his thoughts gave over to how those curves and silk might feel beneath his fingers, his lips….

Regardless of whether she took Mama's money or not, she was attractive and fiery and…something more. Something he would dearly love to sample.

Whether it was good for him or not.

# Four

Bailey visited every employment agency she could find, unfortunately with little success. Although initially there seemed to be some prospects, they turned out to be either charity work or commission-based jobs, like knocking on doors.

Time and again she'd been asked about qualifications. No high school diploma. One year of an apprenticeship at a hair salon. She'd been a school crossing guard, helping kids cross streets for a while. Mainly she'd performed waitress work.

She'd been directed to a hospitality recruitment agency. Placements were available at exclusive establishments but she didn't have the experience necessary to be put forward as a candidate. Many courses to enhance her skills, however, were available. But they cost money and Bailey didn't have the time to spare. She needed to start earning. Needed to start paying back and showing Mateo Celeca she wasn't a con artist but merely someone who'd needed a hand up.

As weary as she felt after a full day trekking around the city, she tried to keep her spirits high. Her mother had always said there was good in every situation. Bailey didn't quite believe that; what was so good about having a stroke take a parent out at age thirty-five? But Bailey did believe in never giving up. Her mother would have wanted her to stay strong and believe in herself, even now when she'd never felt more alone.

In the busy city center, with traffic and pedestrians grinding by, she'd pulled out her bus timetable and had found a suitable link when a familiar voice drew her ear. Masculine. Tense. The tone sent simultaneous chills and familiar warmth racing over her skin. She hadn't heard that voice in over a year. Back then it had told her not to come home begging.

Her heart beating high in her throat, Bailey looked carefully over her shoulder. Her father stood on the curb, phone pressed to his ear, announcing his displeasure over a jury verdict gone wrong.

In an instant, Bailey couldn't draw enough breath. She had the bizarre urge to run—both toward her father and away from him. Never would she have simply waltzed up to his door and thrown out her arms, and yet—with him available such a short distance away—she couldn't help but relive those much earlier days...times when her dad had taken her horseback riding, or suffered answering inane questions from an eight-year-old while he worked on depositions. When she'd come down with tonsillitis he'd rushed her to the doctor. He'd even taken time off to nurse her back, complete with spoon-fed antibiotics.

And that was a full year after her mother had died.

Bailey's throat convulsed at the same time her eyes misted over.

*He was right there.*

A now-or-never feeling fell through her middle as she

moved one foot forward, and another. Maybe he hadn't meant to sound so harsh. So final. Maybe he *wouldn't* turn her away. She was his only child, after all. Perhaps he'd cry out in surprise and wrap his arms around her. Tell her that he'd missed her and ask that she come home with him now. Straight away.

An uncertain smile quivering on her lips, she'd cut the distance separating them by half when a cab swung into the curb. Before Bailey could think to call out, Damon Ross had flung open the door and, phone still at his ear, slid into the backseat. Her hand was in the air, a single word on her tongue, when the cab cut into a break in traffic and shot away.

Her hand lowered and stomach dropped. Blinking furiously, she fought back the bite of rising tears and disappointment. But, no matter how much it hurt, that bad timing was probably best. The cab swerving in at that exact moment had saved her from herself. Her father had said she'd regret dropping out of school and while that was one thing he'd been right about, there was a whole lot more that had never needed to be said. But it was too late for those kind of regrets. Nothing could be done about the past.

Determined, Bailey walked a straight line to the bus stop.

Now the future was all that mattered.

She'd told him five, but Bailey didn't get back to Mateo's mansion until six. Answering the bell, he threw open the door, took in her appearance and frowned. Bailey drew herself up, entered the foyer and fought the impulse to ease the sandals off her feet, grimy with city dirt. God, she must look like an urchin in need of a warm meal and a bath.

He closed the door. "No luck on the job front?"

"There are a few possibilities." She firmed the line of her mouth and almost succeeded in squaring her shoulders. "I'll be out again tomorrow. I just wanted to let you know I haven't skipped town. I have every intention of going through with my end of the deal." Taking up his offer of a loan and signing a contract that would legally commit her to paying every penny back, the sooner the better. She wanted this episode of her life over as much as Mateo must, too.

But then she stopped to take in his attire—custom-made trousers and a black jersey knit shirt that covered his shoulders and chest like a dream. His scent was hot and mouth-wateringly fresh. His shoes were mirror polished.

"Are you on your way out?"

Seemed she was destined to show up on his doorstep whenever he was about to head off.

"I spoke with a friend today," he said. "We went to university together. I delivered his baby boy."

"Having an obstetrician friend must come in handy."

He conceded a smile. "Alex's wife worked in real estate," he went on in that rich deep voice that resonated like symphony base chords through the foyer. "Rental properties. Natalie still works a couple of days a week to keep her hand in."

"Smart lady."

*And you're telling me all this...why?*

As if reading her thoughts, he explained. "Since my trip's been delayed, I suggested we catch up for dinner. Alex thought you might like to come."

At the same time a muscle in his jaw flexed, a wave of anticipation, and apprehension, rippled between them and Bailey fought the urge to clear her ears.

"Your friend doesn't know me. You barely know me and, call me paranoid, but I have the impression you don't like me much."

His closest shoulder hitched and dropped. "We have to eat." She narrowed her eyes at him. Since when had "he" and "she" become "we"? "Unless you have other plans," he finished.

Her only other plans entailed checking into an affordable hotel. The more interesting question was, "How did you explain me to your friend?"

"I told him the truth."

"That I took money from your grandmother and you don't mean to let me out of your sight until I've paid back every cent?"

"I said you were a friend of Mama's returned to Australia."

Bailey held that breath. His expression was open. Given she'd kept her word and come back today, were his suspicions about her character being unfavorable starting to wane? Not that his opinion of her should matter…only, if she were completely honest, for some reason they did.

He thrust his hands in his trouser pockets. "Of course, if you're not hungry—"

"*No*. I mean, I *am*." In fact, now that food had been mentioned, her empty stomach was reminding her she hadn't eaten since a muffin several hours earlier. But…wincing, she looked down and felt the day's dust on her skin. "I'll need a shower."

"Table's not booked till seven-thirty."

Bailey nibbled her lower lip. There was something else. Something any female would be reluctant to admit. "I, um, don't have another dress." From the look of Mateo's crisp attire, jeans and a T-shirt wouldn't cut it.

When his gaze skimmed her frame, her eyes widened. She'd felt that visual stroke like a warm slow touch.

He gave a sexy slanted grin. "What you're wearing," he said, "will be fine."

Twenty minutes later, showered and somewhat refreshed, Bailey followed Mateo to the garage. She was determined not to drink in the way the impression of his shoulder blades rolled beneath that black shirt or recall how delectable that back had looked so bronzed and bare in the moonlight last night.

As much as she'd like to, she couldn't deny she was physically attracted to the man. That didn't mean she should dwell on bone-melting images of him as she had done while standing beneath the showerhead mere moments ago. She hadn't been able to pry her thoughts from memories of Mateo strolling among those lifelike statues. Worse, she couldn't help but speculate on how those strong toned arms might feel surrounding and gathering her in, or how the bow of his full lower lip might taste grazing languidly back and forth over hers….

Now another image faded up in her mind—Mateo Celeca, gloriously naked and poised above her in that beautiful big upstairs bed. Her throat immediately thickened and beneath her bodice, nipples peaked and hardened. Slowing her step, Bailey pushed out a breath. She might have been engaged to Emilio but he'd never affected her this way. No man had. Why should that be so when, not only had she and Mateo locked horns, they'd only known each other a day?

In the garage, he showed her to the passenger side door of an expensive low-slung vehicle. A Maserati, if she wasn't mistaken. Odd there wasn't at least one or two other sports cars housed in the overly spacious garage. Or, perhaps, something classier to more aptly suit his station, like a Bentley or Rolls.

The garage door whirred up and soon they were cruising down the tree-lined drive and out on to a quiet street bordered by wide immaculate sidewalks where women in designer tracksuits walked poodles showing off diamanté collars. These people couldn't have the foggiest idea how the other half lived.

"I phoned someone else today," Mateo said, changing gears.

"Mama?" She guessed, and he nodded. "I wanted to be half settled before I called or wrote her."

"She figured that."

"Did you tell her that you invited me to stay last night?" She asked, feeling a little awkward over it. Not that Mama would mind in the least.

"I told her you rested at my house overnight and you were out looking for a job." Large sure hands on the steering wheel navigated a corner. "She said you should stay until you were earning and set up some place."

Closing her eyes, Bailey groaned as her cheeks grew hot. Mama was a lovely lady. She was only showing that she cared. But, "I'm sure you told her I'd be fine."

"I said I'd offer."

"You *what?*"

"I said you could stay for a couple of days until things were sorted out."

Bailey thought that statement through. "You mean things like our loan agreement?"

He gave an affirmative grunt. "And it's not as if the house isn't big enough to accommodate one more." He skated over a defining look. "For a few days."

Before she could argue, he turned the conversation toward the couple they'd be dining with that night—Natalie and Alex Ramirez. But Bailey's thoughts were stuck on Mateo's offer to stay in his home. She didn't want to sponge. But a few days grace to set herself up would be heaven-sent. She was willing to work at anything to get her life back on track, and quickly. Surely a job would turn up in the next day or two.

When they pulled up at a well-to-do address, Bailey's stomach flipped. She shouldn't be surprised that the Ramirez abode almost rivaled Mateo's in size and grandeur. Of course his friends would be wealthy. But beyond that, despite her nerves, she was curious to meet people the doctor liked to spend time with and perhaps learn a little more about the enigma that was Mateo Celeca. She only wished she was dressed more appropriately, and that she had a better pair of shoes to wear out. Dinner with this type meant more than pulling up a chair in a pizza joint.

Mateo slid out of the car. When he opened her door, she accepted his hand and a flurry of sparks shot like a line of lit gunpowder up her arm. Easing out into the forecourt, although her heart was thumping, Bailey managed to keep her expression unaffected. She'd felt this buzz before, when he'd caught her yesterday and, holding her chin, had looked into her eyes. Tonight the effect was even more pronounced. If an everyday act like hands touching caused this kind of physical reaction, she couldn't fathom how something of consequence might affect her…like a no-holds-barred penetrating kiss.

Did Mateo feel it too?

A stunning brunette holding a young child dressed in a blue jumpsuit, and a tall, dark-haired man answered the door. At the same time the man—Alex Ramirez—stepped aside to show his guests through, his wife put out her free hand. Her nails were French tipped. The princess-cut diamond solitaire was enormous. "You must be Bailey. I'm Natalie and this little fellow is Reece." She bounced the baby and he smiled and squealed again. "Come in, and bring that handsome devil with you."

Mateo leaned in to brush a light kiss on Natalie's cheek before shaking his friend's hand heartily then returning close to her side again, as if he could sense her anxiety. As if they might be a genuine couple.

As they all moved into a sumptuous living room, furnished with contemporary leathers and teak, Bailey took in Natalie's exquisite dress. Cut just below the knee, the lilac fabric shimmered beneath strategically placed downlights. The effect was dazzling, bringing out her complexion and intensity of her long dark hair. Her shoes matched the dress, lilac, delicate heels. Her toenails were painted red. Had she enjoyed a professional pedicure earlier that day?

Glancing down, Bailey cringed.

Her own toes hadn't seen a lick of polish in too long to remember.

Everything in Casa Buona had been so relaxed. She hadn't needed much, although, in order to travel light—to leave quickly when she had—she'd left a number of pretty skirts and tops behind, casual bright wear that suited work at the taverna. Despite the way it had all ended, she'd enjoyed being part of the staff there, serving tables, joining in on the songs and chatter afterward when the kitchen had closed for the night.

How would *this* evening end? With brandy and cigars in the study for the men, most likely. Perhaps flutes filled with Cristal offered to the ladies. And when Mateo drove her home…

Standing beside the liquor cabinet, Alex rubbed his hands together. "What can I offer you to drink?"

"I'm fine," Bailey replied, "thank you." Given her inquisitive thoughts regarding Mateo, better she stayed well clear of beverages that would only weaken inhibitions.

"Ice water for me, Alex," Mateo said, moving to stand alongside her, close enough to soak in the natural heat emanating from his body. "You and Natalie can indulge a little tonight."

"It's true." Natalie rubbed her nose with her baby's. "It isn't often we get a night off."

The little boy giggled and held his mother's cheeks. When his fingers caught in her perfectly coiffed hair, Natalie only laughed, but then worried over a strand wrapped around one tiny finger. Alex walked over, unwound the hair from around his boy's finger then kissed the baby's palm with a loud raspberry that sent the child into peals of laughter.

Bailey's chest squeezed. This trio was the picture of the perfect family. The happiness they so obviously shared lit all their faces. What they had couldn't be bought.

That's what *she* wanted one day. The kind of marriage that took a person's breath away. The kind of love her parents had once shared. They'd been so happy. When she was young, she'd never stopped to think it might not last.

When she refocused, a feathery feeling brushed over her. She looked across. Mateo was looking at her, a curious light shining in those dark eyes, a sexy grin curving one side of his mouth. A pulse in Bailey's throat began to beat fast. She blinked then, uncertain of where to look, concentrated on Alex who sent her an ambiguous smile before returning to the bar to see to the drinks.

Natalie spoke to her husband as he poured a water then what looked like scotch for himself.

"Honey, I might change his diaper for Tammy before we go." Natalie explained to Bailey, "Tammy's the wonderful lady who looks after Reece when I go into the office a couple of times a week. She's catching up on her knitting in the family room until we leave."

"Mateo mentioned that you work outside of the home."

"It's a great balance. Only four hours each day—" Natalie rubbed noses with her baby again "—and then I'm dying to get back to him." She met Bailey's gaze. "Want to help me change him?"

Bailey's knees locked. She'd done some babysitting but never one so young. "I'm not sure I'd be any help."

Natalie only smiled. "You look like a quick study."

They left the men, who were busy discussing football, and moved into a nearby room—a downstairs nursery. Bouncing the baby, Natalie crossed to a white lacquered changing table where she gently lay her bundle down then set about unbuttoning his suit.

"Mateo mentioned you know Mama Celeca?"

"I lived in her town for a few months."

"I've heard so much about her. Alex says she's the biggest darling ever. He went with Mateo to Italy one summer a long time ago. Apparently Mama tried her best to get both of them married off."

She seemed so genuine, Bailey couldn't help but like her. Couldn't help but feel relaxed and at home, even in a dress that looked more like a rag next to Natalie's exquisite creation.

Bailey brushed a palm over the baby's soft crown and carried on the thread of their conversation.

"Lucky for you Mama's matchmaking didn't succeed."

"Lucky isn't the word." Natalie peeled back the diaper and let out a pleased sigh. "I love when there's no messy surprises. Could you hand me a fresh diaper, please?" Natalie cast a glance to her right. "They're in that lower drawer."

Bailey dug one out while Natalie cleaned up, shook on powder then slid the fresh diaper under the baby's bottom.

"Mateo mentioned that you're in between jobs," Natalie said, pressing down the diaper tabs.

"I was out looking today." *All* day.

"Find anything?"

"Not yet."

Natalie took both the baby's feet and clapped the soles together, but the baby's smile was a little slow to bloom this time. Must be past his bedtime, Bailey thought.

"What are you interested in?" Natalie asked, scooping her baby up. "Do you have office skills?"

"Afraid not. I've been waitressing, serving and general cleanup."

"In Italy?" Bailey nodded and Natalie beamed. "What an adventure."

Bailey arched a brow. "It certainly was that."

"I don't know of any waitressing positions, but we're always after good cleaners for rentals at the agency."

Bailey's heart leapt. "Really?"

With the baby's head resting against her shoulder, Natalie headed for the door. "You're probably not interested—"

"No," Bailey jumped in. "I mean, *yes*. I *am* interested. When do you think I could start?"

"I'm going in Monday. I'll give you the address."

"I'd appreciate that." A *lot*. "Thank you."

Natalie's pace had slowed. The baby's eyelids were drooping now. He was about to drift off. "Would you like a cuddle before we leave?"

Bailey gave a nervous laugh. She would. He was so adorable and full of smiles. But what if she took him and he cried? She'd feel terrible. But, as if to reassure her, little Reece stretched his arms out to her and found a drowsy smile.

"Seems at least one of you wants a cuddle," Natalie joked. But then she saw Bailey's hesitation. "He's a darling, honest. The worst he'll do is pull your nose."

Bailey blew out a shaky breath. "Well, I've never had my nose pulled before." She put out her arms.

The baby weighed more than she thought. Close up, his heavy-lidded eyes looked even bluer. And he smelled divine— all fresh and new. No wonder Natalie and Alex were so happy. They had it all.

"He likes your bracelet." Natalie touched the dangling charms that Reece was fingering too. "So do I. Did you get it overseas?"

"It was a gift." And then Bailey admitted what she hadn't in a very long while. "A gift from my mother."

"Then it's doubly precious. Do your parents live in Sydney?"

"My father does. My mother passed away."

Natalie's beautiful face fell. "Oh...I'm so sorry, Bailey."

"It was a long time ago."

The sudden lump in Bailey's throat made speaking a little difficult. Over a decade had passed since her mother's death. Not everyone would understand why her grief hadn't faded. But something about Natalie made Bailey feel as if she would. As if the two of them could be more than acquaintances. That, maybe, they could be friends.

Still, she didn't want to mire down the conversation, not when Reece was mumbling adorable things she couldn't quite understand and hiccuping in such a cute way.

But Natalie's expression had grown alarmed. Slanting her head, she held out her arms.

"I think you'd better give him back."

Bailey's heart sank. "Did I do something wrong?"

"No, no. It's just I think he's about to—"

Natalie didn't move quickly enough. Reece gave another hiccup. Heaved a little. Then a lot. Next his dinner came up.

All over the front of Bailey's dress.

# Five

When Natalie barged into the room, Mateo and Alex had been discussing the state's current public hospital concerns. Mateo immediately dropped the conversation and peered past Natalie's shoulder. Bailey wasn't in tow and Natalie's hands were clasped tight before her. Seemed unlikely—Natalie was one of the sweetest people he knew. But Bailey was a relatively unknown quantity. Had the women had a disagreement?

Natalie pulled up in front of her husband. "Can you ring and let the restaurant know we'll be late?"

Standing, Alex caught her arm. "Is the baby all right?"

"Too much milk after dinner, I'm afraid."

Alex lowered his hand. "Another accident?"

"All over poor Bailey."

Mateo was no stranger to babies' assortment of surprises. He not only cared for pregnant women before and during delivery, he looked after their concerns postpartum. Many days, his practice was filled with the sights, sounds and smells of children of all ages. He'd been chucked up on more often than some people brushed their teeth. Part of the job. He wasn't sure Bailey would be quite so cool with it, particularly given the trying day she'd had.

Setting down his glass, Mateo rose too. "I'll take her home."

"No need. Bailey's fine," Natalie said. "Other than needing a quick shower and a fresh change of clothes, and I have a stack of outfits in my pre-baby wardrobe she can wear." She ran her hand down her husband's sleeve. "Tammy's settling the baby now. I'll go see how Bailey's doing."

As she sailed away, Alex fell back into his chair. The grin on his face said it all. "She's an amazing woman, isn't she?"

"You're a lucky man."

Alex leaned closer and lowered his voice. "So, now we know they'll be occupied for a while yet, tell me about it."

"Tell you what?"

"About your date."

"She's not a *date*."

"She's an attractive female accompanying you to dinner. If she's not a date, what is she?"

"Difficult to work out," Mateo admitted. "Like I said on the phone, she appeared on my doorstep yesterday morning." He went into more about the engagement and her dramatic flight from Italy, the loan and Bailey's search for a job to pay it back. "When I phoned Mama today, she confirmed that she'd told Bailey to drop in." Mateo dropped his gaze to the glass he rotated between his fingers. "Mama also asked me to watch out for her until she can make amends with her father."

"Trouble there too?"

"I'm sure whatever's gone on before could be sorted out with one or two calm conversations."

"Family rifts aren't usually that easy to solve." Alex took a long sip of scotch.

"Either way, it's none of my business."

"So where's Bailey staying?"

"I said she could stay with me—just for a few days." Alex coughed as if his drink had gone down the wrong way. Mateo frowned. "What?"

Alex tried to contain his amused look. "Nothing. I mean, Bailey seems very nice."

"But?"

"But nothing, Mateo. I'm only surprised that you've opened your home to her. You haven't done that in a while."

"You mean since Linda." Mateo slid his glass onto the side table. "This isn't the same."

Alex studied his friend's face and, inhaling, nodded and changed the subject.

"What's happening with the vacation?"

"I haven't made any firm decisions yet."

"But you're still going to France, right?"

It was more a statement than a question. His annual pilgrimage to Ville Laube was a duty he never shirked. But, of course, it was more than simply an obligation. He enjoyed catching up with the people who ran the orphanage. Although seeing the children conjured up as many haunted feelings as good. Each year he saw so many new faces as well as those who had lived there for years.

One little boy was a favorite. Remy had turned five last visit. Dark hair and eyes, solemn until you pitched him a ball—any kind. Then his face would light up. He reminded Mateo of himself at that age. Leaving Remy last year had been difficult.

When he returned this year, Mateo hoped that little boy was gone. He hoped he'd found a good family who would love and support him. He wondered what kind of man Remy would grow into. If he would learn from the right influences. Whether he'd always have plenty to eat.

Mateo confirmed, "I'll go to France."

"Maybe Bailey would like to go too."

Mateo all but lost his breath. Then he swore. "You're not trying to step into Mama Celeca's matchmaking shoes, I hope."

"Just an idea. You seem…interested."

"You saw us together for less than a minute."

"It was all the time I needed to see that you think she's different."

"Hold on." Mateo got to his feet. "Just because you've found the one, doesn't mean I need to be pushed down any aisle."

"Maybe it'd make a difference if you didn't fight it quite so hard?"

"Fight what?"

Both men's attention flew in the direction of that third voice. Natalie stood in the living room doorway. While Mateo withered—*was Bailey a step behind, within earshot?*—Alex pushed to his feet and crossed to his wife.

"Nothing, honey," he said, stealing a quick kiss. "Is the baby okay? How's Bailey?"

"Judge for yourselves."

When a stylish woman, wearing an exquisite pink cocktail number and glittering diamond drop earrings, slid into the room, Mateo did a double take then all but fell back into his seat.

*Bailey?*

While the bikini-girl turned glamour-queen crossed the room, looking as if she'd worn Chanel all her life, Natalie clasped her hands under her chin and exclaimed, "Isn't she gorgeous?"

Mateo knew he was smiling. He wanted to agree. Unfortunately he was too stunned—too delighted—to find his voice.

"The first time Mateo and I came to this place, we were twenty-two," Alex explained as a uniformed Maxim's waiter showed the foursome to a table next to the dance floor.

"Twenty-three," Mateo amended, his hand a touch away from Bailey's elbow as they navigated tables of patrons enjoying their meals and tasteful atmosphere, including tinkling background music. "You'd just had a cast off your arm after a spill on your skateboard."

"You rode a skateboard at twenty-three?" Natalie laughed as she lowered into a chair the waiter had pulled out for her.

Alex ran a finger and thumb down his tie. "And very well, might I add."

While the waiter draped linen napkins over laps, Bailey tried to contain the nerves jitterbugging in her belly. She'd dined at similar establishments, although not since her mother had died. In the old days her family had enjoyed dinner out at least once a week, but never to this particular restaurant. Wearing this glamorous dress and these dazzling earrings, not to mention the fabulous silver heels, she felt as if a magic wand had been waved and she'd emerged from her baby throw-up moment as a returned modern-day princess. For a day that had started out horrendously, she was feeling pretty fine now. Not even tired. Although catch-up jet lag would probably hit when she least expected it.

Until then she'd lap up what promised to be a wonderful night.

Some people you couldn't help but like. Natalie and Alex were that kind of folk. And Mateo...she'd wondered what he'd be like in friends' company. His smile was broader. His laugh, deeper. And when his gaze caught hers, the interested approval in his heavy-lidded eyes left her feeling surreal and believing that tonight they might have met for the first time.

"I must confess," Natalie said, casting an eye over the menu. "I love not having to think about the dishes."

"I help with that," Alex pointed out, teasing.

"And I love you for it." Natalie snatched a kiss from her husband's cheek then found Bailey's gaze. "Do you like to cook?"

"I'm no expert. But I would like to learn how to prepare meals the way they do in Italy." The dishes she'd enjoyed there had been so incredibly tasty and wholesome.

Natalie tipped her head toward Mateo. "You know your date's a bit of a chef?"

Her *date?*

Hoping no one noticed her blush, Bailey merely replied, "Really?"

"We go over for dinner at least every month," Natalie added.

Mateo qualified, "Nothing fancy. Just a way of remembering home."

"His crepes are mouth-watering," Natalie confided.

Bailey thought for a moment. "Aren't crepes French?"

"Mateo spent his first years there." As soon as the words were out, Natalie's expression dropped. "That probably wasn't my place to say."

While Mateo waved it off, Bailey puzzled over what the drama with France could be. He must have seen her curiosity.

"I lived in an orphanage the first six years of my life."

All the air left Bailey's lungs as images of dank, dark corridors and rickety cots with children who lacked love's warm touch swam up in her mind. She couldn't imagine it, particularly not for Mateo Celeca. Her lips moved a few times before she got out a single, "Oh."

"It wasn't so bad," Mateo said, obviously reading her expression. "The people who ran it were kind. We had what we needed."

"Mateo sponsors the orphanage now," Alex chipped in as, wine menu in hand, he beckoned a waiter.

Bailey sat back. Of course. Yesterday Mateo had mentioned he was a benefactor. She hadn't thought beyond the notion that any donations would be the act of someone who had the means to make a difference to others' lives. She hadn't stopped to think his work in France might be more personal. That he was paying homage to a darker past and wanted to help those who were in the same underprivileged position he'd once been.

"It's difficult for them to find funds," Mateo was saying, pouring more water. "A small bit goes a long way."

"You're too modest," Alex said.

Natalie added, "Wouldn't surprise me if one day you come back with someone who needs a good home."

"I'm hardly in a position."

Mateo's reply sounded unaffected. But Bailey detected a certain faraway gleam in his eye. Would Mateo consider adopting if he *were* in the position? If he were married?

She tried to focus on Natalie's words...something about looking forward to dessert. But, as much as she tried, Bailey couldn't shake the vision of Mateo playing with a child of his own with a faceless Mrs. Celeca smiling and gazing on. Not her, of course. She wasn't after a husband—or certainly not this soon after her recent hairy experience. One day she wanted to be part of a loving couple—like Natalie and Alex—but right now she was more than happy to be free.

Did Mateo feel the same way? Natalie wondered, stealing a glance at the doctor from beneath her lashes. Or could Mama's perennial bachelor be on the lookout for a suitable wife slash mother for an adopted child?

\* \* \*

Finishing dessert, a moist, scrumptious red velvet cake, Bailey gave a soft cry when some chocolate sauce slipped from her spoon and caught the bodice of her dress. She slid a fingertip over the spot to scoop up the drop, which only smeared the sauce. Bailey didn't wear these kinds of labels, but she knew something about the price tags. Often they cost more than her airfare home.

With dread filling her stomach, Bailey turned to Natalie. "I'll pay to have it dry-cleaned."

But Natalie wasn't troubled.

"Keep the dress, if you want. It's too snug on me after the baby anyway. In fact, there's a heap of things you could take off my hands, if you'd like."

Eyes down, Bailey dabbed the spot with her napkin. She was grateful for the offer but also embarrassed. Over dinner, they'd discussed her travels and lightly touched on the Emilio affair. Mention had been made of Mateo's suggestion she stay a couple of days as well as Natalie's proposal of work. Now the offer of a designer wardrobe...

She was beginning to feel as if she constantly had her hand out.

Bailey set aside the napkin. "That's very kind, Natalie. But you don't need to do that."

"Chances are I won't wear them again. Some mothers are eager to get back their pre-baby bodies but I quite like the fuller me."

"Hear, hear," her husband cooed close to her ear. "Now if you've finished dessert, what say we dance? Just you and me."

Natalie laughed. "Oh, you love when the three of us dance together in the living room."

"Of course." Alex kissed her hand and found his feet. "But this moment I'm happy to have only you in my arms."

As they headed for the dance floor, Bailey sighed.

"You're right. They're a magic couple. Have they been together long? The way they look at each other, anyone would guess they'd fallen in love yesterday."

"They've been together a couple of years."

"I thought they might have been school sweethearts," she said, watching them slow dance to the soft strains of a love song drifting through the room while misty beams played over their heads.

"Natalie grew up in far different circumstances than she enjoys now. Very humble beginnings."

Bailey was taken aback. "She looks as if she might've been born into royalty."

"Tonight, so do you."

Bailey's breath caught high in her chest. Was he merely being polite or was the compliment meant to have the reaction it did? Suddenly she didn't know where to look. What to say. But her mother had said to always take a compliment graciously. So, gathering herself, she lifted her eyes to his and smiled. "Thank you."

Her heart was thumping too loudly to maintain that eye contact, however, so she found Alex and Natalie on the dance floor. Natalie was laughing at something her husband had said while Alex gazed down at his wife adoringly. They radiated wedded bliss.

"It was a good day," Mateo said.

"Which day?"

"The day I helped bring their son into the world."

Elbow on the table, Bailey rested her chin in the cup of her hand. "I bet you had everything prepared and everyone on their toes."

"Quite the opposite. When she went into labor, we were at Alex's beachside holiday house. It happened quickly." He peered over toward the couple. Natalie's cheek was resting on Alex's shoulder now. "She'd miscarried years before. Alex was concerned for mother and child both."

"But nothing went wrong?"

Mateo smiled across. "You saw Reece tonight."

Bailey relaxed. "Perfect."

"Alex had always longed for a son."

"I suppose most men do," she said, wondering if she'd get a reaction.

"Most men…yes." Then, as if to put an end to that conversation, he stood and held out his hand. "Would you care to dance?"

Bailey's throat closed. Perhaps she should have seen that coming but she was at a loss for words. Mateo looked so tall and heart-stoppingly handsome, gazing down at her with those dark, penetrating eyes. Eyes that constantly intrigued her. She wanted to accept his offer. Wanted the opportunity to know the answer to her earlier question—how it would feel to have his arms surround her. Here, in this largely neutral, populated setting, she could find out.

She placed her hand in his. That telling warmth rose again, tingling over her flesh, heating her cheeks and her neck. His eyes seemed to smile into hers as she found her feet and together they moved to the dance floor, occupied by other couples, some absorbed more in the song than their partner, others locked in each other's arms and ardent gazes.

Bailey couldn't stop her heart from hammering as Mateo turned and rested a hot palm low on her back while bringing their still-clasped hands to his lapel. Concentrating to level her breathing, she slid and rested her left hand over the broad slope of his shoulder at the same time the tune segued into an even slower, more romantic song and the lights dimmed a fraction more.

They began to move and instantly Bailey was gripped by the heat radiating from his body, burrowing into and warming hers. Her senses seemed heightened. She was infinitely aware of his thumb circling over the dip in her back. Her lungs celebrated being filled with his mesmerizing scent. Strangely, all the happenings around them faded into a suddenly bland background. When a corner of his mouth slanted—the corner with that small scar—her pulse rate spiked and her blood began to sizzle. She'd wanted to know. Now she did. Having Mateo's arms around her—soothing and at the same time exciting her—was like being held by some kind of god.

"So you'll be working for Natalie's agency?"

"While I was dressing—make that *re*dressing—Natalie explained they'd lost three cleaners in the past couple of weeks."

"You don't mind the work?"

"I'm grateful for it. And it won't be forever."

He grinned. "Sounds as if you're making plans."

Seeing her father today cemented what she'd already come to realize. Education was the key to independence. "I'm going to apply to college."

"Do you know what you'll study? Teaching? Nursing?"

"Maybe I should become a doctor," she joked. "Dr. Bailey Ross. Neurosurgeon." She laughed and so did he, but not in a condescending way. "I want to do something that makes people happy," she went on. "That makes them feel good about themselves."

"Whatever you choose I'm sure you'll do well."

"Because you know I'm an A student, right?"

"Because I think you have guts. Persistence will get you most places in life."

Unless you were talking about her father. The more she'd tried, the more he'd turned his back. Cut her off. There came a time when a person needed to accept they should look forward rather than back.

But then she retraced her thoughts back to Mateo's

words—*I think you have guts.* She gave him a dubious look. "Was that another compliment?"

A line cut between his brows. "Tell you what. We'll make a deal. I promise not to mention the money you owe Mama in a derogatory way if you promise something in return. It has to do with my vacation."

She couldn't think what. Except maybe, "You want me to house sit?"

"I want you to come with me to France."

Bailey's legs buckled. When she fell against him, bands of steel stopped her from slipping farther. But the way her front grazed against his, his help only made her sudden case of weakness worse.

Siphoning down a breath, she scooped back some hair fallen over her face. "Sorry. Did you just say you want me to go to France with you?"

"I got the impression you hadn't seen Paris."

"I was saving it for last. I never got there."

His smile flashed white beneath the purple lights. "Now's your chance."

She took a step back but more deep breaths didn't help. She cupped her forehead.

"Mateo, I'm confused."

He brought her near again and flicked a glance over his shoulder at the couple dancing nearby. "Blame Alex. He suggested it."

She tried to ignore the delicious press of his body, the masculine scent of his skin, the way his hard thigh nudged between hers as he rotated them around in a tight circle. "You know I don't have money for a ticket to Europe." Her jaw hardened. "And I won't take any more charity."

"Even if you'd be doing me a favor, keeping me company?" His dark gaze, so close, roamed her face. "One good turn deserves another."

"That's not fair."

His mouth turned into a solemn line. "There wouldn't be any conditions."

Bailey blinked. Maybe because he was Mama's grandson, she hadn't considered he might be trying to buy more than her company.

With the lights slowly spinning and couples floating by, oxygen burned in her lungs while she tried to come up with an appropriate reply to a question that had knocked her for a loop. After an agonizingly long moment, she felt the groan rumble in his chest and his grip on her hand loosen.

"You're right," he said. "Crazy idea."

"It's not that I wouldn't *like* to go." She'd always wanted to see Paris. It was her biggest disappointment that she'd planned to save France for last rather than enjoying that country first. "But I've just got back," she explained. "I'm starting that job Monday." She finished with the obvious excuse. "We don't know each other."

He dismissed it with a self-deprecating smile. "Like I said. Forget I spoke."

But as his palm skimmed up her back and he tucked her crown under his chin while they continued to dance, although she knew she really should, Bailey couldn't forget.

At the end of the evening, she and Mateo dropped Natalie and Alex off then drove back to his place in a loaded silence.

Her breathing was heavier than it ought to be. Was his heartbeat hammering as fast as hers, or was she the only one who couldn't get that enthralling dance and tempting offer out of her mind? Mateo had asked her to jet away to France with him. What had he been thinking? What was she thinking still considering it after having already told him no?

Bailey pressed on her stomach as her insides looped.

Admittedly, she was uniquely attracted to Mateo Celeca; he had a presence, a confidence that was difficult to ignore. But how did she feel about him beyond the physical? Yesterday, after he'd tried to degrade her over the money she'd loaned, she'd thought him little more than a self-serving snob. And yet, tonight, when she'd met his friends…had been his *date*…

Her stomach looped again.

After that episode with Emilio, the last thing she wanted was to get caught up in a man. Any man. Even when he gave generously to the orphanage where he'd spent his earliest years. Even when she felt as if she'd found a slice of heaven in his arms.

Since that dance, the air between them had crackled with a double dose of anticipation and electricity. If, when they got home, they started talking, got to touching, she didn't know if she'd want to stop.

After they pulled into the garage, Mateo opened her door and helped her out. Their hands lingered, the contact simmered, before his fingers slipped from hers and he moved to unlock the internal door and flick on the lights. Gathering herself—straightening her dress and patting down her burning cheeks—Bailey followed into the kitchen.

"Care for a nightcap?" he asked, poised near the fridge.

Bailey clasped the pocketbook Natalie had loaned her under her chin and, resolute, made a believable excuse.

"I'm beat. Practically dead on my feet. Think I'll go straight up and turn in."

As she headed out, Bailey laughed at herself. He might not even *want* to kiss her. She could be blowing this awareness factor all out of proportion. But prevention was always better than cure. She'd accepted his invitation to stay a couple more nights. She didn't want to do something they both might regret in the morning. And if they got involved that way, there *would* be regrets. Neither was looking for a relationship. She certainly didn't want to get caught up in a man who, only yesterday, had as good as called her thief. A man who might set her pulse racing but who could never get serious about a woman in her situation.

And yet, he had asked her to France....

When Mateo reached the foot of the staircase, he stopped and turned to face her. Standing there, simply gazing at one another in the semi-darkness, she had this silly urge to play down the scene, stick out a hand and offer to shake. But, given past experience, probably best they didn't touch.

"Thank you for the lovely evening," she said.

"You're welcome."

Still, he didn't move.

"Well..." Clutching her pocketbook tighter, she set a foot onto the lowest stair. "Good night."

"Good night, Bailey."

When she began to climb, he started up too. They ascended together until they hit a point where the stairs divided into separate branches. A fork in the road.

Her stomach twisting with nerves, she chanced a look across. He was looking at her too, a masculine silhouette a mere arm's length away.

Swirling desire pooled low in her belly and she frowned. "You're not moving."

"Neither are you."

Rolling back her shoulders, she issued a firm and final, "Good night."

She hiked the rest of the stairs, right to the top. But before she could head off down to her suite, curiosity won out again. She edged a gaze over her right shoulder, to where she'd left Mateo standing seconds ago. What she saw sent her heart dropping in her chest.

He was gone. And wasn't that what she'd wanted? What she knew was best for both their sakes?

Still, she stared at that vacant spot a moment more, feeling strangely empty and no longer so pretty in her pink designer dress. Shifting her weight, she finally rotated back…and ran right into Mateo's solid chest.

Her heels balanced on the edge of the stairs, Bailey toppled back. But before she could fall, his arm hooked around her waist, pulling her effortlessly against him. *Déjà vu*. With the bodice of her dress pinned to his chest—with every one of her reflexes in a tailspin—she worked to catch her breath before croaking out, "I thought you were tired."

"*You* said you were tired." His dark eyes gleamed. "I'm wide awake."

When she felt his hardness pressed against her belly, she gulped down another breath only to feel him grow harder still. Any doubts she may have had were blown away. The way her own blood was throbbing, taking this steadily growing attraction further seemed frighteningly inevitable.

"Maybe…" She wet her suddenly dry lips. "Maybe we should have that nightcap after all."

His gaze dropped to her lips. "What kind of nightcap?"

"What would you like?"

His mouth came to within a whisper of hers.

"I'd like you."

# Six

He didn't waste time waiting for her reply. Bailey supposed he saw all he needed to know in her eyes. He angled and, before she could think beyond *I need you to kiss me*, she was in his arms and he was moving down the hall, away from her suite, headed for his.

The tall double doors of his suite were open. He didn't bother to kick them shut after he'd carried her through. Nor did he switch on any lamps. What she could make out in the shadows was courtesy of the light filtering in from the hall as well as the moonbeams slanting through a bank of soaring arched windows that looked out over that garden and its statues below.

He stopped at the foot of his bed and his voice dropped to a low rasp.

"This is what you want?"

Instinctively, her palm wove around the sandpaper of his

jaw. She filled her lungs with his scent then skimmed the pad of her thumb over the dent in his chin.

"Yes," she murmured.

His chest expanded, his grip tightened then he lifted her higher in his arms as his head came purposefully down. When his mouth claimed hers, Bailey couldn't contain the moan of deepest desire the sensation dragged from her throat. She didn't want to contain *anything*. And as his mouth worked magic against hers and his stubble grazed and teased her skin, she pressed herself up and in, needing to feel even closer. Needing him as close as it got.

Her fingers wound through his hair while his throat rumbled with satisfaction and the kiss deepened. Even as her mind and body raged with desire, she was lucid enough to recognize the simple truth. Whatever it was that had sparked when they'd met, it had grown to a point where now they were downright hungry for each other. *Starving* for each other's touch in a primal nothing-held-back, nothing-taboo, kind of way. She could never get enough of this burn...of the flames that already leapt and blazed nearly out of control.

When his lips gradually left hers, she felt dizzy. Her eyes remained closed but she heard and felt his breathing. At the edges of her mind, she wondered...why was this coming together so intense? So combustible?

He dipped to sit her on the edge of the mattress. With moonlight spilling in, she dragged the dress up over her head then, in her lingerie, watched as he wound the shirt off his shoulders, the sleeves from his arms. When he was naked, he bent near, slid an arm around her waist and drew her up to stand again. Holding her chin, he ran the wet tip of his tongue along the open seam of her mouth while, at her back, he unsnapped the strapless bra with one deft flick. His palm pressed down the dent of her spine and slipped into the back of her panties. She whimpered as her womb contracted and quivered…a tantalizing prelude to the climax she couldn't wait to enjoy.

His fingertips pressed and seared into her flesh while his mouth covered hers completely again, and all the time her insides clenched and pulsed while her limbs and mind went to mush. She wanted this heaven to go on forever. But even more, she wanted him bearing down on top of her. Inside of her. Filling and fulfilling her *now*.

Her hands ironed down his sides. When she reached his lean hips, she urged him forward, toward her and the bed. With their mouths still joined, she felt his smile before he broke the kiss long enough to wrench back the sheets. With a determined gleam in his eyes, he crowded until the back of her legs met the cool edge of the mattress. His big hands ringed her waist and her feet left the ground long enough for him to lay her gently down. He followed a heartbeat behind.

Looming above her, everything seemed to still as he searched her eyes in a world of midnight shadows. His deep low voice seemed to fill the room.

"I didn't ask you to stay here for this."

She drew an aimless pattern through the hair at the base of his throat.

"I know."

"Although I'm not sorry you agreed."

She matched his grin. "I'm not sorry you asked."

He dropped a tender kiss at the side of her mouth, a barely there touch that shot a fountain of star-tipped sparks through her every fiber.

"Come with me to France," he murmured against her lips.

She groaned. The temptation was huge. She'd said no and had meant it. She was starting a job Monday. She didn't want to take more charity. But those considerations didn't seem quite so solid since he'd carried her to his bed.

Closing her eyes, she sighed. He was kissing the sensitive spot beneath her left lobe.

"What if I say please?"

She bit her lip. He was *killing* her.

"I'll tell you what." She filed her fingers up over his burning ears, through his hair. "I promise not to say no again if you promise not to ask."

He moved lower to nuzzle the arc of her neck. "I don't like when you say no."

"To everything but that, Mateo…" She hooked her leg around his hip and drew him close. *"Yes, yes, yes."*

Mateo couldn't stop to think about how his unexpected encounter with Bailey Ross had come to this. How they'd gone from strangers to opponents to lovers in less than two days. As he tasted a leisurely line along the perfumed sweep of her shoulder, he only knew these sensations were too intense to analyze. More intense—more vital—than he'd ever had before.

When her heel dug into the back of his thigh, letting him know again she was on the same page, he ground up against her but then grit his teeth and blocked that insistent heady push. Tonight would be sweet torture. He'd need every ounce of willpower to keep this encounter—his pleasure—from peaking too soon.

Working to steady his breathing, his pace, he sculpted a palm over the outside of one full breast as he shifted lower. His mouth covered that nipple before his teeth grazed up all the way, tugging the tip of the bead. Her hands had been winding through his hair but now she dug in and held on as she shuddered and moaned beneath him. He heard her desperate swallow and listened, pleased that her breathing sounded more labored than his own. Savoring the way her breasts rose and fell on each lungful of air, he twirled his tongue around that tip and tried to ignore the fact his every inch was ready to explode.

With her leg twined over the back of his, her pelvis began to move in time with the adoring sweep of his tongue. She murmured something he didn't catch. But he wouldn't ask and stop the bone-melting rhythm their bodies had fallen into. He didn't want to interrupt for a moment the feel of her body stirring beneath his. He could lie here all night, doing precisely this.

If only his erection wasn't begging for more.

He repositioned again, higher to savor the honey of her lips at the same time his touch wove down: over her ribs, the curve of her waist, the subtle flare of a hip, then up over the same terrain. He was performing a repeat descent, stroking and playing—anticipating the added treasures he'd discover this time around—when she grunted, shifted and pushed against his chest.

He froze. Then, eyes snapping open, he rolled away. What was wrong? Had he hurt her?

When she slid over too—on *top* of him—he held his brow and almost laughed with relief.

"What are you doing?"

Crouched on his lap, she slid her hips one way and the other then tossed back the hair fallen over her face. "What do you think?"

She slid *up* a little this time then down over his throbbing shaft. That sent him reeling way too close to the edge. He was thrilled she was so completely in the zone that she wanted to take the reins, but any more of that kind of maneuvering and he'd reach the finish line way too soon.

He flipped her over so she lay on her back again, him firmly on top. While she peered up at him, a saucy glint in her eyes, his hand burrowed between them, down the front of her panties, and his erection grew heavier still. She was warm and moist. When his touch curled up between her folds and pressed against a woman's most sensitive spot, she let out a time honored sound that told him she was ready.

Leaning over, he opened his bedside drawer, found the pack then tore a single foiled wrap with his teeth. As he rolled on protection, her fingers sluiced up and down his sides. Oh, he wanted to take this slower. Make it last. But this time, with this lady, that wasn't going to happen.

Sheathed, he positioned himself, took a long slow kiss from her welcoming mouth then eased inside. Her walls clamped around him at the same time her hips lifted and she opened her mouth wider, inviting him deeper.

With one arm curled around her head, he drove in and clenched every muscle as a mind-tingling burn hardened him more. He felt as if he was drowning in a lake of fire. All exposed nerve endings and profound sizzling need.

Bailey trailed her fingers down his neck, felt the cords bulging and pulsing, and melted more. The way he moved with her left her breathless while his mouth on hers raised her up. She wanted this moment to go on forever. Never wanted the steep waves of pleasure to wane or fade. And yet they both needed to go that bit further. Needed to be thrown up to the stars and explode on their way back down.

He was snatching slow kisses from her brow, from her cheek, holding her hip securely as his strokes grew ever stronger and longer. The friction was scolding, the pleasure beyond what she could take.

And then his kisses stopped and his body grew still and hard. She sensed his every tendon stretched trip wire tight, could feel his heart thumping and pounding in his ears. The mind-altering fire at her core intensified, somehow changing in dimension and in shape. Then, in one finite moment, in less time than it took to suck down a breath, all the universe contracted into a single high-voltage speck. Beyond that nothing existed. Nothing but black.

When he thrust again—when he hit that secret wanting spot—she threw back her head, spread her wings and flew.

# Seven

"Tell me more about France."

At the sound of Bailey's voice filtering though the predawn mist, Mateo lifted his head off the pillow and dropped a kiss on her silky crown.

They'd made love well into the night. The first time had been incredible. Incomparable. But over far too quickly. The second time they'd slowed down enough to thoroughly explore each other's bodies and share their most intimate needs. The third time they'd come apart in each other's arms might have been the best…the time when he'd truly begun to see that this joining meant more than simply great sex. The connection they shared, the amazing way they fit, was special.

That didn't mean he'd changed his mind about getting serious. About settling down. Invariably marriage meant children. Children of his own. But his practice was his life. He'd put all he had into doing his best and building a home that was his. He had everything he needed. Everything and more. He felt secure, and that was life's most valuable gift.

If he were to become a husband...a father...well, he couldn't think of a more vulnerable place to be. There were concerns over the complications in the womb, worry about childhood disease, not to mention the fact that in this world he had no living family now, other than Mama. If fate stepped in and left his child without parents...

Mateo swallowed against the pit formed in his throat.

This is why he never let himself analyze relationships too deeply, particularly following the "after all she could get" Linda incident. He was a man of influence and means who could choose what course his life should take. Tonight he'd chosen to act on the undeniable chemistry he shared with Bailey. Given she'd asked about France a moment ago, he hoped they could continue to enjoy the attraction a while longer. For however long it might last.

Nestled in the crook of his arm, she twined to rest her chin on her thatched hands, which lay on one side of his chest.

"What's it like?" She asked, looking beautifully rumpled and sleep deprived but content. "Everyone seems to love Paris. Did you ever get into the city when you were young?"

"As a child?"

"Uh-huh."

"I didn't know Paris existed."

She sat up a little, bracing her weight on an elbow as she searched his eyes in the misty light. Outside, the morning sun peeked over the distant rise, painting a translucent halo around her head.

Her voice softened when she asked, "Were you very lonely there? At the orphanage, I mean."

Mateo's jaw tensed. His first instinct was to push her question aside. If anyone, including Alex or Natalie, brought up his childhood, he rarely gave away too much. The past was past…even if it was never forgotten.

But lying here with Bailey after the extraordinary night they'd shared, he felt closer to her this minute than anyone he'd known. That shouldn't be. He'd loved and respected Ernesto. He adored Mama. He had friends he would do anything for and, he was certain, vice versa.

And yet, he couldn't deny it. Whatever drew him to Bailey Ross was a force unto itself. He wanted to share more than his bed with her tonight. He wanted to open up…at least this once.

"I wasn't lonely," he began. "I had many friends and adults I knew that cared for us all." He thought more deeply and frowned. "I did feel *alone,* which is different, but I was too young to understand why. I never knew my parents. No one explained about the 'who' or the 'when.' I didn't realize a life outside the orphanage existed until my fifth birthday."

Sitting up, she wrapped the sheet around her breasts, under her arms. "What happened on your birthday? I don't suppose you had a party."

"From what I can recall, the day was pleasant enough. Everyone sang to me after lunch. I got a special dessert along with two friends I picked out." He searched his memory and blinked then smiled. "I received a gift. People from town donated them. I tore open the paper and found a wooden train. Green chimney," he recalled. "Red wheels. I thought I was made." But his smile slipped. "Then my best friend said he was going away. That a mother and father were taking him home."

Bailey tucked her knees up and hugged her sheet-clad legs. "It mustn't have made sense."

He flinched at a familiar pang in his chest and for a moment he wanted to end that conversation and talk about the France people found in travel books. The "gay Paree" with which Bailey would identify. But she wasn't listening to this story to snatch some voyeuristic thrill. He saw from her unguarded expression that she wanted to learn more about the man she'd made love with tonight. He wanted to learn more about her too. So, to be fair, he took a breath and went on.

"I knew some children were there with us, then, suddenly, they weren't. No one spoke about it, or if they did, I didn't have the maturity to latch on and work the steps out. But this time, with Henri, I began to see."

"You realized something was missing."

He nodded.

*Yes, missing. Exactly.*

"From a second-story window," he said, "where the boys slept, I watched Henri slide into a shiny white car and drive away with two people, a man and woman. I shouted out and waved, but he didn't look up. Not until the last minute. Then he saw me. I think he called out my name, too."

With her blue eyes glittering in the early dawn light, she tipped nearer and held his arm.

"Oh, Mateo…that must have been awful."

Not *awful*. "Eye-opening. Unsettling. From then on I was more aware of others leaving. More aware that I was left behind. I tried to find him a few years back. It would be great to see him again. Hear if his memories match mine."

Henri had been his first friend.

Mateo touched the scar on his upper lip—the one he'd received when Henri had thrown a ball too hard and he'd missed catching it—then, dismissing the pang in his chest, he swung his legs over the side of the bed and reached for the water decanter. After pouring two glasses, he offered her one.

She drank, watching him over the rim of her glass.

"How did Mama Celeca find you?" she asked, handing the empty glass back.

"Not Mama. Ernesto." He took another mouthful and set both glasses down. "Years before, he'd been in love with a woman who'd carried his child. A friend, returning from France, let Ernesto know he'd heard that Antoinette had given birth in a town called Ville Laube and had offered her baby boy up for adoption there. Ernesto flew straight over. He found the orphanage his friend had described but not his boy."

Clutching the sheet under her chin, Bailey sagged.

"I thought you'd say that *you* were Ernesto's child."

"Not through blood. But apparently my parents were Italian, too. I was left there when I was three, but I don't remember any life before the orphanage."

She shifted and he waited until she'd settled alongside of him.

"One day after Henri had gone," he went on, "I saw this sad looking man sitting alone in the courtyard under a huge oak. His hands were clasped between his thighs. His eyes were downcast. When I edged closer, I saw they were bloodshot. He'd been crying. I knew because some times in the mornings I had bloodshot eyes too."

His throat closed as the memory grew stronger and flooded his mind with a mix of emotions, sounds and smells from the past. The scent of lavender. The noise of children playing. The deepest feeling that, if only he knew this sad man, he would like him.

But, "I didn't know why the man was unhappy. I had no idea what to say. I only knew I felt for him. So I sat down and put my hand over his."

Mateo looked across. In the growing light, he thought he saw a single tear speed down Bailey's cheek. Ironic, because after that day he couldn't remember ever crying again.

"And he took you home," she said.

"Home to Italy, yes. And later here to Australia."

"So Mama Celeca isn't your real grandmother?"

"She's always treated me as though she is. She accepted me from the moment Ernesto brought me back to Casa Buona. I helped Ernesto in his office during the day and hung out with Mama in the kitchen in the evenings."

"Where she taught you to cook."

Remembering the aromas and Mama's careful instructions, he smiled and nodded. "The old-fashioned way."

"The *best* way." She turned more toward him. "Did Ernesto find his boy?"

"No." And that was the tragedy. "Although he never gave up hope."

"Did he ever marry?"

"Never. He died two years ago."

"I remember. Mama told me."

"He wanted to be buried back home. Mama was heartbroken at her son's death, but that, at least, gave her a measure of comfort." He voiced the words that were never far from his heart. "He was a good son. A good father. Last year I had a call from a woman, Ernesto's biological son's widow. After he'd been killed in a hit-and-run, she'd found papers from the orphanage that helped her track Ernesto down. She'd wanted him to know."

She lowered her head and murmured, so softly, he barely heard. "Is all this why Natalie thinks you might bring home a child from France one day?"

"Adoption rules were more flexible in the country back then."

"You'd have no trouble proving you could care for a child. I haven't known you long but I know you'd make a good father…like Ernesto."

A knot twisted in his chest. Sharp. Uncomfortable. He'd already explained.

"I'm too busy for a child." He looked inside and, flinching, admitted, "Too selfish."

When his temple throbbed, he turned to plump up his pillow. They ought to get some sleep, Bailey especially.

They lay down again, front to front, curled up tight. Mateo was drifting when she murmured against his chest.

"When are you expected in France?"

"Next week."

"I told Natalie I'd start work for her in two days' time." She lifted her head to glance out the window at the ever-rising sun. "Make that tomorrow."

Mateo was suddenly wide awake. If Bailey was thinking about changing her mind and coming with him…

"Natalie won't hold anything against you for taking a week off."

In fact, he was sure she'd be happy at the news. Natalie made no secret of the fact that she would love to see her husband's best friend settled with someone nice. Not that that was in the cards.

She snuggled into him more. "I'd feel as if I were copping out."

"Visiting the Eiffel Tower, the Louvre, perhaps. But the orphanage?" He skimmed a hand down her smooth warm arm. "It's not a cop-out."

After several minutes, her breathing grew deeper and he thought she was finally asleep. He was letting oblivion overtake him too when she spoke again.

"Mama's right."

He forced his heavy lids open. "About what?"

She rubbed her cheek against his chest and murmured in a groggy voice, "You are a good man."

# Eight

As Mateo predicted, Natalie wasn't the least bit upset when the following day, Bailey rang to explain.

"I know I'm only starting," she began, sitting behind Mateo's desk in his home office. "I'm so grateful for the chance, but I was wondering if I could possibly ask for the week after next off?"

"Are you all right?"

"I feel great." In fact, better than great. "Mateo asked whether I might like to fly with him to France."

Bailey jerked the receiver from her ear as Natalie squealed down the line.

"Sorry," Natalie said. "I'm just excited for you. For you both. And I'll need to go through my wardrobe with a fine-tooth comb. In late October, you're going to need some warm clothes over there."

The following day Bailey dived into the first of her cleaning jobs. The work was constant and anything but glamorous, but she rolled up her sleeves and took pride in making sure the floors were spotless and that the kitchens and bathrooms sparkled. She was being constructive, pushing forward, earning her way and feeling rewarded because of it.

When Friday came, Bailey was exhausted by the time she got to Mateo's place. But she was also elated. When he opened the door for her, she threw out her hand.

Mateo took the slip of paper she held. "What's this?"

"A printout of the receipt from my transfer."

Mateo had set up an account solely for the purpose of her loan repayments.

When he smiled, he truly looked pleased.

"We should celebrate."

"What do you suggest?"

"Dinner at this little Italian taverna five minutes from here. Unless you're too tired…"

"No." Suddenly she was feeling pepped up. She *should* celebrate. This was a noteworthy step toward reaching her goals. "But on one condition. I pay my way."

One brow hiked up. "You're supposed to be saving, not spending."

"We go dutch or we don't go."

They went and enjoyed a carafe of Chianti, twirled and slurped spaghetti, paid half each and, when they arrived home, made love as they'd done every night since their first.

Afterward, as they lay tangled in each other's arms and Mateo stroked her hair, Bailey thought back on the week, feeling happier than she had in a long while. She'd had fun backpacking around Europe and she'd enjoyed herself in Italy—before Emilio had cornered her the way he had. But now, here with Mateo, she'd stepped up to a different level of understanding.

Funnily enough, she felt settled. Living in this grand palace with a strong-minded millionaire doctor…unbelievable, but she felt as if she belonged.

But this hyper exhilaration was only temporary. It wasn't real. Wouldn't last. Staying in this extraordinary house with this extraordinary man was a fairy tale she happened to fall into. Clearly, Mateo had been with other women but he'd never committed, as Mama had told her more than once. There was no reason to believe that what they'd shared this week would last either.

She was a big girl. She was fine with that.

Smoothing a palm over his chest, she smiled softly. This time with Mateo might be temporary, but she planned to enjoy each minute and, when it was over, cherish every memory. It was a temporary happy ending to an unpleasant episode in her life. And Paris was yet to come!

Two days later they flew halfway around the world on the sumptuous private jet Mateo hired. Nibbling on mouth-watering cheese and fruit platters, feeling as if she were lounging at a luxury retreat rather than an aircraft, Bailey was certain she would never view air travel the same again.

It was early evening when they landed at Charles de Gaulle. The weather was cool in the City of Light, but the darkening sky held no threat of rain or sleet. Bailey tugged Natalie's silk-lined designer jacket higher around her ears and, loving the chilly nip on her nose—so different from the warm weather in Australia this time of year—slid into the back of the chauffeur driven limousine, with Mateo entering behind her. She guessed her mother would have felt just as excited when she'd arrived in this famous city years before.

As the driver performed a pared down city tour, she lapped up the scenery while Mateo pointed out noteworthy spots. The iconic spire of the Eiffel Tower, the history effused Arc de Triomphe. Then they passed the Louvre and the Pyramid.

Bailey sighed. "I wonder if there's a person in the world who doesn't want to see the *Mona Lisa*."

His hand found hers and squeezed. "We'll spend an entire day there."

"Before or after we've spent a morning strolling along the Seine? And I want to sip coffee at a gorgeous sidewalk café and gaze up at the obelisk at the Place de la Concorde."

Mateo nuzzled her hair. "We'll do it all. I promise."

They checked into one of the best hotels in the city, only steps from the Champs-Elysees. Bailey held her pounding heart as she took in magnificent glittering chandeliers, mirror polished floors, classic marble statuettes and fountains of fresh scented flowers. She wasn't interested in being wealthy. Money did *not* buy happiness—ask her father. But this kind of experience was different. It was about appreciating another culture. About absorbing history. Enriching one's life by seeing how others communicated and lived. This hotel was a prime example of crème de la crème. Tomorrow they would move among the less fortunate…children without family or homes of their own. Children who lived as Mateo had once done.

As Mateo checked in at the reception desk, Bailey absorbed his effortless sophisticated air. Calling into that orphanage each year must be a bittersweet experience. Were his memories of that place still sharp or were those long ago days more like a dream…as these days would no doubt be to her in a few years' time?

When they reached their suite, Bailey drifted toward a twinkling view, visible past a soaring window, while Mateo wasted no time coming up behind and enfolding her in his arms.

"It's said that Paris in daytime is only resting," he murmured against her hair. "That the city only comes to life at night. So," his breath felt warm on the sweep of her neck, "are you ready to take on the town?"

"I'd love to say yes, but I need sleep." And she didn't want to be dead on her feet tomorrow when they reached their first and most important destination—the orphanage.

"Hungry then?" He twined her arms around his and pressed her extra close. "Or perhaps we ought to check out that fine piece of furniture."

Eyes drifting closed, she hummed out a grin. He meant that canopied bed.

Turning her back on the view—on the glittering spectacle of Paris at night—she rotated until they were facing one another then gifted his stubbly jaw with a lingering kiss.

"I like that idea," she murmured. "Let's freshen up first."

"Only if we do it together."

He led her through to a marble finished room, featuring a classic clawfoot tub, big enough for two. After kissing her thoroughly, a toe-curling taste of what was to come, he left to order up refreshments.

Floating, Bailey ran the gold gooseneck faucet, added salts and bubble liquid into the rising water then, humming, twirled her hair up and set it with a single pin. After stripping off her shoes and Natalie-sponsored clothes, she threaded her arms through an oversized courtesy robe but stopped when she caught her reflection in the window.

Holding her fluttering stomach, she wanted to imprint this precise moment…this dreamlike feeling…into her memory forever. Beyond that pane, Paris was buzzing with music and laughter and life. Even more amazing, beyond that door, Mateo Celeca was looking forward to sharing this bath with her.

Tying the robe's sash, she lowered onto the edge of the bath's porcelain rim and took stock.

Two weeks ago she'd been near desperate to get home,

for the chance to start again. Two weeks ago she'd thought constantly about her father...reliving those earlier happier years...regretting that their relationship had come unstuck. When she'd seen Damon Ross in the city during that exhausting second day back in Australia, her heart had screamed out for her to walk over. To give them another chance. The cab's timely arrival had put a stop to that idea, thank heaven, because there was nothing she could say that she hadn't said before. Nothing she could do that would mend those flattened fences. She'd tried in the past, over and again. The more she'd persisted, the more her father had only wanted to push her away.

One day, perhaps, they'd talk again, Bailey decided, swirling a hand through the deepening warm bubble-filled pool. But that couldn't happen until she'd proven herself to herself. She was young. With the right attitude she could accomplish anything. Go anywhere.

Right now, however, she wanted to help Mateo accomplish his goals here in France. Of course, she also wanted to enjoy this time they had here as lovers. Still, she was mindful of keeping this whirlwind romance in perspective. It would be ridiculously easy to fall in love with an amazing man like Mateo Celeca only to be left behind.

After this time together, that he was so successful and she was so definitely not didn't worry her so much. His state of mind, as far as commitment was concerned, did. She'd briefly wondered whether he might want to find a wife and adopt that little boy he'd spoken about. But Mateo was married to his career and wanted to keep it that way. He'd confessed he was too busy for a family of his own. Too selfish.

Despite his mansion back home and all his lavish possessions, she couldn't believe he was self-centered. Although Mateo kept him well hidden, the orphaned boy he'd once been was still there deep inside. The boy who'd had no one and nothing. She felt the bracelet heavy on her wrist and smiled softly. People had different ways of dealing with the past.

The adjoining door fanned open and Bailey, brought back, pushed herself to her feet. Mateo entered the room carrying a silver service tray holding two champagne flutes and a dish of sliced pear. At the sight of him, the tips of her breasts tingled and her blood instantly heated. But for the white serving cloth draped over his forearm, he was naked.

Her gaze drank him in…tall, toned and completely comfortable in his own gorgeous bronzed skin.

"I hope you didn't answer the door to room service dressed like that," she said, holding off tightening her robe's sash.

"I doubt they'd bat an eye."

With his gaze lidded and hot, he sauntered closer. After placing the tray on a ledge next to the bath, he poured the champagne then handed over a flute. The glasses pinged as they touched.

"To Paris," he said.

"To Paris," she agreed and sipped.

As the bubbles fizzed on her tongue then slid down her throat, Mateo selected the largest piece of pear, bit in and watched juice sluice down his thumb.

"Delicious," he said and licked his lips.

He offered her a taste. But when she moved to take a bite, he lowered the fruit and touched the piece to the hollow of her throat, drawing a calculated circle before sliding the pear farther down.

Pulse rate climbing, Bailey closed her eyes and waited for the cool to glide between the dip of her cleavage, under the folds of her robe. Instead Mateo lowered his head and sucked at the juice slipping a single line down her throat.

Soaking up each and every thrilling sensation, Bailey sighed and let her neck rock back.

As his mouth slid lower, the sash at her waist was released. A moment later, cool air feathered over her exposed breasts, her thighs, at the same time a big palm trailed the plane of her quivering belly then higher, over her ribs and tender swell of each breast.

He nipped her lower lip and spoke of the near overflowing tub. "That bath needs attention."

Winding her arms around his neck, she whispered in his ear, "Me first."

# Nine

Although the morning was far too fresh to leave the top down, Mateo arranged a late model French convertible for the road trip.

From Bailey's wide-eyed expression as they cruised beyond the city limits, she was in thrall of the unfolding country scenes…roads lined with trees whose leaves had been kissed with the russets and reds of autumn and far-reaching vineyards busy with the business of harvest. She marveled at the *colombage* houses with their geometric half-timber patterns. Mateo had obliged when she'd begged to stop at a rustic farmhouse with a leaded-glass feature that highlighted a coat-of-arms on the lintel above.

And there was so much more ahead of them.

He didn't dwell on the niggling doubts that had surfaced since she'd accepted his invitation to join him on this trip, although at times he had found himself wondering if he'd acted too quickly—whether he was a fool believing Bailey was cut from a different cloth than Linda. But they were here now, and he intended for them both to make the most of it.

"After we visit the children," Mateo said, stepping on the gas, "we'll go back to Paris and spend a couple of days. Longer if you want."

"Two days will be wonderful," Bailey said, focused on a tractor trundling over a patchwork of fields. "I told Natalie I'd be back on deck by next Monday."

"She won't mind—"

"I know she wouldn't," Bailey said, looking over at him, "but I've taken up enough slack. Natalie was good enough to offer me a job. I need to step up to the plate."

Changing down gears to take a bend, Mateo was deep in thought. That Natalie had offered Bailey a job didn't bother him in the least. What did rankle was the fact that she scrubbed floors to pay back money he would never miss. After the time they'd spent together, the intimate moments they'd shared, if he didn't know that she'd argue, he'd tell her to forget the debt. He'd much rather set her up in an apartment and, if she followed through with the idea, finance her way through university, like Ernesto had done for him.

Of course he'd be clear that any arrangement would not include a marriage proposal. From what she'd told him of her experience with Emilio Conti, she'd be glad of the clarification. She'd had one close call. She wouldn't be looking forward to the sound of wedding bells.

That made two of them. He liked children but he did not want the responsibility of bringing his own into this world. Life was too uncertain. No one could convince him otherwise.

They reached the town by eleven. Five minutes later, the convertible made its way up the long dirt ruts that led to the Ville Laube Chapelle, a fine example of early French architecture which had been restored over time and transformed into a children's home last century. Bailey sighed, taking in the hundred-foot steeple and angels carrying the instruments of Passion adorning the ornamental gables. Unpolished strong buttresses contrasted with the intricate foliage friezes and elevated stained-glass windows that captured then speared back the sun's late morning light.

Mateo's throat thickened enough he had to clear it. So many years on and still, whenever this scene greeted him, he was six again…feeling uncertain again.

As they parked and slid out from the car, a girl with short-cropped, blond hair, standing beneath the enormous oak Mateo remembered, gawped, dropped her skipping rope and raced inside. A moment later, children poured out through opened double doors that near reached the sky. Eager women, alternatively clapping hands to order the scattered children and patting down their dresses, followed. One lady, with chestnut hair that bounced on the shoulders of her yellow blouse, hurried to line the children up in the yard. Madame Nichole Garnier, Mateo's contact and current director of the orphanage.

Many girls held bouquets, flowers plucked from the home's gardens or nearby meadow. Every boy had their shoulders pinned back. When the assembly was reasonably quiet, beaming, Madame Garnier swept up to greet her guests.

"Monsieur Celeca, it is wonderful to see you again," she said in French. Light green eyes sparkled as she came forward and kissed him, first on one cheek then the other. She turned to Bailey. "And you've brought a friend."

"Madame Nichole Garnier." Mateo spoke in English, knowing Madame would follow suit. "This is Bailey Ross."

"Mademoiselle Ross."

"Call me Bailey."

Madame held one of Bailey's hands between the palms of her own. "And you must call me Nichole. I'm very happy you are here." Smiling, Madame held Bailey's gaze a moment longer before releasing her hand and speaking again with Mateo. "The children have been eager for your arrival." She pivoted around and beckoned a boy standing at the middle front of the group: six or seven years of age, dark hair and chocolate brown eyes fringed with thick lashes.

Mateo's chest swelled as he smiled.

Remy.

After Remy strode forward then pulled up before them, Nichole placed her hand on the boy's crown. "You remember Remy, Monsieur."

Mateo hunkered down. He'd hoped that, since last time, someone might have seen the same special qualities and warmth *he* saw in this child. He'd hoped that Remy would have found two people who would love and adopt him. Still, in another sense, he'd looked forward to seeing him again. From the boy's ear to ear grin, Remy hadn't forgotten him either.

"*Bonjour,* Remy," Mateo said.

The boy's mop of hair flopped over his eyes as he smiled and nodded several times. Then, without invitation, Remy reached and took Mateo's hand and Mateo's heart melted more as he was dragged off. He hated whenever he left, but he really ought to come more often.

Bailey looked on, feeling the connection, subtle yet at the same time unerringly strong. These two—Mateo and Remy— had a history. An ongoing solid relationship. When Natalie had suggested Mateo might bring home a child, was she speaking of anyone in particular? Did the Ramirezes know about this boy?

His little hand folded in a much larger one, Remy drew Mateo nearer the other children, still lined up and standing straight as pins. Bailey fogged up watching the girls hand over their flowers and the boys beam as they shook their benefactor's hand.

Exhaling happily, Nichole folded her arms.

"We so look forward to his visits."

"How long has Mateo been coming back?"

"This will make eight years. Two years ago he helped with dormitory renovations. Last year he sponsored the installation of a computer network and fifty stations. This year I'd hoped to discuss excursions. Perhaps, even an extended stay in Paris for the older ones."

Bailey was certain he'd like that idea.

Her gaze ran over the remarkable building that looked something like a smaller version of Notre Dame, without the gargoyles. How many stories those walls must hold.

"Has this place changed much since Mateo's time?" Bailey asked.

"The structure has been renovated many times over the centuries. Some of the furniture and facilities will have been upgraded since Mateo's time, much of it via his own pocket."

Bailey studied the children again, well dressed, obviously well fed, not a one looking discontent. The word orphanage brought up such Dickensian images…never enough food, never enough care or love. But Bailey didn't feel that here. She only felt hope and commitment.

When Mateo had greeted each child, Remy still stood beside him, a mini-me shadow.

"Remy seems quite attached to Mateo," Bailey pointed out.

"I think Mateo is quite attached to *him*." But then Nichole rubbed her arms as if she were suddenly cold. "Remy lost his mother when he was three," she confided in a lowered voice. "His father dropped him here saying he would return when he could. Four years on…" She shrugged.

*No sign of him.*

Bailey's chest tightened. At least she'd had her mother until she was fourteen. Had a father too, although he'd been emotionally absent these later years. But looking at that little boy…

Bailey angled her head. "Remy seems happy enough. Lively."

Was it because he was too young to fully understand there was another way to live…with a family, a mother and father?

"He's a joy." Then Nichole hesitated. "Although he doesn't speak often. There's nothing wrong with his hearing. Seems he simply doesn't care to talk most of the time." Her expression softened. "But he and Mateo have a relationship that extends beyond words."

A thought struck and Bailey's smile wavered. "Do you think Remy's father will ever come back for him?"

"I can only say Remy will always have a home here if he doesn't."

Nichole Garnier meant it as a comfort but Bailey heard a dirge rather than a choir. From the little she'd seen, this establishment was well run, with genuine carers who were dedicated to their work. Still, any comprehending child would rather be with his parents in a real home if there were any way, even if that father had once abandoned him…wouldn't he?

Hand cupped to his mouth, Mateo called out.

"Bailey, the girls want to meet you. The boys too."

Laughing, Mateo ruffled Remy's hair and Bailey and Nichole moved forward.

"Have you known Mateo long?" Nichole asked as they walked together and bands of birds warbled nearby.

"Not very."

"He's a good man."

Bailey grinned. "I keep hearing that." She'd even said it herself.

"He gives others so much joy. He deserves every happiness."

Bailey heard the tone in Nichole's voice…the suggestion theirs might be a relationship that could bloom into love and marriage. Perhaps she ought to set the older woman straight. She and Mateo might be lovers, but that didn't translate into anything permanent. He didn't *want* anything permanent.

As they met again and Mateo took her hand and introduced her, Bailey reaffirmed to herself—right now, she didn't want permanent either.

After the children dispersed, Nichole Garnier showed them around the buildings and grounds.

Although the kitchen facilities, plumbing and sleeping quarters were all twenty-first century, the exterior was undoubtedly restored medieval; and the interior, including the lower chapel, retained much of its original decoration, including intricate paintings. Having grown up in a young country like Australia, Bailey was in awe of the sense of history these children were surrounded by every day. The hallowed atmosphere made her feel insignificant, humbled, and at the same time part of the very heart of this sacred place, as if she, herself, might have strolled these soaring halls in a former time.

They enjoyed a lunch of soupe a l'oignon and quiche aux legumes after which the children sang for their adult audience. Although she understood little, Bailey couldn't remember a performance she'd enjoyed more. At the concert's close, she and Mateo provided a standing ovation while the children all bowed and grinned.

Mateo had a meeting with Nichole in the afternoon, so Bailey spent time with the children playing escargot—a French version of hopscotch—and le loup and cache-cache, or hide and seek. One little girl, Clairdy, stole her heart. Only five, Clairdy had white blond hair and the prettiest violet colored eyes. She never stopped chatting and singing and pirouetting. By the end of the afternoon, Bailey's stomach ached from laughing and her palms were pink from applauding.

For dinner they gathered in the dining hall. When Nichole said a prayer before the meal, Bailey's awareness of her surroundings swelled again and, from beneath lowered lashes, she studied her company, particularly the man seated beside her. How amazing if she could see all the world with Mateo. Even more incredible if, in between, they could stay here together in France.

Bailey bowed her head and laughed at herself.

*If fairy tales came true…*

After the meal, she and Mateo said good-night to the children, Madame Garnier and the others, saying they would be back the next day, then slipped outside and back into the convertible. As they drove down those same dirt ruts, Bailey searched her brain. At no time had Mateo discussed where they would be staying.

"Have you booked a room in town?" She asked, rubbing her gloved hands, relishing the car's heat.

"I own a property nearby."

"Well, it can't be the Palace of Versailles," she joked, thinking of his three story mansion in Sydney. But he didn't comment, merely smiled ahead at the country road, shrouded in shadows, stretching out ahead.

Within minutes, Mateo pulled up in front of a farmhouse, similar to the one they'd stopped to study earlier that day. With the car's headlights illuminating the modest stone facade, Bailey did a double take. No immaculate grounds. No ornate trimmings. This dwelling was a complete turnaround from Mateo's regular taste.

As Mateo opened her car door and, offering a hand, assisted her out, Bailey slowly shook her head, knocked off balance.

"We're staying here?"

"You don't like it?" he asked, as he collected their bags.

"It's not that. In fact…" Entranced, she moved closer. "I think it's wonderful." She had only one question. "Does it have electricity?"

"And if it didn't?"

"Then it must have a fireplace."

"It does, indeed." His smile glowed beneath a night filled with stars as they walked to the door.

"In the bedroom?" she asked, imagining the romantic scene.

"Uh-huh."

She studied his profile, so regal and strong. "You never stop surprising me."

At the door, he snatched a kiss. "Then we're even."

A light flicked on as they moved inside and unwound from their coats. The room smelled of lavender and was clean—he must have had someone come in to tidy up—with a three seater settee, a plain, square wooden table and two rattan backed chairs. Bailey's sweeping gaze hooked on the far wall and she let out a laugh.

"There's a fireplace in here too."

He'd disappeared into a connected room, reemerging now minus their bags. Crossing over, he stopped long enough to brush his lips over hers before continuing on and finding matches on the mantel.

"Let's get you warmed up."

Feeling warmer already, she unraveled the scarf from around her neck while taking in the faded tapestries on the walls as well as the flagstone floor, hard and solid beneath her feet. Feeling as if she'd stepped into another dimension—another time—she fell back into the settee and heeled off her shoes.

"How long have you owned this place?"

"I stayed here the first year," he said, hunkering down before the fireplace. "I came back and bought it soon after."

She hesitated unbuttoning her outer shirt. "Eight years ago?"

He'd struck a match. His perplexed expression danced in the flickering shadow and light as he swung his gaze her way.

"Why so surprised?"

"Why haven't you pulled it down and built something more your style?"

When his brows pinched more than before he turned and set the flame to the tinder, Bailey's stomach muscles clenched. She wasn't certain why, but clearly she'd insulted him. He was all about working hard to surround himself with fine things. Possessions that in some way made up for being cast off with nothing as a child. She'd have thought that here, next door to the heart of those memories, his need for material reassurance would be greatest. It was obvious from Madame's testimony and the well-equipped state of the orphanage that Mateo wanted those children to benefit from pleasant surroundings.

Still, whatever she'd said, she didn't want it to overshadow the previous mood.

"I'm sorry," she said, curling her chilled feet up beneath her legs.

"No need to be," he replied, throwing the spent match on the pyre. "You're right."

Finding a poker, he prodded until the flames were established and the heat had grown.

"I had planned to build something larger," he said, strolling back toward her. "But after I spent a few nights under this roof, I found I didn't want to change a thing. In some ways I feel more at home here than I do in Sydney."

Not so odd, Bailey thought as he settled down beside her. Roots and their memories run deep.

His gaze lowered to her hands. Holding up her wrist, he smiled. "Do you know you play with this bracelet whenever you're uncertain?"

Studying the gold links and charms—a teddy bear, a heart, a rainbow—she shrugged. "I didn't know, but I guess it makes sense."

He rotated her wrist so that the flames caught on the gold and sent uneven beams bouncing all over the room. Bailey moved closer. The heat of his hand on her skin was enough to send some of her own sparks flying.

"I've never seen you with it off your arm," he said.

"My mother put it together for me. A charm for each birthday."

Lowering her wrist, he searched her eyes.

"Until you were fourteen?" he said. *Until the year your mother died.*

"I knew about the bracelet all those years before. It was supposed to be my sweet-sixteen gift. But then Dad refused to give it to me, so…"

"You took it anyway?"

"*No.* This bracelet belonged to me but I would never have taken it without my father's consent. When my sixteenth birthday came and went, I begged for him to give it to me. It was a connection…a link to my mother that I'd waited for all that time. He said he wasn't certain I could look after it, but he didn't have the right to keep it from me."

"He gave it to you in the end."

"He never really spoke to me again after that."

"Sounds as if you both miss her very much. You'd have a lot of memories you could share."

She huffed. "You tell him that."

"Why don't you?"

"He wouldn't listen."

"You've tried?"

"Too many times."

He sat back, absorbed in the crackling fire. After a time, he said, "I'd give anything to speak with my biological father."

"What would you say?"

He thought for a long moment and then his eyes narrowed.

"I'd ask him *why*. But I'll never have the opportunity." He found her gaze again. "What would you say to your father if you could?"

She pondered the question as she never had before.

"I guess I'd ask why too."

"One day you'll have your answer."

When she shivered he wrapped his arms around her, bringing her close to the comfort of his natural warmth. His breath stirred her hair.

"Is that better?"

Looking up into his eyes, she spoke from her heart. "Everything's always better when you hold me."

When his brow furrowed, Bailey shrank into herself. Despite the atmosphere, she'd said too much. Not that her words were a lie. She'd never meant anything more in her life. She felt safe, protected, in his arms. But the way that admission had come out...

Too heavy. She'd bet that kind of "I can't live without you" talk had got a number of his previous love interests gently bumped away. But it wasn't too late to reshape her confession, to season it with the tone they were both more than comfortable with.

Pressing closer, she skimmed her lips across his sandpaper jaw, then hummed over the full soft sweep of his mouth. "On second thought, I think I need to have you hold me a little closer."

She felt his smile, heard the rumble of approval vibrate through his chest.

"But there's something stopping that," he murmured as his palm cupped her nape and she nuzzled down to find a hot pulse throbbing in his neck.

"What's that?"

"Clothes."

Delicious heat flushed through her. They'd made love so many times these past weeks, she'd lost count. But something about his voice, his touch, tonight went beyond anything that had come before. Every cell in her body quivered and let her know…whatever they shared would never get any better than this.

But this time she wanted to be the one to lead…to tease and control and drive the other insane with want.

She lifted her face to his and let his lips touch hers before she slid away from his hold and stood in the firelight before him.

"You build a good fire," she said.

He sat straighter. "You're warm now?"

"Beyond warm."

She caught the hem of her lighter shirt and drew it up over her head. The heat of the flames kissed her bare back while Mateo's intent gaze scorched her front. Her heartbeat thudding, she reached around and released her bra and let the cups fall from her breasts to the soft-pile rug at her feet. When he tipped forward, her flesh tingled and nipples hardened beneath his gaze.

She could see in his eyes that he wanted to drag her to him…wanted to kiss and taste her as much as she wanted to devour him too. But she didn't go to him. Instead she recalled how he'd entered the hotel suite bathroom the night before, without a stitch on, ready to stroke and tease.

She first released the clasp above the zip of her dress pants then eased the fabric past her hips, down her thighs. As the pants came down, she leaned over, nearer to where he sat and waited. Close enough for him to reach out and touch. When she straightened, only one item of clothing separated her from her birthday suit.

His breathing was elevated now, his chest beneath that black shirt rising and falling in the firelight. She recognized the fiery intent in his gaze. How long would he go before hauling her in?

She edged a step closer and a muscle in his jaw began to jump. When she reached for his hand and set his hot palm low on her belly, he came forward and traced his warm mouth over her ribs. Trembling inside, she drew his hand down over the triangle of silk at the apex of her thighs then slowly, purposefully, back up again. His kisses ran higher, brushing the burning tip of one breast as his touch trailed and fingers twined around the elastic of her panties sitting high on her hips.

Groaning, he nipped her nipple at the same time he dragged the scrap of silk down.

Time melted away when his head lowered and his mouth grazed what a second before her panties had concealed... tenderly and then deeply as he cupped her behind and urged her ever closer. She didn't resist when he lifted her left leg and curled her calf over his broad shoulder. She only knotted her fingers in his hair as he continued to explore, his tongue flicking and twirling at the same time the heat at her core kindled, sparked and caught light.

A heartbeat from flashpoint, she recalled she hadn't wanted to surrender to these burning sensations this soon. Now it was too late. This felt—*he* felt—too good to stop.

As she was sucked into that void, all her muscles locked, the fire raged and, dropping back her head, she gave herself over to the tide and murmured his name.

She was barely aware of being lowered down upon that soft pile rug or Mateo's hard frame lowering on top of her. As the waves began to ease and, sighing, she opened her eyes, she found the wherewithal to smile. He hadn't taken the time to take off even his shirt before he thrust in and entered her, filling her in every sense while whispering French and Italian endearments in her ear.

Her legs twined around the back of his thighs as her palms grazed up the hot, hard plate of his chest. He began to move, long measured strokes that built on that fire again. Each thrust seemed to nudge precisely the right spot as his lips sipped lightly from her brow, her cheek. When he drove in suddenly hard and fast, she gripped his head and pulled his mouth to hers. His tongue probed as his body tensed and burned above her. Then she felt the warm touch of his palm sculpting over her breast, the pad of his thumb circling the nipple before he rolled the bead and she gasped as a bright-tipped thrill ripped through her.

His mouth left hers as he levered up. Amid the flickering shadows she could see his muscles glistening and working as his hips ground against hers. She trailed her fingertips down the ruts of his abdomen. Then, scooping them lower, she fanned his damp belly before she gripped his hips, closed her eyes and moved with him, feeling the inferno growing, wishing this sensation would never end.

When he groaned and stiffened above her—when he thrust another time and never more deeply—she reached, held on to his neck and joined him, leaping off that glorious ledge again.

# Ten

Later they moved into the bedroom. While Bailey slipped under the covers, Mateo built a fire before joining her. Wrapped in each other's arms, they didn't wake until after eight. He couldn't let her leave the bed until they made love again.

An hour later, Mateo met Nichole at the orphanage. They plotted a workable scheme for regular excursions to the city and surrounds, the first planned in the spring to visit the Louvre with a weekend stay over at a boardinghouse. Nichole was beyond excited for the children, many of whom had never set foot much beyond this district. With a deep sense of satisfaction, Mateo signed his name to the draft document. Opening the world could be an invaluable experience for any child, with regard to education as well as a sense of self. He should know.

They ended their meeting on another high note. A child—Nichole wasn't obliged to say who at this time—would leave the orphanage today for a new home and bright new future. Mateo left the room wondering…

Could this child be Remy? He would only be happy for him if it was.

Mateo had promised Bailey a trip to the neighboring village where she could soak up more of the rustic atmosphere she enjoyed so much. But when he found her in the large undercover area, she and her company looked so enthralled he didn't have the heart to disturb them. Bailey was playing house with a few of the younger girls, one of them Clairdy, a blond angel who Remy was fond of.

As the girls' conversation and laughter filtered through the cool late-morning air, Mateo rested back against that enormous oak-tree trunk and crossed his arms. This was the place he'd wanted to escape as a child. These were the grounds he still recalled in disturbing abstract dreams at least once a year. And yet, whenever he visited, the longer he stayed, the more difficult it was to walk away. Today— this minute, watching Bailey play with the girls—he felt that contradiction more strongly than ever. He couldn't seem to settle the opposing forces playing tug-of-war in his mind. Memories reminded him how much he'd once wanted to leave this place and yet something else whispered for him now to stay.

This, of course, was absurd. He had a practice, friends, a life back home. Here, at times, he felt almost like a ghost.

Bailey saw him and arced an arm through the air. "Mateo, come over! Clairdy and Eleanor are baking cookies. You could help."

Clairdy and an equally small Eleanor chattered on in French as they rolled and cut play dough then put the tray into their playhouse oven. Mateo smiled. Reminded him of when he'd helped Mama in the kitchen all those years ago.

"What cookies are you baking?" Mateo asked, sauntering over.

*"C'est notre recette spéciale,"* Clairdy said. *It is our special recipe.*

"Remember not to have the oven too hot or the bottoms will burn," he pointed out.

Eleanor immediately pretended to alter a temperature dial.

Clairdy patted her friend on the back and exclaimed, *"Bon travail!" Good job!*

"These two are inseparable," Bailey said. "I've never seen two children get along so well."

Clairdy was tugging Mateo's sleeve. "Would you like to try one, Monsieur?" she said in French.

Mateo leaned down, hands on knees. "Will they need to cool first?"

Clairdy put her hands on her hips and nodded solemnly at the oven before she told Eleanor two minutes longer and then the cookies needed to cool.

Mateo ran a palm down Bailey's back and whispered, "After the cookies, I'll take you into town."

"Perhaps the girls would like to come."

His brows lifted. *No doubt.* But, "If we take these two, they'll all want to go."

Bailey nodded earnestly, as Clairdy had done a moment ago, then said, "We could hire a bus."

He laughed. "Perhaps we could."

"How did things go with Nichole this morning?" she asked turning more toward him. Her blue eyes had never looked more vibrant.

"We worked out an excursion schedule for next year. The older children will go first."

Bailey's chin came down. "But no one will miss out."

"Everyone will get a trip," he assured her.

Happy with that, she maneuvered in front of him then wrapped his arms around her middle. Her head dropped back against his shoulder as she sighed and took in the industrious scene playing out before them. Eleanor was stepping into a fairy costume; Clairdy was handing her glittering silver wings.

Bailey snuggled back more. "I like it here."

"The climate suits you." He grazed his lips near her temple. "Brings out the pink in your cheeks."

"What about my lips?"

Mateo's physical responses climbed to red alert. With the children engrossed in their game, he pulled her around a cozy corner, gathered her snug against him and purposefully slanted his head over hers. She immediately melted against him, making him feel invincible...taller and stronger than that five-hundred-year-old oak. When their lips softly parted, he wanted to forget where they were and kiss her again.

"It's only early," he murmured against her cheek. "Perhaps we should visit home before trekking off for lunch."

She dropped a lingering kiss on the side of his mouth. "Maybe we could stay here and eat with the kids."

Frowning, he pulled back. "Am I losing my charm?"

A teasing glint lit her eyes. "Would that bother you?"

"Only as far as you were concerned."

He cupped those pink cheeks and kissed her slowly, deeply, until all the world was only them and this embrace. She might have thought he was only flattering her but his last remark was sincere. Today, that other world—with its busy office and appointments and investments and antiques—wasn't important. He wanted to think, and feel, only her.

When his lips drew away a second time, her eyes remained closed. Leaning against the stone wall at her back, she hummed over a dreamy smile.

"Perhaps we should stay here forever."

His stomach slowly twisted. Not because he disagreed but because as outlandish and flippant as her suggestion may be, he was attracted to the idea. As far as he and Bailey were concerned, this trip was supposed to be about nothing more than short-term companionship. Was meant to be about acting on physical attraction. This minute physical attraction was dangerously high…but he was feeling something more. Something new. And he wasn't entirely sure what to do with it.

A woman's voice, emanating from around the corner, brought him back. It was one of the caregivers, the auburn-haired Madame Prideux. Bailey obviously heard too. Her dreamy look evaporated a second before she straightened her blouse and patted away the long bangs from her blushing face.

"Is she looking for you?" Bailey whispered.

"No. Eleanor. She wants her to wash up and come to the office."

"Is something wrong?"

Mateo remembered Nichole's comment about a child leaving.

"My guess is," he said, "that this is little Eleanor's lucky day."

They came out from behind the corner. Eleanor was holding Madame Prideux's hand as they walked together toward the main building. Clairdy sat by herself on a miniature kitchen chair. Mateo felt this little girl's jumbled feelings as if they were his own.

"Don't worry, Clairdy," Bailey said. "Monsieur says Eleanor isn't in trouble."

Not understanding, Clairdy gave Bailey a blank look, let out a sigh then spoke in French. Bailey's eyes widened at the words Mama and Papa. Clairdy knew Eleanor wasn't in trouble. To Clairdy's mind her friend was being rewarded for being the best little girl at the orphanage.

Bailey lowered into the second tiny chair and spoke to Mateo. "Is she saying what I think she's saying?"

He nodded. "Nichole explained this morning that a couple, who've been waiting years, have jumped through the final hoop and obtained consent to adopt."

"Eleanor?"

"It would appear so."

They both studied Clairdy watching her friend walk away toward a different tomorrow. And as Mateo's gut buckled and throat grew thick, he was reminded again of all the reasons he loved coming back. And why he hated it too.

Bailey gazed down at the little girl who a moment ago had been bubbling with life. Now Clairdy's tiny jaw was slack and her shoulders were stooped. When she held her tummy and spoke to Mateo, Bailey guessed the ailment. The innocent she was, Clairdy would be happy for Eleanor finding a mother and a father—a mama and a papa—but how could she not also miss her friend? Likely envy her.

"Does Eleanor get to say goodbye to her friends?" Bailey asked as they escorted a pale Clairdy back to the dorms.

"I have no doubt."

"That's something at least. Not that I'm unhappy for Eleanor," Bailey hastened to add. "It just must be so hard on the ones left behind." She examined Mateo's intense expression as they walked. "But you know that better than me."

"There'll be someone for Clairdy too one day."

She read his thoughts—*for them all, I hope*—and had to stop herself before she blurted out, *I wish it could be me.*

But she'd known this child a couple of days. Even more obvious, she was in no position to think about children in that context and hadn't before this moment. But the brave way Clairdy held her head as they strolled up the main path brought a stinging mist to Bailey's eyes. She might have lost her mother but she'd known and loved her for fourteen beautiful years, and, as difficult to understand as he was, her father had never considered putting her up for adoption. Damon Ross cared about his daughter. These past years, he simply hadn't been able to show it.

They were all three entering the nurse's office as Remy showed up, a scuffed football clamped under his arm. When they came out a few minutes later, Remy was still there, waiting to see how Clairdy was. Something older than his years shadowed that little boy's eyes; he knew she needed a friend more than medicine. Remy said a few words to Mateo—something in French, of course. Mateo nodded and Remy took Clairdy's hand and led her upstairs to the girls' dorm to rest.

They both watched until the pair disappeared around the top balustrade. Bailey let out a pent-up breath. She couldn't stop thinking about what her mother would've done in this situation.

"We could stay and read her a story," she suggested and stepped toward the stairs, but Mateo's hand on her arm held her gently back.

"She might like to be alone with Remy now."

Bailey wanted to argue, but it was as much herself as Clairdy she wanted to console. This was a small taste of what Mateo must see each time he visited. There was the fabulous welcome and smiling familiar faces, time set aside to make plans for improvements he knew would be appreciated. But those same faces who were overjoyed to see him couldn't help but be sad when he drove away. He must want to take each and every one of these children home with him, and realizing he couldn't...

Bailey hung her head.

A lesser man might simply send a check.

As they moved away from the building toward that big sprawling tree out front, Mateo circled his arm around her waist. "Let's take a drive."

She hesitated but then nodded. If they went out, talked, her mind, and his, would be taken off a situation over which they had no power. And she had to be happy for Eleanor and pray that Mateo was right. A perfect family was around the corner for Clairdy. Remy too.

Mateo drove over that ancient stone-bridge and into the village with a towering gothic church, two restaurants, one bakery…and right on through.

Bailey shot over a glance. "Where are we going?"

"Thought you might like to see something a little different. A fortress. A ruin now. Word is it's haunted."

Determined not to be sullen, she set her mittened hands in her lap. "I'm in."

After a few more minutes traveling along the country road, they reached the foot of a rocky cliff that jutted over the river. Ascending a series of rock slabs that served as steps, Bailey, with Mateo, reached near the summit a little out of breath. But given their incredible surroundings, she soon forgot her tired legs.

"Nine-hundred-years ago this began as a motte—a large mound—and wooden keep," Mateo told her. "An earlier word for keep is *donjon*."

It clicked. "As in dungeon?"

He winked, took her hand and led her toward the ruins. "By the fifteenth century, the fortress consisted of three enclosures surrounding an updated keep. Only the château of the second enclosure still stands."

Bailey soaked up the sense of history effused in the assorted moss-covered arches, sagging stone steps, the remnants of sculptures hanging to cold gray walls. Above what once must have been an imposing door rested a worn coat of arms. Shading her eyes, she peered up. A giant might have taken a ragged chomp out of the second story wall.

"Who are the ghosts?" she asked. "Why do they haunt?"

"It's said that a lord once kept his daughter locked in this tower. Apparently no man was good enough, but everyone knew the true reason. The lord didn't want to lose his only child." Holding her elbow, he helped her over rubble through to a cool interior that smelled of mold and earth. "Then, one day, a knight rode through and was invited to stay for the evening meal. The knight heard the maiden singing and crying. He asked if he could speak with her. But the lord wouldn't allow it."

Bailey had been picking her way up the stairs. Now she swung around to face him. "Don't tell me they both died while the knight was trying to rescue her?"

"The knight succeeded in freeing his lady and they rode away that night to be wed. The father was furious and set out on horseback to bring his only child back. Taking a jump, his horse faltered and the lord broke his leg. Infection set in. He took six weeks to die, but he moaned and howled for his daughter's return until his last breath. He wanted her forgiveness," he added.

Bailey studied the lonely crumpling walls and coughed out a humorless laugh. "Funny thing is that lord never enjoyed his daughter's company while he had it."

Reading between the lines, Mateo crossed the dirt floor and joined her midway up the steps.

"If you'd like to see your father when we get back," he said, "I'd be happy to go with you."

She cupped his bristled cheek. "Thanks, but I can't see any happy ending there either."

"I'm sure if you gave him a chance—"

"Maybe he should give me one for a change." Gathering herself, she blew out a breath. She didn't want to discuss it. There was no point. "I wish it were different, but it's not."

A muscle in his cheek pulsed as he considered her response.

"I suppose it's not easy."

Bailey frowned. Did he mean for her or her father? How would he handle the situation if he ever became estranged from his child? How would he handle any situation as a father? She wanted to ask. And now seemed the time.

"Natalie mentioned at dinner that night she wouldn't be surprised if one year you came home with a child from France."

His face hardened. "Natalie's sweet but she doesn't have all the facts."

"What are the facts?"

"For a start, nowadays the adoption process in France is a longwinded one."

"So you've looked into it?"

"Madame and I have conversed for many years."

Be that as it may, he hadn't answered the question. "Then you've never considered adopting?"

His voice and brow lowered. "Remy will find a perfect home."

"Maybe it could be with you."

The muscle pulsed again before he headed back down the steps. "It's hard, Bailey, I know, to think about leaving those kids behind. But they're well looked after. I do what I can."

Bailey let out a breath. Of course he did, and far more than most people would. Resigned, she admitted, "It's probably best we're leaving tomorrow or I might never want to go. Those kids have a way of wrapping themselves around your heart."

From the foot of the stairs, he found her gaze. "That's the

way it is. When you have to stay, you don't want to. When you're free to leave…" His gaze dropped away.

That's the way it was for her with Mateo, Bailey realized walking with him back out into the open. When she'd had nowhere to go and Mateo had convinced her to stay to rest up, she'd been intent on leaving. She'd ended up sharing his bed for two weeks then flying with him here. And in these few days she'd become frighteningly used to the sight of him sitting before a flickering fire in their cottage. Used to his earnest evaluating walks around the orphanage, as well as his warm smile when any one of the children brought him a drawing or sang him a song. She felt so *close* to him. As if they'd known each other before.

What would happen when they returned to Australia? She'd be earning her own money…would be free to live her own life. She had no real reason to stay at the Celeca mansion any longer.

Only now she wasn't so keen to go.

# Eleven

Mateo looked over the children playing in the late October sunshine and ran damp palms down his trouser legs. He and Bailey had spent three days at the Chapelle. At the end of each day they returned to his stone cottage to talk and make love into the night. The French countryside this time of year, the children's laughter mixed with memories…he didn't want to leave.

Bailey didn't want to go either. If she hadn't seemed so determined to start work again next week, he'd tell her they would stay a few more days. She seemed to fit here among the trees and the quiet.

He wanted to see more of her when they returned to Australia. But he also wanted to be clear on his position. He was not after marriage. Children of his own. If she accepted that, he'd be more than happy to continue what they shared for however long it lasted.

Bailey was strolling along the paved path with Madame

Garnier. Clairdy walked a step behind, looking a little recovered from her news yesterday about her friend leaving. Shoving his hands in his pockets, Mateo headed toward them. All those years ago, he'd been overjoyed when Ernesto had taken him away from here, like his friend Henri had left before him. The friend he'd so love to know again. It hurt to see that little girl's malaise but that's all he could wish for each of these children. That one day soon they would find a family of their own.

A stiff breeze tugged at his coat. He examined the sky. Rain on the way. He should call Bailey now, say their goodbyes and, if they were going, head off.

Bailey and Madame strolled over.

"Are you ready to leave, Monsieur?" Madame asked.

Mateo folded Bailey's gloved hand in his. "We'd best go now or the mademoiselle will miss out on seeing Paris."

Nichole clapped twice, loudly, and children, coming from everywhere, promptly lined up.

"Monsieur Celeca must leave now," Nichole said in French. "Would you all thank him and the mademoiselle for visiting?"

In unison, the children said in French, "Thank you. We will miss you."

But even as Mateo's chest swelled at the sight of so many adoring little faces and their heartfelt words, his gaze skated up and down the line and soon he frowned. One was missing.

"Where's Remy?" he asked.

"Remy is a little under the weather today." Madame reached into a pocket. "He asked that I give you this."

She fished out a handmade card. When Mateo opened the paper, his heart torqued in his chest then sank to his knees.

*Don't forget me, Monsieur.*

There was a drawing of a smiling boy holding a football.

Mateo groaned, then, setting his jaw, started off. "I'll go see him."

But Madame's firm hand on his arm pulled him up. Her green eyes glistened with sympathy and understanding.

"I think, Monsieur, it is best that you don't. I'll keep an eye on Remy. He'll be fine, I promise."

Mateo held Nichole's gaze for a long tortured moment as his thoughts flew and a fine sweat broke on his brow. She knew that if he went upstairs to Remy he would want to take him. And he *couldn't*. For so many reasons. He had to go and let Remy find a couple who wanted a family. That boy didn't need an overworked, set-in-his-ways bachelor.

After the women and Clairdy hugged, he and Bailey headed to the car, and the children began to sing. Emotion biting behind his eyes, Mateo fought the urge to look back. Seeing out the corner of his eye that Bailey's hands were clenched together, it was all he could do not to. But he was scared that if he did, he would see Remy, standing as *he* had once stood, at a second-story window, wondering if two friends would ever meet again.

Mateo barely spoke the whole drive to Paris. Whenever Bailey tried to make conversation, he answered and that was all.

From the first, she'd been aware of the connection he and Remy shared. Now Mateo felt terrible leaving that little boy behind. More terrible than she felt leaving Clairdy, and that was bad enough. But as Mateo had said, he did what he could. Neither of them was in a position to do any more…even if they desperately wanted to.

Still, she wished she could have the happy, talkative Mateo back again.

As the convertible hurled them ever closer to Paris and away from the Chapelle, Bailey told herself not to dwell on the possibility of Mateo being a father to Remy as Ernesto had been a father to him. Watching farmhouses and fields whiz by, she reminded herself that Mateo had a bachelor lifestyle—a busy career—that didn't correlate with having children. Remy deserved a family who were prepared to give up anything and everything to adopt him. When Mateo flew over next year, Remy might well be gone. And that was best.

Wasn't it?

They checked into the same hotel on the Champs-Elysées and, as if neither of them wanted to dwell on where they had been—how different it felt to be back in the bosom of luxury as opposed to snuggling beneath the patchwork quilt of their stone cottage—they had their bags taken to their suite and immediately set off to sightsee.

As they strolled arm in arm along the Champs-Elysées, Mateo explained, "The people of Paris refer to this avenue as *la plus belle avenue du monde*. The most beautiful avenue in the world."

Bailey had to agree. Finally soaking up the sights she'd heard so much about felt amazing. The atmosphere was effused with so much history and courage and beauty. Every shop and tree and face seemed to greet her as if they were old rather than new friends.

She cupped a hand over her brow to shield the autumn sun from her eyes. "It seems to go on forever."

"Two kilometers. It ends at the Arc de Triomphe, the monument Bonaparte built to commemorate his victories."

They strolled beside the clipped horse-chestnut trees and lamplights, passing cinemas, cafés and so many speciality shops, before stopping for lunch at a café where the dishes marked on a chalkboard menu ranged from sweet-and-sour sea bass and lobster ravioli to more casual fare such as club sandwiches. After taking a seat among the pigeons at one of the many sidewalk tables, Bailey decided on the crab and asparagus salad, while Mateo liked the sound of braised lamb with peaches.

"Is this a favorite café when you're in town?" She asked, sipping a glass of white wine.

"This is my first time eating here."

"Then I think today we've found the perfect place to simply sit and watch."

He raised his glass. "A favorite Parisian pastime. Keeping an eye out for the unique and the beautiful."

Bailey had been watching a pair of young lovers, laughing as they meandered down the avenue. Now her focus flicked back to Mateo and the intense look in his dark eyes made her blush. He wasn't looking at the beautiful view. He was looking at her.

They enjoyed their meal then headed off to the Louvre on the bank of the Seine. Bailey couldn't stop from beaming. So much to take in…over thirty-five thousand works of art dating from antiquity to modern times…Da Vinci, Rubens as well as Roman-Greco and Egyptian art collections…she felt deliciously lost as more and more worlds unfolded before her. She adored Michelangelo's *The Slave* and openly gaped at the *Venus de Milo*. But she fell completely in love with Canova's *Psyche Revived by Cupid's Kiss*.

Cupid's wings were raised behind him, his head slanted over the unconscious Psyche's as he held her close. Bailey was in awe of the depth of emotion the master had captured in marble.

"This is my favorite," she decided. "You can see how in love with her he is."

"Legend has it that Venus was jealous of Psyche's beauty," Mateo said, wrapping his arms around her from behind. "She sent her son, Cupid, to scratch Pysche with an arrow while she slept. When Psyche awoke, she would fall in love with the first man she saw: a hideous creature that Venus planned to plant in the bed. But Cupid woke Psyche and, startled, he accidentally scratched himself as well. Under the arrow's spell, they fell instantly in love."

"And lived happily ever after?"

"They had a spat and Venus put some more obstacles in the way. The last sent Psyche into a dead sleep, that only Cupid's kiss could cure."

She sighed. "Like in *Sleeping Beauty*."

"Like you in the mornings," he murmured against the shell of her ear.

She smiled and admitted, "I'm not the lightest of sleepers."

"Waking you is my favorite time of the day."

He brushed his lips down the side of her throat and the backs of her knees turned to jelly. But she was well aware of their public surroundings.

"You want to get us thrown out."

He chuckled. "We're in *France*."

While Mateo continued to nuzzle her cheek, she thought again of the sculpture and its legend. "What happened at the end of their story?"

"Our old friend Zeus blessed their union and gifted Psyche immortality. She and Cupid had a daughter, Voluptas, the goddess of sensual pleasure."

Bailey's eyes widened. "*Voluptas*. Bet she has a story or two of her own."

Laughing—his old self again—he led her away.

They cruised around the exhibits until the museum closed up at ten. But outside they found the city sparkling and very much awake. Making their way along the Seine, they drank in the river's shimmering reflections and music floating over the cold night air.

He released her hand and drew that arm around her waist. "What would you like to do tomorrow?"

"That's easy." She cuddled in as they walked. *"Everything."*

"In a single day?"

"We have a day and a half," she corrected. "And I put myself entirely in your hands."

"Entirely?"

"And exclusively."

He growled playfully, "I like the sound of that," then turned her in his arms to steal a bone-melting kiss that sparked a wanting fire low in her belly and kept it burning.

They found a warm place to enjoy coffee and share a pastry, then walked again. When dawn broke—a palette of pink and gold soaking across the horizon—cold and worn out, she yawned and couldn't stop.

Mateo raised his hand to hail a cab. "Time to turn in."

"But—"

"No buts," he growled before opening the back passenger door of the cab that had pulled up. "We have another big day coming up."

She didn't like when he was bossy. Even if he was right. Nestled in the back seat, she rested her cheek against his shoulder. Smiling drowsily, she found she couldn't keep her eyes open. As her lids closed, all the sights and sounds and smells of their day in Paris flooded her mind. She snuggled more against his warm hard chest and murmured, "I loved our night. Love it here. I love…*I love*…"

Mateo waited for Bailey to finish. But, with the sun rising—with the full day they'd had—she was asleep before her last words were out. After pressing a kiss on her brow, he too closed his eyes.

When they arrived at the hotel, he roused himself and eased away. But Bailey didn't wake, so he carefully scooped her up in his arms and, entering the lobby, asked the doorman to follow him to an elevator and help him into his suite. A few minutes later, the concierge swiped open the suite's door and, on Mateo's orders, hurried to draw back the bed's covers before bidding him a hushed very good morning.

Searching Bailey's contented face, Mateo carefully laid his sleeping beauty upon the sheets. She stirred when he removed her coat and shoes but after he stripped and lay down to join her, she curled up against him and huddled deeper as he drew the covers up around her chin. His body cried out for rest but he didn't want to give into sleep.

The view was too good.

As he stroked her hair and watched growing light play over the contours of that button nose, the curve of her lips, Mateo's chest grew warm. Despite lingering memories of the Chapelle earlier today, he'd never known this depth of peace. The feeling that he had what he needed to survive, to be happy, was right here with him now in his arms.

He'd mulled it over before. Now his mind was made up. No more wondering if Bailey was anything like his manipulative ex. When they were home again in Sydney, he'd make it official. He would make their current living arrangement more permanent. No contracts. No rings. Just an agreement to share each other's company.

And his bed.

# Twelve

At nine the next morning, a soft caress at the shell of Bailey's ear stirred her from her dreams. Smiling, stretching and sighing, she rolled over and remembered where she was and with whom. In Paris with the most incredible man.

Mateo dotted a kiss on her nose, on her cheek.

"You were sleeping soundly." His voice was deliciously husky the way it always was first thing in the morning, and she found herself sighing at her body's reaction to the desire evident in his hooded eyes and slanted smile. Coiling her arms around his neck, she brought his lips to hers while his hot palm trailed up her side. Within seconds her heartbeat was racing.

She couldn't remember the last of that cab ride last night. Couldn't remember how she'd arrived back in this suite. She did know, however, that this minute she felt amazingly snug, wonderfully safe. She remembered their agreement… today she was entirely, exclusively his. How she wanted to pull the covers up over their heads and spend the next few hours in bed.

Reluctantly breaking the kiss, he murmured against her lips. "It's time to get up."

Groaning, she dragged the back of her hand over her tired eyes. *Bossy again.* "What time is it?"

"Time to see Paris."

A second passed when she could have smoothed her fingers over his muscled shoulder and drawn his mouth back to hers. But this was their only full day left in France. She couldn't pass that up, even for such a compelling reason.

With not nearly enough sleep, Bailey was slow to shower and dress. But the moment they were back on the Parisian streets, coats pulled up around their ears, she was bubbling with excitement.

They visited Notre Dame, the legendary home of the hunchback, then went on to an artist's paradise, Montmatre et Sacre Coeur, situated on a hill in the north of Paris. It boasted the famous Moulin Rouge at its base and the famed Sacre Coeur Basilica, with its inspirational equestrian statue of Joan of Arc, at its summit. She made sure Mateo took plenty of snapshots.

After changing for dinner back at their suite, they took the elevator to the top of the Eiffel Tower where they caught the last of the sunset. Gazing over the city's buildings and monuments draped in a coat of gold, Bailey tried to imprint her mind with every inch of the breathtaking panorama. Mateo circled his arm around her waist and handed his camera to a German tourist who ensured the moment was captured.

He thanked the man then asked her, "Are you hungry?"

"I'm starving." They'd had a bagel on the run, but that was hours ago. "What do you have in mind?"

"A special treat."

As they descended, Mateo revealed his biggest surprise of the day. He'd booked well in advance a table at The Jules Verne, one of Paris's most exclusive restaurants, situated on the tower's second floor.

They were shown to a table by a window facing north across the fountains and enjoyed a night of exquisite cuisine, the best of champagne, while surrounded by a glittering blanket of city lights.

When the waiter removed their dessert dishes, Mateo slid a hand across the white linen tablecloth. His fingers folded around hers.

"Did you enjoy the meal?"

"I enjoyed *everything.*"

He grinned, and the smile lit his eyes. His index finger had begun to toy with her bracelet's charms…the heart, the bear…. He looked down but then frowned and took a closer look.

"You ought to have that catch checked out. It's near worn through."

Worried, she inspected the clasp then each of the charms to make certain none were missing. "Guess it should be worn. I don't take it off." Bailey's stomach looped and knotted at the thought of losing it. "After so long, I wouldn't feel whole without this around my wrist."

"We'll get a safety chain for it tomorrow."

"I'll look after it when we get home."

Mateo didn't look pleased. But it wasn't his place to insist.

He reached and took her hand again, angling her wrist to study the charms. "Have you added to it since your sixteenth?"

"It's never felt quite right. It'd have to be a really special charm." She didn't own much, but this possession was sacred. Not that her father would understand that. Even now he probably thought she was a day away from harming or losing it.

"What about you?" She asked, looking up from their twined hands; hers looked so small and pale compared to his. "Do you have any childhood mementos hidden away?"

Mateo's gaze grew distant and his brows knitted before he shook his head. "No. Nothing material."

Bailey's heart went out to him. Given all his chattels back in Sydney, that answer made sense.

"But I do have something," he said. "A memory I treasure."

She sat straighter. "Memories are good."

"The day Ernesto came back to the Chapelle for me. It was spring and everyone was playing outdoors. He called me over, beside that old oak and he said, 'Mateo, if you'd like to be my son…'" His Adam's apple bobbed before he seemed to come back from that distant spot. Then he shrugged and gave an offhanded smile. "How's that. I've forgotten the rest."

From the way his dark eyes glistened, she didn't think so. But she understood. Memories were the most valuable of all keepsakes. He was entitled to protect his. He'd certainly given her some amazing memories these past days to cherish.

Leaning closer, she confessed with all her heart, "I'll never forget our time here."

When his gaze darkened more and his jaw jutted almost imperceptibly, Bailey sat back as a shadowy feeling slid through her. They'd shared so much. Seemed to have gotten so close. But was that open admission too much? Had she sounded too much the lovesick schoolgirl?

But then a smile swam up in his eyes and the tension seemed to fall from his shoulders. He lifted her hand, dropped a light kiss on the underside of her wrist and murmured against her skin, "I won't forget either."

After dinner they strolled again, but the weather had turned even chillier and, while they'd been lucky so far, Bailey smelled rain on the way. She tried her best but when she couldn't keep her teeth from chattering, Mateo stopped to turn and envelope her in his coat-clad arms.

"I'll take you back to the suite," he said.

Her heart fell. "I don't want to go in yet."

"We can always come back."

*Come back?* She searched his eyes. Was she reading him right? "You mean…to France?"

"And sooner than I usually plan."

Bailey couldn't take a breath. It was a generous, wonderful offer but…should she read more into it? She supposed she ought to ask herself, *How much more did she want?* They'd been sleeping together, enjoying each other's company, but did she want a relationship, *if* that's what he was saying?

Her smile quavered at the corners as she tried to contain her whirling mix of emotions. As they headed for a cab stand, she smiled a jumpy smile and said, "I'd like that."

# Thirteen

Mateo made love to Bailey that night feeling both content and never more conflicted. Caressing her silken curves as they played upon the sheets…kissing every sensual inch of her and only wishing there were more. He couldn't deny that he wanted to keep this woman in his life even if, with every passing hour, he felt himself treading farther into dangerous ground.

After the Emilio affair, it was safe to presume Bailey wasn't interested in exchanging vows and wedding bands. He'd invited her back to Paris and she'd agreed. Would she presume, too, that he would also invite her to live under his roof on a more permanent basis? In time, would she expect more? Deeper commitment?

Diamond rings?

Mateo slept on the problem and when they stepped out to bid the City of Light good morning, with Bailey looking so vibrant and fresh on his arm, he made a decision—one he hoped she would be happy with. But now wasn't the time to discuss it.

He arranged for them to spend the morning on a cruise, absorbing the sights from a different point of view. They boarded near the Pont-Neuf Bridge.

"Its name literally means the new bridge," Mateo said as they settled into window seats beneath a Perspex roof that allowed an unhindered view of the sights, including the many graceful arches of the stone bridge. "But this is the oldest bridge in Paris."

Bailey narrowed her gaze on a distant point then tipped forward. "Look there."

She pointed out a couple standing at the center of this side of the bridge in the midst of a passionate kiss. Before their lips parted, the man swept the woman up in his arms and twirled her around. They were both laughing, bursting with happiness.

Bailey melted back into her seat. "I bet he just proposed."

Mateo's chest tightened at her words, at her tone. Shifting, he got comfortable again and explained, "The *Pont-Neuf* is rumored to be one of the most romantic places in the city."

She laughed. "Is there anywhere in Paris that *isn't* romantic?"

He gave an honest reply. "Not this trip."

All expression seemed to leech from her face before she blushed...her cheeks, her neck. From the look, she'd gone hot all over. That made him smile but also made him want to pull back. He really ought to rein it in. Although she knew his mind on the subject, he didn't want to confuse the issue. Companionship was good. A marriage proposal was not.

After a leisurely time enjoying the sights from the river, he helped her off the boat. Her posture and thoughtful look told him she wasn't looking forward to leaving this behind and boarding that jet. But he had one more surprise before they left. One that would, hopefully, surpass all the others.

As they meandered along the avenue, she said, "Suppose we'd better get back to the suite and pack."

He kept a straight face. "I need to duck in somewhere first."

"Souvenir shopping?"

He twined her arm around his. "In a way."

He hailed a passing cab. When they arrived at their destination, Bailey didn't seem able to speak. Her eyes merely sparkled, edged with moisture, as she clasped her hands under her chin.

"It didn't seem right that we leave without visiting here," he said, stepping out from the cab.

"The Paris Opera," she breathed.

"I have tickets, but the matinee starts soon." He extended his hand to help her out. "Let's hurry."

He escorted her toward a magnificent facade adorned with numerous towering rose-marble columns. The highest level was bookended by two large gilded statues. The interior luxury, including mosaic covered ceiling and multiple chandeliers, had been compared to the corridors in Versailles. When Bailey spotted the 98-foot high marble grand staircase—the one his own was based on—she gasped and held her throat. As he took her arm and escorted her up the flight, she looked over and beamed.

"I don't need a ball gown or glass slippers. No one could feel more like Cinderella than I do now."

When they emerged from the theater, she was floating. She literally couldn't feel her feet descending those incredible grand stairs. The performance was a thoroughly beautiful ballet Bailey knew she would dream about for months.

As they made their way toward the exit, all those amazing

sparkling chandeliers lighting their way, Mateo checked his watch.

"We have a little time yet before we need to head off to the airport. What would you like to do?"

She remembered a mention of souvenirs earlier and piped up. "Buy a gift."

"Who for?"

"I wanted to get Natalie something to thank her for taking me on then letting me have this week off. But then I thought she'd appreciate something for Reece far more."

Chuckling, he wound her arm more securely around his. "You're right. She would."

"Maybe some kind of stuffed toy. A Gallic Rooster." Her step faltered at his unconvinced look. "It's this country's national animal, isn't it?"

"But Reece isn't a baby. He'd appreciate something more—" he thrust out his chest "—masculine."

She slanted her head. Okay. "How about a football?"

"Too young."

"Suggestion?"

"That we go to the experts."

"And that would be?"

He quickened his step and propelled her along with him. "The oldest and largest toy store in Paris."

Soon they arrived at Au Nain Bleu, the massive store that had been serving French children's play needs since the mid-nineteenth century. There were lots of stuffed floppy-eared rabbits. Bailey seemed especially taken with a pair of bunny slippers. But Mateo ushered her through to a spot where boys' toys ruled.

They looked at trucks, action figures, miniature drums. Bailey drifted toward a nearby girls' section while Mateo kept searching. After a few more minutes, satisfied, he called and gestured toward a shelf.

Bailey hurried over from a jewelry stand and picked up the pack. "A builder's kit, suitable for eighteen months to three years," she said. With a plastic hammer, automatic wrench, an "electric" drill that buzzed when you pressed a red button. "But Reece is only twelve months."

"Believe me, he'll grow into it quickly."

She quizzed Mateo's eyes and smiled.

"You would have liked this when you were young?"

"More than anything, I wanted to be a builder."

"And you ended up becoming a doctor?"

"Ernesto wanted me to make the most of my grades."

She smiled knowingly. "But there's still a part of you that wants to hammer and saw and create."

He rolled that thought over and admitted, "I suppose there is." Although he hadn't thought about it in decades. He straightened his shoulders. "Anyway, I'm sure you'll be a hit with Reece with this."

At the counter, Mateo pulled out his wallet but Bailey held up a hand. "I have money enough for this."

He wanted to argue but finally put his wallet away while she extracted some French currency. He hadn't known she'd exchanged any cash. But given her backpacker history, of course she'd be well up to speed on such things.

The lady behind the counter insisted on gift wrapping. Mateo was checking his watch again as they headed for the exit when a large well-dressed man materialized directly in front of them. With a stony expression, he studied Bailey who, looking uncertain, slid a foot back. Mateo wasn't uncertain. He was annoyed. They had a jet to catch.

Before Mateo had a chance to speak up, the man addressed Bailey in French.

"I am a security officer for the store. Please empty your pockets."

Bailey clung to his arm. "What's he saying?"

Mateo stepped in front of Bailey and demanded of the officer, "What's this about?"

"I have reason to suspect your wife has something in her pocket for which she did not pay."

Bailey's hushed voice came from behind. "Why is he upset, Mateo?"

He looked over his shoulder. "He thinks you've shoplifted."

Her eyes rounded. "That's crazy."

Yes. It was.

And yet he couldn't help but wonder why a security officer from a well reputed store should stop them if there was no basis to the accusation.

Stepping beside her again, Mateo assessed her knee-length coat. "He wants you to empty your pockets."

"What on earth does he think I stole?"

"The quickest way to end this, Bailey, is show him the contents of your pockets."

If she had nothing to hide, she would have nothing to fear and, doing his job or not, he would then demand an apology from this man. If, of course, the security guard was right…

As shoppers swirled around them and a toddler, trying a mini slide, squealed close by, Bailey reluctantly dragged something shiny from her right pocket then held out her hand, palm up. The officer preened his moustache before leaning in to take a better look. Mateo didn't need to. He knew what Bailey had hidden in her pocket.

The officer angled his head and frowned. "What is this?"

Sheepish, Bailey found Mateo's eyes. "You were right. The clasp broke when I was looking through a display. It fell in with some necklaces. I put it in my pocket and was going to have it fixed, first thing, when we got home."

Mateo let out a lungful of air. Her charm bracelet. She was lucky she hadn't lost it. He knew how much it meant to her. He should have *made* her listen.

Mateo explained the situation to the officer who accepted the story with an apology before allowing them to be on their way.

"I know what you're thinking," she said as they walked out onto the pavement. "It could have slipped off without me knowing." She cringed. "I hate to think what my father would say."

"He wouldn't be happy."

"I'm used to that. But you don't need to be upset."

He didn't reply.

As they cabbed it back to the suite, Mateo mulled over the incident. What really bothered him was that for a moment he'd been prepared to think the worst of Bailey—again. But it had been a misunderstanding, something similar to when he'd jumped to conclusions the second she'd confirmed she'd taken that money from Mama. But that hiccup was long behind them. Bailey wasn't dishonest. Wasn't manipulative.

He stole a glance at her profile as she watched the Parisian streets flash by in her borrowed designer clothes, perhaps thinking of her visit to the Champs-Elysees, and confirmed she wasn't that type. She couldn't be.

He couldn't feel this deeply about someone who was nothing better than a fraud.

Or, more correctly, he couldn't make that mistake again.

They packed, checked out and boarded the jet with time to spare. Bailey felt as if she were grieving for a friend as she gazed out the window, bid goodbye to France and the jet blasted off. She felt as if she were leaving home, leaving her family—Nichole and the children at the orphanage.

Mateo had said they would visit again, and she was over the moon about that. But now, more than before, she also needed to know what would happen to "them" when they arrived back in Australia.

As the jet climbed higher and clouds began to interfere with the view of the receding ground below, she considered hedging around the subject, trying to get an answer without sounding needy or obnoxious by asking directly. Because she hadn't the money to find her own place and wanted to pay that loan back as quickly as she could, she'd agreed to live at Mateo's home…his *mansion*.

But as close as she believed they'd become—as close as she'd come to acknowledging feelings she'd been determined to stay away from less than three weeks ago—she had to know where they were in their…well, their *relationship*. She couldn't land in Sydney and simply walk through his front door as if she owned the place. She needed to know what the next step was, and the best way was to ask straight out.

She set her magazine aside. "You know, with the wage I'll make cleaning, I should have that loan paid back in a couple of weeks."

He looked across, smiled. "That's great."

When he looked back at his obstetrician periodical, she folded her hands firmly in her lap. Since that incident at the toy store, he'd seemed distracted. A silly part of her wondered if, for just a second, he might have believed the security buffoon's accusation. But she hadn't pilfered a thing in her life. He might have set out thinking she'd shammed his grandmother but surely, after the week they'd spent together, he knew her by now. She'd even begun to think that he might be falling a little in love with her. That left her feeling dizzy and, perhaps, even a bit hopeful.

She shook herself. This mooning wasn't getting her any closer to finding out what came next. If either of them truly *wanted* a next.

She drummed four fingertips on the magazine page. "I thought I should start shopping for a place to live before then."

He froze then lowered the periodical and studied her eyes. "Do you want to find a place of your own?"

Bailey swallowed a fluttery breath. What kind of question was that? What kind of reply did she give? Honest, she supposed.

"Depends. Do you want me to?"

His gaze dropped to her hands and again she realized how naked she felt without that bracelet on her wrist. She was squirming a little when he announced, "I thought you might like to stay with me."

Her entire body lit with a blush. She coughed out a laugh, shrugged, tried to find words while attempting to sort out if she really did want to "live with a man" so soon after her pseudo engagement catastrophe, even if that man was the uber attractive, thoroughly irresistible, Mateo Celeca.

Bowing her head, she let out a shuddery breath. This was a thousand times different from Italy. She and Mateo had a connection, something she wanted to pursue...if he did.

She took a breath and looked him in the eye. "Are you sure?"

He waited two full beats where Bailey could only hear her heart pounding in her ears. Then he leaned close, stroked her cheek and murmured against her lips.

"I'm sure."

# Fourteen

A week later, Bailey sat at the meals table next to Mateo's chef-standard kitchen. She'd been struggling all morning with a question. A problem. Finally now she'd made up her mind.

She pushed her coffee cup away and announced, "I'm going to do it."

Sitting alongside of her, Mateo shook out his Sunday paper, looked over and announced, "Fabulous." Then he frowned and asked, "Do what?"

Bailey let her gaze roam the hedges and statues in her favorite of Mateo's gardens—the one that reminded her so much of their time in France—then she studied the bracelet, repaired and back on her wrist. Her stomach turned and she swallowed the lump formed in her throat.

"I'm going to see my father."

The day after they'd returned, she'd gone back to work, cleaning for Natalie's firm; she'd decided to keep Reece's gift until she and Mateo saw them all together. He'd put the rest of his vacation plans on hold and seemed content to play golf and catch up with local friends. He'd said that seeing as Mama hadn't expected him, she wouldn't be disappointed and that he'd visit her and Italy sometime soon. Every night they came together but, although the words almost escaped, she didn't bring up his suggestion that they would return to France one day. There were moments when she'd caught a distant, almost haunted look darkening his eyes. At those times she guessed his mind was back at the Chapelle, wondering how little Remy was doing, as she often thought about Clairdy. She wanted to talk about it but his demeanor at these quiet times told her not to. He might not admit it but he felt guilty about leaving that boy. She understood his reasons. She wondered some times if Mateo did.

What she owed for her return airfare had been paid back and to set all the records straight she spoke to Mama on the phone, admitting that she'd taken her money under false pretenses, that she'd never planned to return to Italy. To Bailey's surprise, Mama had said she'd guessed as much and understood. She might be a dear friend of Emilio's grandmother, but she had never been a big fan of that boy... not since Emilio had tried to fight her Mateo so many years earlier.

Mama had gone on to say that when his ring had returned in the mail, Emilio had spread word that his Australian fiancée had indeed run out on him. But he hadn't pined for long. Emilio was seeing another lady, this one a visitor from Wales. Mama said she was a nice young woman and she would keep an eye out for her too.

Now that her more recent past issues were ironed out, Bailey felt a need to at least try to make some kind of amends with her father. They hadn't spoken in over a year and she'd grown a great deal since then. Perhaps it was foolish hoping but maybe he'd grown too. Whereas a couple of weeks ago, when she'd seen him on the street, she hadn't known if she were strong enough, now, this morning, in her heart she believed she could not only face her father, but if their meeting turned sour—if he still shunned and criticized her—she could do what was needed to go forward with her life.

She could forgive him and walk away.

Now the inquiring smile in Mateo's eyes dimmed and he scraped his chair to turn more toward her. "You want to go see your father now? This morning?"

When she nodded, he ran a hand through his hair, smiled and pushed his chair back. "In that case I'll get the car out."

He got to his feet but, before he could head off, she caught his arm.

"Mateo, you don't have to come."

His dark brows knitted. "Do you want me there?"

A spool of recent memories unwound…how Mateo had helped her with the money she'd owed Mama. How he'd given her a roof over her head, even when she'd insisted she didn't need one. The way he'd invited her into his life, through friends like Alex and Natalie and Nichole. The amazing time he'd shown her in France.

He'd trusted her enough to admit that he would give anything to ask his own father *why*. She'd realized that was precisely what she needed to ask too.

Decided, she pushed to her feet. "If you'd like to come, that would mean a lot."

As they pulled up outside the familiar Sydney address, Bailey dug her toes into her shoes and told herself to get a grip. She wasn't a kid anymore. She was here not because she needed her father but because she *chose* to see him. If he turned her away…well, she'd deal with it. She'd been through worse. And with Mateo standing alongside of her, she could face anything.

Mateo's strong, warm hand folded around hers.

"You'll be fine."

She tilted her head at the front yard. A good part of the greenery lay hidden behind a massive brick and iron fence.

"I grew up playing on that lawn," she said. "The summer after I got a bike for Christmas, my father built a track on the other side of that garage, complete with dirt jumps and dips. He said he'd take me to moto-X competitions, if I wanted."

"Not your thing?"

"I turned seven that year and discovered my destiny. I was going to be either a Labradoodle breeder or a Russian circus fairy."

His eyes crinkled at the corners at the same time his mouth slanted and some of the stress grabbing between her shoulder blades eased.

"I ditched after-school circus skills mid-third term," she explained. "I still love poodle crosses though. Dad said he'd set me up with my own breeder's kennel when I was older."

Mateo curled a loose strand of hair behind her ear. "Everything will be fine."

"Promise?"

"I promise you won't regret coming here today," he said, then pushed open his door.

Together they walked up the path to the front door. Mateo stood back while she flexed her hands a few times then rang the bell. Her heartbeat galloping, she waited an interminable time, but the hardwood door she knew so well failed to open.

Feeling beads of perspiration break on her brow, she glanced across. Mateo cocked his chin at the door and, with a shaky hand, she thumbed the bell again. After several more nothing-happening moments, she surrendered and threw up her hands.

"All that build-up and he's out."

She pivoted on her heel, ready to leave, but Mateo only stood firm.

"It's Sunday morning," he said, running a reassuring palm down her arm. "Give him a chance to put down the paper. Set his coffee cup on the sink."

Listening to a kookaburra laugh from a nearby treetop, Bailey gathered her failing courage and faced that closed door again. A neighbor, trimming hedges, popped his head over the fence. Smiling, Mateo nodded at the curious gray-haired man. But Bailey only blew out a done-with-it sigh.

"If my father's in there, he's not coming out."

After a few seconds, Mateo reluctantly agreed. They'd turned to leave when that heavy door cracked open. A man in a weekend checked shirt squinted at them through a shaft of steamy morning light. While Bailey's chest tightened, Damon Ross's eyes flared and his grasp on the doorjamb firmed as if his knees had given way.

"Bailey…?" His head angled as he took in more of her. "It is you, isn't it?"

She tried to swallow but her throat was suddenly desert dry. So, although it wobbled at the corners, she tried a smile instead.

"How are you, Dad?"

Stepping back, her father ran his gaze up and down again as if she might be an apparition come back to haunt him. But then his expression softened and the stern voice she'd come to know over these last years softened too. He even partway smiled when he said, "I wasn't sure I'd ever see you again."

She shrugged. "I didn't know if you wanted to see me."

Her father moved forward, hesitated, and then reached his arms out. Bringing her in, he hugged his only daughter close and for a bittersweet moment she was transported back to that day when they'd desperately needed each other. The day her mother had been laid to rest.

Bailey gave herself over to the feeling. This is how she'd dreamed this meeting would unwind. The smell of his aftershave, the warmth of his bristled cheek pressed to hers. As tears stung behind her eyes, she wanted to say how much she missed him but as he released her and edged back, she gathered herself. Hopefully, there would be plenty of time for that.

Damon Ross acknowledged the third person standing nearby. The older man drew back his shoulders and extended his hand.

"We haven't met."

Mateo, several inches taller, took her father's hand. "Mateo Celeca."

"Have you known my daughter long?"

"Only a few weeks."

Her father's calculating lawyer's gaze took Mateo in before, obviously approving, he released another smile and waved them both inside.

"Are you from Sydney, Mateo?" Her father asked, escorting them through the foyer that wasn't a quarter as large as Mateo's.

"Originally from Italy."

"The name, the complexion…" Damon Ross lobbed a knowing look over his shoulder. "I guessed Mediterranean."

The aroma of coffee brewing led them to the kitchen. While the men made small talk, Bailey discovered the cups in the same cupboard and poured three coffees before they sat down in the adjoining meals area.

The table was stacked with journals and assorted papers relating to her father's work. The rest of the room looked clean. Almost too tidy. Didn't seem so long ago that her mother's easel and paints had occupied that far corner, the one that offered the best natural light. Ann Ross had always kept a spare pair of slippers right there by the door. Of course, they were gone now. But her parents' wedding portrait still hung in the center of that feature wall. Sipping coffee, Bailey wondered whether their bedroom had changed. Whether her mother's clothes were still hanging in the wardrobe all these years later.

"You had a good time overseas?" Her father's dark-winged eyebrows arched as he lifted the cup to his pursed lips.

"Yes." Bailey fought the urge to clear her throat. "Thank you. I did."

"I'm glad." Her father held his smile. "You must have been busy."

A little nervous, she laughed. "Pretty much."

"You enjoyed it then?" Damon Ross went on.

Her fingers tightened around the cup. He was pushing the point that he had advised her not to go abroad alone. Digging to see if, true to his prediction, anything had gone wrong.

"I'm glad I went," she said, her smile verging on tight now. "I'm glad I'm back."

Her father nodded, but his buoyant expression had slipped a touch, too.

"I wasn't sure what to think," he said.

Out of the corner of her eye, Bailey saw Mateo roll back one shoulder a second before she replied. "About what?"

"About how you were doing," her father expounded as if he were telling her B followed A. "Whether you were in any kind of trouble."

"You didn't need to worry, Dad."

Damon Ross laughed with little humor. "It's not as if I've never had to worry before."

A retort, fast and hot, leapt up her throat but before she

could say a word, her father changed his tone…upbeat again.

"So," he pushed his cup aside and threaded his fingers on the table, "did you find work while you were over there?"

"I did some waitressing."

"Well, as long as it kept you out of trouble."

Bailey's face burned. There was that word again. Or was he merely being inquiring, genuinely concerned, and she was being overly sensitive? Now that she was here, shouldn't she be the better person and let any slights, intended or otherwise, sail over her head? She was mature enough to handle this.

"How did you two meet?" her father asked Mateo while Bailey took a long sip of hot coffee.

Mateo replied, "Through a mutual friend."

"Bailey's mother and I met at a church function." Damon blinked several times then dropped his faraway gaze. "But that was a long time ago."

"We recently returned from France," Mateo chipped in, sharing a covert you'll-be-fine wink with her.

Her father's wistful smiled returned. "My wife and I visited Paris on our honeymoon. Ann was taken with the country scenery. She said she felt as if she'd stepped into a Monet." His gaze wandered to his daughter and he sat back. "So, what are you doing with yourself nowadays?"

"I'm working," she announced. "For a real estate firm."

Mateo stepped in again. "Bailey and a friend of mine clicked. Natalie said Bailey had what her agency was looking for." He caught her gaze. "Didn't she, darling?"

Bailey's heart lifted to her throat. Mateo had only ever addressed her by name and yet he'd chosen this moment to call her an endearment. A well-educated, respected professional in his field, Damon Ross was challenging his daughter and Mateo was defending her without causing waves, by letting her father know she was his "darling" and insinuating she was selling properties rather than cleaning bathrooms.

She hoped the smile in her eyes told Mateo she appreciated his efforts. But honestly, she'd sooner he didn't intervene. Whatever came today, she needed to stand up for herself, not as a child standing toe to toe with a disapproving parent, but as the self-respecting adult she'd become, and without too much of her father's help.

"Bailey's going back to school," Mateo was saying.

Her father looked half impressed. "Well, well. I said one day you'd regret dropping out." While Bailey set her teeth, Damon Ross spoke again to Mateo. "My daughter didn't attain her high school diploma," he said under his breath as if she hadn't learned to spell her own name.

Bailey studied that wedding portrait and, hands on the table's edge, pushed her chair out. She'd come here hoping— she'd wanted to make their father-daughter relationship work—but she was only hurting herself. Still, she wouldn't argue. Neither would she sit here a moment longer.

As she rose, her father stopped talking and looked up at her with eyes that, for a moment, were unguarded.

"Are you pouring more coffee?" he asked.

"Actually, Dad, we have to go."

Her father got to his feet. "You only just arrived."

"We can stay awhile longer," Mateo said, standing too.

But she pinned Mateo with a firm look that said he was wrong.

"Mateo," she said, "it's time to go."

While her father muttered that he didn't know what the rush was all about, Mateo's furrowed gaze questioned hers.

She peered up at the ceiling and almost groaned. She appreciated Mateo coming—appreciated everything he'd done—but this was her business. *Her* life. She'd gone through this game with her father too many times already.

Bailey walked away and the men's footfalls followed. At the door, she leaned toward her father and pressed a quick kiss to his cheek. When she drew back, her father's gaze was lowered on her wrist. On the bracelet.

"I see you haven't lost it yet," he said.

Her gaze went from the bracelet to her father's cheated look and a suffocating surge of hurt, and guilt, bubbled up inside her.

He just couldn't let her leave without mentioning that.

On the edge, she flicked open the bracelet's new clasp. "Know what, Dad?" Slipping the chain and its jingling charms from her wrist, she handed it over. "I want you to have this."

His brow furrowed. "But I gave it to *you*."

"Not the way I needed. The way she would've wanted you to."

"Don't start on—"

"Mum didn't ask to die," she plowed on. "She didn't want to leave us. I don't need this to know she loved me. It's sad but," she slapped the bracelet in his palm, "I think you need this more than me."

She headed down the path.

Mateo remote-unlocked his car a second before she reached for the passenger side handle. Churning inside, she kept her burning, disappointed gaze dead ahead while Mateo slid into the driver's side. He belted up, ignited the engine, shifted the gear into drive. Trying to even her breathing, she felt his gaze slide over.

"Your father's waiting on the doorstep," he told her. "Don't you think you ought to at least wave?"

Her stomach kicked and she screwed her eyes shut. "Don't try to make me feel guiltier than I already do."

Not about her father's behavior but because she *had* almost lost that bracelet, and she would never have forgiven herself if she had.

Mateo wrung the steering wheel with both hands. "He was a little out of line. But, Bailey, he's your father. We were there ten minutes. Do you really want to walk away, cut him off, again?"

Eyes burning, she continued to stare ahead. Mateo might want the chance to sit down and speak with his biological father, but she knew now hers would never listen. Would never understand. He wasn't the only one who'd felt lost when Ann Ross had died.

And while they were on the subject—if she was running away, hadn't Mateo in a sense run away too, from that little boy who would love to be his son?

But she wouldn't mention that. If she did, they'd have an argument and the way she was feeling—the way she'd thatched her fingers to stop her hands from shaking—she wouldn't be the one to back down.

While she glared out the windshield, Mateo sucked in an audible breath and wrenched the car away from the curb. They drove in silence home. When she got out of the car, she tried to make her way through the house and up that staircase before any tears could fall, but Mateo had other plans. Catching up, he grabbed her arm from behind. Tamping down hot emotion, she lifted her chin and turned around.

The chiseled plains of his face were set. "We need to talk."

"Not now."

She tried to wind away but he held her firm. "Don't let this get to you."

"I'd have thought you'd approve of me walking away."

Mateo had once said he was selfish. He was wrong. He was a hypocrite. Mateo might have had a good relationship with Ernesto, but there was a little boy back in France who had silently begged for years for the monsieur to accept him. Not so different from the way she wanted to be accepted by her father.

She shook her arm free and started up the stairs. It was better they didn't discuss it.

Mateo's steps sounded behind her. "I'm not the one you're angry with."

Her throat aching, she ground out, "Please. Mateo." *Please.* She continued up the stairs. "Leave me alone."

When an arm lassoed her waist and pitched her around, she let out a gasp as she fell. But before her back met the uneven ramp of the stairs, that arm was there again, scooped under and supporting her as Mateo hovered over her, daring her to try to walk away from him again.

But he didn't speak, and the longer he stayed leaning over her as she lay on the steps, his eyes searching hers, the more her tide of anger ebbed and gradually seeped away. But the hurt remained...for herself as well as for Remy. She doubted that would ever leave.

Her words came out a hoarse whisper.

"Why does he do that?"

Mateo exhaled and stroked her hair. "I don't know."

"I won't ever go back."

"You don't have to...if that's what you want."

Frustration sparked again. "I know what I want, Mateo."

His lips brushed her brow. "I know what *I* want."

She shifted onto her elbows. "Do you?"

He hesitated a heartbeat before his mouth slanted over and took hers.

His kiss was tender and at the same time passionate. Dissolving into the emotion, needing to completely melt away and forget, she reached for his chest and struggled with his shirt buttons. As the kiss deepened, he shifted too, rolling back each shoulder in turn as she peeled the sleeves off his powerful arms.

When his mouth finally left hers, her blood felt on fire. She didn't want to think about anything but this. Not her father or France or her bracelet. Only how Mateo made her feel time and again. She couldn't deny it any longer. As much as she'd set out to keep her head and her heart, she'd fallen in love with Mateo, an emotion that consumed her more and more each day.

His eyes closed, one arm curled around her head, he murmured against her parted lips. "Perhaps we ought to take this upstairs."

She sighed against his cheek. "If you want."

His brow pinched. Before he kissed her again, he said, "I want you."

# Fifteen

Finished tapping in the final answer on the last form, Bailey held her breath and hit send. If everything went according to plan, in a couple of months she'd be busy studying, sending off her first assignments, on her way to getting that degree.

Sitting back in Mateo's home office chair, she had to grin over the majors she'd chosen. What were the odds? Then again, what were the odds she'd come to feel this way, this *deeply*, about Mateo?

A week had passed since their surprise visit to her father's house…since Mateo had defended her, challenged her, then pinned her on the stairs where they'd made love in a frenzied, soul stirring way they never had before. Her skin flashed hot to even think of the avalanche of emotions he'd brought out in her that day.

Mateo cared about her. He enjoyed her company. But even more, Mateo Celeca *believed* in her. Yes, for her sake he hoped she and her father could somehow, someday, make amends, but he respected her enough not to push. The same way she wouldn't push about Remy, no matter how strongly she felt those two should be together.

More and more she was coming to believe she and Mateo should stay together too. More than common sense said he could have his choice of companions, and yet he chose to be with her. Had asked her to stay. She couldn't help but wonder....

Exhaling, Bailey pushed that thought aside and, before signing off the computer, decided to check emails. A message from her friend Vicky Jackson popped up in reply to the email Bailey had sent when she'd discovered that first day back that her friend was out of town. Vicky was dying to hear all the news. Had she seen her dad yet? Had she met anyone wonderful? As always, Vicky wanted the gossip, just like the old days, bolts and all.

Bailey glanced around Mateo's red leather and rosewood office. So many amazing collectors' items. Even the ornate silver letter opener looked as if it belonged in a museum. Would her friend since school believe what had happened over the last few months? From backpacking around Europe, to settling down in Casa Buona, to being cornered into an engagement that had sent her on a desperate flight home to Australia. Best of all she'd gone and lost her heart. A huge romantic, when Vicky found out, she would go berserk!

Fingers on keys, she jumped right in.

Vicky! You wouldn't believe how I've lucked out. So much has happened since we saw each other last. But the main thing is that I found *the* guy. A keeper!

I'm sitting here now in his home study. Make that mansion! I'm actually cleaning houses atm. Long story.

But that's only temporary. I have *so* many plans—BIG plans—and Doctor Mateo Celeca is at the center of them all—

Bailey stopped, pricked her ears and listened. Mateo's car was cruising up the drive.

She tapped out a super quick "Talk soon," hit send, then jumped up. Mateo had said she could use this laptop anytime. She didn't feel guilty about taking him at his word. In fact, she'd come to feel wonderfully at home here. But, with him being gone for four hours, she was excited to have him back. Whenever she thought of him striding toward her, that dazzling smile reaching out and warming her all over, her knees went weak. She needed his kiss. More and more she wanted so much to let him know how deeply she felt.

What would he say if she did?

Mateo entered the house aware of the weight in his shirt pocket and the broad grin on his face.

Not so long ago he'd had no intention of getting overly involved with a woman. And yet, with Bailey, he was involved up to his chin. He'd spent his whole life avoiding the ghosts and hurdles of his past. He'd only needed his friends and the possessions he surrounded himself with. To open his heart—to consider marriage and children of his own—would mean to invite in vulnerability. Take on risk.

But late last night in the shadows, after he and Bailey had made love and he'd felt so at peace, he'd questioned himself. Searched his soul.

Did he *love* Bailey Ross?

Moving down the central hall now, Mateo rolled the question over in his mind but still the answer eluded him. He did know, however, that he had never felt this attracted to a woman before. He enjoyed, without reservation, Bailey's conversations and smiles. He looked forward to seeing her, kissing her, letting her know how much he valued her. And they were certainly beyond compatible in the bedroom.

In Paris he'd made a decision. To offer her commitment—a home, his affection—without unnecessary encumbrances. This morning he'd come to a different conclusion.

He may not be certain that he loved Bailey but he was wise enough to know he would never find this connection with anyone else. Today he intended to utter words that previously had not existed in his personal vocabulary. As soon as he found her, wherever she was hiding, he intended to ask her to be his bride.

He entered the kitchen, swung a glance around. Empty. Out in "their" garden, no sign of her among the statues either. A hand cupped around his mouth, he called out, "Bailey. I'm back."

He waited but the house was quiet. Then he had a thought. Before he'd left this morning, she'd asked if she could use his computer. A bounce in his step, he headed for the office.

A few seconds later he discovered that room empty too. But from the doorway he saw the internet browser on his laptop had been left open. The world was full of hackers, scammers, looking for a window to wiggle into and defraud. A person couldn't be too careful. Needing to log off, he crossed over and saw a message hadn't been closed. He moved the curser to save the draft at the same time a few words caught his eye.

BIG plans... A keeper...

His gaze slid to the top of the screen. He skimmed the entire message, lowered into his chair and read it again. After a fourth time, Mateo's hand bunched into a tight ball on the desk. There had to be a different way to interpret it. A different light from the murky one he'd latched on to. But, for the life of him, he couldn't grasp any other implication from this message than the one hitting him square between the eyes.


You wouldn't believe how I've lucked out. I found...a keeper!

Actually cleaning houses...that's only temporary... BIG plans—and Doctor Mateo Celeca is at the center of them all—


His gut kicked then twisted into a dozen sickening knots while his hand drifted to his shirt pocket. His fingers curled over the velvet pouch inside and tightened. Was her meaning as obvious as it seemed? Had he been wrong about Bailey? Emilio then Mama...Had she wormed her way into his feelings to manipulate him too?

Had he played the fool *again?*

"Mateo!" Bailey's call came from down the hall. "Where are you?"

He snapped back to the here and now and dabbed his clammy brow with his forearm. He had to think.

*"Mateo?"*

The call sounded close. He looked over and saw Bailey standing at the office door, looking slightly flushed, a brilliant smile painted across her face. She rushed forward and wasted no time plopping onto his lap and snatching a quick kiss.

"Guess what I did today?" She asked, beaming.

Although his mind was steaming, he kept his tone level. "Why don't you tell me?"

"I enrolled."

He forced a smile. "You did?"

"After looking into all the faculties' courses and searching myself about what I really wanted to accomplish, you won't believe what I've decided to be."

Out the corner of his eye, that email seemed to taunt him. "What did you decide?"

"I want to study law. Not criminal, like Dad, but human rights. I want to do my best helping those who don't have the education or means or, in some cases, the status to help themselves."

"That sounds…worthy."

Absently watching the motion, she curled some hair behind his ear. Where normally he would lean in against her touch, this minute it was all he could do not to wince. She had big plans.

Who was this woman?

Did he know her at all?

"Bridging courses are the first step," she went on, "a chance to catch up on high school stuff before tackling the full on units." She let out a happy sigh. "I'm so excited." Nuzzling down into his neck, she murmured against his jaw. "I missed you today. Where have you been?"

Mateo thought of the item in his pocket, and the rock that filled the space where his heart used to beat grew harder still. He shut his eyes and groaned. God, he wished he'd never seen that note.

Her cuddling stopped. Her lashes fluttered against his neck an instant before she drew away and searched his eyes, head slanting as she reached to cup his cheek.

"Is something wrong?"

His gaze penetrated hers as his jaw clenched more. He should ask her point blank, lay it on the table, and this time he wouldn't be hoodwinked. How could he be when the truth was there on that screen in black and white?

"You left your inbox open," he ground out.

She bit her lip. "Sorry. I rushed off when I heard your car."

"You sent a message to a friend."

She blinked. "That's right."

"It didn't go through."

Her brow furrowed and her gaze shot to the screen before it slid back to him. He could sense her mind ticking over. "Did you read it?"

When he moved, she shifted and he got to his feet.

"Mateo…"

He headed for the door. His throat wouldn't stop convulsing. He needed fresh air. Needed to get out of here and be alone for a while. But she stayed on his heels.

"Mateo, tell me what's wrong."

He peered down toward the foyer, to his elaborate staircase that, as large and grand as it was, didn't really lead anywhere…except to more furniture and art and antiques. He'd accumulated so much. Right now he felt as if he'd been stripped of everything.

When she touched his arm, his stomach jumped. He tried to find his calm center as he edged around. Her beautiful pale blue eyes were clouded with uncertainty, the indigo band around each iris darker than he'd ever seen. Blood pounded and crashed in his ears. She'd been caught and she knew it.

The words—his accusation—were on the tip of his tongue when the doorbell sounded. He thought of ignoring it, but he couldn't get what he needed to off his chest with some unknown person lurking on his doorstep. Leaving a desolate Bailey, he strode over, opened the door and was caught between a groan and smile.

Alex Ramirez stood with his hands in his pockets. Natalie, looking as beautiful as ever, was at her husband's side. Reece sat perched on her hip.

"We were on our way to a picnic," Alex said, sliding his

shades back on his head. "We thought you guys might want to join us."

"It's such a gorgeous day," Natalie added breezily, but a certain shadow in her eyes let him know something was amiss. Perhaps she was just overly tired.

"A picnic?" Bailey came forward. "I'd love to get out," she said as she looked across, "but Mateo might have something planned."

Mateo stepped aside. "Come in out of the heat."

"We have plenty of food and drink." Natalie entered the foyer while Reece kicked his legs as if he was riding a horse. "There's chicken and homemade potato salad. And plenty of room in the car. When you start a family you need to trade sports cars for roomier, safer options."

Mateo didn't miss the emphasis Natalie placed on *safer* or the way Alex's lips pressed together as he looked down and crossed his arms.

Mateo folded his arms too as he shared a look between them. "Is something wrong?"

Alex said, "No," at the same time Natalie said, "Actually, we wanted to speak with you—"

Alex groaned out a cautionary, *"Nat."*

"—about France," she finished.

And something else. Something important enough for them to show up unannounced. Not that he minded friends dropping in, but beneath the cheery exterior, some kind of trouble was upsetting Nat and Alex's usual state of marital bliss. And it seemed Natalie, at least, wanted him to referee.

Unfortunately, this was far from the ideal time. But he couldn't simply turn his good friends around and on their way. Not when Natalie's eyes were pleading with him to leave with them.

Mateo unfolded his arms. "Sure," he said, smiling, "we'd love to go."

Bailey spun on her heel. "Let me just race upstairs for a moment."

Natalie headed down the hall. "Do you mind if I use a bathroom? Reece sicked up a little on his shirt. He's had a cough."

"Of course." Mateo ran an assessing eye over the baby, but he didn't look flushed or ill. A little restless perhaps. "You know where the closest one is."

Alex waited until Natalie was out of earshot before he stepped closer.

"Sorry about this."

"No need to apologize. You're welcome any time."

There were simply more convenient times than others.

"It was Nat's idea we drop in. She values your opinion." Alex shrugged. "I do too."

"What's the problem?"

"Nat wanted to pin you down to get your take on—"

"All set!"

Alex stopped mid-sentence and both men's attention swung to the stairs. Bailey was bouncing down, a big bag over her shoulder. When she reached the foyer floor, she glanced around. "Where's Nat?"

"Here we are."

Natalie emerged, baby Reece resting on her hip, his cheek on her shoulder. Carefully, she handed him over to Alex. "I'm afraid he's getting a little too heavy for Mummy to carry."

"Babies do grow up," Alex said, swinging Reece onto his own hip.

"But they still need protecting."

"In lots of ways," Alex pointed out.

Mateo opened the door. "We should go."

As they headed out the door, Bailey went to loop her arm through his but he hadn't forgotten that email. How the truth had made him feel. Grinding his back teeth, he hastened his step, caught up with Alex and helped him put Reece in his seat.

As they all buckled up and Alex pulled out down the drive, Bailey tried to keep her spirits high even though she felt completely off balance.

When Mateo had come home she'd been on cloud nine. Now, for reasons she couldn't explain, there was nothing but tension all around. Between Mateo and her. Alex and Natalie. Even Mateo and Alex! Hugging the gift bag containing that builder's kit close, she studied Reece when he coughed. Even the baby didn't seem overly happy.

As if to prove it, the little guy barked again.

Natalie swung around to check on him but Alex put his hand on her arm and spoke to those in the back, as if he wanted to divert the focus.

"So tell me, has Paris changed?"

Mateo was glaring out the window. "The Louvre's still there."

"So you said hello to the *Mona Lisa?*"

Bailey answered Alex this time. "It was amazing to see her for real."

"And the orphanage?"

Mateo again. "Going well."

"Did you see that little boy? Remy?" Natalie peered around again. "Is he still there?"

"Quite a few have found families," Mateo said, and Bailey almost shivered at his tone. A stay-away-from-that-subject-today timbre.

Still, Natalie persisted. "But not Remy? He hasn't found a home yet?"

When Mateo's hands bunched on his lap, Bailey answered for him.

"Remy's still there. Barely says a word. But his little girlfriend makes up for it. Clairdy never stops talking."

"How old is he now?" Natalie persisted. "Five? Six?"

Mateo leaned forward. "This is a good park. Plenty of shade. Great views of the harbor."

Alex pulled in and they unloaded the picnic basket from the back while Natalie and Bailey took care of the baby. They found a shady spot overlooking the blue water and spread out two large checkered blankets.

"Would you like to go again?" Natalie placed Reece down and fished for a toy to occupy him from her diaper bag. "To France, I mean?"

"Actually, we'd kind of discussed that." Bailey slid a glance over.

Mateo's chest tightened as he took in her curious look. "Depends on my schedule," he replied as he found the thermos.

Bailey could go to France again but it wouldn't be with him. She'd exchanged paying back the price of her ticket home from Italy for an all-expenses first-class trip to Europe. She'd done well. And when they were alone again, he'd tell her exactly that—a moment before he told her to pack her bag and leave.

He'd had doubts from the start. And when that security guard had delayed them in Paris, he'd suffered more than a niggle. Now he knew why. There was reason to be suspicious. Hell, even her own father didn't trust her.

"Which part did you like best?" Natalie was saying, handing Reece a clear ball with jigsaw cut-outs and corresponding shapes inside.

"There were so many amazing things." Bailey fumbled as she laid out the plastic plates and they went in all directions over the blanket. "I couldn't choose just one."

Reece threw the ball then let out another cough and another. Mateo's doctor antennae went up.

"Has he had that long?"

"A couple of days," Natalie said.

Alex added, "But the doctor explained he couldn't give him his scheduled shots until he's completely well."

"*If* we decide he should be immunized," Natalie said.

Alex ran a hand through his hair. "Nat, we've discussed this."

"No. *You* made a decision for all three of us."

Reece began to grumble. Making *shushing* sounds, Natalie folded down beside him and handed back the ball.

Alex set his hands on his hips. "Mateo, save me. Tell her children need to be immunized."

"But there are side effects," Natalie interjected. "Sometimes serious ones. There are risks, aren't there, Mateo?"

Mateo considered the two of them—Natalie so passionate about protecting her boy from possible harm, Alex in exactly the same position, just looking at possible dangers differently. No one ever said parenting was easy. This decision might be a no-brainer for a lot of folks. For others, whether or not to immunize was the beginning of a whole host of moral battles associated with the responsibilities of being a mother or father. He should thank Bailey for inadvertently showing him her true colors and saving him from all this.

"In my professional opinion," he began, "I would have to say that the benefits far outweigh any possible dangers."

Natalie's slim nostrils flared then she dropped her gaze. "It's not that easy when it's your own child, Mateo." Holding her brow, she pushed out a breath and apologized. "I'm sorry. There was just this horrible story on the news the other night about the possible effects of shots. The footage was shocking. And then Sally from work said she knew of a couple who had a similar experience with their toddler. He was never the same again." Natalie peered up with haunted eyes. "Some kids *die*. Once it's done you can't take it back."

Mateo scrubbed his jaw. Natalie did need sleep. And reassurance. This decision obviously meant a lot to her. To both of them. As it should. But it wasn't *his* decision.

When Reece began to whimper, confused at seeing his mother upset, Alex crossed over, kneeled beside his family and hugged them tight. He brushed the words over his wife's crown. "We'll work it out, darling. Don't worry."

Mateo sat down with his friends and while Bailey made chicken sandwiches, he spoke to Natalie and Alex candidly. With any vaccination there could be side effects, but most often minor ones. Immunization was a way to curb and even eliminate deadly diseases in both children and adults. Ultimately the burden of research and decision was on the parents' shoulders.

But he conceded…Natalie was right. Rationalizing must sound pat when the child concerned wasn't your own. Natalie seemed reassured somewhat.

In the dappled sunshine, they finished their sandwiches— Reece ate almost a whole one. The packing up had begun when Bailey remembered. "I left something in the car."

She returned with a gift bag and handed it to Natalie. "This is for Reece. Mateo picked it out."

Mateo averted his gaze. He'd been happy to choose the gift but memories of the day also brought back the image of that security guard and his own suspicions. Come to think of it, Bailey hadn't emptied her pockets that day. She'd merely pulled out the bracelet.

But that was all water under the bridge. As charming as she was, that email had proven her more mercenary nature beyond a doubt. Duped by her own hand. He didn't care what excuses she came up with.

Natalie helped Reece unwrap the gift. He instantly grabbed

the hammer and thumped the ground. He squealed with delight when the tool squeaked and whistled.

Alex gently ruffled his son's head. "That's my boy."

Mateo took in the scene and knew he ought to be happy for them. But, even when he wanted to deny them, the truth was that other emotions were winning out. Ugly emotions like envy and disappointment.

This morning he'd come home thinking that soon he would be a married man. He'd been prepared to do what three months ago no one could have convinced him to try. He'd wanted to risk. Was willing to try for a family of his own. After finding the truth out about Bailey, he would never consider taking that kind of risk again.

After they'd packed up, Alex and Natalie dropped them home. Mateo headed for the door without waiting. He knew Bailey would follow, and out of the earshot of neighbors, he'd tell her precisely what he thought.

Bailey stood, stunned, watching Mateo's broad shoulders roll away as he ascended the stairs to his porch then unlocked and entered the house. She held her sick stomach, unable to comprehend how he could be so angry over that email to Vicky. Yes, she'd been pretty open in suggesting she thought there was—and wanted there to be—a future for them. She knew how he felt about marriage and children. God knows she hadn't wanted to get this involved either.

But now he was acting as though she was some weirdo with an attachment disorder. After the way he'd treated her—like a princess—*dammit,* that just wasn't fair. He'd led her on, set her up to trust him and…yes, *love* him. She thought he was falling in love with her too.

Back straight, she started for the stairs.

If he thought she would cower in a corner and accept this

behavior—the way Mateo had intimated she ought to take her father's sorry treatment—he was sadly mistaken.

When she strode in the door, he was waiting for her by the stairs. Given her dark expression, he knew what to expect. She was primed to defend herself, but he wasn't prepared to let this demise ramble on. He'd get to the point. Then she could leave.

"These past years I thought I had everything I could ever want," he told her as she crossed over to where he stood. "I thought I was content. And then I met you."

A range of emotions flashed over her face. First happiness. Lastly suspicion. "I'm not sure what you're saying."

"When I came home earlier I intended to ask you to marry me."

He extracted the blue jewelry pouch from his shirt pocket, loosened the string and tipped the ring into his palm. Five carats. The jeweler said his fiancée would love it. More than ever, Mateo felt certain that she would have.

Her incredulous gaze drifted from the ring to his eyes. Then her cheeks pinked up and her throat made a muted high-pitched noise.

"When you were out this morning you bought this?"

He inspected the diamond, tipping the stone so the light caught then radiated pale geometric patterns on the walls.

"I wasn't sure of the fit," he said. "The jeweler said I could take it back." That was precisely what he intended to do now. His fingers closed over the stone and his voice lowered to a rough-edged growl. "You have no idea how betrayed I felt when I read that email."

Bailey simply stared, looking as if she were taken aback and even annoyed. "Betrayed is a pretty strong word."

He almost sneered. "I shouldn't feel manipulated when you told that friend you wouldn't be cleaning floors for long?"

"I said that because eventually I'll get my degree."

"What you said was that you had big plans. That you'd lucked out."

"Well, I did feel lucky to have—" she stopped, blinked, then coughed out a humorless laugh.

"Wait a minute. You think I'm here...that I share your bed..." Her eyes glistened at the same time her face pinched as if she'd swallowed a teaspoon of salt. "You think I'm sleeping with you for your *money?*"

He huffed. "I'm sure as hell not sleeping with you because of yours."

When her eyes filled with moisture and hurt, Mateo cursed as a blade sliced between his ribs and twisted.

He inhaled deeply. "I apologize. I shouldn't have said that."

"Mateo, if you felt you needed to say it, believe me, I needed to hear it."

She wound around him and started up the stairs.

He called after her. "So you're going."

She stopped at the same spot where they'd made love a few days before. Her face was pale. Her hands trembled, even as they gripped the banister. He imagined she felt determined... and maybe, with her plans ruined, even crushed.

Join the club.

"You truly believe I'm nothing but a gold digger?"

He should have been prepared for it. The threat of tears. The indignation. Of course she wasn't going to admit it. "Bailey, there's no other way to read it."

Through narrowed eyes, she nodded as if she were seeing him for the first time.

"I'm such a fool."

"And how does that feel?"

She ignored his sarcasm. "Could you believe I thought you

were upset because you'd found out I'd fallen in love with you?"

His head kicked back but then that certain coldness rose up again. "Don't play with me."

"This morning I thought I'd really found the perfect guy, that fate had finally smiled on me again. An intelligent, good-looking professional with a sense of humor who had a heart to boot. Hell, I thought you were way too good for me." She dropped over her shoulder as she continued up the stairs, "Turns out I'm too good for you."

# Sixteen

Bailey had been packed and gone from Mateo Celeca's house in ten minutes flat. He wasn't anywhere around, and she was glad of it. Nothing he could say would change her mind about leaving, and if she'd seen his supercilious face, she would have needed to let him know again how disappointed she was. Disappointed in herself as well. For believing and hoping too much.

Now, a week later she was entering Natalie's real estate office. The receptionist buzzed through and a moment later Natalie breezed out from a back office, the smile wide on her face. She beckoned Bailey inside.

"I wasn't expecting you."

"I just finished cleaning my last house for the day. I hope this isn't an inconvenient time." Bailey took a seat while Natalie shut her office door then lowered into a chair behind her orderly desk.

"What can I do for you? Personal or private?"

"Both. You obviously don't know yet. Mateo and I broke up last week."

Her expression dropped. "I can't believe it. You said you'd had such a perfect time in France."

"We did. So perfect I fell in love with him."

Natalie nodded as if she understood. "He hasn't tried to contact you since you left?"

"No. And I don't want him to."

"He's always said he didn't want to know about vows and rings." Annoyed, Natalie flicked a pencil away. "I love Mateo but he's so stubborn on that. People come into our lives. Things change."

"Actually, Mateo bought a ring. The most beautiful ring I've ever seen."

Natalie's eyes rounded. "He proposed and you said no?"

Bailey relayed the story about the email, how Mateo had misinterpreted the message and how he wasn't prepared to view it from a different, more flattering light.

"I'm sorry," Natalie said, "but it sounds like a timely excuse to me." Bailey waited for her to explain. "For Mateo to have gone so far as to buy a diamond, he *must* be in love with you. But it doesn't sound as if he's ready to look beyond the past."

"I know he has issues with family. That he feels as if his parents abandoned him, his biological father particularly."

That was a big part of the reason he kept his emotions concerning Remy reined in so tight.

"There's something else," Natalie admitted. "Mateo was in love once before, many years ago. From what Alex tells me, she was not a nice type. She preyed on Mateo's good nature and generosity. He gave and gave but nothing was ever enough. They'd have arguments then make up. Alex said Mateo wasn't prepared to ever go through that kind of rollercoaster affair again. It scared him to think what would happen if he married a self-centered woman like that and they had a family. If he died and she abandoned the children."

Bailey tried to absorb the details as she gazed blindly at some document on the desk. "He wanted to marry her and she used him…."

"She didn't so much use him as bleed him dry."

Bailey's gaze flew up. "I wasn't with Mateo because of his money, what he could give me—"

"Oh, honey, I know."

Natalie skirted the desk and put her arms around her, but that didn't help Bailey from feeling gutted. She understood his reasoning a little better, but whatever lay in his past, Mateo was wrong to have jumped to any conclusions without giving her an opportunity to explain. She was tired of feeling as if she weren't good enough. As if she continually had to prove herself.

Moving away, Natalie leaned back on the edge of the desk. "Would you like Alex to talk to him?"

Bailey shook her head. "I'm here about my job. After the break you gave me, I wanted to give you plenty of notice. I've enrolled in classes and I'll be starting work in the university canteen closer to the time. If you don't mind, I'd like to stay on till then. I found a small place to rent and, frankly, I need the money."

The apartment wasn't much more than a room with a tiny bath attached. But it was affordable and clean and, most importantly, all hers.

"Of course you can stay on as long as you need to," Natalie said. "And I'm so pleased for you about the classes. But I do wish you'd let Alex have a word with Mateo."

Bailey found her feet. "It wouldn't work. Even if we got back together, he'd always wonder about my true feelings. Whether or not I'm a fraud." And, right or wrong, she didn't think she could ever get over the anger and disappointment that consumed her whenever she thought of his mistrust. "Still, I hope he finds someone who can make him happy."

Natalie sighed. "Alex and I thought he had."

The two women hugged and promised to keep in touch after Bailey handed in her notice. She was on her way out when she remembered to ask, "Did you and Alex come to a decision about Reece's shots?"

"We're going to take him in next week."

Bailey smiled. "I'm sure he'll be fine."

As she made her way to the bus stop, she rolled over in her mind their conversation. Given Mateo had gone so far as to buy her that ring, Natalie seemed convinced that he loved her. Bailey hadn't confessed that he'd barely batted an eye when she'd admitted that *she* loved *him*. Then again, given his doubtful nature—his ill-fated affair—he would only think she'd been playing her trump card to keep her foot in his door and her body in his bed.

Cringing, she walked faster.

She may not be a virgin but she would only ever sleep with a man if she wanted to share that most intimate part of herself with him. She hadn't been prepared to do that with Emilio, not that Mateo needed to know. The truly sad part was that she'd been burned enough by her Italian episode. Once bitten... Now, like Mateo, she couldn't imagine trusting anyone that much again. To know that he believed she would barter sex for a well-to-do lifestyle—that what they'd shared was essentially a lie—made her want to give up on relationships altogether.

As she neared the bus stop, a tall, suited figure stepped out from behind the shelter. When she recognized the height, the profile, every drop of blood froze in her veins. She was ready to turn straight around and walk away. She didn't want to see him. Didn't need to talk. But another, more resilient part propelled her on at the same time as that man came forward too.

She was shaking inside, but that didn't stop her from standing tall when she pulled up before him.

"What are you doing here? How did you know where to find me?"

"Since you left that morning after our argument," her father said, "I've kept track of your movements. I was about to take a deep breath and knock on your Mateo's front door before I saw you storm out. I contacted Mateo. He explained you two had had a falling out, and he told me which agency you worked for. The lady at the desk explained you were on their books to clean properties. I've waited around every day since, working through what I'd say when I saw you next."

Bailey swallowed against the emotion rising in her throat. "What did you come up with?"

"I don't know if she ever told you," Damon Ross said in a thick, graveled voice, "but your mother and I chose that bracelet together."

She wanted to clamp her hands over her ears. Instead she held them up. "I'm done fighting over that."

"I wanted to get you a gold pin with your name on it," he went on. "But, like always," his smile was both sad and fond, "Ann had her way. And, I'll give it to her, usually she was right. But not always." In his pristine jacket, his shoulders stooped. "Sometimes she was dead wrong."

Bailey's chest ached so badly she didn't want to take another breath. Her father had never opened up like this before. As if he genuinely wanted to help her understand. Still, that lesser part of her whispered in her ear. *Walk away. Say something that will hurt him for a change.* But she couldn't. When everything was said and done, he was her father and he was reaching out. But she needed to make him understand too.

"I know you miss her," she said, "but, Dad, I miss her, too."

He nodded slowly as his gaze trailed off.

"I thought something was wrong," he admitted. "We can all have trouble remembering where we put the keys. We've all missed appointments. But when she couldn't coordinate your activities…when she forgot to pick you up from school…" His features hardened and he thrust out his chin. "I told her I was taking her for a checkup. Yes, she was a free spirit. That's what I loved about her most. She always wanted to do it her way. But just that once—"

He paused and air leaked from his chest before he went on.

"Just that once, I wish she'd have listened." His chin firmed up again. "I should have insisted. Taken her to the doctor myself instead of buttoning my lip when she insisted it was nothing."

Her throat clogged, Bailey's thoughts raced. She couldn't get her mind around what he was saying.

"You blame yourself for her stroke?"

"Sometimes…yes, I do. Her grandmother died of an aneurysm at a young age. Her own mother died of similar complications the year before she passed." His eyes met hers and he smiled. "You're so like her. So headstrong."

"Is that why you pushed me away?"

"Makes no sense to say it aloud but I didn't want to lose you too. I made a pact the day we buried your mother that no matter how much I might want to give in to you, you'd do as you were told. I was going to protect and guide you and I didn't care if you ended up hating me because of it."

"I never hated you." Her voice cracked. "I just couldn't understand why you were so…distant. When Mom was alive, everything seemed so simple." So warm and so safe. "When she died, it felt like the biggest part of me died with her. After the funeral I felt so alone. I got mixed up with the wrong crowd and dropped out because I didn't think anyone cared."

He closed his eyes for a moment as if wishing he could take all those hurt feelings away. "Every day since you left I told myself that I shouldn't be so hard on you. I should be happy to watch you grow, make your mistakes."

She admitted, "I made a few."

"Most of them because I wasn't there the way I should have been."

He fished into his suit jacket pocket. When his hand opened, the gold chain and charms shone out like the treasure that it was. His eyes glistened with unshed tears.

"This is yours."

He took her hand and laid the bracelet in her palm. She gazed down, remembering those happy childhood days—her mother and the father she'd loved so much—and her heart rolled over. Tears ready to fall, she rested her cheek on her father's shoulder and Damon Ross at last brought his daughter close.

Mateo downed the last of his scotch, set his glass on the clubhouse counter and gestured to the bartender. He needed another drink. Make that a double.

Beside him, Alex held up a hand. "No more for me. I told Nat I'd be home by six-thirty."

Mateo argued. "We only got off the course an hour ago."

"And I'm ready to gloat to my wife about how I beat you on both the front *and* back nine." Alex's mouth shifted to one side. "Not that you've been focused on anything much lately."

Two weeks had passed since Bailey had walked out. Admittedly, he'd been preoccupied. Mateo was gesturing to the bartender again.

"I'll be back at work soon."

"And you think that'll help?"

Mateo pretended not to hear that last comment. It was high time he got back to the practice. He was going crazy hanging around that big house. Nothing to do. Only ghosts to talk to. When he'd been with Bailey he'd been happy to postpone visiting Mama. Since she'd gone, he'd considered flying to Italy to fill in the time more than anything, but he knew if he happened upon Emilio he might just punch him in the nose.

"Why don't you come back and have dinner at home with us," Alex said. "Natalie would love to see you. Reece too. I told you he had his shots earlier this week."

"A couple of times. I'm glad there weren't any serious side-effects."

Alex raised his brows. "You're not the only one. So, what about dinner?"

"Thanks. I'll have something here."

Mateo collected his fresh glass while Alex asked to settle his tab.

As Alex brought the leather booklet closer and looked over the items, he asked, "Ever heard the saying, love never comes easy?"

"I'm not in the mood for a lecture." Mateo swirled his ice.

"What about some sound words from a friend then?"

"She's gone, Alex." Mateo took a long sip. Swallowed and enjoyed the burn. "No happily ever afters here."

Alex signed and waited for the bartender to leave before he thatched his hands on the timber counter and asked, "Why do you hold on to it so fiercely?"

"Hold on to what?"

"You're not losing anything by admitting you love her."

"You know, you're right." Mateo found his feet. "Time to go."

"To that great big empty house," Alex reminded him,

following out of the crowded room filled with nineteenth hole chatter.

At the exit, Mateo stopped and rotated around. "I let Bailey know I thought she was a con."

Alex shrugged. "You were wrong."

"Yeah. I was wrong."

He'd let Bailey walk away that day two weeks ago, telling himself he had no choice. He was protecting himself. Doing the right thing. But he'd printed off that email and as the hours and then days passed, he read it over again and again. Bailey had insisted that her dialogue in that email had been that of a woman in love. In love with him. He hadn't wanted to listen. Even when his heart wanted to believe it, his brain didn't want to take the risk. Because this kind of decision was only the beginning. When you were a couple, you had to tend the garden every day, do everything you could to make certain the union survived. And if it didn't...if the marriage failed and you had kids...

Mateo headed for the cab stand.

Better that things had turned out the way they did.

Alex was on his tail. The sun was lying low, getting ready to set. The air was muggy. Stifling. Mateo was a whisker from ripping off his shirt.

"So admit it."

Mateo looked at Alex, striding beside him. "Admit what?"

"That you were wrong."

"Just did."

"To *her.*"

"Sure. I suppose I could kick it off with something like... 'Hey, Bailey, I was wondering if you could ever forgive me for being the world's biggest jerk.'"

Alex tugged his ear. "That's a start."

Mateo confessed, "I found that message and—" What felt

like a sharpened pencil drove into his temple. Growling, he waved off the rest. "Ah, forget it."

But Alex wasn't letting him off. "And what?"

Mateo stopped and studied his feet. His heart.

"And suddenly…I felt as if I had nothing. Was nothing. It's weird. I have so much. Too damn much. But where it counts…" He shut his eyes. *Oh God.* "I'm empty."

"You don't have to be."

Mateo's jaw shifted as his stomach sank more. "I never knew my biological parents."

Alex rested his hand on his friend's shoulder. "You'd make a great father."

"Bailey said that to me once."

"She's a wise lady."

"And I'm a jackass."

"Not usually but in this instance…"

Mateo looked over. Alex was grinning.

He would've liked to smile back but he shrugged instead. "How do I fix this? What on earth do I say?"

"The sixty-four million dollar question." Alex flagged down a cab. "The truth is always a good place to start."

# Seventeen

"Just shout if it's a bad time to drop in."

Knowing that voice, feeling her heart instantly crash against her ribs, Bailey gathered herself in record time and turned to face her attractive, uninvited guest.

"Okay," she said, devoid of emotion. "It's a bad time to drop in."

She angled back to climb her building's first flight of stairs. Mateo Celeca was right there beside her, his arms out, offering to carry her grocery bags.

"I'll help with those," he said.

Ignoring him, she kept climbing.

"Nice complex," he said when they reached the first landing.

She leveled him a glare—*Go away!*—and went on walking.

"Nat said you handed in notice at the real estate agency," he said.

She groaned and kept walking. "Whatever it is you've come to say, please, just say it."

"I thought we could catch a coffee some place."

"Thank you. No."

She tackled the last of the stairs and crossed to her apartment's front door.

"Bailey, I want to say I'm sorry."

His words hit her so hard she lost her breath. But apologies didn't make a difference in how she felt. She bolstered her resolve.

"Terrific." She placed her bags on the ground, found her key and fit it in the lock. "Goodbye."

"Also, I need to mention I was an idiot. I made assumptions and I shouldn't have."

She bent to retrieve the bags, but he'd collected them and was already moving around her and inside. Her tongue burned to let loose and tell him to get out before she called security. But why not let him see how she lived now? He might need all his "stuff" but she certainly did not. Cozy suited her just fine.

"A bit different from what you're used to," she said as he slid the bags on the modest kitchenette counter.

His brows knitted, he cast a glance around. "It's, ah, very clean."

Then, as if she'd invited him to stay, he pulled out a stool. Not happening. Since speaking with her father—making amends there—she'd progressed by leaps and bounds this last week. New place, new job and new life on the way. She wasn't prepared to take a backward step now. She would not let her past feelings for Mateo hoodwink her into thinking for a moment "this" was anything other than over.

"I understand you must feel bad about what you said and even worse about how you acted. You should. But you've said sorry. Hell, I'll even accept the apology. Now," she fanned the door open, "have a nice life."

Not quite a smile, his mouth tugged to one side. "You don't mean that."

"Actually, I don't. But *I wish you nothing but happiness* would've been even harder to believe."

A muscle leapt to life in his cheek as he pushed to his feet. By the time he'd strolled over, Bailey's pulse had climbed so high, she swore it hit a bell. But he didn't sweep her up into his arms and carry her away. He didn't even try to crowd her back against the wall and kiss her. He merely closed the door, then gestured for her to take a seat.

Holding her ground, Bailey crossed her arms.

"It's over, Mateo. I can spell it out for you if you like, but other than that, if you don't mind I have things to—"

She'd reached to turn the door handle. In an instant, his hot hand had covered hers and her gaze jumped to his, his face set and passionate. God help her, he'd never looked more handsome.

"Bailey, what we shared is a long way from over."

Wrenching back, she moved well away. She didn't need to get that close to him. Didn't need to smell his musky scent. Feel that animal heat.

"Do you think that little of me?" She asked. "*Turn on the charm and she'll forget how I suggested she could be bought.* Dr. Celeca, you could be the richest, most powerful, best looking man in the world and it wouldn't make a scrap of difference as to how I feel about you now."

"I understand."

She looked at him sideways then blinked.

"Well…*good.*"

"From the moment we met," he said, "I made assumptions. I was hard on you, suspicious. Not because of Mama and

Emilio. I'm sure I believed you on both counts near to the start."

"So you made me feel like a felon because it rains on Tuesdays?"

A smile curved his lips as he prowled two steps nearer.

"I was hard on you because you made me look at myself. Not the doctor or investor or benefactor. At the *stripped down* me with absolutely nothing to hide behind. And, *Dio buono*, that scared me like you wouldn't believe."

Breathing shallow, she rotated away. *I don't want to hear this. It won't make a difference.*

"Before I met you," he went on, "I knew what I wanted. Success. Security. If I had somewhere solid where I felt I belonged, I had everything I needed. But all the possessions in the world could never be enough because what I need can't be bought."

She shrugged. "Take a bow."

An arm wound around her waist but not firmly enough. She maneuvered out and held up both hands.

"This has gone on long enough. I'd like to say we could be friends but—"

"Dammit, Bailey, I want more than your friendship."

He hadn't raised his voice but something in the timbre set her nerves jangling and her blood racing even faster.

"I know what you want," she said. "But I'm happy the way I am. There are goals I want to accomplish and I want to achieve them my way."

"There's no room for *our* way?" he asked.

She thought of her father's admission—of how her mother hadn't wanted his help when she'd needed it most—and a sliver of doubt pierced her armor.

"I've thought long and hard about this," Mateo said, coming close again. "The way I see it, this is about trust. I needed to trust you. Now you need to trust me."

She huffed and stepped back. "Sorry. Tried that."

"And I let you down."

"Damn right you did."

"But love is about forgiveness."

"No one mentioned *love*." At least he hadn't.

"I have something for you."

She lifted her brows at his change of subject. She guessed what his something was.

"I'm not interested in your big diamond ring, Mateo."

"It's not a ring. I only hope you like it enough." He reached into his trouser pocket and retrieved something small and gold.

Bailey's heart pounded as she gazed down at the Eiffel Tower trinket nestled in the palm of his hand. She couldn't help it. Her eyes misted over and she suddenly felt so weak... so *vulnerable*.

"France was only a week out of our lives."

"The most important week," he said. "The week we fell in love. I love you, Bailey. You loved me then. I'm here because I need to know...do you love me still?"

She searched his eyes...searched her heart. The truth wasn't that simple.

"I don't know," she said.

"Because I made a mistake." Before she could answer, he went on. "An unbelievably huge mistake." Pressing her lips together, she nodded. "Your father made mistakes too. You've made mistakes."

"I don't know that I can forgive you that one."

"I understand." He stepped nearer. "I do." His palm trailed her cheek, her chin. "I'd do anything to take it back."

She closed her eyes to shut out the bitter sting and ache of emotion. "I never wanted your money."

"I always wanted you." A light kiss dropped on the side

of her mouth. "Marry me, Bailey. Be my wife. I need you in my life and you need me. Every day. Every night."

"Because you love me."

He groaned against her lips. "So much."

"And because…"

His hand covered hers and the charm. "Because…?"

Overcome with emotion, finally beaten and glad of it, she gazed into his eyes and admitted.

"Because I love you."

His eyes flashed a heartbeat before his mouth lowered and captured hers.

She was helpless to deny the pleasure, couldn't stop herself from pressing in. As one palm cradled the back of her head and his steaming hard body curled over hers, Bailey could only cling to his shoulder, grateful tears squeezing from her eyes, heart filled to overflowing.

When his lips reluctantly left hers, her head was spinning. But his smile, so close, and his hands, so warm, left her wonderfully anchored.

"Marry me," he whispered.

Another tear slid down her cheek as she took a breath and surrendered. "Yes, Mateo," she murmured. "I'll marry you. I want to be your wife."

A tingling wave of desire and contentment spiraled through her as the man she couldn't help but adore—the soul mate she couldn't help but trust in—kissed her once more. Bailey held on, smiling…belonging…believing…

All the world lay in the palm of their hands.

# Epilogue

Mateo had decided this should be a surprise. Bailey argued; everyone liked to be given at least some notice before guests drop by. When he pulled up outside Ville Laube's Chapelle and Madame Garnier's face lit with amazement, then a group of children edged forward, he laughed and, leaning over, snatched a kiss from his beautiful bride's cheek.

"You see," he said. "Sometimes it's good to be caught off guard."

"I know someone who's going to be a little more than that."

But they'd already agreed. Mateo would give Remy his gift in private. There were other bombshells to drop first.

As the new Dr. and Mrs. Celeca moved forward and the crowd of kids grew larger, someone in the tower rang the bell. Nichole Garnier was one of the first to meet them. Holding her face, she looked lost for words.

Mateo kissed both Madame's cheeks.

"I don't understand," Nichole started. "We only said goodbye. How long are you staying?"

"A while." He and Bailey shared a look. *A long while.*

Mateo was about to explain when he caught sight of Remy, standing by the side, one mitten cupping his brow.

"Remy!" Mateo called out. "Come say hello."

By now children were racing around them, hugging their guests' legs and singing as if school was out for a year.

Laughing too, Madame demanded to know. "Tell me! What are you doing here?"

"Bailey and I have decided to move to France permanently. There's still a mountain of forms to fill out and sign, but—"

*"Mon dieu."* Madame interrupted. *"Here?"*

"Actually, over there."

When he waved toward his cottage, Nichole failed to catch her yelp of delight.

Clairdy was there dancing around, first like a ballerina then a break dancer. Laughing, Bailey crouched down beside her little friend. "Do you understand, Clairdy?"

Nichole ran a hand over the little girl's head and spoke in French. Up to speed now, Clairdy's eyes sparkled before she cartwheeled away and back again. She was telling the other children. *Monsieur and Mademoiselle are married and living here with us!*

Remy must have heard; he came running up, full speed. Mateo bent to catch his hare. The momentum swung them both halfway around. After the commotion settled enough, Mateo drew Remy away, out of others' earshot.

"I have some other news, Remy." He held the boy's hand and continued to speak in French. "Bailey and I would like you to live with us."

But Remy didn't react the way Mateo had hoped. His face filled with uncertainty and his wide eyes darted first right then left. Frowning, Mateo shifted. He hadn't explained properly.

"Remy, if you want me to be your father..." He inhaled deeply and said the words he'd held back for too long. "I'd like you to be my son."

But the boy's expression furrowed more. He looked as if he'd been given the biggest gift under the tree but for some reason couldn't open it.

With a knuckle, Mateo gently tipped up his chin. "What's wrong?"

"Monsieur, I cannot go." The boy held a hand out to where his friend stood dancing with the others. "I cannot leave Clairdy behind."

"You want Clairdy to come with us?" Mateo smiled. "To be your sister?"

"She will be good," Remy promised. "She won't talk too much. I'll tell her."

Mateo chuckled. "We've already thought about your Clairdy. If she'd like to join our little family, we'd love to have her."

Remy gave a *yip!* then raced off to tell Clairdy the good news while Mateo raveled his wonderful wife into his arms.

"I'm thinking we need a dog. How about a Labradoodle?"

Bailey wrapped her arms around his neck and stole a kiss. "You remembered?"

"Why don't we name him after your father?"

"Damon the Labradoodle?" She nodded. "I like it. He can keep you and Remy company while you work on the cottage."

"Yes. Another couple of rooms."

"A cubbyhouse out back."

Letting out a breath, he took in his surroundings...the majesty of the Chapelle surround by a pile of noisy children. "How strange that I should end up back here."

"I think it's perfect. Well, *almost* perfect." She stroked his cheek and spoke earnestly. "Mateo, now I have a surprise for you."

She tilted her chin over his shoulder.

A man was walking up and for a moment Mateo thought he knew him…the hawkish nose, those kind, light gray eyes. Something unique about the way he walked. Mateo's mind wound back, further and faster. Absently he touched the scar on one side of his lip then shook his head slowly.

It couldn't be.

The name came out a threadbare croak.

*"Henri?"*

Upon him now, the man hugged him tight and then Mateo knew for certain. His childhood friend who had left all those years ago. Mateo never thought they'd see each other again.

"You are the same," Henri said, laughing and clapping Mateo's shoulder.

Beaming, Mateo brushed the top of Henri's head. "You're taller!"

Henri's gaze hooked onto Bailey, her hands clasped under her chin. He exclaimed, "This is the lady we have to thank for finding and bringing us here."

Mateo pinned Bailey with a curious look.

*You did this?*

Looking set to burst, she nodded. Now Mateo was the one lost for words.

"I hear you're married, Mateo. And after marriage," Henri said, "comes children. I'm afraid you have some catching up to do." Henri stepped aside. A woman with three children stood behind him. "My wife, Talli. These three rascals belong to us."

The rascals, introduced as Mimi, Luc and Andre, asked if they could play then ran off to join in the other children's games while Nichole rushed inside to have more settings placed for lunch. While Talli and Bailey chatted, Mateo and Henri caught up. Henri lived many miles from the Chapelle. His adoptive father had died and his adoptive mother married again. Change of name, a few changes of address. It made sense that Mateo's search for him had come up empty.

"Until Nichole and your beautiful wife put their heads together. They left no stone unturned."

Mateo explained about Ernesto, his move to Australia and how he'd decided to give up his practice there to live and enjoy a simpler life here.

When Nichole called everyone in for lunch, Mateo held Bailey back.

"I have never been so surprised," he told her as he brought her close and searched her adoring eyes. "Thank you." And then he kissed her with all that his body and soul could give.

When their lips softly parted, he kept her near. He couldn't put into words how much he loved her. How her love had saved him.

Smiling, he shrugged. "You have given me *everything*."

Bailey's heart glistened in her eyes as she replied in French, "Then, *mon amour,* we are even."

\* \* \* \* \*

# KING'S MILLION-DOLLAR SECRET

**MAUREEN CHILD**

To Rory, Scott and Joaquin
at Building and Construction Contractors,
the heroes who rebuilt my kitchen,
put up with my constant questions
and made a palace out of a pup tent!

Thanks, you guys.

# One

Rafe King liked a friendly wager as much as the next guy.

He just didn't like to lose.

When he lost though, he paid up. Which was why he was standing in a driveway, sipping a cup of coffee, waiting for the rest of the work crew to show up. As one of the owners of King Construction, it had been a few years since Rafe had actually done any on-site work. Usually, he was the details man, getting parts ordered, supplies delivered. He stayed on top of the million and one jobs the company had going at any one time and trusted the contractors to get the work done right.

Now though, thanks to one bet gone bad, he'd be working on this job himself for the next few weeks.

A silver pickup truck towing a small, enclosed trailer pulled in behind him and Rafe slanted his gaze at the driver. Joe Hanna. Contractor. Friend. And the man who'd instigated the bet Rafe had lost.

Joe climbed out of his truck, barely managing to hide a smile. "Hardly knew you without the suit you're usually wearing."

"Funny." Most of his life, Rafe hadn't done the suit thing. Actually, he was more comfortable dressed as he was now, in faded jeans, black work boots and a black T-shirt with King Construction stamped across the back. "You're late."

"No, I'm not. You're early." Joe sipped at his own coffee and handed over a bag. "Want a doughnut?"

"Sure." Rafe dug in, came up with a jelly-filled and polished it off in a few huge bites. "Where's everyone else?"

"We don't start work until eight a.m. They've still got a half hour."

"If they were here now, they could start setting up, so they could start working at eight." Rafe turned his gaze to the California bungalow that would be the center of his world for the next several weeks. It sat on a tree-lined street in Long Beach, behind a wide, neatly tended lawn. At least fifty years old, it looked settled, he supposed. As if the town had grown up around it.

"What's the job here, anyway?"

"A kitchen redo," Joe said, leaning against Rafe's truck to study the house. "New floor, new counter. Lots of plumbing to bring the old place up to code. New drains, pipes, replastering and painting."

"Cabinets?" Rafe asked, his mind fixing on the job at hand.

"Nope. The ones in there are solid white pine. So we're not replacing. Just stripping, sanding and varnishing."

He nodded, then straightened up and turned his gaze on Joe. "So do the guys working this job know who I am?"

Joe grinned. "Not a clue. Just like we talked about, your real identity will be a secret. For the length of the job here, your name is Rafe Cole. You're a new hire."

Better all the way around, he thought, if the guys working with him didn't know that *he* was their employer. If they knew the truth, they'd be antsy and wouldn't get the work done. Besides, this was an opportunity for Rafe to see exactly what his employees thought of the business and working for King Construction. Like that television show where employers went undercover at their own companies, he just might find out a few things.

Still, he shook his head. "Remind me again why I'm not firing you?"

"Because you lost the bet fair and square and you don't welsh on your bets," Joe said. "And, I warned you that my Sherry's car was going to win the race."

"True." Rafe smiled and remembered the scene at the King Construction family picnic a month ago. The children of employees spent months building cars that would then race on a track made especially for the event. In the spirit of competition, Rafe had bet against Joe's daughter's bright pink car. Sherry had left everyone else standing at the gate. That would teach him to bet against a female.

"Good thing you let your brothers do all the talking at the picnic," Joe was saying. "Otherwise, these guys would recognize you."

That's just the way Rafe liked it, he thought. He left the publicity and the more public areas of the business to two of his brothers, Sean and Lucas. Between the three of them, they had built King Construction into the biggest construction firm on the West Coast. Sean handled the corporate side of things, Lucas managed the customer base and crews, and Rafe was the go-to guy for supplies, parts and anything else needed on a site.

"Lucky me," he muttered, then looked up at the rumble of another truck pulling up to the front of the house. Right behind him, a smaller truck parked and the two men got out and walked toward them.

Joe stepped up. "Steve, Arturo, this is Rafe Cole. He'll be working the job with you guys."

Steve was tall, about fifty, with a wide grin, wearing a T-shirt proclaiming a local rock band. Arturo was older, shorter and wearing a shirt stained with various colors of paint. Well, Rafe thought, he knew which one of them was the painter.

"We ready?" Steve asked.

"As we'll ever be." Joe turned and pointed to the side of the house. "There's an RV access gate there. Want to put the trailer in her back yard? Easier to get to and it'll keep thieves out."

"Right."

Joe positioned his truck and trailer through the gate and in minutes, they were busy. Rafe jumped in. It had been a few years since he'd spent time on a site, but that didn't mean he'd forgotten anything. His father, Ben King, hadn't been much of a dad, but he had run the construction arm of the King family dynasty and made sure that every one of his sons—all eight of them—spent time on job sites every summer. He figured it was a good way to remind them that being a King didn't mean you had an easy ride.

They'd all grumbled about it at the time, but Rafe had

come to think that was the one good thing their father had done for any of them.

"We did the walk-through last week," Joe was saying and Rafe listened up. "The customer's got everything cleaned out, so Steve and Arturo can start the demo right away. Rafe, you're going to hook up a temporary cooking station for Ms. Charles on her enclosed patio."

Rafe just looked at him. "Temporary cooking? She can't eat out during a kitchen rehab like everyone else?"

"She could," a female voice answered from the house behind them. "But she needs to be able to bake while you're fixing her kitchen."

Rafe slowly turned to face the woman behind that voice and felt a hard punch of something hot slam into him. She was tall, which he liked—nothing worse than having to hunch over to kiss a woman—she had curly, shoulder-length red hair and bright green eyes. She was smiling and the curve of her mouth was downright delectable.

And none of that information made him happy. He didn't need a woman. Didn't want a woman and if he did, he sure as hell wouldn't be going for one who had "white picket fences" practically stamped on her forehead.

Rafe just wasn't the home-and-hearth kind of guy.

Still, that didn't mean he couldn't enjoy the view.

"Morning, Ms. Charles," Joe said. "Got your crew here. Arturo and Steve you met the other day during the walk-through. And this is Rafe."

"Nice to meet you," she said. Her green eyes locked with his and for one long, humming second there seemed to be a hell of a lot of heat in the air. "But call me Katie, please. We're going to be spending a lot of time together, after all."

"Right. So, what's this temporary cooking station about?" Rafe asked.

"I bake cookies," she told him. "That's my business and I have to be able to fill orders while the kitchen is being redone. Joe assured me it wouldn't be a problem."

"It won't be," Joe said. "Of course, you won't be able to cook during the day. We'll have the gas turned off while we work on the pipes. But we'll set it up for you at the end of every day. Rafe'll fix you up and you'll be cooking by tonight."

"Great. Well, I'll let you get to it."

She slipped inside again and Rafe took that second to admire the view of her from the rear. She had a great behind, hugged by worn denim that defined every curve and tempted a man to see what exactly was underneath those jeans. He took a long, deep breath, hoping the crisp morning air would dissipate some of the heat pumping through him. It didn't, so he was left with a too-tight body and a long day staring him in the face. So he told himself to ignore the woman. He was only here long enough to pay off a bet. Then he'd be gone.

"Okay," Joe was saying, "you guys move Katie's stove where she wants it, then Rafe can get her set up while the demolition's going on."

Nothing Rafe would like better than to set her up—for some one-on-one time. Instead though, he followed Steve and Arturo around to the back of the house.

The noise was incredible.

After an hour, Katie's head was pounding in time with the sledge hammers being swung in her grandmother's kitchen.

It was weird, having strangers in the house. Even

weirder paying them to destroy the kitchen she'd pretty much grown up in. But it would all be worth it, she knew. She just hoped she could live through the construction.

Not to mention crabby carpenters.

Desperate to get a little distance between herself and the constant battering of noise, she walked to the enclosed patio. Snugged between the garage and the house, the room was long and narrow. There were a few chairs, a picnic table that Katie had already covered with a vinyl tablecloth and stacks of cookie sheets waiting to be filled. Her mixing bowls were on a nearby counter and her temporary pantry was a card table. This was going to be a challenge for sure. But there was the added plus of having a gorgeous man stretched out behind the stove grumbling under his breath.

"How's it going?" she asked.

The man jerked up, slammed his head into the corner of the stove and muttered an oath that Katie was glad she hadn't been able to hear. Flashing her a dark look out of beautiful blue eyes, he said, "It's going as well as hooking up an ancient stove to a gas pipe can go."

"It's old, but it's reliable," Katie told him. "Of course, I've got a new one on order."

"Can't say as I blame you," Rafe answered, dipping back behind the stove again. "This thing's gotta be thirty years old."

"At least," she said, dropping into a nearby chair. "My grandmother bought it new before I was born and I'm twenty-seven."

He glanced up at her and shook his head.

Her breath caught in her chest. Really, he was not what she had expected. Someone as gorgeous as he was should have been on the cover of *GQ*, not working a construction site. But he seemed to know what he was doing and she had to admit that just looking at him gave her the kind of rush she hadn't felt in way too long.

And that kind of thinking was just dangerous, so she steered the conversation to something light.

"Just because something's old doesn't mean it's useless." She grinned. "That stove might be temperamental, but I know all of its tricks. It cooks a little hot, but I've learned to work around it."

"And yet," he pointed out with a half smile, "you've got a new stove coming."

She shrugged and her smile faded a little into something that felt like regret. "New kitchen, new stove. But I think I'll miss this one's occasional hiccups. Makes baking more interesting."

"Right." He looked as if he didn't believe her and couldn't have cared less. "You're really going to be cooking out here?"

The sounds of cheerful demolition rang out around them and Katie heard the two guys in the kitchen laughing about something. She wondered for a second or two what could possibly be funny about tearing out a fifty-year-old kitchen, then told herself it was probably better if she didn't know.

Instead, she glanced around at the patio/makeshift kitchen setup. Windows ringed the room, terra-cotta-colored tiles made up the floor and there was a small wetbar area in the corner that Katie would be using as a cleanup area. She sighed a little, already missing the farmhouse-style kitchen that was, at the moment, being taken down to its skeleton.

But when it was finished, she'd have the kitchen of her dreams. She smiled to herself, enjoying the mental images.

"Something funny?"

"What?" She looked at the man still sprawled on the tile floor. "No. Just thinking about how the kitchen will be when you guys are done."

"Not worried about the mess and the work?"

"Nope," she said and pushed out of the chair. She walked toward him, leaned on the stove top and looked over the back at him. "Oh, don't get me wrong. I'm not looking forward to it and the thought of baking out here is a little high on the ye gods scale. Still, the mess can't be avoided," she said. "As for the work that will be done, I did my research. Checked into all the different construction companies and got three estimates."

"So, why'd you choose King Construction?" he asked, dragging what looked like a silver snake from the back of the stove to a pipe jutting out from the garage wall.

"It wasn't easy," she murmured, remembering things she would just as soon put behind her permanently.

"Why's that?" He sounded almost offended. "King Construction has a great reputation."

Katie smiled and said, "It's nice that you're so protective of the company you work for."

"Yeah, well. The Kings have been good to me." He scowled a bit and refocused on the task at hand. "So if you don't like King Construction, what're we doing here?"

Sighing a little, Katie told herself she really had to be more discreet. She hadn't meant to say anything at all about the King family. After all, Rafe and the other guys worked for them. But now that she had, she wasn't going to try to lie or squirm her way out of it, either. "I'm sure the construction company is excellent. All of the referrals I checked out were more than pleased with the work done."

"But…?" He patted the wall, stood up and looked at her, waiting for her to finish.

Katie straightened up as he did and noticed that though she was five foot nine, he had at least four inches on her. He also had the palest blue eyes she had ever seen, fringed by thick eyelashes that most women would kill for. His black eyebrows looked as though they were always drawn into a frown. His mouth was full and tempting and his jaws were covered with just the slightest hint of black stubble. His shoulders were broad, his waist narrow and those jeans of his really did look amazingly good on him. A fresh tingle of interest swept through her almost before she realized it.

It was nice to feel something for an ordinary, everyday, hard-working guy. She'd had enough of rich men with more money than sense or manners.

He was still waiting, so she gave him a bright smile and said, "Let's just say it's a personal matter between me and one member of the King family."

If anything, the perpetual scowl on his face deepened. "What do you mean?"

"It's not important." She shook her head and laughed. "Honestly, I'm sorry I said anything. I only meant that it was hard for me to hire King Construction, knowing what I do about the King family men."

"Really." He folded his arms over his chest and asked, "What exactly do you think you know about the Kings?"

His gaze was narrowed and fixed on her. She felt the power of that glare right down to her bones and even Katie was surprised at the tingle of something tempting washing through her. Suddenly nervous, she glanced over the back of the stove to look at the pipes as if she knew what she was seeing. Still, it gave her a second to gather her thoughts. When she felt steady again, she said, "You mean beside the fact that they're too rich and too snobby?"

*"Snobby?"*

"Yes." Katie huffed out a breath and said, "Look I know you work for them and I don't want to make you uncomfortable. I only know that I never want anything to do with any of them again."

"Sounds ominous."

She laughed at the idea. Katie doubted very much that Cordell King had given her a second thought since he'd abruptly disappeared from her life six months ago. No, the Kings steamrolled their way through the world, expecting everyone else to get out of their way. Well, from now on, she was going to oblige them.

"Oh, I don't think any of the Kings of California are staying up nights wondering why Katie Charles hates their guts."

"You might be surprised," he said, dusting his hands off as he looked at her. She shifted a little under that direct stare. "You know, I'm a curious kind of guy. And I'm not going to be happy until I know why you hate the Kings."

"Curiosity isn't always a good thing," she said. "Sometimes you find out things you'd rather not know."

"Better to be informed anyway, don't you think?"

"Not always," Katie said, remembering how badly she'd felt when Cordell broke things off with her. She'd just had to ask him *why* and the answer had only made her feel worse.

Rafe smiled at her then and she noted how his features softened and even his eyes lost that cool, dispassionate gleam. Her heartbeat jittered unsteadily in her chest as her body reacted to the man's pure male appeal. Then, as if he knew exactly what she was thinking, that smile of his widened and he actually *winked* at her.

But a moment later, he was all business again.

"Your temporary gas line is hooked up. But remember, we're shutting the gas off during the day. We'll let you know when it's safe to use the stove."

"Okay. Thanks." She took a single step backward and Rafe walked past her, his arm brushing against hers as he did. Heat flashed through her unexpectedly and Katie took in a deep breath. Unfortunately, that meant she also got a good long whiff of his cologne. Something foresty and cool and almost as intriguing as the man himself. "And Rafe?"

"Yeah?"

"Please don't repeat any of what I said about the King family. I mean, I probably shouldn't have brought it up and I don't want to make anyone uncomfortable while you're working here."

He nodded. "Won't say a word. But like I said, one of these days, I'm going to hear the rest of your story."

Katie shook her head and said, "I don't think so. The Kings are part of my past and that's where I want to leave them."

By the end of the first day, Katie was asking herself why she had ever decided to remodel. Having strangers in and out of her house all day was weird, having *noisy* strangers only made it worse.

Now though, they were gone and she was left alone in the shell of what had been her grandmother's kitchen. Standing in the center of the room, she did a slow circle, her gaze moving over everything.

The floor had been torn up, right down to the black

subfloor that was older than Katie. The walls were half torn down and the cabinet doors had been removed and stacked neatly in the back yard. She caught a glimpse of naked pipes and groaned in sympathy with the old house.

"Regrets?"

She jumped and whirled around. Her heart jolted into a gallop even as she blew out a relieved breath. "Rafe. I thought you left with the others."

He grinned as if he knew that he'd startled her. Then, leaning one shoulder on the doorjamb, he folded his arms across his chest. "I stayed to make sure your gas hookup in the back room was working."

"And is it?"

"All set."

"Thanks. I appreciate it."

He shrugged and straightened up languidly as if he had all the time in the world. "It's my job."

"I know, but I appreciate it anyway."

"You're welcome." His gaze moved over the room as hers had a moment before. "So, what do you think?"

"Honestly?" She cringed a little. "It's horrifying."

He laughed. "Just remember. Destruction first. Then creation."

"I'll try to remember." She walked closer to where the sink had been. Now, of course, it was just a ripped-out wall with those naked pipes staring at her in accusation. "Hard to believe the room can come back from this."

"I've seen worse."

"I don't know whether to be relieved or appalled at that statement," she admitted.

"Go with relieved," he assured her. He walked closer, stuffing his hands into the back pockets of his jeans. "Some of the jobs I've seen took *months* to finish."

"So you've done a lot of this work?"

"My share," he said with a shrug. "Though this is the first job site I've worked on in three or four years."

The house was quiet...blessedly so, after a full day of hammers crashing into walls and wood. The decimated kitchen echoed with their voices, and outside, the afternoon was fading into twilight. There was a feeling of intimacy between them that maybe only strangers thrown together could experience.

She looked at him, taking her time to enjoy the view, and wondered. About him. About who he was, what he liked—and a part of her wondered why she wondered.

Then again, it had been a long time since she'd been interested in a man. Having your heart bruised was enough to make a woman just a little nervous about getting back into the dating pool again.

But it couldn't hurt to *look,* could it?

"So if you weren't doing construction, what were you doing instead?"

He glanced at her, long enough for her to see a mental shutter slam down across his eyes. Then he shifted his gaze away and ran one hand across the skeleton of a cabinet. "Different things. Still, good to get back and work with my hands again." Then he winked. "Even if it *is* for the Kings."

He'd shut her out deliberately. Closing the door on talking about his past. He was watching her as if he expected her to dig a little deeper. But how could she? She had already told him that she felt curiosity was overrated. And if she asked about his past, didn't that give him the right to ask about hers? Katie didn't exactly want to chat about how she'd been wined, dined and then unceremoniously dumped by Cordell King either, did she?

Still, she couldn't help being curious about Rafe Cole and just what he might be hiding.

"So," he said after a long moment of silence stretched out between them. "Guess I'd better get going and let you get busy baking cookies."

"Right." She started forward at the same time he did and they bumped into each other.

Instantly, heat blossomed between them. Their bodies close together, there was one incredible, sizzling moment in which neither of them spoke because they simply didn't have to.

Something was there. Heat. Passion.

Katie looked up into Rafe's eyes and knew he was feeling exactly what she was. And judging by his expression, he wasn't much happier about it.

She hadn't been looking for a romantic connection, but it seemed that she had stumbled on one anyway.

He lifted one hand to touch her face and stopped himself just short of his fingertips tracing along her jaw. Smiling softly, he said, "This could get…interesting."

Understatement of the century.

# Two

"Meeting's over," Lucas King muttered. "Why are we still here?"

"Because I've got a question for you," Rafe answered and looked up at his brothers. Well, two of them, anyway. Sean and Lucas, his partners in King Construction. Just looking at the three of them together, anyone would know they were brothers. They all had the King coloring, black hair and blue eyes. Yet their features were different enough to point to the fact that they each had different mothers.

But the man who had been their father had linked them not just by blood, but by fostering that brotherly connection in their childhoods. All of Ben King's sons had spent time together every summer, and the differences among them melted away in the shared knowledge that their father hadn't bothered to marry *any* of their mothers.

Lucas, the oldest of the three of them, was checking his watch and firing another impatient look at Rafe. Sean, typically, was so busy studying the screen of his cell phone while he tapped out messages to God knew who, he hadn't noticed that Lucas had spoken.

The brothers held weekly meetings to discuss business, to catch up with whatever was going on in the family and simply to keep up with each other's lives. Those meetings shifted among each of their houses. Tonight, they were gathered at Lucas's oceanfront home in Long Beach.

It was huge, old and filled with what Lucas liked to call character. Of course, everyone else called it outdated and inconvenient. Rafe preferred his own place, a penthouse suite in a hotel in Huntington Beach. Sleek, modern and efficient, it had none of the quirks that Lucas seemed so fond of in his own house. And he appreciated having room service at his beck and call as well as maid service every day. As for Sean, he was living in a remodeled water tower in Sunset Beach that had an elevator at beach level just to get you to the front door.

They had wildly different tastes, yet each of them had opted for a home with a view of the sea.

For a moment, Rafe stared out at the ribbons of color on the sunset-stained ocean and took a deep breath of the cold, clear air. There were a few hardy surfers astride their boards, looking for one last wave before calling it a day, and a couple was walking a tiny dog along Pacific Coast Highway.

"What do we know about Katie Charles?" he asked, taking a swig from his beer.

"Katie who?" Sean asked.

"Charles," Lucas said, irritation for their younger brother coloring his tone. "Don't you listen?"

"To who?" Sean kept his gaze fixed on his cell phone. The man was forever emailing and texting clients and women. It was nearly impossible to get Sean to pay attention to anything that didn't pop up on an LED screen.

*"Me,"* Rafe told him, reaching out to snatch the phone away.

"Hey!" Sean leaned out and reclaimed his phone. "I'm setting up a meeting for later."

"How about instead you pay attention to *this* one?" Rafe countered.

"Fine. I'm listening. Give me my phone."

Rafe tossed it over, then turned his gaze to Lucas. "So?" Rafe asked. "You know anything about Katie Charles?"

"Name sounds familiar. Who is she?"

"Customer," Rafe said, picking up his beer and leaning back in the Adirondack chair. "We're redoing her kitchen."

"Good for us." Sean looked at him. "So what's bugging you about her?"

Good question. Rafe shouldn't have cared what Katie Charles thought of the King family. What did it really matter in the grand scheme of things? Still, ever since leaving Katie's house earlier, he hadn't been able to stop thinking about her. And it wasn't just the flash of heat he felt when he was around her that was bugging her. She was pretty, smart, and successful, and she hated the Kings. What was up with that?

"Katie Charles," Lucas was muttering to himself. "Katie Charles. Kitchen. Cookies." He grinned and said, "That's it. Katie's Kookies. She's building a real name for herself. She's sort of a cottage industry at the moment, but people are talking about her."

"What people?" Rafe asked, frowning. "I've never heard of her before."

Sean snorted. "Why would you? You're practically a hermit. To hear about anything you'd have to actually talk to someone. You know, someone who isn't *us*."

"I'm not a hermit."

"God knows I hate to admit Sean's right. About anything. But he's got a point," Lucas said, stretching his long legs out in front of him. "You keep yourself shut up in that penthouse of yours most of the time. Hell, I'm willing to bet the only people you've actually talked to since last week's meeting are the room service operator and the crew you worked with today."

Rafe scowled at Lucas, but only because he didn't have an argument for the truth. He didn't have time to date every model in the known universe like Sean. And he had no interest in the corporate world of movers and shakers like Lucas. What the hell else was he supposed to do with his time?

"Oh, yeah," Sean said with a grin. "I forgot about that bet you made. How's it going, being back on a job site?"

"Not bad," Rafe admitted. Actually, he'd enjoyed himself more than he had expected. Being on a site with hardworking guys who didn't know he was their boss had been…fun. And there was the added plus of being around a woman who made his body tight and his brain fuzz out. Until, of course, Katie had confessed that she hated the King family.

"So," Sean asked, "if you had such a good time, why do you look like you want to bite through a box of nails?"

"You do look more annoyed than usual," Lucas said with a shrug. "What's up? And what's it got to do with Katie Charles?"

"Neither of you knows her?"

Sean and Lucas looked at each other and shrugged. "Nope."

"Somebody does."

"Somebody knows everybody," Lucas pointed out.

"Yeah, but the somebody who knows Katie is a King."

Sean snorted. "Doesn't narrow the field down by much."

"True." Hell, there were so many King cousins in California, they could probably start their own county.

"What's the deal?" Lucas picked up his beer, leaned back in his chair and waited. "Why's she bothering you?"

"Because," Rafe told him, standing up to walk to the balcony railing, "she hates the Kings."

"Hates us?" Sean laughed. "Impossible. Women *love* King men."

"That's completely true," Lucas said with a self-satisfied smile.

"Usually, maybe," Rafe said, his gaze sweeping across the froth of waves on the darkening ocean. Although his ex-wife would probably argue that point. "But this woman doesn't. Hell she barely could say the word *King* without shuddering."

"So why'd she hire us if she hates us so much?"

He turned to look at Sean. "Our company's reputation, she says. But she's not happy about it."

"And you think somebody in the family turned her against all Kings?" Lucas asked.

"What else could it be?" Rafe looked at him and shrugged.

"The real question here is," Sean said quietly, "why do you care?"

"That is a good question." Lucas looked at Rafe and waited.

Too good, Rafe thought. Hell, he didn't know why he cared, either. God knew, he didn't want to. He'd been down this road before and he'd already learned that not only didn't he know how to love, but according to his ex-wife, he was actually *incapable* of it.

So why bother with romancing a woman when you knew going in it was doomed to fail? No, he kept his relationships easy. Uncomplicated. A few hours of recreational sex and no strings attached.

Better for everyone when the rules were clear.

Yet, there was Katie.

She stirred him up in a way he'd never known before, though damned if he'd admit that to anyone else. Hard enough to get himself to acknowledge it.

"Yeah, it is a good question," Rafe muttered. "Too bad I don't have an answer."

Katie was getting used to the noise, the dust, the confusion and the presence of strangers in her house. One week and she could barely remember what quiet was like. Or privacy. Or being able to move around her kitchen to the sounds of late-night radio.

Now, her kitchen was an empty shell of a room. She glanced out one of the wide windows into the backyard and sighed. There was a small trailer parked on her grass, its doors wide open, revealing tools and equipment enough to build four kitchens.

Pickup trucks belonging to Steve, Arturo and Rafe

were also parked on her lawn and the piles of her discarded kitchen were getting bigger. Broken linoleum, old pipes, her *sink*—a beautiful, cast iron relic—lay tilted atop one of the mountains of trash and just for a second, Katie felt a twinge of panic.

This had all seemed like such a good idea at the time. Now though, she had to wonder if she'd been crazy. What if the new kitchen wasn't as good as the old? What if her new stove didn't cook as reliably? Where would she ever find another sink so wide and deep? What if her business went belly up and she'd spent her savings on a kitchen she wouldn't be able to afford?

"Oh, God…"

"Too late for panic now," a deep voice assured her from the doorway.

She turned around to look at Rafe and caught the knowing gleam in his eyes. She forced a smile. "Not full-blown panic yet. Just a little…okay," she admitted finally, "panic."

He laughed and she had a moment to think how devastating he really was before the smile on his face faded. He walked into the room and looked out at the view she'd been staring at. "It looks bad now, but it's going to be great when it's finished."

"Easy for you to say."

"Yeah, it is. This isn't my first rodeo, you know. I've done a lot of remodels and the owners always have that wild-eyed look you have right now." He lifted one shoulder in a shrug. "But they're always happy when it's over."

"Because it's over or because they love what you did to their houses?"

"A little of both, maybe," he acknowledged. "Just

wanted to let you know we found a leak in a hot-water pipe."

"A *leak?*" Katie instantly had mental images of a rising flood beneath the house.

"Relax," he said. "It's just an old, slow leak. The joint on the pipes is bad. We're going to replace it, we just need to show it to you first and get you to sign off on the work, since it's extra to the contract."

She blew out a relieved breath. "Right. Okay then. Lead the way."

Katie followed Rafe out of the patio, across the yard and through the back door to the kitchen. She couldn't even reach her favorite room in the old house by walking down the hallway. It was crowded with her refrigerator, tables holding all of her pantry items and towers of pots and pans.

The sun was blazing down out of a clear blue sky and she was grateful for California weather. If she'd had to do this remodeling job in a place renowned for rain, it would have been far worse.

Rafe held the door open for her and she walked inside to a room she barely recognized. The old subfloor was black and littered with dust. The skeletons of the cabinets stood out like picked over bones on the walls. The pipes looked forlorn somehow, as if they were embarrassed to be seen.

Steve, the plumber, was crawling up out of a hole in the floor. Katie just managed to hide a shudder. You couldn't pay her enough to crawl under the house where spiders and God knew what other kind of bug lived. When he was clear, Steve turned to flash her a smile. "If you come over here, I can show you the leak."

"Great. Leaks." She picked her way across the floor, stepping over scattered tools and bits of old wood. She stopped alongside the long, narrow opening in the floor and squatted beside Steve. He held a flashlight pointed beneath the floorboards and said, "There it is. Probably been dripping like that for years. Hasn't done any damage, so that's good. But we should put in a new copper joint."

Katie nodded solemnly as if she understood exactly what he was talking about. But the truth was, she didn't see a leak. All she noticed was a damp spot on the earth beneath the floor that probably shouldn't be there. If she actually admitted she couldn't see the leak, they might insist she go down there to see it up close and personal. So Steve's word would be good enough for her. "Okay then. Do what you have to."

"Excellent." Steve turned and said, "Hey, Rafe, why don't you show her the new sink you brought in this morning."

"My new sink's here? Already?" Now this she was interested in. As far as pipes went, all she cared about was that they carried water whichever way they were designed to carry it without leaks, thanks very much. She didn't need to understand how they did it. Hard to get thrilled over copper piping.

"I was at one of our suppliers and saw a sink I thought you'd like, so I picked it up. We'll just store it in the trailer until it's time to install." Rafe led her out of the kitchen, down the back steps and across the lawn.

Arturo had the cabinet doors spread across makeshift sawhorse work tables and was busily scraping off the old finish before sanding them. Everything was happening. Only a week and already she was seeing progress. Maybe they'd get it all done in two weeks, Katie thought, then smiled wryly to herself. And maybe she'd sprout wings and fly.

"Here it is." Rafe stopped at the trailer, reached in and drew out a huge sink, one side much deeper and bigger than the other.

"Isn't that heavy?" she asked, remembering the loud *clunk* her old cast-iron sink had made when tossed to the top of the junk pile.

"Nope. It's acrylic." He held it in one hand to prove his point. "Tougher and won't chip or rust."

She smoothed her fingers over the edge and sighed a little. It was perfect. Looking up at him, she said, "Thank you. It's great."

"Glad you like it." He tucked it back into the trailer and draped a protective work blanket over it.

"I thought the contractor was supposed to pick up the supplies for the job," she said.

He turned back to look at her and shoved both hands into the pockets of his jeans. "Joe asked me to pick up a few things at the home store. I saw the sink and..."

"How'd you know I'd like it?"

"Took a shot," he admitted.

"It was a good one."

His blue eyes were shining and a cool wind tossed his black hair across his forehead. He was tall, broad-shouldered and looked *great* in those faded jeans, she thought, not for the first time. In fact, she had dreamed about him the night before. In her dream they were back in her kitchen, alone, as they had been yesterday. But in her fantasy, Rafe had kissed her until her toes curled and she had awakened so taut with desire and tension she hadn't been able to go back to sleep.

Even her unconscious mind was working against her.

"So, Rafe Cole," she asked, "how long have you been in construction?"

She thought his features tightened briefly, but the expression was gone so quickly, she couldn't be sure. Now why would that simple question get such a reaction?

"My dad started me out in the business when I was a kid," he said, staring off at the house, keeping his gaze deliberately away from hers. "I liked it and just sort of stuck with it."

"I get that," she said, trying to put him at ease again, to regain the easiness they'd shared only a moment ago. "My grandmother started me out baking when I was a little girl, and, well, here I am."

He nodded and glanced at her. "How long have you lived here?"

"I grew up here," she said. "My dad died before I was born, and my mom and I moved in here with Nana." Her gaze tracked across the familiar lines of the old bungalow. The windows were wide, the roof was shake and the paint was peeling in spots. But the house was home. It meant security. Comfort. "I moved out for college, then mom died and a year ago, I inherited the house from Nana."

"Oh," he said softly. "I'm sorry."

It took her a second; then Katie laughed and told him, "No, she didn't die. She just moved. Nana and her sister Grace decided to share an apartment at the Senior Living Center. They figure there are lots of lonely men over there looking for love!"

He laughed at that and once again, Katie felt a rush of something hot and delicious spread through her. The man should smile more often, she thought and wondered why he didn't. The other guys working here were forever laughing and joking around. But not Rafe.

He was more quiet. More mysterious.

Just…*more*.

Rafe sat opposite his brother Sean at a local diner and waited for his burger. As for Sean, he was typing out a message or thirty on his cell phone. Okay, as far as Rafe was concerned. Gave him more time to think about Katie Charles.

The woman was haunting him.

He couldn't remember being so fixated on a single woman—not even Leslie, before he married her, had so completely captivated him. While that should have worried him, instead he was intrigued. What was it about Katie that was getting to him?

She was beautiful, sure. But lots of women were. He wanted her, but he had *wanted* lots of women. There was something else about her that was reaching out to him on so many different levels, he couldn't even name them all.

"Hey," Sean said with a laugh. "Where'd you go?"

"What?" Rafe swiveled on the bench seat and looked at his younger brother.

"I've been talking to you for five minutes and you haven't heard a word. So I was wondering just what exactly had you thinking so hard."

Rafe scowled a little, irritated to have been caught daydreaming. Jeez. Thoughts of Katie were taking up way too much of his time. "Not surprising I was thinking of something else, since you were so busy texting."

"Nice try," Sean said, still grinning. "Distract me with insults so I won't ask if you're still thinking about the cookie woman."

Rafe shot him a glare. "Her name's Katie."

"Yeah, I know."

"Anyone ever tell you how irritating you are?"

"Besides you, you mean?" Sean asked, giving their waitress a bright smile as she delivered their dinners. "You bet. All the time."

Rafe had to smile. Sean was absolutely the most laid-back King ever born. Most of them were type A's, ruthlessly pushing through life, demanding and getting their own way. Not Sean. He had a way of slipping up on whatever he wanted until it just naturally fell into his hands.

He was damn hard to annoy and almost never lost his temper. In the world of the King family, he was an original.

Once the waitress was gone, the brothers dove into their meals. This hamburger joint on Ocean Avenue had been a popular spot since the forties. Rafe and Sean were on the outside patio, where they could watch traffic and pedestrians in a never-ending stream of motion. Kids, dogs, parents with digital cameras poking out of their pockets fought for space on the crowded sidewalk. Summer in a beach town brought out the tourists.

"So," Sean said, reaching for his beer, "let's hear it."

"Hear what?"

"About the cookie lady," Sean countered, both of his eyebrows wiggling.

Rafe sighed. Should have expected that his brother would be curious. After all, Rafe hadn't talked about a woman since Leslie walked out. He remembered his ex-wife looking at him sadly and telling him that she felt "sorry" for him because he had no idea how to love someone. That he never should have married her and sentenced her to a cold, empty life.

Then he thought about Katie and it was like a

cool, soft breeze wafted through his mind. "She's…
different."

"This gets better and better." Sean leaned back in his
booth and waited.

Frowning, Rafe took a sip of his beer. When he spoke,
it was a warning not only to his brother, but to himself.
"Don't make more of this than there is. I just find her
interesting."

"Interesting." Sean nodded. "Right. Like a bug
collection?"

"What?"

Laughing, his brother said, "Come off it, Rafe. There's
something there and you're looking. And about time too,
I want to say. Leslie was a long time ago, man."

"Not that long," Rafe countered. Although, as he
thought about it, he realized that he and Leslie had been
divorced for more than five years. His ex-wife was now
remarried to Rafe's former best friend, with a set of
toddler twins and a newborn, last he heard.

"Long enough for her to move on. Why haven't
you?"

Rafe shot Sean a glare that should have fried his
ass on the spot. Typically enough though, Sean wasn't
bothered. "Who says I haven't?"

"Me. Lucas. Tanner. Mac. Grady…" Sean stopped,
paused and asked, "Do I have to name *all* of our brothers
or do you get the point?"

"I get it, but you're wrong." Rafe took a bite of his
truly excellent burger and after chewing, added, "I'm
not carrying a torch for Leslie. It's over. Done. She's a
mother, for God's sake." And if he was to be honest, he
hadn't really missed her when she left. So what did that
say about him?

"Yet, you're still living in a hotel suite making do with the occasional date with a beautiful airhead."

"I like living in a hotel and they're not all airheads."

"Good argument."

"Look," Rafe said, reaching for his beer. "Katie's a nice woman, but she's off limits."

"Why's that?"

"Because she's got white picket fence written all over her," Rafe explained. "She's the settle-down-and-get-married type and I've already proven I'm not."

Sean shook his head and sighed. "For a smart guy, you're not real bright, are you?"

"Thanks for the support."

"You want support?" Sean asked, digging into his burger. "Then stop being an idiot."

"Shut up. I tried the happily-ever-after thing and it blew up in my face. Not going to do it again."

"Did you ever consider that maybe the reason it didn't work was because you married the wrong woman?"

Rafe didn't even bother answering that jibe. What would have been the point?

Monday morning, the guys were still fighting with the pipes and Katie was ready for a week in Tahiti. She'd hardly slept all weekend. Though the peace and quiet were great, she'd been so busy filling cookie orders she hadn't had time to appreciate it.

Now she sipped at a cup of coffee and winced every time the whine of a drill shrieked into the air.

"The noise is worst the first week," someone from nearby said.

She turned to look at Joe Hanna, the contractor. "You're just saying that so I won't run away."

He grinned. "Once the new pipes and drains are

installed, the rest will be easier for you to live with. I promise."

He had no sooner made that vow when a shout came from the kitchen. "Arturo! Shut off the water! Off! Off!"

"Crap." Joe hustled across the yard just behind Rafe while Arturo sprinted for the water shutoff valve out front. Katie was hot on Joe's heels and stepped into the kitchen in time to see Steve crouched over a pipe with water spraying out of it like a fountain in Vegas.

Katie backed out of their way while the men grabbed towels. Then Arturo got the water off and the three men in the kitchen were left standing around as what looked like the incoming tide rolled across the floor and under the house.

"That fitting wasn't on there right, damn it," Steve muttered and dropped through the hole in the floor.

"Should have checked it out with the water on low," Joe pointed out and got a glare from Rafe in response.

"What happened?" Katie asked and both men turned to look at her.

"Nothing huge," Joe assured her. "Just got to tighten things up. Looks worse than it is."

Katie hoped so, because it looked like a lake was in her kitchen and she couldn't think that was a good thing.

Joe slapped one hand on Rafe's shoulder and said, "I should have checked his work personally before we tested it. Rafe's been out of the game for a while, so he may be rusty. But he's got potential."

Katie saw the flicker of annoyance cross Rafe's features and she shared it.

"Isn't Steve the plumber?" she asked pointedly.

"Yeah," Joe said, "but Rafe did the joint work on that pipe."

"It was fine," Rafe said. "That shouldn't have happened."

"Sure, sure," Joe told him, then looked at Katie. "My fault. Like I said, I should have kept a closer eye on the new guy's work."

Rafe was biting his tongue, no doubt worried about defending himself and maybe losing his job. Then she realized that he could be fired anyway, if Joe decided that his work was too sloppy. So before she could stop herself, she stepped in to defend him. "Rafe does excellent work. He set up my temporary kitchen, allowing me to keep my business going. He's stayed late everyday cleaning up and making sure I'm inconvenienced as little as possible. I'm sure that whatever happened with that pipe was unavoidable."

"Yeah," a voice came rumbling up from under the house. "Found the problem. The first joint worked itself loose, so the water had to go somewhere. My bad. I'll get it fixed and we'll be back in business."

Katie gave Joe a look that said quite clearly, *See? You blamed the wrong man.* She smiled at Rafe and left them to clean up the mess and get back to work.

"What was that all about?" Joe wondered.

Steve poked his head up from under the floorboards and smiled widely. "Sounds to me like the boss lady has a thing for Rafe. Lucky bastard."

"Shut up, Steve," Rafe said, but his gaze was locked on the empty doorway where Katie had been standing only a moment before.

Joe was riding him because he could and Rafe would take it because it was all part of the bet he'd lost. Good-natured teasing was all part of working a job. But Katie's defense of him had surprised him. Hell, he couldn't even remember the last time someone had stood up for him—not counting his half-brothers and cousins.

Katie Charles was like no one he'd ever met before. She didn't want anything from him. Wasn't trying to get on his good side. But then, that was because she thought his name was Rafe Cole.

It would be an entirely different story if she knew he was a King.

# Three

Rafe was late getting to the job site.

Despite the bet he was in the process of paying off, he had his regular job to do, too. And dealing with a supplier who wasn't coming through for them was one of the tasks he enjoyed most.

"Look Mike," he said, tightening his grip on the phone. "You said we'd have the doors and windows on site at the medical complex by noon yesterday."

"Is it my fault if things got hung up on the East Coast?"

"Probably not," Rafe conceded, "but it's your fault if you don't get this straightened out in the next—" he checked his watch "—five hours."

"That's impossible," the older man on the other end of the line argued.

"All depends on how determined you are, now doesn't it?" Rafe wasn't going to listen to the man's excuses.

This was the second time Mike Prentice had failed to come through for King Construction. It would be the last.

Rafe didn't put up with failure. Mistakes happened to everyone, he knew that. But if a man couldn't keep track of his own business, then he was too disorganized to count on. The Kings required the people they worked with to have the same diligence they showed. "You have the materials at the job site by end of day today."

"Or…?" Mike asked.

A slow smile curved his mouth. Mike couldn't see it, but he must have heard it when Rafe answered, "You really don't want to know, do you?"

"Things happen, Rafe," the man continued to try to defend himself. "I can't stay on top of every supplier I have, you know."

"Don't see why not," Rafe countered. "I do."

"Right. Well, I'm betting that every once in a while someone stiffs the Kings, too."

"Yeah, they do." He glanced around his office at King Construction, already moving on from this particular problem. "But it doesn't happen often and it never repeats itself. This isn't the first time we've had this conversation, Mike. I took your explanation last time, but this is your second chance. I guarantee you, we'll never have this discussion again. If you can't get the supplies to us in five hours, King Construction will find a new supplier for this job."

"Now just wait a minute, let's not be hasty."

"You get *one* second chance with King Construction, Mike," Rafe told him flatly. "And this was it. Now, you have the materials there, as we agreed, or I'll put the word out to every construction outfit in the state that you can't be trusted. How many jobs you think you'll get then?"

A long moment of tense silence passed while the other man did some fast thinking. Rafe knew what was going through the guy's mind. He'd already ruined his rep with the Kings, but he still had hundreds of other construction outfits to do business with. Unless he messed this up further.

"It'll be there," the man said, but he didn't sound happy about it. "You're a hard man, Rafe."

"You should've remembered that, Mike."

Rafe hung up then, leaned back in his desk chair and spun it around until he could look out the window at the ocean scene stretching out in front of him. The King Construction building sat directly on Pacific Coast Highway and each of the brothers had an office with a view. One of the perks of being an owner.

Another perk was reaming guys who failed them.

Standing up, Rafe leaned one hand on the window, feeling the cool of the glass seep into his skin. Was he a hard man? He supposed so.

His ex-wife sure as hell thought so.

Just another reason for him to keep his distance from Katie Charles.

A woman like that didn't need a hard man in her life.


"Now, isn't this a nice view?"

Katie rolled her eyes and laughed at her grandmother. "You're impossible."

Emily O'Hara grinned, fluffed her stylishly trimmed silver hair and then winked at her granddaughter. "Honey, if you don't like looking at handsome men, they might as well bury you."

They were standing at the edge of the yard, watching the action. The men worked together seamlessly, each of them concentrating on a certain area, then helping each other out when needed. Naturally, Nana had noticed Rafe right away, but Katie could hardly blame her. The man was really worth watching.

Katie's gaze went directly to Rafe, on the opposite side of the yard. Since that morning when she'd stood up for him to Joe, Rafe had been avoiding her. She couldn't quite figure out why, either. Maybe it was a guy thing, embarrassing to have a woman defend his honor? She smiled to herself at the thought.

"Well, well. I can see now that you're doing plenty of noticing." She draped one arm around Katie's shoulders. "He's quite the hunk, isn't he?"

"Hunk?" Katie repeated with a laugh.

"You betcha. The question is, what're you going to do about it?"

"What can I do?" Katie watched Rafe as he grinned at something Arturo said and she felt a delicious flutter in the pit of her stomach.

"Honestly," Nana said with a shake of her head, "youth really is wasted on the wrong people. Katie, if you want him, go for it."

"He's not a cookie I can grab and wrap up."

"Who said anything about wrapping him up?" Nana laughed and advised, "I was thinking more that you should *unwrap* him. Just grab him and take a bite. Life's too short, honey. You've got to enjoy it while you can."

"Unbelievably enough," Katie said, "I'm not as freewheeling as my grandmother."

"Well, you could be." Nana shook her head and said, "I loved your grandfather, honey, but he's been gone a long time and I'm still alive and kicking. And, so are *you*. You've been burying yourself in your work for so long, it's a wonder you can step outside without squinting into the sun like a mole."

"I'm not that bad!"

"Didn't used to be," her grandmother allowed. "Until that Cordell twisted you all up."

Katie frowned at the reminder.

"There's a whole wide world full of people out there and half of them are men," Nana told her. "You can't let one bad guy ruin your opinion on an entire gender."

Is that what she was doing? Katie wondered. She didn't think so. Sure, Cordell King had hurt her, but she wasn't hiding. She was working. Building her business. Just because she hadn't been on a date in…good night. She hadn't been on an actual date with an actual man since Cordell and that was more than six months ago now.

How had that happened?

She used to be fun.

She used to call her friends and go out.

She used to have a life.

"Oooh, here comes the cute one," her grandmother whispered.

Katie came out of her thoughts and watched Rafe approaching them. He wasn't cute, she thought. He was dark and dangerous and so sexy just watching him walk made her toes curl. Golden retrievers were cute.

Rafe was…tempting.

"What'd you say his name was?"

"Rafe. Rafe Cole."

"Hmm…"

Katie looked at her grandmother, but the woman's expression was carefully blank. Which usually meant there was something going on in Nana's mind that she didn't want anyone else to know about. But before Katie could wriggle the information out of her, Rafe was standing in front of them. She made the introductions, then Rafe spoke up.

"I just wanted to tell you that we'll be shutting down early tonight. Joe's got a meeting and he wants Arturo and Steve there."

"Not you?" she asked.

He shook his head. "No reason for me to be there. I'm just a worker bee. Anyway," he said, with a smile for her grandmother, "it was nice to meet you."

"Good to meet you too, Rafe," Nana said with a smile.

When he walked away, Katie's gaze was locked on him. His long legs, the easy, confident strides he took, the way the sunlight glinted on his black hair. And yes, she admitted silently, she liked the view of his butt in those faded jeans, too.

Finally though, she turned her gaze to her grandmother. The thoughtful expression on her Nana's face had her asking, "Okay, what's going on? What're you thinking?"

"Me? Only wondering if he has a grandfather as good looking as he is."

"You're hiding something," Katie said, narrowing her eyes.

"Me?" Emily slapped one hand to her chest and widened her eyes in innocence. "I'm an open book, sweetie. What you see is what you get."

"Nana…"

She checked her wristwatch and said, "Oh, I have to fly. Grace and I have a double date tonight with a couple of frisky widowers. I'm meeting Grace for manicures in half an hour."

Katie laughed and gave her a hug. "You're amazing."

"So are you, when you give yourself a chance." Emily slid a look at Rafe again. "Why not invite that boy to dinner? Live a little, Katie. You like him, don't you?"

"Yeah," Katie said, shifting her gaze back to Rafe. "I do. I mean, I've only known him a week, but I've spent so much time with him, it feels like longer. He's a nice guy, Nana. A regular guy. Nothing like Cordell King and believe me, that's a good thing. I've had it with the idle rich."

"Not all rich guys are idle," Emily pointed out. "Or, jerks for that matter."

"Maybe," Katie said, but she wasn't convinced. Granted, she hadn't had a lot of experience with rich men. Cordell had been the one and only billionaire she'd ever known. But if he was an example of their breed, then he was more than enough to last her a lifetime. "From now on though, I'm only interested in regular, hardworking guys."

"You have your mother's hard head, God bless her." Nana blew out a breath and said, "Fine. This Rafe seems nice enough and he's surely easy on the eyes."

"That he is," Katie agreed, letting her gaze slide back to the man whose image had been filling her dreams lately.

"But you never really know a man until you've hit the sack with him."

"Nana!" Katie groaned and shook her head. "What kind of role model are you, anyway?"

"The good kind." Emily laughed, clearly delighted at being able to shock her granddaughter so easily. "I'm just saying, it might be interesting to take him out for a test drive, that's all."

Katie loved her grandmother, but she was in no way the free spirit Emily O'Hara was. But then Nana hadn't always been this outspoken and full of adventure. Right after Katie's mother died, Nana had seemed to realize just how short life really was and she'd thrown herself into the mix with abandon.

And while Katie admired that adventurous style and certainly understood, she just couldn't bring herself to behave the same way. Nana had had the great love of her life and now she was looking for fun.

Katie was still looking for love.

Still, the fact was, Nana was probably right about Rafe. Katie was more drawn to him than she had been to anyone, up to and including Cordell King. So maybe it was time she took a chance. Pushed herself out of the cocoon she'd wrapped herself in.

"Not interested in a test drive." Okay, that's a lie, she amended silently when that little buzz of interest popped in her veins again. "Not yet, anyway," she said aloud. "But dinner would be good. I do like him and he's so different from Cordell King."

"Uh-huh."

"What?"

"Nothing. Not a darn thing." Emily pulled her in for a hard, tight hug and said, "I'm off for some fun. I suggest you do the same. Gotta run."

Alone again, Katie silently studied Rafe Cole as he stood in the sunlight laughing with Arturo.

Fun sounded like a good idea.

"The guys are gone," Rafe said.

He had stayed deliberately, after the crew left for the

night, just to get a few minutes alone with her. Hadn't asked himself why, because he wasn't sure he'd like the answer. But he'd fallen into the habit of being the last man to leave and he actually looked forward to the times when it was just him and Katie at the house.

The neighborhood was quiet, but for the muffled, heartbeat-like sound of a basketball thumping in someone's driveway. A dog barked from close by and the ocean wind felt cool after a long day in the sun.

Katie had her curly red hair pulled back in a ponytail and her green eyes were shining in the afternoon light. A soft smile curved her mouth and Rafe felt a punch of need slam into him. He knew it would be a mistake to get her into bed. After all, not only was she so not his type, but she hated the King family. If they had sex and she found out he'd lied about who he was, it could only get ugly.

But damned if logic had anything to do with what he was feeling at the moment.

"How'd it go today?" She stepped out of the house and started for the garage. Rafe walked with her.

"We got the drywall up over the pipes and the plumbing's finished."

"Really?" She stopped and grinned. "No more naked pipes!"

The smile on her face made her eyes shine brighter and Rafe felt a tug of something hot and wicked. The woman could turn him hard without even trying. He couldn't even remember a time when he'd been this attracted, this quickly to anyone. Not even Leslie, the ex-wife from hell, had had this effect on him.

After a moment or two, he cleared his throat and said, "Yeah. It should move pretty quickly now, as long as all of your supplies come in on time."

She held up both hands, fingers crossed, and said, "Here's hoping. I really miss having a kitchen."

"Maybe, but from the smells coming from your temporary setup, it's not slowing you down any."

Laughing, she opened the garage door and stepped into the gloom. Rafe stayed with her, not ready to leave yet. He took a quick look around the garage. It was tidy, like the rest of her house. Storage shelves on one wall, washer and drier on another. There was an older model, red SUV parked dead center and a few lawn and garden tools stacked along the last wall.

"Baking the cookies is easy enough thanks to you setting up the stove for me," she said, with a nod of her head. "But oh, I miss my counter when it comes time to decorate and wrap. I've got tables set up all over the patio now, but…"

"You want your life back," he finished for her.

"*Yes,*" she agreed with a sigh. "Funny, but you go along every day and you hardly notice your routine—" She paused and smiled. "You'll notice I said routine, not *rut*."

"I noticed," he said with a grin.

She stopped beside the shelves and bent down to pull a bag of charcoal free. He bent down at the same time and suddenly, their mouths were just a kiss apart. Time staggered to a standstill. His gaze dropped to her lips and everything inside him clenched when her tongue slipped out to slide along her bottom lip.

Rafe wanted a taste of her. More than he did his next breath. But her eyes told him she wasn't ready for that and if there was one thing Rafe King knew, it was how to be patient. So he straightened up and grabbed the bag.

"Let me get that for you."

She stepped back with a soft *thanks,* then continued with what she'd been saying. "Then you get ripped out of that routine and all you can think about is getting it back. That doesn't make any sense at all, does it?"

"Sure it does," he said, idly noting how the sunlight drifting in through the small garage windows shone on her hair like fire. His body was tight and his breath was strangling in his lungs. But he didn't let her know that.

"Nobody likes having their place invaded and their life turned upside down."

"What about you?" she asked. "Do you have a routine you don't want upset?"

He gave her a quick grin and set the bag of charcoal at his feet. "Men don't have routines," he corrected. "We have schedules."

"Ah." She leaned against the front fender of the van. "And your 'schedule'?"

"Same as everyone else's I guess," he said after a long minute, when he took the time to remind himself to be vague. He couldn't exactly tell her about time spent with his brothers, or at King Construction. "Work, home. Play."

"I know what you do for work. What's your idea of playtime?"

"Well now," he mused thoughtfully, meeting her gaze and allowing her to see exactly what she was doing to him, "that's an interesting question."

She sucked in a breath of air and straightened up and away from her car. He liked seeing her nervous. That told him she was feeling the same kind of attraction he was. Good to know. But he'd let her catch her breath before he pushed any harder. He wasn't used to dealing with a woman like Katie.

The women he generally spent time with were, like Rafe, only interested in a few hours of pleasure. There were no hidden agendas, no emotional traps and no expectations. Katie was different. She was new territory for him and damned if he wasn't enjoying himself.

"So?" he asked, picking up the bag of charcoal, "Barbecuing?"

She looked grateful for the reprieve. "Yes. Hamburgers sounded good to me and they're just not the same if they're not barbecued."

"Agreed," Rafe said, turning for the door. "Want me to set it up for you?"

"Only if you'll stay for dinner."

He stopped, half turned and looked at her. A slow smile curved his mouth. If he was here for dinner, he'd be damn sure staying for dessert, too. "That'd be great. But if it's all the same to you, I'll go home and shower and change first."

"Sure, that's fine."

She looked nervous again, chewing at her bottom lip. His gaze locked on that action and his insides tightened even further. Oh, yeah. He'd make it a cold shower, too.

"Okay," he said, "give me an hour? I'll get the barbecue going when I get back. I'm good at starting fires."

"That," she said, "I absolutely believe."

# Four

"It doesn't mean a thing," Katie told herself while she quickly mixed up a batch of pasta salad to go with the burgers. "It's just dinner. A barbecue. Friendly. Non-threatening. Not sexual in any way…"

Oh, even *she* didn't believe that. She'd felt the tension mounting between them when they both went to reach for the bag of charcoal. For a second, she had been sure he was going to kiss her and she still wasn't sure if she'd been relieved or disappointed that he hadn't. And, she had seen his eyes when he promised to start her fire for her. He probably knew that he'd already started it.

Cooking helped center her. It always had. As a girl, she'd helped Nana out in the kitchen and slowly learned her way around a recipe. Then, she started creating her own. And she had learned early that no matter what else was happening in her life, the kitchen was her comfort zone.

She chopped celery, then mushrooms, carrots and broccoli, and added them to the cold pasta, giving it all a good stir together with the homemade pesto. When she was finished, she stored the bowl in her fridge and started on dessert.

She had to keep busy. If she stopped long enough to think about what she was doing, she'd talk herself out of it.

That brought her up short.

"Out of *what* exactly, Katie?" she demanded. "He's coming for dinner. Nobody said anything about sex."

Oh, boy.

The problem was, she really wanted Rafe Cole. She'd been around him almost nonstop for the last week and every day, he'd gotten to her just a little bit more. He was friendly and helpful and, boy, he looked darn good in his jeans. Those blue eyes of his were starring nightly in her dreams and her fingers itched to slide through his thick, black hair.

Yep, she was in bad shape and no doubt asking for trouble by instigating this dinner. But maybe it was time she had a little trouble in her life. She'd always been the good girl. Always done the "right" thing. The *safe* thing.

Heck, she'd dated Cordell King for three months and hadn't slept with him. She'd wanted to take it slow because she'd been so sure that he was the one.

It had seemed, at the time, as if fate had thrown them together. After all, it wasn't as if she stumbled across billionaires all the time in her everyday life. He had ordered an extra-large cookie bouquet to be delivered to his assistant, who was taking off for maternity leave. Katie's delivery girl hadn't been able to take the runs that day, so Katie had done the job herself.

Cordell had slipped out of his office to watch as his assistant cooed and cried over the beautifully frosted cookies that Katie presented to her. And after that, he'd walked Katie to her car and asked her to dinner. After that night, they'd been together as often as each of their schedules had allowed.

Looking back, Katie could see that she had been flattered by Cordell's attention. That the thought of a rich, successful man being interested in her had fed the flames of what she had believed was the start of something amazing. He was so handsome. So attentive. So damned sexy. Her heart had taken a leap before her mind could catch up.

Shaking her head, she realized that she had felt at the time as if she were living in a fairy tale. Where the handsome prince swooped into her poor but proud cottage and carried her off to her castle.

"Silly," she whispered, thinking back to her own actions. Thank God she hadn't slept with him. That would have only fed the humiliation when she looked back on a time where she had been involved in what she thought was something special.

As it turned out, of course, the only thing special they shared was that they were both in love with Cordell.

Grumbling under her breath, Katie let the old, hurtful memories fade away as she focused instead on the evening to come. She spooned fresh whipped cream into old-fashioned sundae glasses. Then she layered chocolate-chip cookie bits with more whipped cream and when they were finished, they too went into the fridge. She would drizzle raspberry syrup over the top of the frothy dessert just before she served it.

When the meal was done, she glanced around the temporary kitchen, checked her watch and realized that

Rafe would be arriving any minute. So she raced to the bathroom and checked her hair and makeup. Stupid, but she felt like a teenager waiting for her first date to arrive.

Nerves bubbled in the pit of her stomach and a kind of excitement she hadn't felt before hummed through her bloodstream. Staring at the woman in the mirror, she gave herself a little pep talk.

"You're going to have fun, Katie Charles. For once in your life, you're not going to think ahead to tomorrow. You're going to enjoy tonight for whatever it turns out to be." She nodded abruptly and pretended she didn't see the flash of nervousness staring back at her from her own eyes. "He's a nice guy. You're both single. So relax, already."

Easier said than done, she knew.

But there was nothing wrong with a little fun.

Right?

"You find out anything from the family?" Rafe asked his brother as he steered his truck down Katie's street.

"Not a damn thing," Sean assured him, his voice crackling with static over the cell phone. "I talked to Tanner, but since he and Ivy got married, he's pretty much useless for picking up stray news. All he talks about is their latest ultrasound picture." Sean sighed in disgust. "Seriously, you'd think they were the only people in the universe to get pregnant."

Rafe let that one go. He was glad for their brother Tanner. Ivy was a nice woman and against all odds, she was turning Tanner into a halfway decent Christmas-tree farmer.

"Then," Sean said, "I called cousin Jesse. But the only thing he knows about Katie Charles is that he favors her macadamia-nut-white-chocolate-chip cookies. His wife Bella says the peanut-butter ones are best, but their boy Joshua likes the chocolate fudge."

Rafe rubbed a spot between his eyes and took a breath. "And I care what kind of cookies they like, because…"

"Because that's the only information they had and now I want a damn cookie," Sean grumbled.

Rafe scowled as he pulled up outside Katie's house. He parked and slanted a glance at the setting sun reflecting off the gleaming front windows. "Somebody in the family knows her and I want to find out who."

"What do you care?" Sean snorted a laugh. "I mean, seriously dude, you've known her for what, a week? What's it to you if she hates the Kings?"

"I don't like it."

"You'd think you'd be used to it," Sean said. "There are plenty of people out there who feel the same."

"Not *women*."

"Good point." Sean sighed and said, "So, this is part of why you find her so interesting, huh?"

"Maybe." He didn't even know. But Katie Charles was hitting him in places he hadn't known existed. And she kept doing it. One look out of those green eyes of hers and his mind filled with all sorts of damn near irresistible images.

And it was lowering to admit that if she knew he was a King, she'd slam her front door in his face and he'd never see her again.

"Fine. I'll go back to the drawing board. Hey, I'll call Garrett," Sean suggested. "He loves a mystery, so if he doesn't have the answer he'll find it."

Sean was right. Their cousin, Garrett King, ran a security company and liked nothing better than delving for secrets. If anyone could find out who was behind Katie's feelings about the Kings, it would be Garrett.

"All right, good. Thanks."

"You busy? I'm taking the jet to Vegas tonight. Why don't you come with me? We'll hit a show, then wipe out the craps tables."

Rafe smiled. Ordinarily, he'd have appreciated the invitation. But tonight, he had something better to do. "Thanks, but I've got plans."

"With the King hater?"

"Her name is Katie, but yeah," Rafe said tightly.

"She doesn't know who you are, does she?"

"No." Irritation hummed inside him again. He'd never before had to disguise himself to be with a woman. Hell, if anything, the King name had women clamoring to get near him.

"Great. Well, pick me up some cookies before she finds out you're lying to her and you ruin what's left of our rep with her."

Rafe hung up a second or two later, his brother's words ringing in his ears. He dismissed them though, because there was no way Katie would find out Rafe's last name until he was good and ready for her to know. And that wouldn't be until he'd romanced her, seduced her and shown her just how likeable he really was.

*Then* he'd tell her he was a King. And she'd see how wrong she was. About all of them.

But for now, he was enjoying himself with a woman who didn't want anything from him beyond barbecuing some burgers.

He got out of the truck and headed for the house. But before he reached the porch, Katie rushed out the door and skidded to a stop when she saw him. Her curly red hair was loose around her shoulders and her long legs looked tan and gorgeous in a pair of white shorts. Her dark green T-shirt made her eyes shine as she spotted him. "Rafe, I'm so glad you're back! Follow me!"

She sprinted down her front steps and past him, headed toward her neighbor's house. She rounded a white picket fence with bright splashes of flowers climbing across it and headed up the driveway. Rafe stayed right on her heels, his mind already racing to possible disasters. Someone dying. Someone bleeding. He reached into his pocket and gripped his phone ready to dial nine-one-one.

Adrenaline pulsed through him as they rushed up the drive to the front porch of a small, Tudor-style cottage with a sloping roof and leaded windows.

"What's wrong?" he shouted.

"Nicole needs help!"

The front door of the house swung open as they approached and a harried woman with short, blond hair and a toddler on her hip sighed in relief.

"Thank God you're here, it's all over everywhere."

Katie made to run inside, but Rafe pulled her back and went in first. He didn't know what the hell was going on around here, but damned if he was going to let Katie run into the heart of whatever trouble it was.

She was right behind him though. He took a moment to glance around, while looking for whatever disaster had happened. He registered the toy cars strewn across the floor and the wooden train set. Then he heard the trouble and his heartbeat returned to normal. No one was dying but it sounded like there was an indoor fountain on full blast.

The woman was talking to Katie, but Rafe was only half listening.

"I can't turn the water off—it's like the valve is frozen

in place or something and there's water everywhere and Connor was crying...."

"It's okay, Nicole," Katie said. "We'll get it shut off and help you clean it up."

He ignored the women and headed for the kitchen, following the loud sound of splashing. Not the way Rafe had planned on this first date with Katie going, but he could adapt. Water was shooting out from under the kitchen sink through the open cupboard doors. Already there was a small flood in the room and a kitchen rug was drifting out on the tide.

Cursing under his breath, Rafe sloshed his way through the kitchen. He crouched down in front of the sink, reached through the cascading cold water and blindly found the shutoff valve. Water poured over him in a never-ending jet. He blinked it out of his eyes, muttered an oath and grabbed hold of the damn valve. Hell, he thought, no wonder Nicole hadn't been able to turn it. It took everything he had to budge the damn thing and it didn't go easy, fighting him every inch of the way. By increments, he slowly shut down the torrent until all that was left was the mess on the floor and a steady drip under the sink.

The sudden silence was almost overpowering. Until the little boy in his mother's arms started laughing.

"Boat!" he cried, pointing to a cell phone as it floated past them.

"Fabulous," Nicole murmured and bent down to scoop it up. "Well, I needed an upgrade anyway."

"Oh, honey, I'm so sorry," Katie said, dropping one arm around her friend's shoulders. She looked at Rafe, soaking wet, and winced. "Rafe Cole, this is Nicole Baxter. Nicole, Rafe."

The woman gave him a tired smile. "I suspect I'm happier to meet you than you are me at the moment."

"No problem. I like an adventure every now and then." He pushed his hair back from his face with both hands, then swept water off his palms. Wet and cold, he caught the glimmer of regret and amusement in Katie's eyes and smiled in spite of everything. "I've got it shut off, but your pipe joint's shot. It has to be fixed."

"Of course it does," Nicole said with a sigh. She hitched her son a little higher on her hip and added, "Thanks. Really, for shutting off Old Faithful. I never would have been able to do it."

"Your husband should be able to replace it without a problem," he told her.

"My *ex*-husband's in Hawaii with his secretary," she said wryly and only then did Rafe see Katie shaking her head at him in a silent signal to shut up.

"Haven't seen him since before Connor was born," Nicole added, kissing the little guy's cheek. "But we do fine, don't we, sweet boy?"

*Perfect,* Rafe thought. He'd made the woman feel even worse now by reminding her of her creep of an ex. A bubble of irritation frothed inside him. What kind of man walked away from his child? Rafe didn't get it. Sure, he knew that marriages didn't always work out. But what man would walk away from his own baby? Shouldn't he try to hold his family together?

While his brain raced, a quiet, rational voice in the back of his mind warned him that he was putting his own issues out there and it was time to draw them back. His old man hadn't been even close to a normal father, but at least Ben King was always there when his kids needed him. Which was more than Rafe could say for Nicole's ex.

Still, looking at Katie's friend, holding her son so closely, reminded him of his own upbringing. Oh, his mother hadn't stuck around or anything. She'd handed him off to an elderly aunt before he was a year old and only showed up for a visit when her money was running out. Ben King hadn't married her, but he'd supported her until Rafe was eighteen.

Once he was grown, his mom had started coming to Rafe for the cash she required to live the kind of life she preferred. He didn't mind paying. It kept her out of his hair.

Now though, watching Nicole and her son brought home to him again how hard the aunt who'd raised him had had it. Oh, she'd had money for plumbing repairs, but she'd been all alone raising a boy. Just as Nicole was. And Nicole didn't have the luxury of calling a King for help.

Lucky for her, there was already a King in the neighborhood.

He looked at Katie and saw the worry for her friend shining in her eyes and he heard himself say, "Why don't you two get the back door open and sweep out as much of this water as you can?"

"Good idea," Katie agreed. "Come on, Nicole, I'll help you get this straightened up."

"You don't have to do that," the blond said. "We'll be fine. Really."

"Sure you will, I can see that," Rafe told her with a shrug, not wanting to wound her pride. "But while you two get the water out of here, I'm going to run up to the hardware store. I'll get a new joint in there and have you up and running again."

Katie *beamed* at him.

And he felt as if someone had just pinned a medal to his chest.

Their gazes locked, and the rest of the world fell away for one long, sizzling moment. Every heartbeat felt measured. Every breath a struggle.

Rafe was caught by the emotion on her face. The pride in *him*. The gratitude and the admiration. He had never known another moment like it. It was amazing, he thought, to have someone look at him as if he'd hung the moon.

And all he wanted to do was walk across the floor, take her into his arms and sweep her into a dip for a kiss that would send them both over the edge of hunger. Need was a gnawing ache inside him. He'd never experienced *that* before, either, he thought. Desire, sure. Want, absolutely.

But *need?*

Never.

"I can't ask you to do that," Nicole said, shattering the moment.

Rafe took a breath to steady himself and shook his head, clearing his thoughts, getting a grip on the emotions suddenly churning through him. As he regained control, he mentally thanked Nicole for shattering whatever it was that had so briefly hummed between he and Katie.

Looking at the blonde, he said, "You didn't ask. I offered. And don't worry about it. Besides," he added with a grin for the toddler, "with this little guy around, you're going to need water, right?"

Katie was still smiling at him as if he were some kind of comic-book hero. And she was still stirring him up inside, so he gave her a smile, then tugged his keys out of his jeans pocket. Best all around if he left now. "I'll be back in a few minutes and we'll get you set up."

"Thanks." Nicole whispered the word. "Really."

Katie gave her a brief hug, then stepped up to Rafe and slid her hand into his. "I'll walk you to the door while Nicole gets the broom and mop."

His fingers curled around hers and he felt the heat of her skin zing through his system like a raging wildfire. At the front door, Katie looked back over her shoulder to make sure Nicole was out of earshot, then said softly, "Thank you for offering to help her like that, Rafe. Nicole couldn't afford a plumber. You're really doing something amazing for her."

"It's not a problem."

"For *you*," she said with another smile. "But for a single mom, it's a catastrophe. Or it would have been. Without you. You're my hero."

Her simple words hit him with a crash. Always before, when people needed help, he wrote a check. Made a donation. It was safe, distant and still managed to salve the urge he had to help those who needed it. He hadn't realized until just now how differently helping felt when it was up close and personal.

"I've never been anybody's hero before."

She looked up at him and he knew he could lose himself in the deep, summer green of her eyes. Her delectable mouth curved at the edges. "You are now."

He reached up and cupped the back of her neck with his palm. "Keep that thought and hold on to it for later, okay?"

"I can do that," she said and went up on her toes to brush a soft kiss across his mouth. Then she stepped away and said, "Hurry back."

His lips were tingling, his breath was still strangling

in his lungs and Rafe was suddenly so damn hard he didn't think he'd be able to walk to his truck without limping.

Some hero.

Nicole and Connor joined them for the barbecue.

Katie told herself she was just being nice—Nicole was still upset and they were all tired out from cleaning up the mess in her kitchen. But the truth was, that moment with Rafe at the front door of Nicole's house had shaken Katie enough that she had wanted someone else around during dinner. Not exactly a chaperone, just someone to keep Katie from jumping Rafe the moment they were alone.

Because that's exactly what she wanted to do. He had been wonderful. Honestly, she thought back to her time with Cordell King and no matter how she tried to imagine it, she couldn't see that man diving under a kitchen sink to fix something as a favor. He was too much a suit-and-tie man. Too focused on the bottom line of his company and not so interested in the "real world."

Rafe though, was different, she thought, watching him gently toss a soft foam ball to Connor. The little boy waved both arms trying to catch it and Rafe laughed with him when he missed. The man was just…

"Amazing," Nicole said, unknowingly finishing Katie's mental sentence.

"What?"

"Him." Nicole smiled at Katie, then shifted her gaze to where her son was playing with Rafe. "That guy is one in a million, Katie."

"I was just thinking the same thing."

"Yeah?" Nicole pushed her paper plate aside, leaned

both arms on the weathered picnic table and asked, "If you think so, why'd you have Connor and I come over and horn in on your date?"

"You're not horning in," Katie argued. In the year she and her son had lived next door, Nicole had become Katie's best friend. They'd commiserated on the rotten tendencies of the men they'd had in their lives and they'd bonded over working from home. Katie had her cookie company and Nicole did the billing for several local companies.

"You're my friend, Nicole, and you're always invited over. You know that."

"'Course I know that." Nicole reached out and covered Katie's hand with her own. "You've been great to us since we moved in here. But Katie, this is the first guy I've seen you date in like forever. Don't you want some alone time?"

Katie stared at Rafe as he scooped Connor up and ran across the yard, the little boy chortling happily. "I do and I don't. Seriously, Nicole, I'm not sure what I want."

"Well I can tell you if he looked at *me,* the way he looks at *you,* I wouldn't have any trouble deciding what I wanted."

"It's complicated."

"I know. Cordell." Giving her hand a squeeze, Nicole sat back and shook her head. "He messed you up bad. But Rafe isn't Cordell."

"You're telling me," Katie said on a sigh.

"Do you really want to risk losing a great guy because you're still mad at a rotten one?"

"Have you been talking to Nana?"

Nicole laughed. "No. I haven't. But if she agrees with

me, then we're both right and you should trust us on this. Give it a shot, Katie. What've you got to lose?"

*Another chunk of her heart,* she thought but didn't say. But then again, if she never risked her heart, she'd never use it, would she? She'd die an old lady, filled with regrets, still holding on to her withered pride like a trophy with some of the shiny worn off.

Her gaze locked on Rafe again as he lifted the little boy high enough for tiny hands to swat at the glossy leaves of an orange tree. Her still-wary heart turned over in her chest as she watched the expression on Rafe's face. He was enjoying himself. He was relaxed, at ease with her friends, in her tiny backyard. Cordell, in the same situation, would have—never mind, he never would have been in this situation. He had preferred five-star restaurants to picnics and three-piece suits to jeans.

Cordell had swept Katie off her feet because she had never been with anyone like him. Now she knew she should have kept it that way.

But Rafe…he was different from Cordell. He was the kind of guy Katie should have met first.

And if she had, she asked herself, would she have been so hesitant to take a chance on him? No, she wouldn't have.

"Ooh, I can see by the look in your eyes you've decided to take a chance," Nicole said. "Want me to take Connor home so you can get going on that?"

Katie shook her head. "Not until after dessert," she said. "Then we'll see what happens."

She stood up and headed for the enclosed patio and her refrigerator. Behind her, she heard Connor's giggles and Rafe's deep laughter.

Her skin tingled and everything in her awoke to anticipation.

# Five

"If that dessert was a sample of your cookies," Rafe said much later, "then I can understand why people are so crazy about them."

"Thank you. I can give you some to take home if you like," Katie said.

Rafe tipped his head to one side and studied her. Nicole and her son had gone home and now it was just he and Katie in the backyard. The summer night was cool, the sky overhead swimming with stars. Moonlight drifted down and did battle with the candle flames flickering in the soft breeze.

"Anxious to get rid of me?" he asked quietly.

"No," she said. "That's not what I meant. I just—oh, for heaven's sake. You'd think I'd never been on a date before." She caught herself and amended, "Not that this is a date or anything…"

Rafe grinned, enjoying that touch of nervousness. "It's not?"

"Is it?"

His smile firmly in place he admitted, "Well, I don't usually do plumbing on a date, but everything else seems about right."

Now she returned his smile and seemed to relax a little. The wind lifted her hair like a lover's caress. "It was fun, wasn't it?"

"Yeah, and it's not over yet."

"Really."

Not a question, he told himself. More of a challenge. Well, he was willing to accept it. "Really."

He stood up, walked to her side of the picnic table and pulled her to her feet. "What're you doing?"

"I want to dance with you," he said simply, drawing her closer.

Even as she went with him, she was saying, "There's no music."

"Sure there is," he told her, wrapping his arm around her waist and capturing her right hand in his left. "You're just not listening hard enough."

She shook her head at him.

"Close your eyes," he said and she did. He looked down at her, so trusting, so beautiful, and his breath caught in his chest. Her hand was warm and smooth in his, her scent—a mixture of vanilla and cinnamon—filling him. He smiled, thinking that she smelled as edible as her cookies.

"Now listen," he urged quietly, his voice hardly more than a whisper of sound.

"To what?" she answered just as quietly.

"Everything."

He swayed with her in his arms and rested his chin

on top of her head. Her body felt perfect aligned along his and he went hard and ready almost instantly. If she noticed, she didn't let him know.

As they moved in the starlight, sounds of the summer night began to encroach. Crickets singing, the distant sigh of the ocean, the wind in the trees. It was as if nature herself were providing a perfect symphony just for the two of them.

She smiled, tipped her head back, and keeping her eyes closed, moved with him as if they'd been dancing together forever. "I hear it now," she whispered. "It's perfect."

"Yeah," he said, coming to a stop, staring down at her. "It is."

Her eyes opened and she met his gaze. "Rafe?"

His hand tightened on hers and he held her closer, pulling her in firmly enough against him that she couldn't miss feeling exactly what she was doing to him. "I want you, Katie. More than I've ever wanted anything."

A tiny sigh slipped from her mouth as she confessed, "I feel exactly the same way."

He gave her a grin and slowly lowered his mouth to hers. "Good to hear."

He kissed her and the instant their mouths met, Rafe felt a punch of desire so hot, so unbelievably strong that it nearly knocked him over. In response, his arms tightened around her, all thoughts of dancing disappearing from his mind. He wanted to move with her, but dancing had nothing to do with the plans quickly forming in his mind. He needed her, more than he would have thought possible. And he wanted her even more.

His hands swept up and down her spine, defining

every curve, every valley she possessed. She moved against him, her body restless, her soft moans telling him everything he needed to know. He slipped one hand beneath the hem of her T-shirt and swept up, to caress the side of her breast. Even the lacy material of her bra couldn't keep him from enjoying the heat of her. The perfectly shaped wonder of her. His hands itched to feel her skin.

Hunger roared through him and he deepened their kiss, his tongue sweeping into her mouth, claiming everything she had and silently demanding more. She gave it to him, surrendering herself to the passion rising between them. Her tongue tangled with his, her breath sighing against his cheek as she met him stroke for stroke. Her hands clutched his shoulders, holding on tightly as she moaned in appreciation.

That soft sound was enough to push Rafe dangerously close to the edge. He tore his mouth from hers, looked down at her through eyes glazed with heat and need and said grimly, "If we don't stop right now, I'm going to throw you down onto this picnic table and give your neighbors a show."

A choked laugh shot from her throat. She didn't release her hold on him though, as if she didn't quite trust herself to be able to stand on her own two feet.

"The picnic table's not nearly as comfortable as my bed," she said, just a little breathlessly.

"Is that an invitation?"

"Sounded like one to me."

"All I need to know," Rafe muttered and swept her up into his arms.

"You don't have to carry me!"

"Faster this way," he told her, nearly sprinting across the yard toward the house.

"That works too," she said, snuggling close to him, stroking the flat of her hand across his chest.

He hissed in a breath, hit the patio door and stepped inside. "Where to?"

"Down the hall, turn left at the end."

He was already moving. His body was hard and aching. He could hardly draw a breath without fanning the flames licking at his insides. His heart pounding, Rafe entered her room and strode straight to the bed. Absently, he noticed the window seat on the front wall, colorful rugs scattered across a gleaming wood floor and a squat bookcase stuffed with paperbacks.

But his gaze was locked on the wide bed covered in an old-fashioned quilt. He stopped alongside the four-poster, tossed the covers back to reveal smooth white sheets and dropped Katie onto the mattress.

She bounced, then smiled up at him. It was all the encouragement he needed. Tearing off his clothes, he watched her as she did the same. In seconds, they were both naked and he was leaning over her. Rafe had been thinking about this moment for days. Dreaming about it every damn night.

She was haunting him, this woman who so hated the King family. She had somehow reached him in a way no other woman had and though that admission bothered him, it wasn't enough to keep him from enjoying what she was offering.

Reaching up to him, she plunged her fingers through his hair and drew his mouth down to hers. Their mouths melded and her taste was as intoxicating as ever. Her kiss sizzled inside him, making the ache in his body almost overpowering. Everything in him urged him to hurry. To take. To ease the need clamoring within him.

But the urge to savor was just as strong. His tongue

entwined with hers, he slid one hand down the length of her body, relishing the glide of her skin beneath his palm. So soft, so curvy. So just right.

Reluctantly, he broke their kiss, shifted position slightly and took one of her hard, pink nipples into his mouth. She gasped and arched against him as he suckled her, using his teeth and tongue to lovingly torture her. He felt every breath she took, heard every sigh and wanted more. Rafe inhaled her scent and lost himself in the glory of her.

She held his head to her breast as if afraid he might stop. But Rafe was just getting started. He moved to give the same attention to her other breast, feeling her heartbeat quicken, as anticipation rolled through her. He smiled against her skin, then lifted his head and looked up into her passion glazed eyes. "I've wanted this since the first moment I saw you."

"Me, too," she admitted, licking her bottom lip in an action that caused everything inside him to clench.

His fingers and thumb continued to tug and pull at her nipple, making her squirm and her breath catch in her throat. When he touched her, he saw exactly what she was feeling on her face. He loved watching her expression shift and change as she gave herself over to him and Rafe knew there was something more here than want.

Something dangerous.

Yet he couldn't have pulled away and left if it had meant his life.

That thought stark in his mind, he leaned over her again, stared down into her green eyes and asked, "What are you doing to me?"

She laughed a little and cupped his cheek in her palm. "At the moment, it's *you* doing something to *me*."

Staring into her eyes, he felt that kick of something he didn't quite recognize and after a long second or two, he let it go. Now was not the time to be thinking.

"So it is," he agreed, dipping his head for one brief, hard kiss. He felt it again. That something *more* between them. That extra jolt he'd never known before. A part of Rafe worried that he might be getting in deeper here than he had planned. But there was no way out now. No other answer but to have her. To feel her body welcoming his. To delve into her heat and take them both where they had been heading from the first.

He'd worry about consequences later. Wonder if this had been a good idea another time. For right now, there was nowhere he'd rather be.

Sliding one hand down the length of her body, he stroked her core with the tips of his fingers until she lifted her hips into his touch. Her gaze never left his. He watched passion flare and sparkle in her eyes and pushed her higher, faster. Her breath came in quick gasps. Her body trembled in his arms and he felt her pleasure as if it were his own.

Rafe couldn't get enough of looking at her face. Every emotion so openly displayed. Nothing hidden. Nothing held back. He'd never been with a woman so honestly enthusiastic. Always before, the women in his life had been controlled. As if playing the role they thought he wanted from them.

Even his ex-wife Leslie had held something back from him, as if she couldn't quite trust him enough to confide her deepest feelings and reactions. But there was no artifice with Katie.

She threw herself into the moment and in so doing, drew him with her.

"Come for me," he whispered, dipping his head

to taste her mouth. He caught her breath as it passed between her parted lips. She tasted as sweet as the cookies she was known for. "Let go, Katie. Fly."

She choked off a half laugh and held on to him, one arm draped around his shoulder. Her hips rocked into his hand and when he dipped his fingers in and out of her heat, she groaned and arched high off the bed. "Rafe…"

"Shatter, Katie. Let me watch you shatter."

Her gaze locked on his, she expelled a breath, took another and did as he asked. Her body shook as she cried out his name, her gaze never leaving his. She allowed him to see exactly what he was doing to her. What he was making her feel. And his own passion exploded in response. She bit down hard on her bottom lip and rode the wave of completion he gave her and all Rafe could think was, it wasn't enough. He had to see her face etched in pleasure again and again.

The last of her tremors had barely faded away when he pushed off the bed, grabbed his jeans off the floor and dug into the pocket.

"What're you…" She stopped and smiled when she saw him pull out a foil-wrapped condom. Stretching her arms back over her head, she sighed and said, "Pretty sure of yourself tonight then, weren't you? You came prepared."

He ripped open the foil, sheathed himself and turned back to her. "Not sure of myself. Just hopeful."

He leaned over her and Katie's arms encircled his neck. "I think, Rafe Cole, that you're *always* sure of yourself and tonight was no different."

Couldn't really argue with that, he thought. But the truth was, he had just wanted to be prepared. Unlike his father, Rafe didn't run around the world leaving illegitimate children in his wake. In fact, he had no intention of ever having children and he for damn sure wouldn't create a life because he was too lazy or too selfish to wear a condom.

None of which Katie needed to know.

Bending his head to claim another hard, fast kiss, Rafe looked into her eyes and said, "I'm not so sure of myself around you, Katie. And that's the truth."

She smiled, a slow curve of her mouth, then reached up to stroke her fingertips along his jawline. "I like hearing that."

Wryly, he said, "Thought you would. Women love to know when they've got a man dazed and confused."

"Are you dazed?" she asked, moving against him.

"With any luck," he told her, "I'm about to be."

He parted her thighs and settled himself between them. He looked his fill of her then, stroking her center with long, leisurely caresses until she was writhing with the tension.

"Yeah," he whispered, more to himself than to her, "dazed, all right."

Outside, the night was cool and quiet. In this room, the only sound was their ragged breathing and the thundering beat of their hearts. All that existed was this moment. This near-electric current of passion was flooding back and forth between them and Rafe knew he couldn't wait one more second to claim her.

For more than a week, he'd watched her, laughed with her. He'd spent more time with Katie Charles in the last week than he had with his ex-wife in the last year of their marriage. And he'd enjoyed it more, as well. She was smart and funny and talented and so damn sexy; one look from her green eyes was almost enough to floor him.

She parted her thighs wider in acceptance and sighed as he touched her. Rafe felt the slam of that soft sound ricochet inside him and ignored it. He didn't want his heart to be involved in this, so it wouldn't be. He wouldn't allow any more connection than the physical between them. And that would be enough, he assured himself.

He just had to have her, and then everything would go back to normal.

Lifting her hips to give himself better access, he slowly pushed himself into her heat. Into the very heart of her. And as her body wrapped itself around his, he hissed in a breath and fought for control.

Instinctively, she moved with him, lifting her legs high enough to wrap them around his waist and pull him in deeper, tighter, harder. He looked down at her and she opened her arms to him. Leaning over, he kissed her as he rocked his body against hers. Retreating and then advancing, he felt the magical slide of her warmth and knew it had never been better for him.

For the first time in his adult life, he wished to hell he wasn't wearing a damn condom. He wanted to feel *all* of her, without that layer separating them. But that would have been nuts, so he pushed that thought aside and moved on her again.

She lifted up from the bed and kissed him, framing his face in her hands, running her tongue along his bottom lip until she pushed him so near the edge there was no restraining himself any longer. He'd wanted to draw this out. Wanted to make it last, because he'd been dreaming of this moment for days now. But there was no more waiting. No slow and seductive.

There was only need and the desperate ache for completion.

Pushing her back onto the bed, he levered himself over her and took her hard and fast.

"Yes," she whispered, moving with him, matching his rhythm eagerly. His body pistoned into hers. Her hunger fueled his and together they reached for what they both needed.

He felt her climax hit her and as she rode out the convulsing waves of pleasure, he erupted, called her name and joined her in time to slide into oblivion, locked together.

"My hero," Katie said when she was sure her voice would work.

"Happy to oblige," he murmured, his face tucked into the curve of her neck.

She smiled to herself and stared up at the pale blue ceiling overhead. The soft sigh of his breath against her skin, the heavy weight of his body pressing onto hers and the throbbing center of her where they were still joined all came together to create perfection.

Running her hands up and down his back, she listened to the sound of his ragged breathing and felt the pounding beat of his heart. It had been so long since she'd been with someone, that maybe she was making too much of this.

But there was a tiny voice inside her, whispering to Katie that this had been *special*. That she had just shared something with Rafe that went far beyond sex.

Her heartbeat jittered unsteadily as that thought settled into her mind. Hadn't she thought what she had with Cordell was special, too? But this was different, her thoughts argued. This was so much more than she had ever felt for Cordell. Rafe touched more than her heart. He'd somehow wormed his way into her soul.

But she was rushing things and she knew it. She wasn't going to be foolishly romantic about a purely physical pleasure. Not again. She wasn't in love, for heaven's sake. Katie was a rational, logical woman and she knew that falling in love just didn't happen in a week's time.

But she could at least admit that Rafe Cole was in her heart. She cared for him or she never would have slept with him. And watching him tonight with Nicole and Connor had only heightened her feelings for him. How could she *not* be touched by a man who was so gentle with a two-year-old? So nice to a single mom who had needed help?

Rafe was the kind of man she used to dream of finding. He was hardworking and honest and kind and so very, very sexy.

"You're thinking," he murmured.

"Yep," she said.

He lifted his head and quirked a smile at her. "Why is it that good sex energizes a woman and makes a man unconscious?"

"I'd tell you," she said solemnly, "but then I'd have to kill you."

He laughed and she felt the jolt of that movement ripple throughout her body. They were still locked together. Every move Rafe made awakened already sensitized flesh and set it sizzling.

"Hmm," he whispered, as if knowing exactly what she was thinking, feeling. He moved in her again, slowly at first, eliciting another sigh from Katie. "Seems we're not finished yet."

"Not nearly," she agreed, moving with him, sliding into the pace he set as if they had been together hundreds of times and knew each other's moves instinctively. It was, Katie thought, as if they had been meant to be together. As if their bodies had been forged specifically to link into place, two halves, one whole. She couldn't help feeling that this was all as it was supposed to be. That this night had been fated in some way. That she'd been given this chance with Rafe in order to make up for the wounded heart she'd lived through months before. And it was working.

In seconds, the fire between them was burning again. Flames licked at her center and spread throughout her body. He touched her and there was magic. He became a part of her body and a corner of her heart never wanted it to end.

She looked up into those deep blue eyes of his and thought how glad she was that she'd taken this chance with him. That she had opened herself up to possibilities. To the magic that could happen between the right people.

And then her thoughts splintered as he pushed her beyond desire into passion that demanded her focus. She felt the quickening within, the first tingle of anticipation that something amazing was about to happen. Katie reached for it eagerly, hungrily, wanting to feel it all again.

He kissed her and she opened her mouth to him, welcoming his invasion. The taste of him filled her and she felt his breath on her face. His body rocked into hers over and over again and she lifted her legs higher around his waist, holding him to her, offering herself up to his pleasure.

To *their* pleasure.

And when the first, shattering jolts hit her system, she

tore her mouth free of his, whispered his name and clung to him desperately. Moments later, while she shivered and trembled in his arms, he allowed himself to follow her and she held him tightly as his body exploded into hers.

# Six

"That's it," he whispered. "Unconscious for real now."

"I feel great," she admitted with a happy sigh.

He looked down into her eyes and shook his head. "You're amazing."

"Why am I amazing?" she asked, reaching up to smooth his thick black hair off his forehead.

Studying her for a moment or two, he finally said, "Most women right now would be either regretting what just happened—"

"Not me," she said.

"—or they'd be silently planning how to make this a little more permanent."

Katie frowned and shook her head. "Also not me."

"I'm getting that," he said and rolled to one side of her, pulling her with him though, so that she rested her head on his shoulder.

Snuggling close, Katie listened to the steady beat of

his heart and the quiet, every-night noises of her old house. Wind rattled her windows and the familiar creaks and groans of the house settling sounded like whispers from friends.

She felt wonderful. Better than she had in too long to remember. But, she had heard what Rafe had to say and she knew he was probably right. A lot of women right now would be plotting how to keep him in their beds. In their lives. And, she had to admit, at least silently, that it would have been easy for her to fall into that category.

But she wasn't going to fool herself or tell herself comforting lies. She knew this one night wasn't the beginning of a "relationship." If not for remodeling her kitchen, she never would have met Rafe Cole. This wasn't your ordinary dating situation, she thought firmly. He hadn't made her any promises and she hadn't asked for any.

She rose up and braced her folded arms on his chest. Her hair was in her eyes, so she shook it back and looked at him squarely. Might as well have this conversation now, she told herself and gave him a sad smile.

"Uh-oh," he murmured. "That's not a this-was-great-let's-do-it-again smile, is it?"

"No," she told him and moved one hand to smooth his hair back from his forehead. If her fingers lingered a little longer than necessary, who was to know? "This was lovely, Rafe. Really. But—"

He frowned at her, did a quick roll and had her under him in the blink of an eye. Now he was looming over her and his blue gaze was fixed and sharp. "But *what?*"

She sighed. "I just don't think we should do this again, that's all."

"You're *dumping* me?"

"Well, we're not really a couple, so it's not really dumping you, but, yes. I guess so."

"I don't believe this." He sounded astonished and Katie admitted silently that he probably wasn't used to women turning him away. Any man who looked like he did had to have women clinging to him like cat hair. She chuckled a little at her pitiful analogy and his frown deepened.

"This is funny, too?"

"No, sorry." She stroked her hand up and down his arm, tracing the line of his well-defined muscles and barely restraining another sigh of appreciation. "No, this isn't funny. I just had a weird thought and—"

He snorted. "Perfect. So not only are you dumping me, but you can't even focus on the task?"

"Why are you getting angry?"

"Why the hell wouldn't I be?"

Katie felt a small spurt of irritation shoot through her. "Just a second ago, you were proud of me for not making more of this than there was."

"Yeah, but—"

"And now you're mad for the same reason?"

He blew out a breath and stared at her for a long second. "This isn't the usual response I get from women, so pardon the hell out of me if I'm a little surprised."

"Surprised, sure. But mad? Why?" Her minor irritation faded and she gave him a patient smile. "You feel the same way, you know you do. I just said it first. I would think you'd be glad for my reaction."

"Yeah, well, I'm not," he muttered, pulling away. He leaned back against the headboard and threw one arm behind his head. Giving her a look that probably should have worried her, he said, "So exactly what was tonight about, Katie?"

"Us," she said and scooted to sit beside him. Absently, she tugged the sheet up to cover her breasts. "We both wanted this, Rafe. And I thought, why shouldn't we have it?"

"And that's it?"

"Yes." Well, not completely of course, she thought. She did care for him and if she spent too much more time with him, she could come to care a lot more. Which would be a huge mistake. Yes, Rafe was a great guy, but she didn't trust herself anymore to know the good guys from the creeps.

Cordell King had seemed like a sweetie at first, too. Then he'd had a diamond bracelet overnighted to her along with a note saying they "were just too different to make a longer relationship work." Translation, she'd always known was really, *I'm rich, you're poor, goodbye*.

So, she'd been wrong about Cordell. And confidence in her character-reading skills was low. Nope. Better she bury herself in work for a year or two and then she'd get back out there. Oh, she was glad she'd had this night with Rafe. But she wasn't going to build a future out of it. Still, she knew now that she could get back into the world and one day she'd look for a man like Rafe, she told herself. Someone strong and kind and honest.

"I don't believe you," he said grimly. "Something else is going on here and I want to know what it is."

"Excuse me?"

"You heard me, Katie. You *like* me. I know you do. So why're you cutting me loose before the sheets are even cold?"

"That doesn't matter."

He grabbed her, pulled her across his lap and held her tightly to him. "Yeah. It does. To me."

Being this close to him really wasn't a good idea when she was trying to be logical and rational, Katie thought. She fought down the impulse to slide her palms across his broad, muscular chest and said, "You're taking this all wrong, Rafe."

"What did you expect? That I'd just get dressed, say thanks for the roll in the hay and then leave?"

"Well…*yes*." Of course that's what she had expected. What man wouldn't enjoy free, no-strings-attached sex?

"Sorry to disappoint," he muttered, then tipped her chin up so that their gazes locked. "I want to know the real reason behind this."

"Rafe…"

"It's him, isn't it? The mysterious member of the King family."

Katie scowled at him, pulled free and scooted off his lap all at once. "If it is, that's my business."

"You just made it my business too, Katie. I'm getting the heave-ho because of this guy. The least you can do is tell me why."

"Because I trusted him, okay?" She blurted it out before she could stop herself and once the words started coming, there was no stopping them. "I thought I was in love with him. I thought he loved *me*. He was sweet and thoughtful and funny."

"And rich," Rafe muttered darkly. "Don't forget rich."

"Okay, yes, he was," she said. "But that's not why I fell in love with him. In fact, it's why it didn't work out in the end."

"What?"

Shaking her head, she pushed out of bed, walked to the connected bathroom and stepped inside. There she grabbed her bathrobe and pulled it on. When it was tied securely around her waist, she felt a little less vulnerable. Though the look in his eyes told her he wouldn't be leaving until he knew all of it. So she would be vulnerable anyway, she told herself. At least emotionally.

"Fine," she said at last. "You want the sad truth? He dropped me because we were too 'different.' Because I wasn't good enough. According to him our worlds were too far apart. Bottom line? Rich guy didn't want poor girl. Big surprise. There, happy now? Feel better getting *all* of my little humiliations up front?"

He simply stared at her. "Not good enough? Who the hell is he to say that about anybody?"

Unexpectedly, Katie smiled, despite the rawness of her feelings at the moment. His outrage on her behalf took a little of the sting out of her memories.

"He's a King," she said with a shrug she didn't quite feel. "Masters of the known universe. Just ask anyone. Heck, ask the guys you work with. They've probably got stories and complaints about the great King family."

He scowled at her. "Actually, the guys *like* working for King Construction. Haven't heard a word against them."

"Probably out of fear of losing their jobs," she muttered. On the other hand, maybe working for the King family was entirely different from trying to date one of them.

Frowning, he asked, "Who is he? Which King, I mean? Tell me who he is and I'll go punch him in the nose for you."

A surprised laugh shot from her throat and Katie was grateful for it. "Still my hero?"

"If you need one."

Tempting, she thought. He wasn't running for the hills. Maybe he was actually interested in her for more than a fleeting encounter. All she really had to do to find out was trust herself. Trust Rafe. She'd like to, Katie realized. But apparently she just wasn't ready.

Shaking her head, she said, "No, but thanks. I think I have to be my own hero first."

"So *you* want to punch him in the nose?"

She laughed louder. "Oh, I did, about six months ago. But I'm over it. I'm over *him*."

"No," he said, "you're not."

"Excuse me?"

He got out of bed and pulled on his jeans. "If you were over him, we wouldn't be having this conversation. We'd still be in bed, doing what we're obviously so good at."

Her amusement died in a flash. "This isn't about him. This is about me. It's about us."

He snorted and tugged on his boots. Then he grabbed his shirt off the floor, shrugged into it and stalked across the floor toward her. He stopped dead within arm's reach and then grabbed her, tugging her tightly to him. "You just told me there is no *us,* Katie, so get your stories straight."

"Let me go."

He did, but frustration simmered in the air around him. Shoving one hand through his hair, he grumbled, "What do you care what a King had to say anyway? Didn't that prove to you the man was an ass?"

"Don't you get it? I thought he was Prince Charming. Turned out he was a frog. But I never saw it." She threw both hands high and let them fall to her sides again. "How can I even trust my own judgment if I was that far off to begin with?"

"You're letting him win, Katie," he told her, bending over her, until their noses were practically brushing against each other. "By doubting yourself, you're giving that guy power he doesn't deserve."

"Maybe," she admitted. "But I'm not ready to make another mistake yet."

"What makes you so sure I'm a mistake?"

"I'm not sure," she told him quietly. "That's the problem."

He eased back a little, laid his hands on her shoulders and slowly drew them up until he held her face between his palms. His gaze was locked on her and Katie could have sworn his eyes were blue enough to drown in.

"You'll miss me."

"I know."

"I'm not going away," he said. "You'll see me every day."

"I know that, too."

Bending down, he kissed her, gently at first and then as the moments ticked past, the kiss deepened until Katie felt as though the ends of her hair were on fire. Finally though, Rafe pulled back to look at her again.

"Tonight isn't the end, Katie. It's just the beginning."

Before she could argue with him, he turned and walked out of the room.

When he got home, he placed a call.

"Sean?" he said when his brother answered. "Did you get hold of Garrett?"

"No can do," Sean said. "He's in Ireland and he's not answering his phone."

"*Ireland?*" Rafe repeated. "What's he doing over there?"

"Exactly the question I asked his twin. Griffin says Jefferson had some problems with a thief in his European company and Garrett went to investigate it."

*Great timing,* Rafe thought in disgust. Jefferson King, one of their many cousins, lived with his Irish wife on a sheep farm in County Mayo. Hard to believe that Jefferson, Mr. Hollywood Mogul, was happy out in the boonies, but he was. And if Jeff had a problem, then there was no telling when Garrett might come back home. To the Kings, *Family comes first* was the unofficial motto. So Garrett wouldn't leave Ireland until he'd turned the country upside down to find the answers Jeff wanted.

"Well, that's great," Rafe grumbled, stalking through the sleek, modern hotel suite he called home. The place was empty, of course, but tonight, it felt…desolate. Rafe had always preferred life in a hotel. It was easy. Uncomplicated. But tonight, it also felt…sterile.

His mind kept returning to Katie's older house with its overstuffed furniture and creaky floors. There was a sense of continuity in that bungalow, as if the walls and floors themselves held the echoes of generations of laughter and tears.

His gaze swept the interior of his own home and for the first time in years, he found it lacking. Irritated with himself, he opened the sliding glass door to his terrace and stepped outside. The cold wind slapped at him and the roar of the ocean growled unceasingly. Streetlamps below threw yellowed circles of light onto the sidewalks and out on the beach. He spotted the dancing flames of campfires blazing in the fire rings.

"So," he asked, "we still don't have any idea which one of the family is the one who messed with Katie."

"Nope," Sean said. "Not a clue. And except for the married ones, it could be anyone."

"This I know already." Rafe shoved one hand through his hair and squinted into the cold sea breeze. His body was still humming from his time with Katie, and his mind was racing, trying to figure out how it had all gone to hell so damn fast.

He didn't have an answer.

"I can ask around," Sean offered.

"Never mind," Rafe told him. "I'll do the asking myself."

"Fine," Sean said, then asked, "Hey, did you get me some cookies?"

Rafe hung up, stuffed his phone into his pocket, then leaned both hands on the wrought-iron railing in front of him. He leaned into the wind, watched the black waves moving and shifting in the moonlight and promised himself that he would find out who had hurt Katie.

A few days later, Rafe was still simmering. He was getting nowhere fast with talking to his cousins. Amazing how many Kings took off during the summer. What the hell had happened to the family's work ethic? But it wasn't just the frustration of trying to find out which of his cousins he should pummel that was making him insane.

It was Katie herself. Until her, the only woman who'd ever turned her back on him was Leslie. And at least she had *married* him first.

"Everything okay here?"

Rafe buried his irritation, turned the electric sander off and faced Joe, the man pretending to be his boss. "Fine," Rafe said shortly and moved the finished cabinet door to one side before grabbing up the next one in line.

Sanding was hot, tedious work, so his mind had plenty of room to wander. Unfortunately, it continued to wander toward Katie.

The woman was making him insane and that had never happened before. Always in his life, Rafe was in charge. He did what he wanted when he wanted and didn't much care about looking out for whoever might be in his way. Since Leslie, women were expendable in his world. Temporary. They came in, spent a few good hours with him; then they were gone, not even leaving behind a residual echo of their presence.

"Until now," he muttered, removing the safety goggles and paper mask he wore to avoid inhaling all the sawdust flying around so thickly in the air.

Joe glanced over his shoulder to make sure no one was close enough to overhear them. "Look, I don't know what's going on, but I just came from talking to Katie and she's wound so tight she's giving off sparks."

"Really?" Rafe hid a smile. Good to know he wasn't the only one. She had managed to avoid talking to him the last few days, so he hadn't known exactly how she was feeling until just this moment. It had about killed him to be here, so near to her every damn day, and not speak to her. Touch her. But he'd kept his distance because damned if he'd be the one to bend. He wanted her. She knew it. Let her come to him. She was, after all, the one who pushed him away to begin with. "She say anything?"

"She didn't have to," Joe told him. "The whole time I was talking to her about her new floor tiles, she kept looking out here at *you*."

Also good to know, Rafe thought and hid a satisfied smile.

"What's going on?"

Rafe slanted a hard look at Joe. He'd known the man for years. Trusted him. Considered him a friend, even. But that didn't mean that he was interested in Joe's opinion on this particular subject. "That's none of your business, is it?"

The older man scrubbed one hand across the top of his balding head. "No, I guess it's not. But I work for King Construction. I've got a good reputation with the company and with our clients."

"You do," Rafe said, keeping his voice down. "What's your point?"

"I've known you a long time, Rafe, and I'm going to say that my business or not, I think you need to tell that girl who you really are."

He snorted. "Not likely."

Hell, she'd kicked him loose thinking he was Rafe *Cole*. If she knew he was actually a King, who knew what she'd do?

Joe huffed out an impatient breath. "She's a nice woman and I don't like the idea of lying to her. I'm sorry I suggested this bet in the first place."

Rafe saw how uncomfortable Joe was and he was sorry for that. But he wasn't telling Katie the truth. Not yet. Not until he'd made her see how much she wanted him. How much she liked him. Then he'd tell her that she was wrong about the King family and him specifically. And she'd have to admit that she had made a mistake.

"Look, Joe," he said, "I'm sorry you're in the middle of this, but we're already too deep in the game to stop. There's no changing the rules at this late date."

"A game? Is that what this is?" Joe's eyes narrowed and Rafe had the distinct impression that his contractor was about to defend Katie's honor.

Well, there was no need.

"I don't mean Katie is a game to me, so relax."

The man's pitbull expression eased a bit and Rafe kept talking.

"Don't get all twisted up over this, Joe." Rafe slapped one hand on the man's shoulder. "We made the bet and I'm honoring it. As for telling Katie the truth, I'll do that when the time's right."

"And when's that?"

"Not now, for damn sure." Rafe narrowed his own eyes in warning. "And don't you tell her, either."

Grumbling under his breath, Joe worked his jaw furiously as if there were a hundred hot words in his mouth that he was fighting to keep inside. Finally though, he grudgingly agreed. "Fine. I won't say anything. But I think you're making a mistake here, Rafe. One that you're gonna regret real soon."

"Maybe," he said and shifted his gaze back to the enclosed patio where Katie was working in her temporary kitchen. Even from a distance, she was beautiful, he thought. But it wasn't just her beauty calling to him. It was the shine of something tender in her eyes. The knowledge that she had wanted him, desired him, without knowing who he was. She didn't want anything from him and that was so rare in Rafe's world that he couldn't let her go.

But his heart wasn't involved here and it wouldn't be, either. He had tried love. Tried marriage and failed miserably at both. Kings didn't fail. It was the one rule his father had drummed into all of them from the time they were kids.

Well, his divorce from Leslie was going to be the *only* time Rafe King failed at anything. He wouldn't risk another mistake. Wouldn't give Fate another shot at kicking his ass.

"Whether or not I regret anything," Rafe told Joe quietly, "is not your business. You just do your job and leave Katie Charles to me."

"Fine. You're the boss," Joe said after a long minute of silence. "But King or not, you're making a mistake."

Joe walked off to the kitchen where Steve and Arturo were jokingly arguing about the plastering job. Inside her temporary kitchen, Katie was busy working on another batch of her cookies and the delicious aromas wafting from the oven wrapped themselves around him. Rafe stood alone in the sunlight while his mind raced with possibilities.

Maybe Joe had a point. But being with Katie, keeping his identity a secret, didn't feel like a mistake to Rafe. So he was going to stick with his original plan. Once a decision had been made, Rafe never liked to deviate. That was second-guessing himself and if he started doing that, where would it end? No.

Better he take the fall for his own decisions than have to pay for unsolicited advice gone wrong.

# Seven

Emily O'Hara was waiting for Rafe outside Katie's house late that afternoon. Again, he was the last man to leave and he had lingered even later than usual, half hoping Katie would get back from the store before he left. He wanted to talk to her. Hell, he admitted silently, that wasn't all he wanted.

Since Katie wasn't home, he was surprised to find her grandmother leaning against his truck when he walked out front to leave. She wore a hot-pink oversize shirt over a white tank top and white pants. Huge red-framed sunglasses shielded her eyes, but when she heard him approach, she pushed them up to the top of her head.

Idly filing her nails, she looked up at him as he got closer and gave him a tight smile that should have warned him something was up. But, he reminded himself, if there was one thing Rafe knew, it was women. Granted, he didn't have much experience with older females, but how hard could it be to pour on some charm and win her over?

Besides, Katie's grandmother had seemed nice enough when he first met her. What could possibly go wrong?

"Mrs. O'Hara," he said, giving her a guileless smile designed to put her at her ease, "Katie's not home."

"Oh, I know that Rafe. It's Tuesday. My girl always goes grocery shopping on Tuesdays. I've tried to shake up her world a little, but she does love a schedule." She straightened up, tucked her emery board into the oversize purse hanging from her shoulder and cocked her head to look at him. "Wait, maybe I shouldn't call you Rafe at all. Maybe you'd prefer it if I call you Mr. King?"

Rafe flinched and a sinking sensation opened up in the pit of his stomach. This he hadn't expected at all. She knew who he was. Had she told Katie? No, he thought. If she had, he'd have heard about it by now. Hell, Katie would have come at him with both barrels blazing. So the question was, why hadn't her grandmother given him up?

"Rafe'll do," he told her and stuffed his hands into his pockets. "How long have you known who I am?"

She chuckled. "Since the moment my Katie introduced you as Rafe Cole." Shaking her head, she ran one finger along the hood of the truck, looked at the dirt she'd picked up, then clucked her tongue and rubbed her fingers together to get rid of it.

"See, Katie's a good girl, but she's single-minded. At the moment, she's so focused on her business that she doesn't see anything else. Sadly, her pop culture knowledge is lacking, too. If she'd read the celebrity magazines more often, as I do..." She paused to give him another one of those cool, measuring stares. "Then she would have recognized you, too. Though I will say, you look different in jeans than you do in a tux at some fancy party."

Inwardly, he groaned. Stupid. He hadn't even thought of that. He'd been in one of those weekly tabloidesque magazines only last month. Photographers at the Save the Shore benefit had gotten shots of him squiring an actress to the affair. Not that he and Selena were a couple or anything. After one date, he'd known that a man could only talk hairdos and tanning tips for so long.

Sliding his hands from his pockets, he folded his arms over his chest in a classic defense posture. Emily might appear to be a sweet older lady, but the glint in her eye told him that he'd better walk soft and careful. But Rafe was used to sometimes-hostile negotiations with suppliers, so he was as prepared for this confrontation as he could be. Bracing his feet wide apart, he waited for whatever was coming next.

"So, not going to deny it at least," she said.

"What would be the point?"

"There is that."

Curious now, Rafe asked, "Why haven't you told Katie?"

"Interesting question," Emily acknowledged with a small smile. "I've asked that of myself a time or two in the last couple of weeks. But the truth is, I wanted to wait and see what you were up to first."

"And?"

"Still waiting." She wagged her finger at him as if he were a ten-year-old boy. She took a step or two away from the truck, walking from sunlight into shade. Her sandals clicked on the concrete driveway. When she turned to look at him again she asked, "So instead of keeping me in suspense, why don't you do us both a favor and tell me what's going on? Why are you pretending to be someone you're not?"

For one moment, Rafe caught himself wondering what it might have been like to have a woman like this one in his life. He had the distinct impression she would be a lioness when protecting Katie. He couldn't blame her for that, Rafe thought, even as he shrugged. He didn't want to be disrespectful, but damned if he'd explain himself to Katie's grandmother, either.

"Long story short," he offered, "I lost a bet so I'm working this job. Easier to work it as a nobody than one of the bosses."

"That explains why you haven't told your crew," she said thoughtfully. "It doesn't explain lying to Katie."

"No, it doesn't."

She blew out an impatient breath and prompted, "And? So?"

One look in the woman's eyes, so much like her granddaughter's, told Rafe that she wasn't going to give up until she had what she'd come here for. He didn't like being put on the spot. Didn't appreciate having to justify his actions. But, if there was one thing Rafe respected, it was loyalty and he could see that feeling ran deep in this woman.

So, though he wouldn't explain himself thoroughly, he was willing to give her the bare bones. "I like her. She hates the Kings. So I'm not about to tell her I'm one of them."

*"Ever?"* Emily asked, clearly dumbfounded.

"I'll have to tell her eventually," he acknowledged, "but in my own time and my own way."

"And when is that, exactly?"

Looking into her eyes, Rafe wondered why he had considered this woman to be just a nice older lady. Katie's nana had steel in her spine. He wasn't used to this. Rafe couldn't even remember the last time anyone had questioned him about anything. He was a King. He didn't do explanations or apologies. And he didn't, for damn sure, wither under a disapproving stare from a suburban grandmother.

Yet, that was just what he was doing.

"When I've convinced her that not *all* Kings are bastards," he admitted. "When she likes me enough, I'll tell her everything, prove to her she was wrong about us and then I'll get out of her life."

Emily blinked at him, then shook her head as if she hadn't heard him right. "That's your plan?"

"Something wrong with it?"

"Let me count the ways," she muttered, with yet another shake of her head.

He didn't care what she thought of his plan, he was sticking with it. But as he stood there, another idea occurred to him and he wondered why he hadn't thought of it before. Could have saved himself, and his brother Sean, a lot of trouble. Taking a step or two closer to Emily, he said, "You know which of the Kings treated her badly, right?"

She frowned so harshly, Rafe was instantly glad it wasn't *him* this formidable woman was mad at. "I do."

"Tell me," he said shortly. "Tell me who he is. I'm trying to find out, but it's taking me too long."

"Why do you care?"

"Because—" Rafe's mouth snapped shut. He took a breath and said, "I want to know who hurt her so I can hurt him back."

"One of your own family?"

He heard the surprise in her voice and a part of him shared it. The Kings always stuck together. It was practically a vow they all took at birth. It was the King cousins against the world and God help anyone who tried to undermine them. The occasional brawls and fistfights notwithstanding, none of the Kings had ever turned on another.

"Yeah," he said, realizing that cousin or not, Rafe really wanted to hit the guy responsible for Katie's defensiveness. No matter who the King cousin—or brother—was, Rafe was going to make him sorry for hurting Katie.

"Again," Emily said quietly, "I have to ask, why do you care?"

He scrubbed one hand across the back of his neck and gritted his teeth in frustration. Rafe wasn't sure himself why he cared so damn much, he only knew he did. The only possible explanation was that he didn't like the idea of a woman like Katie hating the Kings. She was…nice. Frowning at that moronic thought, he grumbled aloud, "You ask a hell of a lot of questions."

"I do indeed. So how about an answer?" she countered. "An honest one."

Rafe met her gaze and wondered if Katie would be as amazing a woman as her grandmother when she was Emily's age. He had to figure that she would. As the Kings were always saying, *it's in the blood.* And a part of him wanted to be around to see Katie as a scary-smart old woman. He dismissed that thought quickly enough though, as he knew all too well that commitment and permanence weren't in him.

Choosing his words carefully, Rafe said, "Honestly, I don't know why I care so much. I only know I do. I don't like knowing it was one of my family who caused her pain. And I don't like knowing she hates the Kings because of that one jerk—whoever he is. So give me a name and I'll take care of it and get out of Katie's life all that much sooner."

She gave him a slow, wide smile and shook her head firmly enough to have her short, silver hair lifting in the breeze. "You know what? I don't think I will."

"Why not?"

"Because, I'd rather watch you play out your plan," she admitted. "My Katie can take care of herself, you know. That guy hurt her, but he didn't break her. You know why? Because she only *thought* she was in love. You might want to remember that, Rafe."

Confusion rose up inside him, but he swallowed it back. "Fine, I'll remember."

"Good. Now, I've got a hot date, so I've got to get a move on," she announced and turned around to leave, only to whirl back to face him again. Pointing at him, she said, "Just one more thing."

"What's that?"

Her eyes narrowed and her voice dropped a couple of notches. There wasn't even the glimmer of a smile on her face. "If you break her heart, I'll hunt you down like a sick dog and make you sorry you ever set foot in Katie's house. Sound fair?"

Rafe nodded, admiration for the older woman filling him again. Family loyalty he understood completely. And he found himself again envying Katie for having someone in her life who loved her so much.

He'd never known that himself. Oh, he had his brothers and cousins, sure. His mother, though, hadn't loved him; she'd only used him as a bargaining chip, to squeeze Ben King for money. The elderly aunt who'd raised him hadn't—she'd only done her duty, as she often told him. Rafe was pretty sure his father had loved him, as much as Ben King was able. Rafe wasn't feeling sorry for himself. Things were as they were. And he'd done fine on his own.

But he had to wonder how it might have been to be raised with the kind of love he saw now, glittering in Emily O'Hara's eyes.

"I hear you."

"Good." She set her sunglasses in place, flashed him a quick smile and said, "As long as we understand each other, we'll be fine."

Then she waved one hand and hurried to a bright yellow VW bug parked at curbside. She hopped in, fired it up and was gone an instant later.

Scowling to himself, Rafe looked back at Katie's house, quiet in the afternoon light. The crew was gone, *she* was gone and the old bungalow looked as empty as he felt.

Talking to Emily had shaken him. Hearing his own plan put into words had made him realize that maybe it was as dumb as Katie's grandmother clearly thought it was. The lie he'd spun and invested so much in suddenly felt like a weight around his neck. He had to wonder if he wasn't doing the wrong thing in keeping it going.

He'd started this as a way to win her affection and respect without her knowing who he really was. But if he pulled it off, what did he really gain? She wasn't caring for the real him if she didn't *know* the real man. The sad truth was, Katie now cared about a lie. A fabrication. He'd done this to himself and couldn't see a way out without risking everything he didn't want to lose.

Rafe didn't like admitting it even to himself, but he suddenly felt more alone than he ever had in his life. And he wasn't sure what the hell to do about it.

* * *

Katie had deliveries to make bright and early the next morning. Any other day, she would have enjoyed being the one to drop off a surprise gift of cookies. She always got a charge out of seeing people's reactions to the elegantly frosted and wrapped creations. Since she'd become busier, she didn't normally have time to make deliveries herself anymore.

Usually, she had a teenager from down the street deliver her cookie orders. It helped her out and Donna made more money than she would babysitting. A win-win situation all the way around.

But Donna was on vacation with her family, so despite being so tired she could barely stand up, Katie had no choice but to load up her car with the week's orders. Specially made boxes lined her trunk and she carefully stored away the cookie bouquets and cookie towers and cookie cakes that she'd spent the last two days making. Each of them were frosted, some personalized and a swell of pride filled her as she looked at them.

She'd built this business out of nothing and she had big plans for it, too.

"And that," she told herself firmly, "is just one more reason to stay away from Rafe."

He was too male. Too overwhelming to every sense she possessed. She couldn't afford to be distracted from her goals, not even by a man who had the ability to sweep her off her feet with a single glance. And, if she hadn't already surrendered to her own hormones, he wouldn't be taking up so much of her thoughts. So she deliberately stopped thinking about Rafe—though it wasn't easy.

For now, she would devote herself to her burgeoning business. She wanted to make an even bigger name for herself. Move Katie's Kookies into a shop down on Pacific Coast Highway. Have several ovens, hire more help, expand her client list and maybe even go into online orders. She had big plans. And nothing was going to stop her from making them come true.

The scents of vanilla, cinnamon and chocolate filled her car and made Katie smile in spite of the fact that she was running on about three hours sleep. But she couldn't blame her sleeplessness entirely on the fact that she'd been baking half the night. Because when she finally did get to bed, she'd slept fitfully, tortured by dreams of Rafe. Of the night they'd had together.

And there he was again, front and center in her brain. Seeing him every day wasn't helping her avoid thoughts of him. Especially since her own body seemed determined to remind her, every chance it got, of just what she'd experienced in his arms.

"Need some help?"

Katie jolted and slapped one hand to her chest as she turned around to look at the very man she had just been thinking about. "You scared me."

"Sorry." He grinned. "I called out to you, but you didn't hear me, I guess."

No, she hadn't. She'd been too busy remembering his hands on her skin. The taste of his mouth. The slow slide of his body invading hers. Oh, boy. She blew out a breath, forced a smile and said, "I'm just preoccupied."

"I can see that," he said, glancing into the back of the SUV. "You've been busy."

"I really have," she admitted, and turned to pick up the last box, holding a dozen pink frosted cookies shaped like baby rattles.

"Let me get that," he said and reached for it before she could stop him.

Truthfully, even though it was a little uncomfortable being around him at the moment, Katie was glad he was there. She'd spent the last few days avoiding being alone with him, allowing herself only a glimpse of him now and then. Having him close enough now that she could feel his body heat was a sort of tempting torture. He looked great in his worn blue jeans and blue T-shirt with King Construction stenciled across the back. And he smelled even better, with the scent of soap from his morning shower still clinging to his skin. She wanted to go to him. To kiss him.

She caught that thought and strangled it. She was so tired, she was nearly staggering. Way too tired to trust her instincts around a man she already knew she wanted. Katie gave herself a quick, silent talking-to. Besides, she still had a full morning of deliveries.

"Thanks."

He set the box in the trunk, then shot her a look. "Are you okay?"

"Yes. Just tired."

He frowned and shifted his gaze to the mass of cookies. "You're delivering all of these yourself?"

She yawned and nodded. "Sorry. Yes. My usual delivery girl is camping in Yosemite with her family so…"

"You can hardly keep your eyes open," he accused.

As if to prove him wrong, Katie opened her eyes as wide as possible and pretended not to notice that they felt like marbles rolling in sand. "I'm fine. Really. I'll have these done in an hour or two and then I'll come home and take a nap."

From inside the kitchen, a saw buzzed into life.

"Well, maybe I'll take a nap," she said with a wry smile.

He didn't return the smile. Instead, he glowered at her, crossed his arms over his chest and said flatly, "You're not driving anywhere."

She blinked at him. "Excuse me?"

Shaking his head, Rafe said, "Katie, you're practically asleep on your feet. You try to drive and you'll end up killing someone. Or yourself."

"You're overreacting," she said and closed the trunk lid. "I can take care of myself."

"Sure you can," he agreed amiably. "When you're awake."

"I'm not your responsibility, Rafe," she argued, fighting the urge to yawn again. See? Just another reason why they wouldn't have worked out as a couple. He was too bossy and she was too stubborn.

God, she was tired. Another yawn sneaked up on her before she could stifle it and she saw his eyes narrow dangerously. Perfect. She had just given him more ammunition for his argument. To head him off before he could say anything, she spoke up quickly. "Look, I appreciate the concern, really. But I'm fine and we both have work to do. Why don't we just get on with what we were doing and let this go?"

"I don't think so." Rafe grabbed the keys from the trunk lock and held them out of reach. "I'm not kidding about this. No way am I letting you drive."

*"Letting me?"* she repeated incredulously as she stared up into his implacable expression. "You don't have a vote in it, Rafe. This is my car. My business, and I say I'm fine to drive."

"You're wrong." He looked over his shoulder at the house. "Wait here."

He might as well have patted her on the head and ordered her to *stay.* As if she were a golden retriever or something. And of course she would wait there. What choice did she have? Katie wondered in irritation. He'd taken her keys.

Anger churned inside her and mixed with the fatigue clawing at her. Probably not a good combination. Okay. Fine. Yes, she really *was* exhausted. But she wasn't a danger to people on the road for heaven's sake. She wasn't a complete idiot. She wouldn't drive if she didn't think she could.

The longer he was gone, the more irritated she became. She paced—in the garage, muttering to herself, rubbing her gritty eyes. One night with the man and he became territorial. Probably a good idea she'd decided to keep her distance. Imagine what he'd be like if they were actually in a relationship.

Then that thought settled in. Instead of making her angrier, it gave Katie a soft, warm glow. Who was she kidding? She'd love for someone to be that worried about her. Oh, not that she was some mindless woman to take orders from anyone. But the idea that a man would care enough to worry about her safety sort of dulled the edges of her anger. Of course, she thought wryly, that could be the exhaustion talking.

So when he finally came back, her tone hadn't softened by much as she said, "Give me my keys."

"Not a chance." He took her arm in a firm, no-nonsense grip, steered her to the passenger side of her car, opened the door and said simply, "Get in."

Stubbornly, Katie pulled free of his hold and took a determined step back. Standing her ground, she lifted her chin in defiance and met him stare for stare. "This isn't funny, Rafe."

His blue eyes narrowed on her. "Damn right it isn't. You're too self-sufficient for your own good."

"What's that supposed to mean?"

"It means that you're so focused on doing everything on your own you don't know enough to ask for help when you need it." He scowled at her as if expecting her to quail before his impeccable logic.

She didn't.

"I don't need help, and if I did, I wouldn't come to you."

He took a quick, sharp breath. "Why the hell not?"

"Because, we're not together and you're supposed to be working on my kitchen."

"We could be together if you weren't so damn hard-headed," he pointed out. "And as for working on your kitchen, I can do that when we get back."

"*We* aren't going anywhere," she argued and felt another yawn sneaking up on her. She twisted her mouth together and clamped her lips shut rather than giving into it.

"Nice try, but I saw that yawn anyway," he pointed out.

"Doesn't mean a thing," she told him.

"Damn it, Katie," Rafe said, his voice quiet, his gaze locked on hers, "Even if you don't want *my* help, you could at least admit that you're too damn tired to think straight, let alone drive."

He was leaning on the open passenger door, just an arm's reach away from her. His blue eyes were locked on her and his dark blue, steely stare told Katie he wouldn't be giving up easily.

So she tried another tactic.

"Rafe," she assured him in a calm, rational tone that completely belied the irritation still spiking inside her, "I'm completely fine. Really."

Then she yawned again.

"Uh-huh," he said, "I'm convinced. Get in. I'm driving."

*"You?"* She looked from him to the kitchen, where the crew was busy doing heaven knew what to her house and asked, "You can't just walk away from your job."

"I told the guys to let Joe know I was helping you out and that I'd be back in a couple of hours."

"You can't do that." Wouldn't he be fired? She couldn't let him lose his job over this.

"Yeah," he said, "I can. Consider us a full-service construction company. Whatever the boss—that's *you*—needs, we provide."

Katie hadn't gone to him, he'd come to her. And there was the slightest chance that he was right and she was too tired to drive all over town. But at the same time, that didn't make it okay for him to ride in and take over.

She thought about it, her mind racing, arguing with itself. Yes, he was being a jerk, but he was also being nice, in a roundabout, tyrannical sort of way. He was glaring at her, but he was worried about her. He was supposed to be working on her kitchen, but instead he was willing to drive her around town making cookie deliveries.

And she would be alone with him in the car for an hour or more. That appealed to her on so many levels it was scary. But could she really be with him and *not* with him at the same time?

Oh, she was so tired, even *she* didn't understand her any more.

"I can practically hear you arguing with yourself," he said after a long moment.

"It's easier than arguing with you," she told him.

"True. And before we start in again, you should know that I don't quit. I don't give in. Never surrender."

She tipped her head to one side and looked up at him. "I don't quit, either."

He shrugged. "Hence the trouble between us."

*"Hence?"* she repeated, smiling in spite of the situation.

Rafe blew out a breath. "Are you getting in, or do I pick you up and *put* you in?" he asked.

Katie sent him a hard glare. "All right, fine," she confessed. "I *might* be a little too tired to drive."

He smiled and Katie's toes curled in her comfortable flats. Oh, boy. For all of her fine notions about keeping her distance, about not letting herself fall for a guy, she was certainly doing a lot of stumbling around him.

"Now that we're on the same page, so to speak," Rafe said, "will you please get in the car?"

Her mouth twitched into a smile at the way he'd changed his command to a request. She nodded, climbing up into the passenger seat. "Thank you."

"You're welcome." He closed her door, walked around to the driver's side and slid her key into the ignition. Then he looked at her and said, "So, how does it feel to be going on our second date?"

Her eyebrows winged up when she turned her gaze on him. "Delivering cookies is a date?"

"If we say it is, yeah." He fired up the engine and looked at her again. "So? Is it?"

Katie stared at him and remembered that night. Then she remembered the last few days, being so close to him and so far away all at the same time. She remembered every haunting dream she'd had and how she would wake up, aching for his touch.

Was she being an idiot by shutting out the first nice,

normal guy she'd met in way too long? Okay, yes, he was a little bossy, but she could handle that. Would it really be so bad to take a chance? To spend some time with Rafe? To see if what she already felt for him might grow? After all, she could concentrate on her business *and* have a life, couldn't she? Isn't that what Nana and Nicole both had been trying to tell her?

Memories of Cordell rose up in her mind, but Katie fought them down with determination.

Watching Rafe, she finally said, "It's not a date unless you spring for a cup of coffee at least."

He grinned at her, clearly victorious. "One latte, coming up."

# Eight

An hour and a half later, Katie looked a little more alert and Rafe was enjoying himself immensely. "No wonder you like doing this," he said, sliding into the driver's seat after making the last of the deliveries. "People are excited to see you when you bring them cookies."

She grinned. "How did the pink baby-rattle cookies go over?"

He laughed and held up a five-dollar bill. "I got a tip!"

He looked so pleased with himself, Katie had to laugh, too. "Congratulations, you're a delivery person."

"She cried, too," he said, handing Katie the five. Shaking his head, he remembered the expression on the woman's face when she opened the door and saw him standing there, holding the basket of pink frosted cookies. "The woman? The new mom? She took one look at those cookies her friend ordered from you and burst into tears. She was laughing and crying and for a minute." Then he added, "it was terrifying."

Katie reached out and patted his arm. "Not what you're used to as a carpenter?"

"No," he said simply, looking into her green eyes. She was so pleased with him, having so much fun, he couldn't help but suddenly feel like a first-class rat for lying to her.

He thought back to his conversation with Katie's grandmother and realized that she had been right. Ever since talking to Emily, he'd been rethinking this whole keep-the-lie-going thing. His lies hadn't seemed like such a big deal when he had started out on this job. But now, every day with Katie made him feel that much more like a jerk. He should have told her the truth before now.

Sure, he'd told Emily that he was sticking to his plan, but she'd made him start to doubt the wisdom in that. But he couldn't think of a good way out of this mess. Because, he realized with startling clarity, the moment he told Katie about his lies, what his real name was, it would all be over between them.

Odd that he hadn't considered that possibility before. But then, he hadn't thought that he would *want* to keep seeing her once this job was finished. Now though, he knew he didn't want her disappearing from his life at the end of this job. He wanted to keep seeing her. And the chances of that happening looked slim.

He imagined blurting out the truth right there and then. Telling her that he wasn't the man she thought he was. And in his mind's eye, he saw her features tighten with betrayal, saw the shine in her green eyes dim and then flash with fury, and he told himself that it didn't matter if he was starting to get uncomfortable with his lies.

She wasn't ready to learn the truth.

He wanted her to care for him before he told her who he was. And then? a voice in his mind whispered. But he didn't have an answer to that yet. All Rafe knew was that he wanted to be with her *now*. And he didn't want the King name ruining that.

So he was stuck with his lies, his plan, whether he wanted to be or not.

"How are you feeling?" he asked, suddenly changing the subject.

"A little more awake, thanks. The latte helped."

"Not enough," he decided. Her green eyes were shadowed and her face was too pale to suit him. The fact that he was worried about her bothered him, but there didn't seem to be anything he could do about that. "You still look tired."

"Well, don't I feel pretty?" she asked wryly.

"You're beautiful." Two words, softly spoken, and they seemed to echo in the air around them. He hadn't meant to blurt that out. It had been a knee-jerk reaction.

"Rafe—"

"Don't," he said quietly, before she could start in on her speech about how nothing had changed and she still wasn't interested in being with him. He could *feel* her reaction to his closeness. Her skin was warm and though her eyes were tired, he still noticed the gleam of desire in their depths.

Leaning in closer to her, Rafe reached out, touched her cheek with his fingertips and tipped her face up for his kiss. "Just, let me…"

She sighed and moved into him, meeting him halfway, taking what he offered, and Rafe was relieved. He didn't know if he could have taken her turning from him or pulling away. He'd been thinking about doing just this for the last few days. Thinking about *her*. The first touch of her mouth to his eased everything inside him, yet rekindled a fire that had been nothing more than glowing embers since their one night together.

His body tightened, his heartbeat thundered in his chest and Rafe had to fight every instinct he possessed to keep from grabbing her and yanking her close to him. He wanted his hands on her again. Wanted her under him, over him. Wanted her body surrendering to his.

He groaned then, knowing he couldn't have everything he wanted right now. And the longer he kissed her, the less willing he would be to stop. So he pulled back while he still could and drew a long, shaky breath.

Resting his forehead against hers, he waited for control to slide back into his body, but it was a long time coming. Especially when he could feel her short, sharp breaths against his face. Well, he thought wryly, so much for her claims of not wanting to be with him again.

Several long moments passed before he gave her a smile, looked into her eyes and said, "There. Told you we weren't done with each other."

Katie shook her head, one corner of her mouth tipping into a reluctant half smile. "You really think now is the right time for I-told-you-sos?"

"What better time?"

"You're impossible."

"I like that." He skimmed his fingers through her hair until his hand was at the back of her neck, kneading her skin with a sure, gentle touch.

"You would," she told him, sighing at his touch.

"Are we going to argue again?" he asked. "Because I warn you, I'm getting to the point where I really enjoy our 'disagreements.'"

"Maybe later." She cupped his cheek in the palm of her hand.

"At least you admit there will be a 'later.'"

"Yes," she said with a slow nod, never tearing her gaze from his. "There will be."

"Tonight." Rafe caught her hand in his. "I want to see you tonight."

"Okay," she said. "Another barbecue?"

"Oh, I think this time we'll let someone else cook. I'll pick you up at seven," he said, easing back behind the wheel.

"To go where?"

"That's a surprise." He shot her a quick grin as a plan formed in his mind while he steered the car into traffic. "All you have to do is dress up. Oh, and take a nap. I want you wide awake tonight."

"That sounds intriguing."

"Count on it."

His mind was already racing with plans and he smiled to himself as it all began to come together.

That feeling lasted until he went home to change.

The minute he walked into his hotel suite, he knew someone was there. Didn't take a genius, after all. There was a designer purse on his couch and a pair of black heels under the glass-topped coffee table.

Rafe's brain raced frantically. Had he already set up a date for tonight? He didn't think so. Hell, he hadn't seen anyone since Selena the Self Involved Actress. So who...?

"Rafe? Is that you?"

The familiar, feminine voice sent a twist of old pain mixed with regret slashing through his middle, but he fought it down and managed to give his ex-wife a half smile when she came in off the balcony.

"Leslie. What are you doing here?"

The cool, elegant brunette flashed him a brief, wry smile. "Well, good to see you too, Rafe."

Irritated at being called to the carpet on his manners when she was the one who'd shown up unannounced and let herself into *his* home, Rafe just stared at her. Waiting.

It didn't take long. Leslie never had been the patient type. "I know I should have called before just showing up here."

"That would've been good," he said.

She stood with the balcony and the bank of windows at her back. Rafe was absolutely sure she knew that the sunlight streaming in through those windows was highlighting her to a beautiful advantage. Leslie always had known how to show herself off in the best way. She was lovely, self-assured and the only woman in the world who had ever told him that he wasn't good enough.

That memory colored his tone when he spoke. "How did you get in here?"

"Oh," she said, giving him a palms-up shrug, "Declan's still the concierge here. He let me up so I could wait for you in private."

Silently, Rafe told himself that he'd be having a little chat with Declan real soon. For the moment though… "I repeat. What are you doing here?"

Leslie frowned slightly, not enough to mar her brow or anything, but he got the message. She had never had any trouble letting Rafe know that he'd disappointed her in some way. Looking back now, he couldn't even remember *why* they had gotten married in the first place.

"You always were a straightforward man," she murmured.

"As I recall, that's one of the things you didn't care for."

Her mouth flattened into a straight line briefly; then, as if she'd willed it to happen, it curved again slightly. "Look at us. It's been years since we divorced and we're still treating each other like the enemy."

He shifted a little at that, since it was true and there really was no point in it. Leslie wasn't a part of his life anymore, so why go on a forced march down memory lane?

"True. So tell me. Why are you here?"

"Honestly?" She shook her head in wonder and admitted, "I can't believe I'm here, either. But I didn't have anywhere else to turn."

She took a small breath, covered her mouth with her fingertips and let tears well in her eyes. Something inside Rafe tightened as he remembered all the times Leslie had been able to turn on the tears. During an argument, to avoid an argument or just to make the point that he was a selfish bastard—out came the tears. When they were dating, he'd felt almost heroic when he could make those tears stop. Because she looked so damn fragile when she cried. Today though, he was no longer moved. Besides, she had a different husband now. Why wasn't she home turning *him* inside out?

"Oh, Rafe," she whispered brokenly, allowing the sunlight to backlight her to perfection. "I hated coming here, truly, but I had no choice."

"Just tell me what's going on."

"It's John," she said and Rafe felt an instant stab of

worry. After all, before he became Leslie's husband, John Peters had been Rafe's best friend.

"Is he all right?"

"Physically, yes," she said with a little shake of her head. "But Rafe, he's lost his job and I don't know what to do."

For one very brief second, Rafe felt a twinge of sympathy for his old friend. He and John had met in college and until Leslie had come between them, they'd been the best of friends. Truthfully, Rafe had missed John's friendship more than he had missed being with Leslie.

A sad statement on a dead marriage.

"What's that got to do with me?" He winced at the tone in his own voice and knew that he'd sounded crueler than he'd intended when her head came up and her eyes narrowed.

"You don't have to be mean."

He sighed and glanced at his watch. He wanted to take a shower, get dressed and pick up Katie. Leslie was his past and his present was looking a lot more promising. So rather than prolonging this conversation, he got to the point. "Leslie, you're my *ex*-wife married to my *ex*-friend. Just how much sympathy do you expect?"

"I knew you wouldn't understand."

"You're right," he agreed, heading for the wet bar along the wall. He suddenly wanted a beer. "I don't."

She walked over to join him and asked for a glass of wine. Once he'd poured it and handed it to her, Leslie took a sip and said, "I need money."

Rafe almost smiled, even as he felt a brand-new sheen of ice coat his heart. He should have known. When it came right down to it, what people wanted from the

Kings was money. Never failed. "Does John know you're here?"

"Of course not. He'd be humiliated."

That much Rafe believed. The man Rafe remembered would have been horrified to know that Leslie was here asking for help. He leaned one arm on the bar top. "Just out of curiosity, say I give you the cash you need, how do you explain that to John?"

"I'll find a way," she said, lifting her chin slightly to prove her point. "I can be pretty persuasive."

"I remember." He remembered a lot, Rafe thought. Leslie had always been able to find a way to get whatever it was she wanted. That much, it seemed, hadn't changed. As he looked at his ex-wife now, he mentally compared her to Katie Charles. Katie with her soft hair and faded jeans. With the laugh that seemed to bubble up from her soul. With green eyes that flashed from humor to fury and back again in a heartbeat.

Leslie was coolly elegant.

Katie was heat and passion and—he shut his brain off before it went on an even wilder tangent.

"Rafe, I wouldn't have come to you if I'd had anywhere else to turn," she said, and for the first time, her voice held an edge of regret.

"Yeah, I know that, too." Rafe thought about Katie again and wondered what she would do if she was in Leslie's position. He didn't like to think about Katie being in trouble. Didn't want to acknowledge that it bothered him more than a little to know that she wouldn't turn to him.

Then he thought about how hard Katie worked at building her business. How she scrambled for a living. How she worked and fought for a future doing something she loved. She would do whatever she had to do to take care of herself. And he realized that Leslie was only doing the same thing now. She never would have come to him for help if she hadn't been desperate. Hell, he could read that much in her tear-sheened blue eyes. Because of Katie, Rafe felt a surge of sympathy for Leslie he might not have experienced just a few weeks ago. What was that about?

However it had ended between them, Rafe knew he couldn't ignore Leslie's request for help. Maybe he was finally letting the past go—along with the regrets and the stinging sense of failure memories of his marriage inevitably dredged up.

"Call my assistant Janice tomorrow," he told her. "She'll give you however much you need."

She let out a relieved breath and gave him a grateful smile. "Thanks. To tell the truth, I didn't really think you'd help."

"But you asked anyway."

"Had to," she said, her gaze steady and honest. "I can't stand seeing John worried and upset."

Rafe studied her. "You really love him."

"I really do," she said simply.

That should at least sting, he thought, but it didn't. Not anymore. And, if he was honest with himself, Rafe could admit that when Leslie had walked out, it had been his pride, more than his heart, that had been affected. What did that say about him? Was Leslie right when she told him that he simply wasn't capable of love?

"Les, when we were married," he asked quietly, studying the label on his beer bottle as if looking for the right words, "did you feel that way about me? Would you have protected me if I needed it?"

"You didn't need me, Rafe," she said softly. "You never really did."

"I loved you."

She smiled and shook her head. "No, you didn't."

Irritation spiked. "I guess I know what I felt."

"Don't be so insulted," she said, giving him a patient smile. "I know you cared, but you didn't *love* me, Rafe. I finally got tired of trying to get through to you."

He straightened up, set his beer down and stuffed both hands into his jeans pockets. "I seem to recall you telling me I was incapable of love."

She blinked at him, stunned. "No, I didn't."

"Yeah, you did," he argued.

"For heaven's sake, Rafe," she countered, "why would I say that?"

"Funny, I asked myself that a few times."

"Honestly, Rafe, this is one of the reasons we didn't work out," she told him with a shake of her head. "You never *listened* to me. I never said you were *incapable* of love. I said you were incapable of loving *me*."

He shifted his gaze from Leslie to the view beyond his windows. The sun was sliding into the ocean, dazzling the waves in a brilliant crimson light. A cool breeze danced in through the open balcony doors and he turned his face into it. "Either way, you were right."

"No," Leslie said. "I wasn't."

She reached out and laid one hand on his arm. "Rafe, don't you get it? You didn't love me and that hurt. So I wanted to hurt you back."

She hadn't hurt him, he realized now. She had just driven home the point he'd learned long before her. That love was something you had to be taught when you were growing up. And that was one course Rafe had never gotten.

Leslie tipped her head to one side and looked up at him. "Who is she?"

"What?" He stiffened, instantly retreating into privacy mode, shuttering his eyes, closing down his expression. He took a long, metaphorical step back and distanced himself as much as possible from the curiosity in Leslie's eyes.

"Wow," she murmured, staring at him as if he'd just performed a magic trick, "you still do that so easily."

"Do what?"

"Lock yourself away the instant anybody gets close. Used to make me crazy," she admitted. "It was as if you were on a constant red alert—just waiting for a sneak attack on your heart so you could defend against it."

He resented the description, but Rafe really couldn't deny it, either.

Shaking her head again, she said, "Don't do it, Rafe. I mean, with her, whoever she is, don't do this. Let her in. Risk it."

"Yeah, because my track record is so good."

"You don't need a track record to love someone," she told him. "All it takes is the *right* someone."

"Like John?" he asked.

"For me, yes. Exactly like John." She let her hand fall from his arm and added, "You know, John misses your friendship. You didn't have to cut him loose because of what happened between us, Rafe."

Yes, he did. Because he couldn't look at his friend without knowing that somehow, John had been able to do something Rafe had failed at. He'd made Leslie happy when Rafe couldn't. Kings didn't like losing, probably because they weren't very good at it. Thankfully, the Kings didn't have to deal with that situation often, since they rarely accepted failure.

But in these last few minutes with Leslie, Rafe could admit that whatever he had once felt at losing her was now gone. She was married, happy and a mother. Leslie had moved on, just as his brothers had said. Maybe it was time he did the same thing. Should he really allow one failure to dictate the rest of his life?

"I've missed John, too," he admitted finally. And since that statement didn't leave a bitter taste in his mouth, he heard himself ask, "How are the kids?"

Her face brightened instantly and her smile went wide and heartfelt. "They're terrific. Want to see some pictures?"

"Sure." It only took her a moment to get her purse and pull out her wallet. Then she was flipping through pictures of two beautiful kids, each of them with her hair and John's eyes. He looked at those shining faces and felt the slightest ping of envy at the proof of his ex-wife's current life.

"Nice-looking kids."

"They're great," Leslie said. "And John's a wonderful father."

"I'm glad for you," he told her and surprisingly enough, he meant it. Odd, Rafe thought. Before, when he'd thought about Leslie, there had always been a thread of sadness sliding through him. His failure. His mistake. Now, he felt nothing like that. Instead, his thoughts were filled with images of Katie Charles. Her smile. Her laugh. The feel of her skin beneath his hands.

Leslie was the past.

Was Katie the future?

"Are you okay?"

"What?"

Leslie studied him. "You looked worried there for a second."

Worried? Him? Rafe frowned slightly. He didn't

worry. He acted. "No. Not worried. Everything's fine." He paused and then surprised himself by adding, "I'm glad you stopped by today, Leslie."

"Yeah?" She grinned. "Now there's something you wouldn't have said even a year ago."

"True," he admitted ruefully. "But I can say it now."

"She must really be something, your mystery woman."

"You know," he said thoughtfully, as the last of his baggage from his failed marriage fell away, "she really is."

"Then don't blow it, Rafe," Leslie told him. "For your own sake, let her in."

He already had, he realized now. Hadn't meant to. Hadn't even been aware of it. But somehow Katie had gotten past his defenses and now he had to figure out what that meant for him. For them.

"I should be going," Leslie said. She picked up her bag and walked over to slip into her heels. "Thank you again for doing this, Rafe, and I will pay you back."

"I know. Just…call Janice tomorrow."

"I will. Oh, and don't be mad at Declan for letting me into your place. I won't do it again."

He nodded, watching her prepare to return to her own life and world.

"There's one more thing," she said softly. "I'm sorry about how we ended."

He snapped her a look and noted that her smile was genuine and the tears were gone. For the first time, Rafe could look at her and see beyond his own failures and disappointments. He realized that there weren't hard feelings anymore. He didn't need to continue to avoid Leslie or even John. The past was done. It didn't matter to him now and with that realization came a sort of peace. So when another thought popped into his mind, he went with it.

"We could always use another legal shark at King Construction," he offered. "Tell John to call me."

Her smile was quick and bright. "He'd love to talk to you again, Rafe. Even without a job offer."

"Yeah," he admitted. "Me, too."

When Leslie left a moment later, Rafe took a second or two to enjoy the unusual sensation he felt. For years, he'd been holding on to the failure of his marriage like a damn battle flag. Internally, he'd waved it any time a woman even remotely seemed to be getting too close. That stamp of failure was enough to ensure he'd never try marriage again. Never allow someone to matter too much. As a King, he didn't fail.

But now, he was beginning to realize that maybe his marriage to Leslie hadn't had a chance from the beginning. He'd never had a shot at making it work because he had married Leslie for all the wrong reasons.

They had both been too young to know what they wanted. Too stupid to see that getting married wasn't the natural end result of dating for a year. He had blindly pushed forward even though a part of him had known going in that it wasn't right.

The problem was, he didn't feel like that about Katie. Being with her felt absolutely right. But would it still feel that way when she knew the truth?

# Nine

After a long nap, Katie felt energized and a little nervous about her upcoming date. So she took moral support along when she went shopping.

"Seriously?" Nicole asked, shaking her head and grimacing. "You're not fifty years old, Katie."

Katie looked down at the dress she had tried on and frowned to herself. It was a lovely beige silk with a high neck, long sleeves and a full skirt that swirled around her knees when she did a quick turn in front of the mirror. "It's pretty."

"It's dowdy," Nicole argued and handed Connor a bottle of juice.

The little boy kicked his heels against the stroller bottom and cried out, "Pretty!"

"Connor likes it," Katie argued.

"He won't when he's thirty." Nicole shook her head again, leaned over to a nearby rack and plucked a dress free. "Try this one. It's your size."

"It's black."

"And...?"

Katie blew out a breath and said, "Fine. Be right back."

They were in a tiny boutique on Second Street. She might have had better luck in a mall, but this was closer and Katie preferred supporting the small businesses around her. After all, she was determined to be one of them someday soon and besides, the big mega stores already had a huge customer base.

She took off the beige and hung it up carefully, giving it one last wistful glance. "Are you sure?" she called out from the dressing room. "The beige one looks so elegant."

"Try the black," Nicole ordered from just outside the door. "Trust me on this."

Sighing, Katie did, dragging the black dress over her head and positioning it just right. When she closed the side zipper, she looked into the mirror and instantly thought about buying a sweater.

"I can't wear this," she complained, still staring at her reflection as if seeing a stranger. "This is so not me."

"Let's see it."

Katie opened the door a scant inch, barely giving Nicole a peek. But her friend wasn't satisfied with that and pushed the door open completely. Her eyes went wide and a slow grin curved her mouth. "Wow."

Uncomfortable, Katie looked back into the mirror. Miles of skin were exposed. She'd never worn anything like this before. And what did that say about her sad, quiet little life?

Two thin black straps snaked over her bare shoulders and the bodice was cut low enough to give an excellent view of the tops of her breasts. The material was slick and clingy and molded to every inch of her body, defining curves even she hadn't been aware of. The hem of the dress hit mid-thigh—another inch or two higher and it would've been illegal.

As it was, it was only embarrassing.

"You look amazing," Nicole said, staring into the mirror to catch her eye.

"I can't wear this."

"Why not?"

"It's just not me," Katie said, fighting the urge to tug the bodice up a little higher.

"That's exactly why you should wear it," Nicole told her, scooping Connor out of the stroller to prop him on her hip. Swinging her blond hair back behind her shoulder, she met Katie's gaze in the mirror and said, "Cordell shot your confidence out from under you."

"True." But she was the one who had allowed it to happen. Katie ran one hand over the front of the dress, smoothing the fabric. She studied her own reflection while her friend continued talking.

"If you keep hiding away, you're letting *him* decide your life for you. Don't you get it?"

Katie's gaze shifted to Nicole's in the mirror. "Yes, but—"

"No buts." Nicole shook her head firmly and ran the palm of her hand across the top of her son's head. "Trust me, I know what it's like to have your self-assurance shaken. Let's pause to remember that my husband walked out on me when I was pregnant."

"Nicole…"

"Not a bid for sympathy," she said firmly. "I'm so over him. My point is, you should be over Cordell, too."

"I am really," Katie told her and realized that she had been "over" Cordell for some time. She'd been nursing her own hurt feelings for too long, but that had stopped when she met Rafe.

Just one of his kisses was enough to sear anyone else from her mind. Her heart. Her breath caught and twisted in her lungs until she was almost light-headed as she thought about the gleam that would appear in Rafe's eyes when he saw her in this dress.

"Then what're you waiting for?" Nicole came up behind her. In the glass, the two women stood side by side, with a toddler boy grinning between them. "If you're really over that creep, then wear this dress tonight. Knock Rafe's socks off."

Katie sent her own reflection a thoughtful smile. Slowly, she straightened up, threw her shoulders back and let the initial embarrassment she'd felt slide away. She did look good. She really liked Rafe and hiding away from what she was feeling wouldn't change that any.

"Atta girl," Nicole whispered as if she could hear what Katie was thinking.

Katie's mind raced. Cordell King hadn't even been a part of her life for very long. Truthfully, she thought now, she had probably built what they'd so briefly shared into something it had never been. Meeting him had been so far out of her orbit that she had taken it as some sort of sign—that he was the one. She had been willingly blinded by the fairy tale, Katie told herself hollowly. Rich, handsome man sweeps poor but honest shopkeeper off her feet and whisks her off to his palatial estate.

She gave her reflection a rueful smile.

When her fantasy ended, she'd crawled back into her narrow routine and pulled it in after her, essentially cutting herself off from everything just so that she couldn't make a foolish mistake again. And who was *that* decision hurting? she demanded silently.

Cordell had gone on his merry way, leaving a diamond token in his wake, no doubt never once thinking about Katie. While she, on the other hand, had not only buried herself in work, but continued to hold off on another relationship just because she'd made one bad judgment call.

Straightening up slowly, she looked her reflection in the eye and asked, *Are you going to be alone for the rest of your life, Katie?*

God no. She didn't want that. She had never wanted that. Ever since she was a little girl, she'd dreamed about having a family of her own. She had heard all the stories from her grandmother and her mother, talking about the great loves of their lives and how they wouldn't have traded a minute of it—even to spare themselves the pain of losing those special men.

What, she wondered, would she look back on one day? A great cookie recipe?

"So just when exactly did I become such a coward?" she whispered.

"What?"

She shifted her gaze to Nicole's reflection and asked, "Why didn't I see this before? Why am I hiding away? I didn't do anything wrong. I just picked a lemon in the garden of love."

Nicole laughed and the baby's giggle echoed her. "Nice way of putting it, but yeah."

Every passing moment filled Katie with more strength. More confidence. Right there in the tiny dressing room, she had the epiphany of all epiphanies. She had closed herself off to life to punish herself for being wrong. It didn't even make sense. Was pain so great that you couldn't risk being happy on the off chance you might get hurt again?

It was as if she could feel her old self clawing her way to the surface, brushing past the hesitant, meek Katie and tamping her down, she hoped, never to rise again.

"Who doesn't pick the wrong guy occasionally?" she demanded.

"Preaching to the choir, girl," Nicole said ruefully.

"That's right!" Katie swung around and draped one arm around Nicole's shoulders. "*Your* guy was a jerk, too!"

Laughing, Nicole said, "Do you have to sound so excited by that?"

Katie shook her head and said, "Sorry, but I'm having a moment here. The problem's not me. It never was me. So I picked the wrong guy? So what? Doesn't mean I'll pick the wrong one again, does it?"

"Nope."

Swinging back around to face her reflection, Katie dismissed the dowdy beige dress from her mind and instead admired the sexy black one she wore. She turned and checked herself out from every angle and finally gave a sharp nod. "You were right, Nicole. This dress *is* perfect. It's going to knock Rafe's socks off."

"Hopefully," Nicole added with a sly grin, "it'll knock off a lot more than his socks."

Katie felt a flush of heat rush through her just thinking about the possibilities. Then she tugged at the zipper and said, "As soon as I'm dressed again, we're headed for the shoe department. I need some sky-high heels, too."

"Now you're talking," Nicole said and took her son out of the dressing room.

Katie thought about what Rafe's reaction to her might be and she smiled to herself. She was through pretending she didn't care about him. Finished trying to protect herself at the cost of her own happiness. Tonight was going to be a turning point for her and Rafe. She was opening herself up to the possibilities.

Katie gave her reflection one last, approving glance. Nana would be so proud.

The restaurant sat high on the cliffs at Dana Point.

There was patio dining and then there were the booths inside, safely tucked behind a glass wall, protecting diners from the cool wind. He'd left their choice of table up to Katie and was pleased when she'd opted for the patio. From here, they could not only see the ocean, but hear the pulse of it as the water met the cliffs.

With the stars overhead and the waves crashing into the rocks below, it was probably one of the most romantic places on the coast. Rafe hadn't been there in years—but he had known it was the perfect spot for the romantic evening he wanted to have with Katie.

Looking at her now, across the table from him, with the ocean breeze ruffling her dark red hair into a tumble of curls, his breath caught in his chest. Her green eyes shone in the soft candlelight burning from behind the safety of hurricane lamps in the center of their table. Her smile was infectious as she admired her surroundings, and the urge to reach out and touch her was damn near overpowering.

He'd never forget his first sight of her when she opened her door to him. That black dress clung to her body in all the right ways. Her creamy skin was displayed to perfection and the heels she wore made her already great legs look amazing.

Everything in him went hard and tight. His heartbeat was crashing in his chest and his mind filled with sensual images of just how he hoped this evening would end.

"This place is gorgeous," she said, shifting her gaze

back to him before turning her head to take in the restaurant behind them and the people sitting behind the glass wall. "I can't believe anyone would choose to be inside instead of out here."

"Me either," he said and reached for his glass of wine. He took a sip, admired the taste of it and silently toasted his cousin Travis, who owned and operated King Vineyards. The bottle of King Cabernet was perfect. As it should be. "But most women prefer to be inside where their hair doesn't get messed up by the wind."

She turned to grin at him, flipping her hair back over her shoulder. "Not me. I love the feel of the wind."

"It looks good on you," he said softly.

Katie took a sip of her wine and smiled. "The wine's good, too, even if it *is* from the King winery."

Frowning a bit, Rafe told himself he should have ordered a different wine, if only to keep her mind off the King family and her resentments toward them. Clearly, tonight would not be the night when he'd make a full confession. He would soon, though. He just had to find the right words. The right way to explain to her who he was and why he'd lied to her.

Just as he was about to change the subject, he thought better of it and decided to plunge in and try to subtly alter her opinion of the Kings.

"They can't all be bad," he said diffidently.

"Maybe not," she allowed and he felt a small stirring of hope that was dashed a moment later. "But people that rich are so removed from everyday life they tend to look at the world differently than we do."

One of his eyebrows lifted. "You know many rich people, do you?"

She smiled. "No. Just the one. But he left an impression."

"Obviously," Rafe murmured, still wishing he knew which member of his family had hurt her so badly.

Reaching across the table, Katie covered Rafe's hand with her own and his fingers trapped hers instantly, holding on to her when she would have pulled back. She tipped her head to one side and said, "The difference between you and a rich guy is that you brought me here because you thought I'd love it. He would have brought me here to impress me. That's a big difference, Rafe."

He shifted a bit in his chair, uncomfortable with her explanation. The truth was, he'd brought her here because he *had* wanted to impress her—but he'd also known that she would love this place. So that was sort of a compromise, wasn't it?

Still holding on to her hand, he stroked the pad of his thumb across her fingers and said quietly, "What if the rich guy really did bring you here because he thought you'd like it?"

She smiled and briefly gave his hand a squeeze. "It still wouldn't have been as special as you bringing me here, because I know that for a working guy, this place is so expensive, you wouldn't come here normally."

The frown he felt earlier came back as he studied her. "You know something? You're a snob, Katie Charles."

"What?" She tugged her hand free and sat up straight in her chair. "No, I'm not."

"Sure you are," he countered, suddenly feeling more relaxed. If he could make her see that she was being prejudiced, maybe she'd take the truth, when he finally told it, a little better. "On the strength of meeting one rich creep, you've decided that all rich guys aren't worth your time. So you're a reverse snob. As far as you're concerned, only poor guys need apply."

"That sounds terrible," she said, reaching for her wine. She took a sip and set the glass down again.

"But it's accurate." Rafe grinned, and took her hand in his again, despite her efforts to wriggle free.

"Nice to know what you really think of me."

"What I think is, you're a beautiful, smart, ambitious woman with one huge blind spot."

She laughed in spite of herself. "That's a heck of a description."

"This guy who treated you so badly," Rafe said, ignoring her last comment. "What was it about him that attracted you in the first place?"

Her mouth twisted a little and she took a breath, then blew it out in a huff. "Fine. I admit it. He was…" She lifted one shoulder in a half shrug. "…exciting. Different. He was rich and handsome and—"

"Hmm," Rafe teased in a thoughtful tone. She'd said exactly what he'd hoped she would say. Made it much easier to score a point here. "So the first thing you noticed about him was that he was rich?"

"Not the first," she argued quickly, then after a second or two she admitted, "but it was in the top two."

"Uh-huh."

"Fine. I see what you're saying." She shook her wind-tousled hair back from her face. "Very clever. So the poor rich man was taken advantage of by a woman who was intrigued."

"Nope, not what I'm saying at all," he told her, keeping her hand firmly in his despite the fact that she kept trying to slip free. "All I'm saying is that you liked that he was rich until it turned on you. So basically, the problem here is that he was a jerk, not that he was a *rich* jerk."

Whatever she might have said in response went

unspoken because their server chose that moment to arrive with their salads. Rafe and Katie stared into each others' eyes as the woman deftly slid icy plates in front of them and asked, "Is there anything else you need right now?"

"No, thanks." Rafe dismissed her with a smile, then turned his gaze back on Katie, who was watching him through narrowed eyes.

"Think you're pretty clever, don't you?" she asked.

"Actually, *yeah*."

She laughed and the sound of it was like music to him.

"Okay, I see your point," she acknowledged, picking up her fork. "And maybe you're a little bit right."

"Only a little?" he asked.

"Yes," she said. "I didn't like him *because* he was rich, but I do admit that was part of the attraction. Mainly since I couldn't understand why he was interested in me."

"I can."

Rafe understood completely what any man would see in Katie. What he couldn't understand was how a member of his family could be so stupid as to walk away from her. To hurt her and toss her aside. That he would never figure out. But if his anonymous relative hadn't walked away from Katie, Rafe wouldn't be with her now. So maybe he owed the bastard a thank-you—after he punched him in the face.

She smiled. "Thanks for that. And I'll think about what you said. Maybe you're right. Maybe it's not rich guys I should be mad at, but the jerks of the world."

He lifted his glass in a silent toast to her, even while thinking that if she was going to condemn the "jerks," wouldn't he technically be one of that crowd? The burden of lies fell on top of him and Rafe couldn't shrug it off anymore. He wasn't looking forward to telling her the truth, but he couldn't see a way around it.

"Deal." He reluctantly released her hand so that she could eat her salad, but he found he missed the warmth of her touch. He watched her in the flickering candlelight and though the restaurant patio was crowded with other diners, it felt to him as though he and Katie were all alone.

He didn't need dinner. Didn't need the wine. All he really needed—*wanted*—was this woman sitting across from him. She was unlike anyone he'd ever known. She didn't want anything from him. Didn't demand his attention—though she had it anyway. In another week or so, her kitchen redo would be complete and he wouldn't have a handy excuse for seeing her every day. That thought settled like a black cloud over his heart and it was just another reminder that he didn't want to let her go.

He wasn't sure if that meant they had a future or not, but what it did mean was he wanted her for more than a few stolen moments.

This had never been about a future with Katie, he reminded himself. This had started out as a way to reclaim the King family reputation. But there was more to it than that now. He had planned to simply woo her, win her and then move on. Go back to his life and leave Katie to hers.

But since that plan wasn't as appealing as it had been before, he clearly needed a new plan.

He only wished he knew what that was.

# Ten

Two hours later, dinner was over and instead of taking her home, Rafe helped Katie down to the beach.

"These heels are *not* made for walking in the sand," she said with a laugh. She stopped and pulled off first one shoe then the other and looked up at him with a grin. "There. That's better."

High above them, diners still filled the restaurant patio. But here on the moonlit beach, they were alone in the shadows, as if they were the only two people on the coast. And Rafe couldn't take his eyes off her. She was the most captivating woman he'd ever known. She thought nothing of kicking off her heels to take a walk on the beach with him. She didn't worry about her hair and she didn't whine about being cold. She was… amazing and he felt a hard, solid punch of something he couldn't identify somewhere around his heart.

She laid one hand on his chest. "Rafe? You okay?"

"Yeah," he told her, "I'm fine."

But he wasn't at all sure. Leading her along the beach, Rafe held her hand and made sure she didn't get wet as the tide rushed in, leaving a foaming layer of lace on the sand. The coast was dark, but the ocean shone with moonlight glittering on its surface.

"Tonight was perfect," she said and leaned her head on his shoulder. "But you didn't have to take me to such an expensive restaurant."

He dropped her hand and laid one arm around her shoulders. "You didn't like it?"

"I loved it," she admitted. "I just don't want you to think you have to spend a lot of money to impress me."

There was a first, he told himself wryly. He couldn't remember anyone ever telling him not to spend money on them. Hell, his own mother only came around when her bank account was empty. And even thinking that made him feel like a child demanding something he couldn't have. Ridiculous. He didn't *need* anybody. He was better alone. At least he always had been. Now, he wasn't so sure. His mind was racing with thoughts that contradicted each other. Back away, one side of him said. Have a few great nights with Katie, then tell her the truth and leave her behind. But there was another voice in his mind now, too. And it was saying something completely different. That maybe Katie was what had been missing from his life. That maybe, if he could find a way to dig himself out of the hole he found himself in, he might actually find *love*.

That thought was both intriguing and terrifying to a man with so little experience with love.

She threaded her arm through his and snuggled closer and his heartbeat quickened even as his brain raced. Damn, what was going on with him? All his body wanted to do was slow down, enjoy her. Hold her. But his mind wouldn't let him relax into the moment. It kept insisting that Katie was different. Special. That she deserved honesty, damn it. That he was risking something potentially wonderful by lying to her.

"What're you thinking about?" she asked, coming to a stop so she could tip her head back to look up at him.

"You," he said.

She reached up and smoothed his hair back from his forehead and the touch of her fingers sent heat jolting through him.

"They don't look like happy thoughts. Should I be worried?"

"No," he said quickly. He threaded his fingers through her hair and she turned her face into his palm. "Did I tell you how beautiful you are?"

"Yeah, I think you mentioned it a time or two."

"Well, since I don't like repeating myself, why don't I show you instead?"

He kissed her thoroughly, completely, parting her lips with his tongue and sweeping into the warmth he'd found only with her. She welcomed him, leaning into his embrace, matching his desire with her own. He held her tightly to him, drawing her as close as possible and still it wasn't enough.

Here on this lonely stretch of beach, with the moonlight spilling down on them, Rafe could only think of her. Nothing else mattered. Only the next kiss and the next. Touching her, being with her. His brain was finally silenced by his body's overwhelming need.

He swept one hand along her side, feeling the curves of her through the silky coolness of her dress. He cupped her breast and she arched into him, a soft moan issuing from her throat. His thumb stroked the peak of her rigid nipple and even through the fabric separating him from her, he could feel her heat reaching for him.

Not enough, he thought wildly. Not nearly enough. He needed to feel her skin. Flesh to flesh. Heat to heat. He shifted her in his arms and while his mouth tantalized hers, his hand swept to the hem of her dress and inched it up, higher and higher. His palm moved over her thigh, sliding toward her core, and she parted her legs for him.

That first touch inflamed him, though the silk of her panties kept him from delving as deeply as he wanted—needed—to. He stroked her center and she shivered, that soft moan erupting over and over again as he brushed his fingertips over her most sensitive flesh.

The sea wind caressed them, the moonlight coated them in a silvery light and all Rafe was aware of was the woman in his arms. The woman he wanted above all things. He pushed the edge of her panties to one side, stroked that one tender spot at the heart of her and felt her tremble in his arms, quaking and shivering. Again and again, he touched her, pushing her higher, faster. He dipped his fingers deep, stroking her, inside and out. Her legs parted farther as she plastered herself against him. Rafe's tongue twisted with hers, he took her breath, each labored gasp, as she twisted and writhed against him, hungry for the climax shuddering just out of reach.

He reveled in her response. Loved knowing that she was as hungry for him as he was for her. He continued to push her, using his hand, his fingers, to urge her toward completion, needing to feel her surrender.

Then it was there, a release crashing down over her with enough force to leave them both shaken.

Her hands clutched at his shoulders, and her hips rocked into his hand, riding him as he took her quickly, inexorably into a shower of stars.

When it was done, when she hung limp in his arms, he tore his mouth from hers. It nearly killed him to stop, but he gathered his strength and rested his forehead against hers, each of them struggling for breath that wouldn't come. After several long seconds, he smoothed her skirt back down and whispered, "Let's go back to your place."

"Yes," she said, her voice husky with satisfaction and growing need. "Let's go now."

He grinned at her, swept her up into his arms and carried her back across the beach to the cement stairs leading up to Pacific Coast Highway.

Laughing, she said, "Rafe, I can walk, you know."

He brushed a quick kiss across her mouth. "Yeah, but I really liked carrying you before. Thought it was worth repeating."

At the head of the stairs, he took a left and made for the restaurant. He was suddenly grateful he hadn't used valet parking. They wouldn't have to stand around and wait for the car to be brought up. Instead, he'd make a dash to the lot and swing back around to pick her up.

Kissing her again, he dropped her to her feet, cupped her face in his palms and said, "Wait here. I'll get the car."

"I can come with you."

"Faster if I run for it and those heels aren't made for running."

"True," she said, glancing down at the sexy black heels she'd stepped into again the moment they were off the beach. "Hurry up."

"Back in a flash," he promised and raced off into the parking lot.

Katie watched him go, her gaze locked on him until he was swallowed up by the crowd of cars and the hazy light thrown from the yellow fog lamps. Her heart was pounding and every inch of her body was tingling, throbbing still from the effects of the orgasm still rattling through her.

The ocean wind was cold now, but it couldn't even touch the heat flooding her body. She smiled to herself, thinking that the splurge on the dress and shoes had been totally worth it. Having him touch her, take her, on the beach beneath the moon had been an experience she would never forget. The man was far too sexy for his own good and his touch was magic.

The whole night had been perfect and was, she told herself with another smile, about to get even better.

She was going to be happy, damn it. She wasn't going to deprive herself of the chance to be with Rafe because of old fears and trust issues. She wouldn't pass up a shot at happiness because of past mistakes. Besides, she had been thinking about what Rafe had said earlier all night.

He had a point. Part of what had attracted her to Cordell had been the fact that he was rich. So what did that say about her? She couldn't really blame his actions on the fact that he had money any more than she could blame her response on the fact that she *wasn't* wealthy.

They were just people.

And people made mistakes, right? The important thing was to learn from them and try not to make the *same* mistakes over and over again.

She remembered the feel of Rafe's arms coming

around her. The slow, intimate caresses. The heat of desire and the warmth of love rushing between them and her breath caught in her chest. She hadn't realized it until just this moment, and now that she had, she couldn't imagine how it had escaped her for this long.

Katie was in love.

Real love. She knew the difference this time and she wrapped herself up in the amazing sensations as they spiraled through her. What she'd thought she felt for Cordell before wasn't even a glimmer of what she felt for Rafe now. He was everything she had hoped to find. He was the man she had been waiting for all of her life.

How had it happened so quickly?

But even as she wondered that, she smiled to herself, remembering that Nana had always said "Love doesn't go by the clock." One moment was all it took when it was real. One amazing moment when the world suddenly became clear and your heart knew exactly what it wanted and needed.

She sighed a little and held her newfound knowledge close. Tonight was a night she would remember forever.

"Katie?" A deep voice called her name. "Katie Charles? Is that you?"

A small thread of something unpleasant unwound throughout her system as Katie turned slowly toward that too-familiar voice. She saw him instantly, but then he was hard to miss. Tall, gorgeous, black hair long enough to lay on his collar and sharp blue eyes fixed on her.

Cordell King.

She stood her ground and lifted her chin as he walked to her. She shouldn't have been surprised to see him.

She knew he lived in Laguna Beach and this restaurant, being the most expensive one in miles, would surely be a draw to him. But what did amaze her was the fact that she felt *nothing* for him. There were no leftover feelings trapped inside her. Not even anger, though as he smiled at her as if they were long lost friends, she could feel a spark of irritation flash into life.

"It's great to see you," Cordell said as he got close enough. He swept her into a brief hug whether she wanted to go or not, then released her. "You look amazing."

"Thanks," she said, even more grateful now that she'd bought the fabulous black dress. Imagine if she'd run into him wearing that beige one.

He glanced around, then asked, "Are you here alone? Can I buy you a drink?"

"No, you can't," she said, amazed that he had even asked. "I'm sure the woman you're with wouldn't appreciate the company."

"No date," he said. "I'm here meeting a couple of my brothers."

"Well, I'm here with someone else. He's just gone to get the car."

"Oh." He shrugged and gave her that slow, easy smile that had first tugged at her. "Well, not surprising you've got a date. You look great."

"You said that already."

"Yeah, I know," he told her. That smile came back, but when she didn't respond, he continued. "Look, Katie. I'm actually glad we ran into each other. I've been doing a lot of thinking about you lately."

Now that was surprising. "Is that right?"

"Yeah," he said, stepping in a little closer. "I was

going to call you, but doing this in person is even better."

"Why's that?" she asked sharply, folding her arms over her chest. "You didn't think breaking up with me was important enough to do in person. You overnighted me a diamond bracelet along with that charming note that said something along the lines of 'Our worlds are just too different.' Remember?"

He had the good grace to wince at the reminder, but it wasn't enough to shut him down completely. *Oh, no, not a King,* she thought.

"Okay, I could've handled that better," he acknowledged. "But I did send you diamonds."

And she'd sold them to help pay for the kitchen remodel, Katie told herself.

"I never asked for diamonds," she pointed out.

"No, but—" He stopped, took a breath and said, "Look, we're getting off the subject."

"Which is?" The toe of her shoe tapped against the cement, making a staccato sound that played counterpoint to the conversation.

"I'd like to give our relationship another chance," he said. "I mean, we had a great time for a while—"

"Until you dumped me, you mean?" she interrupted, that spark of irritation flashing into quite the little blaze.

"Yeah, well." He shrugged as if that were water under the bridge. "That was then, this is now. And, babe, looking at you now makes me think we could work things out if we tried."

*"Babe?"* she repeated, taking one step toward him. "Don't you call me 'babe.'"

"Hey." He lifted both hands in the air as if he were

surrendering, but that meant nothing. "Relax, I just thought—"

"You just thought that I'd what? Leap into your arms at the *gracious* offer of being able to go out with you again?"

He smiled and that simply infuriated her. Cordell King had bruised her heart so badly, she'd completely lost sight of who and what she was. He'd shattered her confidence and made her question her own ability to judge a person's character.

"All I'm saying is—" he started.

But Katie cut him off with a single wave of her hand. She was through. She didn't want to hear his lame excuses. He'd hurt her and now he behaved as though it had never happened. Well, maybe most of the Kings were able to skate through life without ever once having to face up to what they'd done, but Cordell was going to get a piece of her mind. At last.

"Don't bother. I'm not interested in what you have to say. Do you really think I would go out with you again after how you treated me? Seriously? Does that sweet smile and charm really work for you?"

"Usually," he admitted, taking a long step back as if finally understanding that she wasn't thrilled to see him. He took a quick look around as if to assure himself that they were alone.

They were. But it wouldn't have mattered to Katie either way.

"Amazing," she said, "that there are so many women out there allowing themselves to be dazzled by good looks and empty promises."

"Now just a minute," he countered in his own defense. "I didn't make you any promises."

"Oh, no," she acknowledged. "Just the unspoken

promise of one human being to treat another with a bit of respect."

"It was a good time, okay? That's all. As for tonight, I saw you and thought—"

"I know exactly what you thought, Cordell, and I can tell you it's never going to happen."

He shook his head, blew out a breath and said, "Okay, I can see that this was a mistake, so—"

The sound of a rumbling engine came to her and Katie glanced at the parking lot. Rafe was driving his truck around to the front to pick her up and as he approached, she pointed at him.

"You see that truck? Driving it is a better man than you'll ever be, Cordell. He's a carpenter. He's not rich, but he's got more class than you could hope to have. He's honest and kind and sweet and—"

"Okay!" Cordell took another step away from her and his features clearly said that he wished he were anywhere but there. "I get the picture."

"Good." She set her hands at her hips and took a deep, calming breath of the cool, fresh air. Katie felt better than she had in months. Being given the chance to face Cordell and tell him exactly what she thought of him had been...liberating.

She was still watching him with a gleam of triumph in her eyes when she heard the truck stop and the driver's side door open and slam shut.

"Cordell?" Rafe shouted as he came closer.

Katie slowly swiveled her head to stare at him. How did he know Cordell?

"Rafe?" Cordell said his name on a laugh. "*You're* the poor but honest carpenter? The paragon of virtue Katie just slapped me upside the head with? *You?*"

Rafe didn't say another word. He bunched his fist

and threw a punch to Cordell's jaw that had the man sprawled out on the cement before he could take his next breath. Then Rafe stood over him, glaring in fury. "You son of a bitch."

"You *know* each other?" Katie asked, her voice hitching higher on every word.

Rubbing his jaw, Cordell scrambled to his feet, his glare burning into Rafe as if he could set fire to him with only the power of his will. "You could say that. Rafe's my cousin."

Katie staggered back a step or two, her gaze locked on the man turning to face her now. "Rafe *King?*"

"I can explain," he said.

She noticed he wasn't denying it.

"So much for the poor but proud carpenter, huh?" Cordell muttered, his gaze snapping from his cousin to the woman staring at both of them as if they'd just crawled out from under the same rock. "Katie, I admit it. I treated you badly and I'm sorry for it. But at least I never lied to you, which is more than I can say for my cousin."

"Shut up, Cordell."

"You want to try another shot at me, Rafe?" he offered. "Go for it."

"Both of you stop it," Katie demanded, suddenly feeling like a bone being tugged between two snarling dogs.

Fury tangled with hurt and mixed into a knot of emotions in the pit of her stomach. She was so shaken she could hardly stand, but still, she had to look at Rafe. She read regret in his eyes, though that didn't do a thing toward assuaging what she was going through.

Tears stung her eyes, but she refused to let them fall. Damned if she'd give her tears to the Kings. Again. No, instead, she went with the fury, letting her anger pulse inside her until she could hardly breathe for the fire churning inside her.

"Was this a game?" she demanded, ignoring Cordell, giving her attention only to the man she had thought she knew so well. "Did you have a good time? Are you going to run off to your country club now with lots of fun stories about how you wormed your way into the cookie queen's bed?"

"You slept with her?" Cordell said.

Rafe sent him a death glare, then focused on Katie. "It wasn't a game. Damn it, Katie, you're...*important* to me."

"Oh, sure," she said, sarcasm dripping from her tone, "I can sense that. Lies are always an indicator of a real depth of feeling."

"I was going to tell you the truth."

"What stopped you?" she asked tightly. "Could it be shame?"

"Katie, if you'll just listen for a second..." He took a step closer and she skipped back in reaction.

"Stay away from me," she muttered, shaking her head as if she could wipe away the memory of these last few minutes. "I can't believe this is happening."

"Katie let me explain," Rafe said.

"This should be good," Cordell murmured.

"Don't you have somewhere to go?" Rafe challenged.

"I'm not going anywhere," his cousin said.

"Then I will," Katie told both of them. She couldn't stand here listening to either one of them.

"Not before you hear me out," Rafe said, grabbing her arm to hold her still when she would have sailed past him.

Katie pulled free, ignoring the instinct to stay within the grip of his warmth. "Fine. Talk."

He shot another look at his cousin, then focused on her as if she were the only person in the world. "I made a bet with Joe. The contractor."

"A *bet?* You bet on me?" Oh, she thought grimly, this just got better and better. Now it wasn't just Rafe lying to her, but Joe, too. And probably Steve and Arturo, as well. They must have had some fun lunchtime conversations talking about how stupid she was. "I can't believe you did that."

"No," he snapped, then ran one hand through his hair. "It wasn't about you. I lost a bet and had to work a job site. Your job site. Then I met you and found out you hated all the Kings because of what this moron did to you—"

"Hey!"

"—so I didn't tell you who I was. I wanted you to get to know me. To like me. Then I was going to tell you the truth, I swear it."

"*That* was your plan?" Cordell asked. "And you call me a moron."

"Be quiet, Cordell." Katie shook her head in disbelief and gave her full attention to Rafe again. His eyes were flashing with emotion, but she couldn't read them and wouldn't have bothered if she could. She was beyond caring what he was feeling. Her own emotions were too wild. Too tangled and twisted to be able to make sense of them. All she knew was that she was hurting and, once again, a *King* was at the center of her pain. "You were going to show me that I was wrong about your family by *lying* to me?"

He scrubbed one hand across his jaw and muttered

something she didn't quite catch. Then he said, "Katie, let me take you home so we can talk this out."

Cordell snorted a short laugh.

Neither of them so much as glanced at him.

"I'm not going anywhere with you, Rafe," she said quietly. Looking up into his beautiful blue eyes for the last time, she silently said goodbye to her hopes, her dreams and the love she had so recently discovered. How could she love a man she didn't even know? And that knowledge made the pain in her heart much more fierce. "Just leave me alone."

She started walking and only paused when he called out, "You need a ride home."

"I'll call a cab," she said without even looking at him.

Katie couldn't bear it for another minute. Couldn't look at him one more time, knowing that he'd lied to her every day they were together. None of it had been real. None of it had meant a thing.

She had fallen in love with a stranger.

And now she was alone again.

As the restaurant valet called for a taxi, she realized that she had been right earlier.

Tonight *was* a night she would always remember.

"So," Cordell asked, "you want to get a drink?"

"Sure," Rafe grumbled, "why not?"

The two cousins headed for the restaurant bar and Rafe didn't miss the fact that Katie's gaze locked on them both as they walked past her. He could almost feel the fury radiating off her and damned if he could blame her for it.

Amazing, he thought, just how fast a perfect night

could go to hell. As they stepped into the restaurant, Cordell shivered.

"Did you feel those icicles she was shooting at us?"

"Felt more like knives to me," Rafe said and led the way into the wood-paneled bar. A dozen or more people were scattered around the glass-walled room at tiny round tables boasting flickering candlelight. Rafe ignored everyone else and headed directly for the bartender. He took a seat, ordered two beers, then turned to look at his cousin as Cordell took the stool beside him. "This wasn't how I saw tonight ending up."

"Guess not," Cordell said amiably. "So how long have you been seeing Katie?"

"A few weeks." Rafe picked up his beer and took a long swallow.

"A few weeks? Hell, I dated her for three months and never got past her front door."

Rafe smiled to himself. That was good to hear. If Cordell had said something about sleeping with Katie, then Rafe would have had to kill him and there would have been hell to pay from the rest of the family.

As it was, he was fighting down an urge to hit Cordell again just for the heck of it. But what would be the point? Katie had made it all too clear that it wasn't just Cordell she was angry at anymore. Seemed there was plenty of outraged fury to spread over the whole King family.

And he'd brought it all on himself.

Rafe rubbed the back of his neck and gritted his teeth against the urge to howl in frustration. Ironic that just when he'd decided to come clean and confess all, he'd lost everything before he had the chance. He should have told her sooner, he knew. But he hadn't wanted to risk what they had.

Now, it no longer mattered because what they had was gone.

His cousin nudged him with an elbow. "So why'd you lie to Katie?"

"Why were you a jerk to her?"

Cordell shrugged. "According to most of the women I go out with, that's what I'm best at."

"That's just great," Rafe said, nodding grimly.

"You're avoiding the question," his cousin said. "Why'd you lie to Katie?"

"You heard me explain it to her," Rafe said, studying his own sorry reflection in the mirror across from him.

"Yeah," Cordell agreed. "But I'm thinking it was more than that."

Listening to his cousin was making Rafe bunch his fists again. He didn't want to be here with Cordell. He wanted to be with Katie. Wanted to make her understand…*what?* What could he possibly say now that wouldn't paint him as the same kind of ass as Cordell?

She had lumped all the Kings into one bad basket and as it turned out, he told himself, she was right.

"What're you talking about, Cordell?"

"Only that you really liked her. And once you found out she hated all Kings—"

"Thanks to you," Rafe added.

Cordell shrugged and nodded. "Thanks to me, then you decided that you didn't want to blow it by telling her the truth."

"Wrong. I had a plan. I was going to tell her."

"Sure you were," his cousin said on a snort of laughter.

"If there's something funny about this," Rafe muttered, "I wish you'd share it. Because I just don't see it."

"I know." Cordell took a long pull of his beer and looked into the mirror, meeting Rafe's gaze with a smile. "And that's the funniest part. Man, if your brothers could see you now."

"You want to step outside and finish that fight?"

"Nope," Cordell said, "and hitting me won't change a thing for you anyway."

"Meaning?"

"Meaning, you're in love with her." Cordell laughed, took another drink of his beer and shook his head. "Another King bites the dust."

"You're wrong." Rafe looked into the mirror, met his own gaze and assured himself that Cordell couldn't have been more wildly off base. He wasn't in love. Had no wish to be in love.

Which was a good thing, he decided grimly. Since the only woman who might have changed his mind about that now wanted nothing to do with him.

# Eleven

Katie spent the next few days buried in work.

There was simply nothing better for taking your mind off your problems then diving into baking. She devoted herself to building cookie cakes, decorating birthday cookies and churning out dozens of her clients' favorites.

The scents of cinnamon, vanilla and chocolate surrounded her, giving her a sense of peace that actually went nowhere toward calming her. Inside, her heart was torn and her mind was still buzzing with indignation and hurt. In her dreams, she saw Rafe's face, over and over again, as he looked at her and said, "I can explain." She saw Cordell laughing, Rafe furious and herself, shattered.

He'd said she was "important" to him. As what? A means to winning a bet? As a personal challenge to change her mind about the Kings? And if she was so important to him, why hadn't he tried to talk to her since that night? Why had he been able to let her go so easily?

God, she wasn't making sense. She didn't want him back, did she? So why should she care that he wasn't calling? Wasn't coming over?

Again and again, she relived that night and each time the images danced through her brain, the pain she felt ratcheted up another notch. Her own fault, she knew. She had trusted. Big mistake. She had known going in that she should keep her distance from Rafe. Instead though, she'd followed her heart again, choosing to forget that that particular part of her anatomy was fairly unreliable.

"How many times are you going to go over this anyway, Katie?" she murmured. Shaking her head grimly, she boxed up a dozen chocolate-chip cookies and tied the pink and white striped container with a cotton-candy-colored ribbon.

No matter what else was happening in her life, at least her business was surviving. Thriving, even. The stacks of boxes waiting to be delivered gave her a sense of accomplishment and pride. And that was exactly what she needed at the moment.

This temporary kitchen was her solace. Here she could remember who and what she was. Remind herself that she was building a future for herself. And if that future didn't involve Rafe Cole—she frowned and mentally corrected, Rafe *King*—she would find a way to deal with it.

While the latest batch of cream-cheese cookies baked, Katie wandered to the windows and looked out at the backyard. It was slowly returning to what it had once been. The piles of discarded flooring and plasterboard were gone. Blue tarps covering the grass had been folded and stored away in the crew's trailer, with only squares of dried grass to mark where they had been. The crew was nearing the end of the job and Katie's heart ached at the thought. Her last connection to Rafe was quickly dissolving.

Despite her determination to be strong and self-sufficient, a small, whiny part of her wanted to see Rafe again. Didn't seem to care that he had lied to her. Repeatedly. There was still a dull pain wrapped around her heart and she knew instinctively that it wouldn't stop hurting any time soon.

She hadn't seen Rafe since that night at the restaurant. Apparently his "bet" with Joe had ended the moment she discovered the truth. Rafe had simply walked away without a backward glance, as far as she knew, and it didn't look as though he'd be back. Really, it was as if he had never been here at all, she thought, watching Steve and Arturo carry in the last of the newly refinished cabinet doors.

Katie had walked through her kitchen only that morning in the pre-dawn silence. The pleasure she would have taken in the remodel was muted by the absence of the man who was taking up far too many of her thoughts.

The kitchen was exactly as she had pictured it. The tile floors and granite countertops were in place. All that was left was the finishing work. A few more doors, installing the new drawer pulls and light fixtures, and then her house would be hers again. The crew would leave and she would be alone, with no more contact with King Construction.

Or Rafe.

That twinge of pain twisted in her chest again and

she wondered if it would always be a part of her. She sighed and so didn't hear a thing when Joe entered the patio kitchen.

"Katie?"

She whirled around, startled, to face the man who had been a part of what she now thought of as the Great Lie. He looked uncomfortable, as he had since discovering that she now knew the truth.

Her voice was cool, but polite. "Hello, Joe."

She actually saw him flinch. Though Rafe hadn't been around, she knew that he had been in contact with Joe to tell him that the jig, so to speak, was up.

He shifted position as if he were nervous. "Just wanted to let you know your new stove will be delivered and installed tomorrow morning."

"That's good, thanks."

"The inspector's signed off on everything so we'll move the refrigerator back into the kitchen this afternoon."

"All right." It was almost over, she thought. She wouldn't spend another day cooking in her temporary kitchen. The batch of cookies in the oven now would be the last she baked in her old stove.

"And," he continued, "the guys will be here to help the installers. Then they'll do the last of the finishing jobs and we'll be out of your hair by tomorrow afternoon."

"Okay."

Katie tucked her hands into the pockets of her jeans and as she stood there watching Joe in his misery, she almost felt sorry for him. None of this was his fault. The morning after that scene at the restaurant Joe had explained what had happened and all about the bet Rafe had lost to him.

He'd apologized for going along with Rafe's lies,

but Katie knew he also hadn't had much choice in the matter, either. As an employee, he could hardly argue with the boss. With that thought in mind, she managed to give the man a small smile.

"I have to admit, I'm looking forward to getting my life back," she said. She wouldn't confess to missing Rafe. Not to Joe. Not to anyone.

"Yeah," he muttered, voice still gloomy. "I'll bet."

She noticed he was crumpling an invoice in one tight fist and asked, "Is that the last one?"

He looked down at the paper as if surprised to see it. Then he smoothed it out before holding it out to her. "Your last payment includes the little extras you asked for along the way that were off contract."

Katie nodded and walked over to take it. She didn't even glance at the total. "I'll have a check for you tomorrow."

"That'll be fine." He turned to leave, then stopped and looked at her again. "I'm really sorry, Katie. About everything."

She flushed and now it was her turn to be uncomfortable. Blast Rafe King for putting her in this position. "It wasn't your doing."

"It was, in a way," he insisted, apparently unwilling to let it go that easily. "You know, Rafe's actually a good guy."

"Of course you'd say that," she told him with a sad smile. "You work for him."

"I do," Joe argued, animation coming into his face at last as he tried to defend his employer. "And that's why I'm in a position to know just what kind of man he is. You can tell a lot about a person in the way they treat the people around them. Rafe's not an easy man, but he's a fair one."

"To whom?" Only moments ago, she'd been feeling sympathetic toward Joe since Rafe had put him in such an awkward position. But now, outrage began to bristle inside her. "Was it fair to lie to me? To force you to go along with the lie?"

Joe scowled and scrubbed one hand over his jaw. "No, it wasn't. But he was paying off his bet to me, so I think we should cut him some slack. Not all employers would have had the spine to honor the debt like that."

"Honor?" A burst of laughter shot from Katie's throat.

"Yeah," he said flatly. "Honor. I don't know what happened between you two and I don't want to know. But I can tell you that Rafe's not a man who goes out of his way to treat people badly."

"Just a happy accident, then?" she sniped and instantly regretted it when Joe winced. Honestly, why was she taking her anger and hurt out on him? He hadn't done anything to her beyond supporting Rafe's lies. It was Rafe who had set everything in motion. Rafe who had slept with her and *still* lied to her. Rafe who had let her believe that something amazing was coming to life between them, all the time knowing that it was a sham.

Katie struggled for control and found it. Forcing a smile she didn't feel, she said, "Joe, why don't we just call this a draw and agree not to talk about Rafe King?"

A moment or two passed when it looked as though he might argue with her. But at last, Joe nodded in surrender. "That's fine, then. I'll just let you get back to work and go see if I can help the boys finish up any faster."

She watched him go, then took a deep breath and tried to push Rafe from her mind. Again.

Naturally, it didn't work.

It had been almost a week since he'd last seen Katie Charles.

Rafe felt like a caged man. He was trapped in his own memories of her no matter what he did to try to shake them loose. Her image haunted his dreams, and awake, he couldn't seem to keep thoughts of her at bay. Didn't matter where he was or what he did, Katie was never more than a thought away.

Hell, he'd even considered calling one of the women he knew, to dive back into his life. Get back in the normal swing of things. But damned if he'd been able to make himself do it. No, he had a charity event he had to go to in a few days, but until then, he wasn't going out.

Didn't have the patience to put up with any of the women he knew and wasn't interested in finding someone new.

He just wanted to be alone. But not by himself. Which didn't make sense even to him.

He had tried holing up in his suite at the hotel, locking himself away with only his racing brain to keep him company. But the hotel rooms felt sterile, impersonal, and the echoing emptiness had pounded on him until he thought he might lose what was left of his mind.

So here he sat, trying to focus on inventory and supply sheets while images of Katie taunted him. To make matters worse, there was Sean. The problem with coming into King Construction offices, Rafe told himself, was that he couldn't really avoid his brothers.

"What is your problem?" Sean asked.

"I'm fine," Rafe insisted, keeping his head down, his gaze on the paperwork scattered across his desk. "Just get off my back, all right?"

Sean laughed. "Trust me when I say, I'd love to. But you're making everyone around here nuts. When Janice was doing some phone work for me, she *begged* me to get you out of the office."

*That's great,* he thought. Always before, Rafe had kept his personal and business lives separate. Now though, it seemed his lousy attitude was bleeding into the office. Hell, maybe he should take some time off. But if he did that, his mind would have far too much time to think about Katie. So whether his assistant was happy about it or not, he wasn't going anywhere.

Rafe scowled and looked up to watch his brother stroll around the perimeter of his office. When Sean stopped at a shelf and plucked a signed baseball off its pedestal, Rafe grumbled, "Put that down." When he complied, Rafe demanded, "Why is *my* assistant doing work for you anyway? Don't you have your own? What happened to Kelly?"

Sighing, Sean walked over and perched on the edge of Rafe's desk. "She eloped last weekend."

"That's the third assistant you've lost this year, isn't it?"

"Yeah. I've got to stop hiring the pretty ones," Sean mused. "Inevitably, they run off and get married and leave me swinging in the wind."

"Well, call the temp agency and get someone in here. Just leave Janice alone."

"Funny," Sean said, his eyes narrowing as he watched Rafe thoughtfully, "she'd rather work for me these days."

Disgusted, Rafe muttered, "Yeah, well, she doesn't."

"Better she work for me than quit. And until you lighten up, nobody wants anything to do with you. So why don't you just tell me what's going on?"

"Work," Rafe said flatly, his gaze giving nothing away as he glared at his brother. "You should try it."

"Just so you know? The whole 'King Glare' thing doesn't work on me. I can do it too, remember?"

Rafe tossed his pen to the desktop and, giving into the irritation flooding his system, jumped out of his chair as if he couldn't bear to sit still any longer. Turning his back on his brother, he stared out the window at the spread of sunlit ocean before him. There were a few sailboats out on the water today and in the distance, fishermen lined the pier. Gray clouds gathered on the horizon and the wind whipped the waves into choppy whitecaps.

"So," Sean asked again, "what's going on?"

He glanced back over his shoulder. He knew his younger brother wouldn't go away until he got some answers. And a part of Rafe wanted to say it all out loud anyway, so he blurted, "Found out which King hurt Katie."

"Yeah? Who?"

"Cordell."

"Should have thought of him," Sean mused with a nod. "He goes through women faster than Jesse used to."

At mention of their now-married cousin, Rafe almost smiled. As a former professional surfer, Jesse King's reputation with the ladies had been staggering. Of course, that was before he married Bella and became a father.

"How'd you find out who it was?"

Rafe muttered an oath and looked at Sean. "Ran into Cordell when I took Katie to dinner."

"Ouch." Sean nodded thoughtfully, clearly understanding the situation.

"Yeah. That about covers it." Pushing one hand through his hair, Rafe looked back at the ocean and said, "It all happened pretty fast. I punched him. Then he told Katie who I was. Then she left."

"And you let her go."

Swiveling his head around, he glared at Sean again. "What was I supposed to do? Hold her captive?"

"Or talk to her?"

"She was through talking," Rafe assured him, remembering the look in her eyes as she faced him down. He'd seen the pain glittering brightly in tears she hadn't let fall. He'd heard the betrayal in her voice and felt the sharp sting of his own lies catching up with him.

"So that's it?" Sean asked.

"That's it." Deliberately, Rafe turned his back on the view, ignored his brother and took a seat behind his desk again. Picking up his pen, he stared blindly at the supply sheets.

"Can't believe you're going to let her get away."

"I didn't *let* her do anything," Rafe muttered, still not looking up at Sean. "Katie makes her own decisions. And now she has more reason than ever to hate the Kings. Most especially, *me*."

Blowing out a breath, Sean stood up but didn't leave. "And you're okay with that?"

"Of course I am," Rafe lied and mentally congratulated himself on just how good he was getting at it. "I always intended to walk away from her, Sean. It just happened a little faster than I'd planned."

God, that was a lie, too.

"Right." Sean slapped one hand down on top of the papers, forcing Rafe to look up at him.

"Butt out, Sean," he ground out.

"Hell no," his brother said, frustration simmering in the air between them. "You're not usually a stupid guy, Rafe. But this time, you're being an idiot."

No, he wasn't. Katie didn't want to see him and he couldn't blame her. Besides, it was better this way. If she was mad at him, she wouldn't stay hurt for long. She'd get over it. So would he. He was no good at love and he knew it. Better he hurt her now than destroy her later.

"Thanks for the input." Rafe peeled Sean's hand off the papers. "Now go away."

"If you don't go after her," Sean said quietly, "you'll regret it."

Rafe already regretted it. Enough that his soul felt as if it was withering and his heart could barely summon the energy to beat.

"I've had regrets before," he finally said. "Let's remember Leslie."

"Uh-huh. Speaking of your ex…I hear you hired her husband."

Rafe sighed. Yes, he had hired John. And he was forced to admit that he might not have if he hadn't met Katie. Being with her had allowed him to face his own past. And the talk with Leslie had been eye-opening enough that he'd been able to reach out to an old friend. Maybe he and John would actually be close again someday.

If they were, that too would be laid at Katie's feet. Her optimism and rosy outlook on life had affected him more than he would have thought possible. Rafe shifted in his chair. He didn't want to talk about any of this. Hell, he didn't want to talk at all.

"So the question is," Sean continued, oblivious to the fact that Rafe wanted him gone, "why is it you can make peace with John and Leslie, but you won't go see the woman you're crazy about?"

Several silent, tense seconds passed before Rafe finally asked, "Are you going to leave? Or do I have to?"

"I'll go," Sean said amiably. "But that won't solve your problem for you."

"Yeah?" Rafe countered. "What will?"

Sean laughed at him and shook his head as he opened the door. "You already know the answer to that, Rafe. You just don't want to admit it."

# Twelve

"It's really gorgeous, honey," Emily O'Hara said as she walked through the completely remodeled kitchen. "I love the floor and the counters are just beautiful."

Katie should have been cooing over her finished kitchen too, but somehow she couldn't muster up the enthusiasm for it. Heck, in the two days since the crew left, she hadn't even made a single batch of cookies in her shiny new stove.

Her gaze swept the remodeled room, trying to see it as Nana was, from the slate gray tiles to the pearlized blue granite counters to the dark blue walls and she felt... nothing. It was all perfect and it meant...nothing.

"All right, sweetie," her grandmother said, coming up to give her a brief, comforting hug. "You've got the kitchen of your dreams, but you're standing there looking as if you just found out cookies had been banned. Tell me what's wrong."

The tears that Katie had been holding at bay for days crested again and before she could stop them, one or two trailed down her cheeks. Her heart ached and it felt as though there were a boulder sitting on her chest. She could hardly draw a breath without wheezing. "Oh, Nana, *everything's* wrong."

"Honey…" The older woman sighed and steered Katie across the room. An ancient, round pedestal table and captain chairs sat before the wide window where sunlight splashed and curtains danced in a soft wind. Emily pushed her granddaughter into one of the chairs, then sat down beside her. "Talk to me."

*Where to start?* Katie wondered. With the fact that she was in love with a man she didn't really know? That she'd allowed herself to get bamboozled by the King family? *Again?* Or should she just admit that she wasn't getting over it this time? That she would *never* get over it? That she couldn't sleep, she couldn't eat, she didn't even want to bake anymore. And that was saying something. She just couldn't bring herself to care about anything but the gaping hole in her own heart.

"It's Rafe," she said, slumping back into her chair. "He lied to me."

"I know."

"What?" Katie blinked at her grandmother and waited for an explanation. But the older woman just sat there in the sunlight, smiling benevolently. "How? What? How?"

Emily reached over, patted Katie's hand, then sighed and leaned back in her chair. "I know his real name is Rafe King, if that's what you're talking about."

"Well, yeah, it is."

"Do you want tea? We should have some tea."

"I don't want tea," Katie said, stopping her grandmother before the woman could get up. "I want some answers. You know about Rafe? For how long?"

She waved one hand dismissively. "Oh, I knew the minute you introduced us."

"How?" Katie just stared at her in rapt confusion. "Do you have some kind of inner lie radar that I didn't get?"

"No, and I don't think I'd want it, either. Sometimes lies can be a good thing," Emily said, her gaze locked on Katie.

"Lying is *not* a good thing. You're the one who taught me that, remember?"

Again, Emily waved a hand, effectively wiping away that little nugget of so-called wisdom. "That was different. You were ten. Now you're an adult and surely you've learned that sometimes a small, harmless lie is far better than a hurtful truth."

"This lie wasn't harmless," Katie argued, remembering the sting of betrayal when she'd discovered Rafe's game. "And you still haven't told me how you knew who he was."

"If you read popular magazines once in a while, you would have known him too," Nana said with a huff. "There's always one King or another's picture in there. I recognized Rafe from a picture taken at a movie premiere."

"A premiere." Katie shook her head and felt her heart drop through the floor. He was used to dating actresses and going to fabulous parties. Oh, he must have gotten such a laugh from the spur-of-the-moment barbecue in her backyard.

Annoyance flickered into anger and soon that hot little bubble of fury was frothing into real rage. "I can't believe it. He must have thought I was an idiot for not recognizing him." She paused for a glare at her grandmother. "And why didn't you *tell* me?"

"Because," Emily said. "You needed your life shaken up a little. Besides, he's a cutie-patootie and you can't hang *all* of the Kings for what one of them did."

"*Two* of them now," Katie reminded her.

"All right, yes, Rafe's not looking too good at the moment," Emily admitted. "But did you give him a chance to explain?"

"Oh, he explained. I was a bet gone wrong."

"Katie…"

She shook her head and held up both hands. "No, Nana, there's no excuse for what he did. He lied to me and that's it."

"I lied to you too, sweetie," her grandmother pointed out in a small voice.

Sighing, Katie said, "Yeah, but you didn't do it to hurt me."

"No, I didn't. And maybe that wasn't Rafe's intention, either."

"We'll never know, will we?" Katie muttered, as anger seeped away into the wide black hole she seemed to be carrying around inside her these days.

"You could find out if you'd stop hiding away in your house and go see him." Emily frowned and looked at her steadily. "Are you really going to become a hermit while he's out having a good time?"

*That* caught her attention quickly enough. Rafe was having a good time? Where? And a moment later the more important question—*with who?*—leaped into mind.

"What do you mean?" Katie asked, voice tight.

Her nana sighed again and reached for the morning paper, still folded and unopened on the kitchen table.

"Honestly, Katie, if you paid a little more attention to current events…"

"What does that have to do with anything?"

Silently, Emily discarded the news section and went straight to Lifestyles. Thumbing through it, she finally found what she was looking for and folded it back. Then she laid it down in front of Katie and stabbed a grainy black-and-white picture with her manicured nail. "It means, you can find out a lot by keeping up with gossip. Like for example…there."

Katie looked at the picture and felt the tightening in her chest ratchet up until she couldn't get any air in her lungs. She was light-headed. That had to be the reason her vision was narrowing until all she could see was the picture in the paper. The picture of an unsmiling Rafe in a tuxedo at a charity fundraiser, with a blond sporting boobs twice the size of Katie's clinging to his arm.

"When was—" She broke off as she read the caption under the photo. "Two nights ago."

"*He's* not curled up in the fetal position like someone else I could mention," Emily murmured.

"That rat. That *creep*." Katie slowly rose from her chair, clutching the paper in her fists. Her gaze still locked on the picture, all she could see was Rafe's face, glaring at the camera as if he were wishing the photographer into the darkest bowels of Hell.

"Atta girl," her grandmother whispered.

"He told me I was *important* to him," Katie said, fury coloring her voice until it quivered and shook with the force of it. "He must have been lying *again*. If I was so damn important, how is he out with this bimbo?"

"To be fair, we're not sure she's a bimbo," Nana said.

Katie glared at her. "Whose side are you on?"

"Right."

"Does he think I'm stupid?" Katie asked, not waiting for an answer. "Did he really believe I wouldn't find out that less than a week after—after—that he'd be dating the rich and pointless again? Does he think I don't read the paper?"

"Well," Emily pointed out easily, "you don't."

"I will from now on," Katie promised, giving the paper a hard shake.

"So, what're you going to do about this?"

Katie finally lifted her gaze and looked into her grandmother's eyes. With cold, hard determination she said simply, "I'm going to go dethrone a King."

Rafe couldn't settle.

He felt uncomfortable in his own skin.

Which left him nowhere to run.

Not that he would. Kings didn't run. Kings didn't hide.

But then if that were true, why wasn't he over at Katie's house right now, demanding she listen to him? Grumbling, he stood up, walked to the window of his office and stared out at the view without even seeing it. The ocean could have dried up for all the notice he gave it. There might as well have been empty sand dunes stretching out into eternity out there. He didn't care. It didn't matter. Nothing did.

He'd tried going back to his life, but it was a damned empty one. Hell, he couldn't even go into his hotel suite anymore. The silence was too much to take. So instead, he stayed here. At the office. He'd been sleeping on the damn couch, if you could call it sleep.

Every time he closed his eyes, he saw Katie, as she had been that last night. Quivering in his arms. Kissing him breathless. Then finally, staring at him out of hurt-filled eyes. And if he had been able to figure out how to do it, he'd have punched his own face in days ago.

The intercom buzzed and he walked to stab a finger at the button. "Damn it, Janice, I told you I didn't want to be disturbed."

"Yes, but there's—" she said, then added, "Wait! You can't go in!" just before his office door crashed open.

Katie stood in the doorway, her green eyes flashing at him dangerously. Her hair was a wild tumble of curls around her shoulders. She wore a black skirt, a red button-down shirt that was opened enough that he could see where her silver necklace dipped into the valley of her breasts. And she was wearing those black high heels she'd been wearing their last night together.

Altogether, she looked like a woman dressed for seduction. But with the fury in her eyes, any man she was aimed at might not survive. Rafe was willing to take his chances. And if she did end up putting him down, he couldn't think of a better way to go.

"Sorry," Janice was saying as she brushed past Katie with a frown. "She got past me and—"

"It's okay, Janice. Close the door on your way out."

"Yes sir," she said and, though curiosity was stamped on her face, she did what he asked and left he and Katie alone.

"It's good to see you," he said, knowing that for the understatement of the century.

"It won't be in a minute," Katie promised and stalked toward him like an avenging angel on a mission. She dipped one hand into the black purse hanging off her shoulder and came back up with a folded newspaper.

Once she had it, she threw it at him. He caught it instinctively and gave it a quick glance. Ah. Now he knew what was behind the fresh fury driving her. And weirdly, it gave him a shot of hope that she wasn't lost to him completely since that picture had definitely pissed her off.

"Did you think I wouldn't see it?" she said, her voice little more than a snarl. "Or was it just that you didn't care if I saw it? Game over, bet won, moving on? Was that it?"

"It wasn't a game, Katie," he said and his tone was as tight as the tension coiled inside him. "I told you that. Or I tried to."

"And I should believe you," she said, dropping her purse onto the closest chair and stabbing one finger at the newspaper he tossed to his desk. "Because clearly you missed me so much you had to rush out and drown your sorrows in that blonde double D."

He grinned at her, even knowing that would only feed the flames of her wrath. Rafe couldn't help himself. Hell, he could hardly believe she was standing here. Even gloriously furious, she was the only woman who could make his heart lift out of the darkness he carried inside him. The only woman who made him want to smile. Who made him want to promise her any damn thing she wanted as long as she never left him again.

He thought briefly about what Cordell had said at the restaurant the other night. *Another King bites the dust.* He'd argued the point then, out of sheer stubbornness and a refusal to see the truth for what it was.

But now that Katie was standing here in front of him, bubbling with a fury that had her green eyes flashing like fireworks, he knew he couldn't deny the facts any longer. Not even to himself. More importantly, he didn't want to.

He was in love for the first time in his life.

And damned if he'd lose her.

"Don't you dare laugh at me," she warned.

"Not laughing." Reaching out, he grabbed hold of her shoulders and only tightened his grip when she tried to twist free. "Katie, that blonde is an actress. Under contract to my cousin Jefferson's film company. I had to go to the charity thing anyway and he asked me to escort her to get her some media."

She wasn't mollified. "And I should believe that *why?*"

"Because she was boring and vapid and I had a terrible time because she wasn't you. And…because I won't lie to you again, Katie."

Some of the fight went out of her. The rigidity in her shoulders faded enough that he risked easing his grip on her. She didn't step away from him when she had the opportunity and Rafe silently considered that a good sign.

"I miss you," he said before he could gauge his words and try to predict her reaction.

Her delectable mouth flattened into a grim line. "I'm still furious with you."

"I get that." But she was *here* and he was taking that as a good sign. She looked up at him with those gorgeous green eyes and Rafe knew that he had only this one shot. This one chance to redeem himself. To somehow salvage the most important relationship he'd ever known.

So the words came slowly, but they came.

Words he had never thought to say to anyone.

"I wasn't ready for you," he started and read the confusion in her eyes. "The bet with Joe? It shouldn't have been a big deal. But then I met you and found out you hated the Kings and I knew if I told you the truth, you'd never look at me again."

She frowned, and bit into her bottom lip as if trying to keep herself from talking so that she could hear him out completely.

"I told myself that I wanted to change your mind about the King family," he said and watched a flash of something in her eyes come and go. "But it wasn't only that. Like I said, I knew you'd never look at me again if you knew. And I *wanted* you to look at me, Katie," he said, shifting one hand to cup her cheek. "I wanted a lot more than that, too."

"You got more, Rafe," she said, her voice so quiet he had to strain to hear her. "You got more than I ever gave anyone before. I *loved* you. So when I found out you had lied to me, it hurt far deeper than anything Cordell made me feel."

"I know," he told her, mentally holding fast to the word *loved*. If she had loved him then, she had to love him still. It couldn't burn out that fast, no matter how angry she was. "I know."

He pulled her close and kissed her once, twice. It was soft and hard, passionate and tender. That one kiss carried his heart and he nearly sighed in relief when she leaned into him to return that kiss, however hesitantly she did it.

Pulling back, he let his gaze move over her features, as if burning this moment, her expression, into his brain. Finally though, he drew away and said, "I told you I wasn't ready for you and that's the honest truth. But I don't know how I could have been prepared for what you would do to me."

"Rafe…"

He shook his head and laid his fingertips over her

mouth. "No, let me say it. You grew up with your grandmother, your mom. You knew you were loved and you knew how to respond to it. I didn't. My dad was a lousy role model and I hardly knew my mother. When I got married, it was for all the wrong reasons and when she left, my ex let me know that it was *my* failings, my inability to love, that ruined everything—"

Katie's eyes shone brightly as she reached up to smooth her palm across his jaw. "She was wrong."

"No," he said, "she wasn't. Because until I met you, I didn't know how to love."

"Oh, Rafe..."

His heart felt light for the first time in days. His soul was warm again because she was near. Rafe knew that this one woman was the center of his world. If he couldn't convince her to take a chance on him—to love him in spite of all the reasons she shouldn't—then he'd never have anything worth a damn.

"Look, I'm a bad bet," Rafe told her, determined to be completely honest with her even if it cost him what he wanted most. "I know that. But I love you, Katie. In my whole life, I've never loved anything else."

Tears glittered in her eyes and his stomach hitched. Happy tears? Or goodbye?

She took a breath, let it slide from her lungs and admitted, "I want to believe you."

Rafe smiled and pulled her in close to him, where she could feel the hammering of his heart in his chest. Where she would feel the strength of his love wrapping itself around her.

"Take a chance on me, Katie," he whispered, dipping his head to kiss the curve of her neck. He inhaled the scent of her and smiled as cinnamon and vanilla surrounded him. "I swear you'll never regret it."

"Rafe?"

He pulled back to look into her eyes and before she could speak again he said, "Marry me, Katie. Marry me and let me live with you in that great old house. Let me make you happy. I know I can. I'll prove to you that I can be what you need."

"Yes, I'll marry you." Finally, a slow smile curved her mouth and she reached up with both hands to cup his face between her palms. "Don't you know that you're *already* everything that I need?"

"Thank God," he whispered and kissed her again, a promise of more to come.

"After all, you did build me a nearly perfect kitchen."

*"Nearly?"* he asked with a grin.

"Well, I've suddenly decided that since I'm marrying a carpenter, he should be able to build me a pantry."

"Anything you want, Katie," he promised with a grin. "But I warn you, as soon as he finds out we're getting married, my brother Sean's going to want cookies."

"For family?" she said, *"Anything."*

Rafe dropped his head and rested his forehead against Katie's, feeling his world, his life slide into place again. The woman he loved was in the circle of his arms, and the future was suddenly looking bright. He was right where he wanted to be. Where he was supposed to be.

With Katie Charles, the cookie queen.

# <u>Epilogue</u>

Katie grinned as she looked out the kitchen window at her crowded backyard. "I never dreamed there were so many Kings in California."

Julie King, married to Travis, laughed as she pulled a bowl of pasta salad from the fridge. "And this isn't all of them by any means."

"Wait until your wedding," Maggie King, wife of Justice warned her. "They'll *all* be there for that."

"Yep," Jericho's wife Daisy agreed. "They never miss a wedding. Jeff and Maura will even come in from Ireland for that."

"It's a little intimidating," Katie admitted, unwrapping a platter of cookies designed especially for their engagement party. There were dozens of golden crowns, frosted in yellow or white, with Katie and Rafe inscribed on them.

She glanced down at the emerald engagement ring

glittering on her finger and almost hugged herself just to make sure she was awake and not dreaming all of this. But remembering the night before, when Rafe had made love to her for hours and then held her as she slept was enough to convince her that yes. Her life really was perfect.

It had been a month since she'd stormed her way into his office and he laid siege to her heart with the truth. And in that time, she hadn't once regretted taking a chance on Rafe. He'd shown her in countless little ways just how important she was to him. He'd built her that specially designed pantry just as he'd promised. He sent her flowers, made her dinner and when she was tired, he gave her a fabulous foot rub that inevitably led to long, lovely hours in bed.

"Uh-oh," Daisy said with a laugh. "I know that smile."

"What?" Katie grinned, embarrassed to be caught daydreaming.

"It's the same one I get when I remember how I ended up with a gorgeous baby girl." Standing up, Daisy smiled. "And speaking of Delilah, think I'll just go and make sure Jericho's not teaching her how to do something dangerous. The man's got a thing about his daughter being the first female Navy SEAL."

"I know how she feels," Ivy King said, rubbing a rounded belly. "Tanner already plans on our poor baby being the next computer genius of the universe. But no pressure."

As Daisy left and the other King wives laughed and chatted about their kids and their husbands, Katie took a minute to enjoy where she was. Her nana had been right all along of course. Which Emily had continued to remind her of over the last month. Love was worth taking a chance on. Because Katie had risked it, she was about to marry the man she loved, become a part of a huge family and, one day, start her own.

Babies. They would come soon. Rafe had already talked about how he wanted to add to the next generation of the King family.

"It's funny," Katie said softly to the women who were already her friends as well as almost-relatives. "Just a few months ago, I hated the Kings."

"Yeah," Jackson's wife Casey said as she unwrapped a sheath of plastic cups, "we all heard about Cordell. If it helps, everyone knows he's a dog."

Maggie chimed in with, "Justice offered to beat him up, as soon as Cordell arrived today, but apparently Rafe already took care of it."

"Yeah, he did," Katie assured them. "But as much as I hate to admit it, without Cordell being a jerk, I might never have fallen in love with Rafe."

"So, it was worth it then?" Jesse's wife Bella asked.

"More than," Katie assured them. Then she glanced out the window to see her neighbor Nicole walking into the yard with her son in tow. "A friend of mine just showed up. I'll be back to finish up the potato salad!"

"No, you won't," Julie told her. "This is *your* engagement party. Go out and enjoy it. We'll take care of the setup."

Smiling, Katie left her beautiful kitchen and walked into the yard. Her grandmother and aunt were in heaven, playing with all of the King kids. The men were gathered around the brick barbecue Rafe had finished building only last week, arguing over the best way to grill steaks. She caught a glimpse of Rafe in the middle of them all and couldn't help smiling. She had been so wrong. The rich weren't snobby. At least, the Kings weren't. They were just people.

"This is some party," Nicole said as she walked up and gave Katie a hug.

"It is. And I'm so glad you came."

"Wouldn't have missed it. As your future matron of honor, it's my duty to sit here and have a beer and eat steak." Nicole picked Connor up and placed him on her hip. "And your ring bearer wants a cookie."

Katie laughed, delighted, and leaned in to kiss Connor. "My special ring bearer can have as many cookies as I can sneak him!"

When two strong, familiar arms snaked around her middle from behind, Katie leaned back into Rafe's chest with a sigh of satisfaction.

"Hi, Nicole," he said, planting a quick kiss on Katie's head. "Glad you could make it."

"Are you kidding? Wouldn't be anywhere else," she told him. Then with a wry smile at the two of them, she added, "I'll just take Connor in to grab a cookie. We'll see you later."

Rafe turned her to face him and Katie flung her arms around his neck. He kissed her hard and long and deep and when her head was buzzing and her balance had completely dissolved, he lifted his head and looked down at her. "Have I told you today how much I love you?"

"You have," she said, "but I never get tired of hearing it."

"Good. I plan to say it often. Just so you never forget it."

"Not a chance," she promised.

He rested his forehead against hers. "So, after meeting the thundering herd of Kings, you still want to marry me next month?"

His tone was joking, but she knew that a part of him

was still worried that something might happen to tear them apart. He might not believe that he was capable of love, but Katie knew differently. Rafe King had more love to give than most men, simply because he'd never known it before. And she knew that once his heart was given, it was forever.

"You're not getting away from me now, Rafe," she said softly. "We're getting married and I am going to love you forever."

His eyes flashed, his mouth curved, and he pulled her in hard against him for a hug that left her breathless. But who needed to breathe when you were surrounded by love?

When he finally let her go, he draped one arm around her shoulders and, together, they walked into the circle of family.

\* \* \* \* \*

# LET'S TALK
## Romance

For exclusive extracts, competitions
and special offers, find us online:

 facebook.com/millsandboon

@MillsandBoon

@MillsandBoonUK

**Get in touch on 01413 063232**

For all the latest titles coming soon, visit
**millsandboon.co.uk/nextmonth**

# WANT EVEN MORE
# ROMANCE?
## SUBSCRIBE AND SAVE TODAY!

'Mills & Boon books, the perfect way to escape for an hour or so.'

**MISS W. DYER**

'Excellent service, promptly delivered and very good subscription choices.'

**MISS A. PEARSON**

'You get fantastic special offers and the chance to get books before they hit the shops.'

**MRS V. HALL**

Visit millsandboon.co.uk/Subscribe and save on brand new books.

# MILLS & BOON
## A ROMANCE FOR
## EVERY READER

- **FREE** delivery direct to your door

- **EXCLUSIVE** offers every month

- **SAVE** up to 25% on pre-paid subscriptions

## SUBSCRIBE AND SAVE

millsandboon.co.uk/Subscribe

# MILLS & BOON

## THE HEART OF ROMANCE

---

## A ROMANCE FOR EVERY KIND OF READER

---

### MODERN

Prepare to be swept off your feet by sophisticated, sexy and seductive heroes, in some of the world's most glamourous and romantic locations, where power and passion collide.
**8 stories per month.**

### HISTORICAL

Escape with historical heroes from time gone by. Whether your passion is for wicked Regency Rakes, muscled Vikings or rugged Highlanders, awaken the romance of the past.
**6 stories per month.**

### MEDICAL

Set your pulse racing with dedicated, delectable doctors in the high-pressure world of medicine, where emotions run high and passion, comfort and love are the best medicine.
**6 stories per month.**

### True Love

Celebrate true love with tender stories of heartfelt romance, from the rush of falling in love to the joy a new baby can bring, and a focus on the emotional heart of a relationship.
**8 stories per month.**

### Desire

Indulge in secrets and scandal, intense drama and plenty of sizzling hot action with powerful and passionate heroes who have it all: wealth, status, good looks...everything but the right woman.
**6 stories per month.**

### HEROES

Experience all the excitement of a gripping thriller, with an intense romance at its heart. Resourceful, true-to-life women and strong, fearless men face danger and desire - a killer combination!
**8 stories per month.**

### DARE

Sensual love stories featuring smart, sassy heroines you'd want as a best friend, and compelling intense heroes who are worthy of them.
**4 stories per month.**

---

To see which titles are coming soon, please visit

**millsandboon.co.uk/nextmonth**

# JOIN US ON SOCIAL MEDIA!

Stay up to date with our latest releases, author news and gossip, special offers and discounts, and all the behind-the-scenes action from Mills & Boon...

 millsandboon

 millsandboonuk

 millsandboon

*It might just be true love...*

# GET YOUR ROMANCE FIX!

# MILLS & BOON
## *blog*

Get the latest romance news, exclusive author interviews, story extracts and much more!

# blog.millsandboon.co.uk

# MILLS & BOON
## MODERN
# Power and Passion

Prepare to be swept off your feet by sophisticated, sexy and seductive heroes, in some of the world's most glamourous and romantic locations, where power and passion collide.

Eight Modern stories published every month, find them all at

## millsandboon.co.uk/Modern